# THE FRENCH GIRL

## The Ant Murders series

### VOLUME TWO

### BY

# Marion Lindsey-Noble

First published in Great Britain in 2021 by Cashmere Publishing

Brompton Regis TA22 9NW, Somerset,
marion.lindseynoble@btinternet.com

A CIP catalogue recorded for this book is available from the British library.

ISBN 978–1–9168859–1-2

Cover Design by Print Guy

Printed by www.Print Guy/books.co.uk

**To Royce,**

**my ever patient and supportive husband and soulmate**

# CHAPTER ONE

'This is so undignified,' Ant shouts into the wind, her green eyes blazing with fury. She is at the top of her farm, not enjoying the sweeping views over Exmoor, but desperately holding on to a low branch of a gnarled oak tree to avoid slipping down the muddy hill. Pelting rains overnight have turned the soil into a slippery slide. She can't even brush away streaks of her brown, long ponytail stuck on her muddy forehead. She has no idea how that happened. The piglets in their enclosure are unperturbed while the mother sows are looking on, bemused, unruffled and unhelpful. When they have satisfied their curiosity about that human being making such a racket, they turn back to munching the mushy banana treats she has brought along to distract them. She has succeeded in that sense, but she still hasn't caught one single piglet, let alone the three she has promised to bring into the local school. Ant steadies herself by leaning against the nearest tree and reminisces.

It had all begun when Ant, hurrying through the aisles of the local supermarket, had met Kathleen Fitzgerald. The woman's trolley had overturned and spilled most of the items already chosen onto the floor. Ant, in her forties, petite, fit and only carrying an empty wicker basket, had rushed to the woman's aid, crouched down and gathered up potatoes, apples, oranges, a couple of butter tubs, a few tins, a packet of pasta and several packets of biscuits.

'Luckily, I haven't reached the eggs, double cream and pickles just yet,' the woman had joked, when almost everything was back in the trolley. 'That would have made a mess!' Ant admired the unexpectedly philosophical cheerfulness, accompanied by a grin from one ear to the other. In contrast to Ant, the woman was tall, built for comfort in a motherly sense; her prematurely grey hair was piled up on her head, a couple of strands having come loose, slightly undermining her subtle air of authority. Her statuesque figure and the cape-like garment she wore were a distinct disadvantage, rendering her unable to crouch down like the agile Ant could. Moreover, Ant was not one to worry about getting her washed-out jeans and thick jumper dirty - to which clung a permanent, faint smell of pigs; only Ant's long, brown ponytail kept getting in the way, falling over her shoulder to the front. When Ant had straightened up and handed the last two items to the woman - a tin of asparagus soup and a paper bag full of doughnuts - she received an unexpected explanation: 'One to keep up my strength, and the others as a treat.' Both women had burst into laughter that afternoon in the middle of the little town's supermarket.

'Time for an introduction: I am Kathleen Fitzgerald,' the woman had said offering her hand.

'Antonia Bell, Ant had replied and had added, 'Ant for short. Lovely to meet you, Kathleen' Ant had, out of habit, wiped her hand on her jeans, before shaking Kathleen's. It felt fleshy, comfortingly warm and wonderfully soft, like a little pillow filled with duck feathers.

'Is Ant your nickname?' Kathleen Fitzgerald had asked with a grin.

Ant had nodded, slightly embarrassed. Kathleen had noticed.

'I shudder to think what sort of nicknames my pupils have given me,' Kathleen had muttered under her breath, followed by a gratefully: 'Thank you so much, Ant,' using the nickname without hesitation. 'You are very kind. I think I would have been blocking the entire aisle for a while without your help,' her self-deprecating giggle was infectious, 'never mind the spectacle of me bending down and trying to get up again!'

'So you are a teacher?' Ant had changed the subject. 'Are you new to the area? I haven't seen you here before.'

'Ah! The Coop, the social hub of the town,' Kathleen had exclaimed, still in high spirits, obviously glad to have met someone of similar age, who wasn't a parent of one of her charges.

'It's better than nothing,' Ant had pointed out. 'Civilisation is a forty-five minutes' drive away along the river Exe or, if you are unlucky, along a flooded road.'

'You are right, I should be more grateful. I have only been here a couple of months, and I am still reeling from the culture shock.'

'Where did you live before?' Ant had asked out of curtesy rather than genuine interest. She needed to get on with her own shopping.

'London.' It hadn't been clear whether Kathleen Fitzgerald had sighed because she missed London or because she remembered the capital's own trials and tribulations.

'And now you are a teacher in Dulverton?'

'Not quite, I am the new Headmistress of the Middle School.' It was stated as a fact, not a boast.

'And what do you do, Ant?'

'I have a farm fifteen minutes from here.' Ant had said, picked up her basket and had made a move to pull away. After all, she had only come in for a few items. As if to stop her, Kathleen had asked promptly: 'Can I buy you a coffee when you have finished shopping? I believe there is a tearoom along the road.' It was now quite noticeable that Kathleen Fitzgerald spoke with an Irish accent, in spite of coming from London.

'Sorry,' Ant had said, 'I need to get back to my animals;' she had suddenly wanted to escape. Closeness amongst women frightened her for some unknown reason; the only friendship with another woman had ended badly: first, the girly outings had fizzled out when a potential husband had turned up, and then, Lucinda had disappeared altogether. Memories of last year's investigation into the disappearance were still raw.

Somehow Kathleen Fitzgerald had sensed Ant's unease: 'Some other time then,' she had replied with genuine regret in her voice.

'Maybe you could come up to the farm sometime and have a look at my pigs,' Ant had blurted out, fidgeting with the handle of her basket. She could have kicked herself a moment later for saying such a thing –as if she didn't have enough to do. Ant has never been that keen on entertaining.

'I would like that,' Kathleen had replied, 'maybe during the next school holidays?' the Headmistress had suggested. 'Tell you what: here is my card. Give me a call when you are free.' Luckily, the next school holidays were weeks away.

'On the other hand, you could come to my place,' Ant had heard Kathleen suggest; 'I live in a little house near the school. It's not glamorous, but I know how to make a decent cup of tea. May I have your mobile number?'

'I haven't got one,' Ant had replied with more sharpness than she had intended and had explained hastily: 'No signal on the Moor.' Ant had suddenly realised how churlish she must sound to this thoroughly nice woman and had scribbled her landline number on the back of her shopping list with a stubby pencil she always kept in her jeans pocket: 'Ring me any time you like. I am usually at home or working outside.'

'Won't you need that?' Kathleen had held the piece of paper aloft. Ant had shaken her head; she remembered the few items she had run out of: tea, milk, sugar, eggs, blueberry muffins, her favourite, and a few ripe bananas for the pigs. She tapped her temple a few times with her forefinger to indicate that she had memorised the list. The women had smiled at each other and then had gone their separate ways.

# CHAPTER TWO

Soon afterwards, on a Saturday morning, they had met again and had made time to pop into the tearoom in Fore Street. They felt surprisingly comfortable in each other's company, and the subsequent visit to Ant's farm was an unexpectedly hilarious success. 'I am not really built for climbing hills,' Kathleen had wheezed but her blue eyes had glinted with mischief. Admittedly, Kathleen had been a good sport and had bravely battled against the unusually steep terrain of Ant's farm and the gusts of wind which had made her long skirt billow to reveal ankle-height rubber boots.

'Very fetching,' Ant had commented with a grin and had been informed by her new friend that she had been a keen Brownie in her youth and hence, always came prepared. With lots of huffing and puffing, they had made it eventually up to the pigs, Ant's pride and joy. Kathleen had to catcher breath, leaning against the gate. No, Kathleen wouldn't be much help on the farm, Ant had mused, but she was good company, which was all that mattered.

'You do this twice a day, I presume,' Kathleen had guessed, shaking her head in admiration. The response was a shrug of the shoulders. Ant was used to it.

'What a view!' Kathleen had exclaimed when they had gone past the pigs' enclosures and reached the top of Ant's land. Their eyes were sweeping over mysterious dark Moor hills in the distance and over a river below dividing fields which were dotted with sheep grazing the sparse winter grass – not another house in sight. 'That's Haddon Hill over there,' Ant had pointed across the valley to an almost black hill - rising above everything else.

'Look at this!' Kathleen had exclaimed again and again, and Ant had been gratified because that had been exactly her reaction when she had first set eyes on the property during her hunt for a new home after her early retirement.

'Yes, it's glorious, isn't it,' Ant had agreed with pride. 'I love living here.' They had walked back down to the pigs in silence, where Ant had suddenly stopped.

'May I introduce: Iolanthe, Agatha and Persephone and their most recent unruly off- spring… Girls, meet Kathleen Fitzgerald, Headmistress of the Middle School,' she had made the farcical introduction, and Kathleen had promptly entered into the spirit: 'Pleased to meet you, ladies,' making a theatrical bow like a courtier in front of the Royals. We are not only of similar in age, Ant had thought; we have even the same weird sense of humour; and if her instincts didn't deceive her, Kathleen was living on her own, too. It didn't happen to Ant often that she took to somebody so easily.

'Are you going to dispatch them any time soon?' Kathleen had asked innocently, 'I like a bit of pork.'

'That's a sore point,' Ant had admitted. Indeed, she had kept some piglets from her first litter for breeding and had sold some at market, hoping that they would go to a good home rather than the abattoir. It had been a wrench, and she had hated every minute of it. She had suddenly discovered that she wasn't really cut out for raising pigs for slaughter. How nice, that Kathleen had sensed and understood Ant's unresolved dilemma; reassuring her that she couldn't contemplate dispatching a living creature either.

During the following couple of school terms, Ant's contribution to their flourishing friendship was to help occasionally out at school fetes and fundraising events for which Kathleen was immensely grateful. It wasn't always easy to keep

11

rivalling mothers focused on the real purpose of such gatherings. 'I'll do it. No change really from supervising pigs,' Ant had joked.

'You don't socialise much,' Kathleen had observed during a tea break at one of those occasions; 'hardly any of the locals know you.' Ant didn't want to explain, but had noticed a few enquiring looks in her direction, too. No, she thought, I don't want that much contact with the outside world; I have seen too much of the dark side of mankind and have become rather cynical about the supposedly innate goodness in people. She simply didn't want to make the effort any more, only to perhaps be proved wrong. It didn't bother her if they thought her odd.

Kathleen was a rare exception. 'Let's say, I like my own company,' Ant had conceded and had left it at that.'

'Were you always a pig farmer?' Kathleen had changed the subject diplomatically.

'No. I bought the farm a couple of years ago.'

'And what did you do before?'

At first, Ant had avoided Kathleen's questioning gaze before taking the plunge: 'I was a forensic scientist,' she had gulped, 'working with the police on murder cases.'

# CHAPTER THREE

At the beginning of Kathleen's second year as the headmistress of the school it was decided to establish a students' exchange with a school in Northern France. Excitement and anxiety were palpable in equal measure amongst pupils, parents and some of the staff - some mutterings against the project could be heard, but Kathleen was a firm believer in bringing up children to be broadminded and to provide them with a window to the world. She could be enormously persuasive and, to the delight of the pupils, she won the argument, at least for a trial run.

The English children, accompanied by two popular young teachers, Miss Barber and Miss Heath, travelled first during the Easter holidays on the Plymouth to Roscoff ferry and stayed for a week with families in a small town called Morlaix, not far along the Britany coast. It was gloriously sunny as the adults had hoped, but had not dared to expect, considering that Northern France often shared the same weather with England. The brave group members, the guinea pigs, had a whale of a time, forming new friendships with their French counterparts who - they discovered to their relief - were more fluently in speaking English than the guests were in speaking French. The pupils from the little school on Exmoor sampled French family life and French food. On the first morning - to give them an idea of the beauty of Morlaix's location - the French teachers, a young woman and her even younger male assistant, took them up a narrow path to the top of the surrounding hills of the Monts d'Arree, showing them proudly the view onto the town's half-timbered buildings, their jewel-like tiny gardens and the ruins of the old walled town. 'Over there,' the young teachers pointed into the direction of the ocean, 'you can see the famous pink granite coast of Morlaix and the estuary of the river Dossen; it is a tidal river, but often dries up in the summer. After admiring the view dutifully for a little while, the English pupils were ready to climb down again to hit the shops in the narrow streets; however, to their disappointment, the teachers didn't turn back to descend, but carried on leading the group further up on the so called Priest's Allee until they reached the first level of a Viaduct, spanning the entire valley, with a magnificent view onto the harbour and its bobbing boats.

After that, the group clambered happily back down to the town to do a bit of sightseeing: they were taken to visit the inside of La Maison de la Duchesse, one of the half-timbered maisons à pondalez, the residences of the wealthy linen merchants in the 16th and 17th centuries whose upper storeys were strangely and precariously overhanging the narrow alleyways.

The harbour looked much like any port in Devon and Cornwall, but they had never seen a river flowing underneath such an imposing viaduct which loomed over the town. The teachers reminded them that, only an hour ago, they had all stood on the viaduct's first level, sixty-two metres up from the ground. What the teachers didn't mention was that the river separated the town into an old, wealthy part, and the one where most of the host families lived. It was all rather exotic and exciting.

The English pupils were glad that only one day of their stay was reserved for a school visit. The school building looked austere like the monastery it had once been. The French pupils were highly disciplined and the lessons were theoretical and boring with little opportunity for teachers and pupils to interact. The students were sitting on old fashioned benches, rigid as if glued to their seats, and nobody said a word unless asked; even the English children didn't dare to fidget or whisper to each other. The teachers hammered the target messages of each lesson home, strict and unsmiling, and at the end of each lesson, they

14

seemed to set hours of homework. The English teenagers were bewildered, glad that they were only visitors, taking away the impression that the French teachers didn't liked children very much, and that their own school in Dulverton with the friendly staff was vastly more preferable.

However, after the obligatory cultural elements of their stay, the English school children were left to enjoy what young people like best: shopping and hanging out with their new pals. They spent hours browsing in Place Allende with its quaint shops which had elegant names like *boulangerie* and *patisserie*, *boutiques* and *kiosque de journaux*, and refreshed themselves in the town's outdoor cafes and bistros; they even sat through an entire film in French which, luckily, some of them had seen before at home in English. The most exciting thing they were allowed to do was to visit the local bar in whose cellar some host parents had organised a disco on the Saturday night - of course supervised discreetly by the teachers from England and a couple of young French colleagues, who, to the children's relief, sat at the bar all evening, drinking, chatting, occasionally dancing and flirting. It seemed quite natural to the French teenagers to spend most of Saturday night until the early hours in the company of deafening music, bottles of pop or something stronger, exhausting themselves by jiggling on the dance floor or shouting to each other across the general din – not something that would have happened in their little hometown in the South West of England. At the end of the week, the English children were reluctant to leave. Even the rough return journey on the ferry across the English Channel added to the excitement and sense of adventure.

Once the English children had returned home, they couldn't wait for their new friends to repay the visit, and they pestered their parents and teachers to organise a 'cool' programme for them. There was a definite buzz to school life in the weeks running up to the guests' arrival.

The Headmistress drowned in organising it all, and Ant understood that for the next few weeks, she would not see much of Kathleen.

And then suddenly, she had a call out of the blue from the school secretary, saying that the guests had arrived, and would she like to give a presentation on her Mangalia pigs - to the assembled crowd of English and French pupils and maybe bring some of the piglets with her. Stupidly, she agreed.

'...got you,' Ant exclaims with relief. She has already played with the idea to cancel the assignment. The piglet squeals and struggles to get out of her grip, but she quickly drops it into a battered, lidded animal basket which had seen a variety of cats, guinea pigs and hamsters, but never a pig. She slams the lid shut, so that it can't escape; however, she cannot drown out the furious squeals and scrabbling noises in spite of having donated an old woollen jumper for the creature's comforts.

'Now we need to give you a name,' she mumbles to herself. Children pay much more attention to talking adults when everything is personalised, and when the animals have a name. She decides on the first thing that comes into her head: Magnus – a bit grand for a wriggling, grunting piglet with flapping ears and a wet nose. It would have to do.

'Mangalia pigs are an unusual type of pig - descended from various Hungarian breeds and wild boars,' Ant begins her talk. As expected, the children are delighted with Magnus, who at one stage escapes and runs around between the legs of the squealing children and, just before he can be caught by a flustered Ant, deposits a smelly brown parcel under a piano stool which sends the audience into hysterics. 'Magnus, Magnus,' they screech at

16

the top of their voices; some even rename him Magnum, probably after their favourite ice-cream. The word chaotic springs to mind, but Kathleen turns up just in time. She has heard the commotion and soon restores calm and order in the assembly hall. There is no doubt, Magnus is a great hit!

'Sorry about that,' Ant says when the children have left for their class rooms and Magnus is safely back in his cat carrier on the backseat of her car. Kathleen laughs: 'They loved it! A great interruption of the curriculum is always appreciated by the pupils. You did a great job in communicating information in an entertaining way. Well done!' Ant is not quite convinced that her friend is not simply kind, but she laughs with her good naturedly.

Ant is relieved that the talk wasn't a total disaster, but makes a promise to herself not to do it again. Once the French boys and girls have gone, she hopes that she and Kathleen will resume their easy friendship in private.

Three days before the French group's departure, Ant receives an unexpected call from the school. This time Kathleen herself is on the phone, her voice strangled with fear, pleading: 'Ant, I need your help!'

# CHAPTER FOUR

Charlotte is one of the girls who had been on the trip to France. Her parents were excited for her, telling her about their honeymoon traveling around France, which in those days was something rather daring. They had told her about the warmth of the people, the stylish women, spectacularly good home-cooking even in the smallest restaurants, constantly changing landscapes of high mountains to wooded hills, from lavender fields to fabulous beaches on the Atlantic or, down south, on the Mediterranean. Charlotte had never seen them so full of nostalgia, exchanging happy giggles after allusions only they understood. They had avoided the Cote d'Azur, sensing that they wouldn't even be able to afford an ice cream in these posh resorts for the wealthy. Charlotte's Mum had therefore, helped happily to buy nice presents for her daughter's host family: chocolates, English tea, marmalade and a set of table place mats with pictures of timbered old pubs. Charlotte had thought the latter an inspired choice.

When she had arrived in the French family, it was rather different: a single parent family consisting of a petite, gaunt-looking nervous mother with straggly blond, shoulder-length hair, dressing in untidy, short skirts and un-ironed blouses, who rushed in and out of the apartment, apparently working all the hours God sent. It was left to Sylvie to do most of the hosting and catering, and they didn't need place-mats for that. Sylvie was a tall, - certainly taller than Charlotte - skinny fourteen year old who looked nothing like her mother: her hair was pitch-black, reaching almost down to her waist. Her skin was tanned, bordering on swarthy and her big, dark eyes in a long face seemed permanently filled with a dreamy sadness. Charlotte had to admit that had she been in Sylvie's shoes- having to do all the hosting, housework and school work - she would not have coped as well as her new friend did. On top of it all, poor Sylvie seemed to be in charge of Bertrand, her wayward, wild younger brother, who took no notice of his sister's desperate attempts at reining him in. Strangely enough, Bertrand looked nothing like Sylvie and rather more like his mother. Food consisted of ready-made, microwaved mush in silver foil trays which nobody seemed to enjoy. There was no sitting down for two hours of lunch with an amicable chat over delicious, steaming food, as Charlotte's parents had described. Bertrand usually ran off, still food in his mouth; Sylvie picked at whatever they were eating and couldn't wait to clear the table and wash up. The table mats had been shoved into a drawer in an old dresser, probably never to see the light of day again. Charlotte took to helping Sylvie with drying up, something she didn't do often at home, as her Mum had a dishwasher. The whole exchange was a bit of a let-down; far removed from what she had expected and what she was used to, until her Mum reminded her over the phone that she had come to France to experience something new, something different, and that she should make the most of whatever there was. She did and also made an effort to get closer to her exchange partner, who seemed to be burdened with tasks and responsibilities too heavy for her slim shoulders.

'Please, not tell teacher!' she had begged Charlotte in broken English, when they had reached a degree of closeness.

'Of course, not,' Charlotte had promised.

'...I not get bursary to go to England,' Sylvie had sighed. 'I must go to England!'

Charlotte understood perfectly, that Sylvie would be looking forward to getting out of her environment and away from her never-ending duties - at least for a week. She even played with the idea that her parents might let Sylvie stay for the summer holidays. However, when she hinted at the idea to Sylvie, the girl shook her head and pointed out that her mother needed her help even more during school holidays, to keep her little brother out of mischief while Mum was working.

My mother goes to work, Charlotte thought; admittedly only part-time, while she, an only child, was at school, but Charlotte was very rarely alone at home, for hours in charge of things, like Sylvie was. Her only daily tasks were to feed and brush the cat and to clean the litter tray regularly. Otherwise, she rarely had to help out because her mother preferred her to concentrate on school work and to practise for her piano lessons. If her mother could be organised, surely, Sylvie's mother could make more effort, too, and not be quite so reliant on her young daughter?

Charlotte felt sorry for her friend, whom she thought immensely glamorous with her long, black hair hanging loose down her back and a fringe which nearly covered her eyes. She liked the way Sylvie frequently blew it, her bottom lip pursed, out of her forehead. Sylvie was tall for her age and looked, compared to the slightly plump Charlotte, like one of those undernourished photographic models featured in exotic fashion journals; maybe it was just Sylvie's natural shape or the fashion in France. Charlotte vowed in her heart that she would make her friend's return visit a special one.

Now, almost at the end of Sylvie's stay, Charlotte has to admit that it hasn't been quite the unqualified success she had hoped for. For a start, Sylvie has been morose when she arrived and all through her visit; whatever they suggested, Sylvie looked unhappy and had no interest in anything she and her parents suggested. She seemed to endure English school life rather than enjoy the comparative freedom of it; nor did she find pleasure in any of the carefully chosen outings; not even a shopping trip to Exeter could lift her spirits. Her room, which she didn't have to share like she did at home, was in a permanent state of mess; the bed remained crumpled as it had been on the first morning after she had slept in it. Sylvie's mother kept ringing every evening at nine, her almost hysterical voice through the receiver did nothing to improve Sylvie's mood. She usually went to bed straight after and wasn't seen nor heard until the morning.

What hurt Charlotte most – not that she blamed her friend – was that the closeness she had worked so hard to achieve while in France, had evaporated and any attempt at renewing it, was firmly rebuffed. Sylvie had become a stranger once more.

'She is probably a bit homesick,' Charlotte's mother had tried to console her daughter, reading the disappointment in her face. She surmises that the pretty Sylvie has come with a lot of emotional baggage. Or it could be, that Sylvie, who is over a year older than the rest of her group and Charlotte's class friends, is feeling isolated. 'Why is she older than all the others,' her mother had asked, and Charlotte had explained that Sylvie had to repeat a year in school to make up for the teaching she had missed while looking after her mother when she was ill. Charlotte and her Mum decide that they can only do their best in being kind to her and to make her stay as pleasant as possible; everything else is out of their hands.

Working in a school for behaviourally challenging children, Mrs Bowers never ceases to be amazed at the resilience of children and their desire to cling to their parents however bad they are; the tenacity to mother the adults and blaming themselves when things fell apart. Poor mites! Now at the end of the exchange, they have to admit that – although Sylvie doesn't quite fall into that category - there is something not right with the girl, something she is hiding.

Patience! Only a couple more days until the group's departure, Mrs Bowers admonishes herself. She knows that Sylvie likes

Hamburgers. I shall make my own, special version, she decides. It will be a rare treat for Charlotte, too. I'll just have to nip into the Coop for a few things. She is cheered by the prospect of the girls tucking into the universally favourite meal 'Sylvie! Sylvie! Wait!' The summer rain lashes the little town. Her soaking wet plaits are beginning to feel heavy on her back and rain drops are running down Charlotte's forehead, dripping into her eyes. She blinks furiously while running to catch up with Sylvie.

Sylvie turns around, and Charlotte nearly bumps into her.

'Sylvie, you misunderstood! You can stay for the choir. I was just not sure whether you would rather go to the library.' Charlotte sincerely wishes she had not even mentioned an alternative to choir practice.

'I go 'ome. Singing is boring. You sing; I speak to my mother.' Sylvie's French accent is endearing, but she is in a particularly bad mood and sounds defiant. Maybe it is better if she does go home; she might even have a headache and doesn't want to say. However, Charlotte isn't quite sure whether her mother will be back from work yet. That question usually doesn't arise, because Charlotte always sticks to what has been arranged.

'I think Mum would prefer you to stay with me. It's only an hour, Sylvie.'

'I know way 'ome; it is ten minutes.' Charlotte loves the French accent, how it turns ordinary English into elegant sounds, into something thrillingly foreign. She smiles at Sylvie: 'I really rather you stayed,' she pleads.

The two girls look at one another. Sylvie is pouting. They really haven't much in common. Nothing is ever 'cool' enough for Sylvie. Charlotte begins to wonder whether there is anything at all her exotic friend is interested in.

Sylvie purses her lips and blows her black fringe out of her eyes: 'My mother ring in 'alf an 'our.'

'Your mother usually rings at nine o'clock,' Charlotte reminds her.

'Not today,' Sylvie contradicts provocatively.

'Is something wrong at home?' Charlotte's heart sinks.

Sylvie shrugs her thin shoulders, as if she didn't care.

Charlotte is at a loss what to do. She is torn between taking part in the choir rehearsal, which she has promised to attend, and her duty as a friend and host to Sylvie. She really doesn't want to make her even more upset than she has been all week.

'I have an umbrella in my satchel. Would you like me to get it?'

Sylvie shakes her head.

'You go home then. Here, take my key, and I see you in an hour!' Charlotte relents.

As Sylvie turns away, Charlotte feels uneasy: 'You will go straight home, Sylvie, won't you? You know the way...' she shouts after her.

'Of course,' Sylvie half turns back, suddenly smiling broadly, and blowing her an unexpected kiss.

# CHAPTER FIVE

'Ant.' Kathleen's cry for help into the telephone sounds, as if she is drowning.

'Kathleen, what's the matter?'

'One of our French exchange students has gone missing! She said she would go straight home after school, but she never arrived.'

'Slow down, Kathleen; kids go missing all the time. What's happened?'

'Sorry,' Kathleen gulps, 'her exchange partner, Charlotte, had choir practice after school, and Sylvie didn't want to stay, so she gave her the key to the house and let her go.'

'…and that was around three-thirty in the afternoon?'

'Yes, just after lessons ended; choir practice starts fifteen minutes later.' Kathleen's horrified whisper is hardly audible.

'Have you asked around - the host families, the other students?'

'We have rung or seen everybody we can think of. We asked in the shops, the post office; the charity shop she likes…Nobody has seen her,' Kathleen stops to take a breath.

'Maybe she is sitting on a bench by the river, feeding the ducks?'

'We looked there as well. The owner of the pub by the river was there all afternoon, but he didn't notice any youngsters,' Kathleen replies miserably. 'He said the town was very quiet; there was hardly anybody about.'

'Ant, is it too early to ring the police?' Ant checks her watch; t is now just past six o'clock. 'Charlotte and her parents are frantic, and so am I!'

'I think there is no need to panic just yet,' Ant stalls. 'When did they discover that Sylvie had not gone home?'

'The mother went to the butcher's just before all the kids came out of school, thinking that Sylvie and Charlotte would be at choice practice until four forty-five . She expected them to come home around five o'clock. When Charlotte arrived home alone, that's when alarm bells rang. They called me, to ask whether I had seen Sylvie. They thought she might have returned to school to pick up Charlotte after she had spoken to her mother in France on the phone... and the girls might have missed each other.' The headmistress's anxious words tumble out like a torrent.

'She might just have gone for a walk and got lost,' Ant speculates. '...or she met one of the other kids in the group and has gone off with them. Carry on with your enquiries and ring the police: they will organise a thorough search – the sooner the better.' Ant can hear Kathleen breathing hard - or is it a sob?

'Don't worry too much,' she tries to console her friend. 'It's terrible when kids go missing, but in most cases, they turn up within a day or so, okay?' Ant hopes she is right.

'...those poor families!' Kathleen moans.

Ant has an idea: 'Do you think she might be with one of the local boys?'

'I haven't heard any rumours, but I shall ask around.' Kathleen clutches at the straw offered which gives her something concrete to do.

'I'll just finish off the pigs, and then I come down and help with the search. With some luck, Sylvie will have turned up by then. '

'I hope so. It doesn't bear thinking about…' Ant can hear in Kathleen's voice that she is desperately trying to suppress tears.

'I'll be with you in half an hour. In the meantime, do ring the police to report her missing, and then you can make discreet enquiries about a possible boyfriend.' It's something to occupy Kathleen's mind and to lessen the panic, Ant hopes.

'Yes, 'Kathleen confirms miserably…Ant…'

'Yes?'

'Do I ring the poor mother in France just yet?'

'Wait until the police are here. It's better to ask them. No point in alerting the poor woman, if there is a good chance that the girl turns up soon.'

'Thanks, Ant. It's good to talk to someone who understands. Everybody else seems to look to me for advice, and I can't think of any; I feel as dreadful as everybody else.'

'Nobody can expect miracles. All we can do is to remain calm, logical and patient.

As soon as the first police officers arrive, young Charlotte, wiping constantly tears from her swollen eyes with an already soaking wet handkerchief, is asked to give them Sylvie's most recent photograph on her phone. Sylvie's mobile lies on her unmade bed, and they soon find a suitable picture: Sylvie pouting moodily, her skinny jeans and a skimpy, washed-out pink T-shirt clinging to her body which is thin as a rake; Sylvie posing in the garden on the day she arrived. The photo is distributed among the leaders of the hastily arranged search parties of Dulverton residents and sent via the Internet to all Police Stations in the county, to airports, train stations and port authorities – just in case. The police are soon joined by every fit person in the community. They walk along the grassy banks of the rivers Barle and Exe; up the little lane to Charlotte's family home; citizens of Dulverton are asked to inspect their properties, particularly outbuildings and cellars for signs of young people having congregated; the school building is searched from top to bottom by the caretakers and a young policeman; members of the amateur dramatic society scour the proud little town hall where they usually perform; and other searches go on at the modern doctor's surgery, which the architect has made to look like the bow of a ship; the tourist information centre - well-frequented in the summer months by hiking, cycling and equestrian tourists, campers and holidaymakers – and the adjacent library, run by volunteers, are next to be searched; the clergy inspect every corner of the church and the church yard, but nothing can be found, which would indicates that Sylvie might have been there. Where else could she be? The familiar quaint, narrow lanes feel suddenly threatening and ominous.

As soon as three more Taunton police cars arrive with flashing lights, the search is widened: up to the surrounding hills on steep, narrow, deserted lanes leading up to the Moor. In a month, the height of summer, Exmoor will turn purple with heather. The search teams make use of the light June evening, until dusk falls and a fine mixture of mist and drizzle - *mizzle,* as the locals call it- drives them home. They will continue tomorrow unless the girl has reappeared.

Kathleen's thoughts sway form hope, that Sylvie is somewhere safe, to the horrific prospect that the girl might have slipped and fallen into one of the rivers, however low they might be now compared to the winter months. But wouldn't people have noticed a foreign girl? This is a community, where people look out for each other.

As everybody falls exhaustedly into bed, the police carry on their search for another couple of hours in the dark under powerful search-lights.

'I shall have to ring our colleagues in Morlaix,' says the policeman in charge, Sergeant William Penhaligon, 'they must contact the mother. I hope the young lady has turned up before then.'

Few people in the little town are sleeping that night. Everybody is thinking about the French girl, and what might have happened to her. Most hope that she has simply been naughty, maybe gone on a secret date or for a ramble on her own. It wouldn't be pleasant for her to be outdoors at that time of night; she might be cold, maybe lost, feeling all alone in a foreign country. The host families count their blessings that all their children had returned safe and sound from France.

Charlotte is wide awake in her bed. Her mother has urged her several times to try and sleep, but how can she? Wild thoughts tumble through her mind: of Sylvie's dreadful home-life; of her poor mother having to worry about the only person who supports her; and Sylvie's unhappiness since she arrived. Does her French friend have secrets? Are there things she hasn't told anybody? She never talks about any other members of her family; Charlotte would love to ask her about her father, but Sylvie never mentions him, and Charlotte wouldn't pry. She doesn't want to make her friend even more unhappy than she already is. Poor Sylvie; she really hasn't much luck in her young life. If only she, Charlotte, had insisted that she stayed with her at choir practice! If only Sylvie hadn't felt that she rather went home or somewhere to be on her own. Had she really expected a call from her mother? Or was that an excuse - to meet someone? Maybe she felt so homesick that she had taken a bus to Plymouth and boarded a ferry home, however far-fetched that sounds? But then the French group were going home soon anyway. Or had Sylvie run away to London, a magnet for thousands of young tourists every year? Maybe she was disappointed that the metropolis was nowhere near Dulverton? Would she have known how to get there? Sylvie hadn't mentioned any such intentions; all group excursions had been organised by the school or the host parents in advance, and going to London had not been considered feasible during the group's one week visit. Thoughts are circling round and round in Charlotte's head like laundry in a tumble-dryer, tormenting her; if she goes over each detail again, maybe she will discover something that she has missed before, something that will point to where Sylvie might be. It is fanciful, but in a night of worries and tension, all sorts of strange ideas lodge in one's head and seem feasible.

Eventually, Charlotte falls into an uneasy sleep, interrupted by wild dreams, frightening scenarios and pictures of Sylvie coming through the door.

# CHAPTER SIX

When neither Kathleen nor Ant have heard from Sylvie's mother or the French police by mid-morning, they decide to ring Mrs Karim from Kathleen's office, just to reassure her that everything possible is done to find her daughter. They tremble in anticipation of a harrowing call. Kathleen catches her on the mobile. Mrs Karim's voice is timid and cracking. They had hoped that the French police would have contacted her by now and informed her about the search for her daughter, but no such luck.

'It's Kathleen Fitzgerald from England. I am the Headmistress of the school in England.' She is immediately interrupted by a panicked voice: 'Is all right with Sylvie?'

Kathleen chooses to ignore the question and asks instead: 'Are you at home, Mrs Karim?'

'Yes; I go to work soon,' Bernadette Karim whispers, as if somebody has robbed her of air.

'Are you on your own, Mrs Karim?'

Kathleen can hear sobs and then a scream: 'Where is Sylvie? What happen?'

Kathleen takes a decision in spite of her fear that she might be the first person to tell the poor woman that her daughter has gone missing. She does so as gently as she can, imagining her at the other end of the phone line, alone, ready for work, hearing the dreadful news.

Once they have communicated that the girl is missing, Sylvie's mother goes understandably and completely to pieces, screaming hysterically into the telephone, as if her brain was about to flip over and her heart would break. Even Ant can hear the screams, standing a few feet away from Kathleen. They can only imagine the poor woman's anguish.

'Ask her for the address,' Ant says in a low voice; 'we need to alert Sergeant Penhaligon and the French police. Somebody should be with her.' When they have finally extracted a sensible answer from Mrs Karim, Ant leaves the room and makes the urgent phone call to Taunton from the school secretary's office next door.

Kathleen holds on to the call, trying to find soothing words for the person at the other end and wishes, her arms could reach through to hold her close.

'Mrs Karim, we are all looking for her. Has she ever run away before?'

She doesn't get an answer; Bernadette Karim cannot think. She only feels pain and numbness. After a while, the screams die down and turn into heart-wrenching sobs intersected by gulps for air. 'Je savais, je savais!' she cries out in agony, as if she had known that something disastrous would happen.

Why aren't the French police by her side yet? Kathleen feels so powerless. In her mind's eyes, she can see the woman crouching on the floor, in a heap, unable to stand up, wailing in mental distress. Kathleen continues to speak to her in a quiet and, what she hopes, reassuring tone about the efforts being made to find her daughter; she tells her that everybody in the little town was getting involved, doing something to help; she mentions the professional efforts of the police who had been called without delay and have returned early this morning with an even bigger team to continue and widen the search. Kathleen speaks for what seems like an eternity, before Ant returns, giving a silent thumbs-up and whispers that the French police are on their way.

It is a relief, when Kathleen can hear knocking in the background through the telephone line. At least someone is coming. Kathleen and Ant are thinking: about time! Maybe they should have contacted them last night after all?

Kathleen can hear Bernadette putting the mobile down somewhere, luckily without cutting her off; she listens to steps going away, accompanied by sounds of thick , heart-wrenching sobs and the sound of a door being opened; a few mumbled words and another cry of anguish and pain – and then silence; only two male voices talking rapidly in French. Bernadette has probably fainted, hopefully into the arms of a police officer.

Someone has taken hold of Mrs Karim's mobile and reassures Kathleen and Ant in broken English that they would take over now. There is no time to explain anything else.

Ant falls into a chair by the desk.

'What did she mean by: Je savais, Je savais?' Ant mutters.

'I think it means something like: I knew it.' Kathleen explains.

'Strange thing to say, isn't it?' Ant raises her eyebrows,

Kathleen shrugs her shoulders. She is exhausted. 'There is no accounting for the things people in distress say,' she guesses. Ant makes a mental note.

In the afternoon, Kathleen has to see off the group of twenty exchange pupils minus Sylvie and their two teachers. The police have hastily taken statements from each one of them that morning. There is no point extending their stay, and they promise to ring the school, should anyone suddenly remember something important they haven't reported yet. It is a sad good-bye of silent hugs, solemn faces and a few tears. They climb into the school bus, subdued and bewildered, which will take them back to Plymouth; they will catch the ferry they had booked originally. The little group of English host children, Kathleen, Ant, Sergeant

32

Penhaligon and the two teachers involved in the exchange wave a few more times, even though the coach has already gone out of sight.

'What's going to happen now?' Kathleen turns to the Sergeant, who shakes his head: 'We do our best. We keep searching.' They look at him in hope, and he feels compelled to add: 'It is early days yet.'

# CHAPTER SEVEN

A day later, Bernadette and a French police woman, Jeanne Charpentier, have come over from Roscoff on the first available ferry, possibly crossing the path of the one which carried the French exchange group home. Standing on the forecourt of the passenger lounge, waiting for the police car to pick them up, they look lost and bewildered. The two and a half hours drive back to Exmoor is spent in near silence, interrupted only by the odd sob escaping Bernadette's throat, while the police officers exchange whispers of basic information about what is to them a rapidly developing investigation.

Bernadette Karim looks absolutely shattered when they finally reach Dulverton. She is emaciated, as if she hasn't eaten for days; her face is crisscrossed with traces of long wept tears like dried up river beds; and the skin is almost translucent with a deathly pallor with features rigid like a mask; her eyelids keep twitching and her lips are cracked and bloodless. She only speaks in staccato, broken sentences which are translated by the accompanying policewoman Jeanne. Bernadette Karim has only brought an overnight bag with her, containing hardly more than a change of clothes, should she need to get out of her black, skinny nylon slacks and the polo-neck pullover in a washed-out shade of beige. Her blond hair falls in straggly strands to her shoulders – having long outgrown any stylish cut if there had ever been one; it looks unwashed, greasy and unkempt which is not surprising under the circumstances. There are big, black rings under her grey eyes, puffy and red from weeping; her elfin figure appears fragile; and she moves, numb with shock, like a wooden marionette. Her dainty, flat ballerina-type shoes are surely bound to make her feet feel every stone on the ground, but she seems oblivious to anything around her as if trapped in the eye of a cyclone while the storm is raging all around her. They stop in the school car park and Kathleen is there to welcome her with a warm embrace; then she takes her guest gently by the shoulder and steers her to the office.

Sitting on the settee, each a cup of strong coffee in front of them on the low glass tale, they introduce themselves one by one, and then Sergeant Penhaligon asks the first question addressed to the French guest: 'Where would you like to go first?' She hasn't listened, so Jeanne, the French police woman, repeats the question in French.

'The family,' her words sound like a faint breath. They understand, and the Sergeant puts a quick call through to the host family, to ask whether they could pay a brief visit. 'Of course, by all means,' Mr Bowers replies with dread in his voice.

'Do I need to come?' Kathleen asks. She has tons of paperwork to catch up on. Fortunately, the Sergeant shakes his head.

'Could you look after Mrs Karim for the rest of the evening?' he probes. 'We have booked two rooms for both of them in the local hotel.' They arrange a time for the change-over.

The two women and the Sergeant climb back into the police car and drive straight to the host family's house. They introduce themselves stiffly as Ken and Christine Bowers. Bernadette, of course, knows Charlotte and shakes her hand. Then, they show the visitors to the room Sylvie had inhabited for almost a week. It is a pretty guest room, in spite of the unmade, single bed and a crumpled bedsheet – they were told by the investigating officers to leave everything as the girl had left it. The rose bud motif on the duvet cover and two pillows is repeated on the wallpaper. Beneath the window, which has a view over the back garden, stands a light-brown wooden desk, a dainty, free-standing mirror on it and Sophie's make-up bag leaning against it. The girl's suitcase rests on the floor against the wall close to the bed, the lid open and the contents in disarray, as if Sylvie had left it after a frantic search. A pair of cheap trainers, scuffed and with brown rimmed soles stand next to it, one overturned. There is a little sink fitting snuggly into the left hand corner behind the door, where Sylvie's toothbrush and paste are kept in a glass and a large piece of English rose soap lies dry and hardly used on the soap indent of the basin.

Bernadette stands lost and lonely in the middle of the room as if to soak up any remaining traces of her daughter. She turns in a full circle, but she can't feel Sylvie's presence. Did Sylvie really sleep here for a week? All she can see are a few shabby items her daughter has left behind.

'Is it possible that Sylvie came home sometime during the day?' asks Jeanne, the French policewoman, in a whisper. 'That suitcase looks as if she was searching for something in a hurry.'

Charlotte, who has kept close behind her mother, shakes her head: 'She didn't have a key. I gave her mine when she didn't want to stay for choir after school… and she was sitting next to me in every lesson that day.'

'Would you like to stay with us?' Christine Bowers offers hospitality, haltingly, questioning the wisdom of the suggestion. Would Sylvie's mother want to sleep in a room from which her daughter has disappeared?

Bernadette can't get herself to sleep in what has been Sylvie's bed: 'Je ne peux pas…,' she whispers, turning to her translator for help, but Sergeant Penhaligon conveys already to the family that she wouldn't. He seems to be speaking a little French.

'It's very kind of you, but it is just too much for her to bear,' Jeanne adds quietly.

'That's all right,' replies Christine with an inner sigh of relief, 'I just thought it might help if she could wrap herself into her daughter's duvet.' They all recognise that it is well-meant.

'Thanks anyway,' the Sergeant says with a faint smile. 'We have provisionally booked her into the hotel.' He is grateful that it isn't fully booked so near to the school holidays. It is not very big, and they were lucky to secure two singles. The regular holiday makers on Exmoor National Park book ahead for the next year before they leave.

On the way there, Penhaligon asks Bernadette, whether she has eaten. She shakes her head and refuses the offer of a meal in the hotel's restaurant, before she is shown to her room. She says something to Jeanne who duly translates: her charge wants to make a phone call to her son.

'I'll ask the manager to let her call from his office whenever she wants. We'll settle the bill at the end.' the Sergeant suggests. 'It's too expensive from her mobile, and there might not always be a signal in this area.'

'Thanks,' says Jeanne, but Bernadette shakes her head and takes a mobile from her holdall. They leave her to go upstairs with the young lady from behind the bar, who will take her to the room, so that the guest from France can make her call in private. Jeanne and the Sergeant reassure her that they would be waiting downstairs at the bar.

'I didn't realise she had a son,' says the Sergeant, when they each have a much needed cup of coffee in front of them. 'How old is he?'

'I don't know. He wasn't in when I picked her up, but he is younger than Sylvie, she told me, and a bit... shall we say: difficult?'

'Who is looking after him now?'

'Hm. Presumably Bernadette has made arrangements. But good point! I think I better send somebody round to the flat to check.'

Penhaligon likes the no-nonsense approach of this young French colleague. He guesses, she is probably in her mid-thirties, to his trained eye, about five foot six, sturdy – certainly a lot sturdier than Mrs Karim - but still looking elegant in the French version of a police uniform. Her thick, blond, hair is short, tucked behind her ears and brushed to one side from a parting. It's always interesting to witness and hear how forces in other parts of the world work and deal with their assignments. One thing baffles him, though:

'Where did you learn such good English?'

'Are you saying, you can speak French?' she teases him.

Sergeant Penhaligon blushes. Jeanne laughs: 'The English have a reputation regarding foreign language skills,' she reminds him. 'Don't worry. My mother was English and part of my schooling was in England. When my dad was recalled to France by his company, I went with them; I didn't fancy the idea of staying behind in a boarding school.'

William Penhaligon sighs; feeling a little vindicated, and changes the topic: 'What do you know about the Karim family?'

'Not much,' Jeanne admits. 'Bernadette lives on some sort of benefit, but she is also working as a cleaner, and on Saturdays, she helps out as a shop assistant – I guess on a minimum wage.'

'So the children don't really see much of her?'

'It looks to me, as if Sylvie is in charge of young Bertrand and the running of the household: shopping, meals, cleaning, that sort of thing.' Jeanne explains.

Penhaligon shakes his head in disbelief: '...the host family and the headmistress told me that far from enjoying her week of freedom, Sylvie was on edge and morose all week. They put it down to homesickness,' Penhaligon remarks.

'She probably worried about her mother and Bertrand – a young carer's syndrome,' Jeanne has dealt with cases like this before.

'It doesn't seem fair.' The Sergeant shakes his head with sadness. Some children are really dealt a bad hand from birth. Not that it was any different on his patch.

'Sylvie is by far not the worst case,' Jeanne breaks into his thoughts.

The thin, pale figure of Bernadette reappears on the stairs, slowly and holding on to the banister, as if afraid that she might tumble down. She has wrapped herself into a black woollen cardigan which reaches to her knees and is held together at the waist by a belt of the same material.

'Everything all right with your son?' the Sergeant enquires with concern.

'Oui, mon fils est avec…'The Sergeant raises his eyebrows in question and looks at Jeanne for a translation.

'He is with his father.' Jeanne repeats quickly.

'I thought she was a single mum.' Penhaligon looks confused from one to the other. 'With a name like Karim, is he … Muslim?' he asks cautiously.

'Not sure. I think it's complicated.' Jeanne hazards a guess.

'Can you find out?' It's more of a request than a question.

'Not tonight,' she pleads with him.

'Of course, not,' he concedes, 'we all need a good night's sleep.'

'I'll speak to her tomorrow,' Jeanne promises.

When Bernadette reaches the two police officers, she agrees to have at least a black coffee.

'I want to see way Sylvie go home from school,' she tries to convey to the Sergeant.

'…tonight?' They are a little aghast, having hoped that they could have their drink and then retire, but they can't really deny her request.

Bernadette confirms the urgency of her wish with an unexpectedly vigorous nod.

'Okay, but it will be dark soon, so we better go when you have finished your coffee.'

Bernadette immediately grabs her cup and gulps down the thick, black liquid, oblivious to how hot it still is. 'We go,' she hurries them on.

Sergeant Penhaligon and his French counterpart take the determined but ever so frail looking Bernadette back to the school. Kathleen, the Headmistress, is still in her office; she can't bear to go home and relax; she has managed to get through quite a lot of work which had accumulated in the chaos of the past couple of days. Ant has just popped in with a couple of sandwiches, when the little group arrive.

'I'll come with you,' Kathleen offers immediately, putting down her half eaten bread. 'I am restless anyway.'

'I'll have to go to do the pigs,' says Ant diplomatically, picks up the last sandwich from the desk, smiling apologetically when a few crumbs fall on the floor, and stuffs it into her rucksack. 'Give me a call if you need anything.'

Kathleen nods: 'Thanks, Ant, you're a brick.' Ant is already out of the door. Kathleen feels very lucky to have her as a friend.

The policeman explains the purpose of this late visit, and Kathleen offers to come with them for a second time 'Let's go,' the headmistress tells the trio and slings a thick, dark green cape around her ample figure. When she sees the French police woman's slightly bemused look, she mutters: 'I know I look like a walking tent, but at least it's warm.' Before they leave the school building, Kathleen shows her visitors the room where Sylvie attended lessons; from where she had started her fateful journey. She switches off lights everywhere and locks the doors behind her. As she looks back to see, whether she has forgotten to switch of a light somewhere, the school has lost its warm familiarity and has turned into an intimidating block of concrete and bricks with the windows gawping in the descending dusk like blind eyes.

The school is the last house on the edge of the little town, surrounded in one direction by meadows and fields. It is an idyllic spot to give the pupils a feeling of freedom, clean air and natural beauty whilst they play at break times. After crossing the school car park, Sergeant Penhaligon, Jeanne, Bernadette and Kathleen have to walk down a slope, sharing the narrow lane with cars; luckily, there is not much traffic at this time; people have already hurried home to prepare dinner and to put the smaller children to bed. The four make their way down to where the road splits into two, turning to the left towards the minute town centre called Fore Street with its pretty shops and cosy tearooms, and to the right into an even narrower and steeper path between a pub and a pottery. It hadn't felt quite as steep driving up to the Bowers' house in the afternoon.

The sun has been shining all day, wonderfully warm, but not enough to warm Bernadette's frozen heart. A sudden and brief bout of rain while they were in Kathleen's office has left the air fresh and unpleasantly cool. Bernadette shivers and pulls her cardigan closer around her.

'Was it dark when ...,' Bernadette can't either get herself to say the words or she can't find them in English, but her companions understand.

'No,' says Kathleen gently. 'It was afternoon, just after lessons had ended; around three-thirty.'

'She was ...with Charlotte?'

'No, Sylvie went home alone. Charlotte had choir practice.' Jeanne translates as soon as the headmistress has finished her sentence. 'She did try to make Sylvie stay,' Kathleen adds, disquieted by how neglectful that might sound.

'Sylvie go 'ome alone.' Bernadette shakes her head disapprovingly; then she falls silent as if storing the information in her memory. It takes her a few moments.

'Yes, Mrs Bowers was due to come home soon afterwards, and Charlotte gave Sylvie her key to the house,' Kathleen explains.

While this is translated, Bernadette bites her lip, uncomprehending, deep in thought, as if trying to solve a complicated puzzle.

'Mrs Karim,' the Sergeant interrupts as the enormity of the situation sinks into everybody's psyche and settles heavily on their hearts: 'Sylvie said she needed to go home because you were going to ring her on the Bowers' landline. Is that true?'

'Non,' Bernadette exclaims, wrinkling her forehead in an effort to find an explanation for Sylvie's lie, looking at each of them in puzzlement. 'I always ring nine o'clock in the evening,' she confirms what they had all known.

'That's what the host family told us,' Sergeant Penhaligon repeats, 'but why would she lie?'

'Maybe she just didn't fancy listening to the choir and wanted a bit of time to herself,' Jeanne volunteers.

'She meet boy?' Bernadette guesses swiftly, resigned to the waywardness of her children, hoping that somebody would reject the idea. They can't.

'We have asked around,' Kathleen tries to soothe thoughts of having failed as a mother and looks firmly into Bernadette's large grey eyes in the thin, pale face: 'Neither Charlotte, nor her parents nor anybody else in the school have seen Sylvie with a boy. She kept very much to herself all week.'

Bernadette nods, as if forcing herself to believe it. 'Anyway,' Kathleen continues, 'people would have noticed a budding romance in a small community like ours. There would have been gossip amongst the teenagers and their parents; rumours tend to spreads like wildfire here.'

'And don't forget Social Media,' the Sergeant reminds them of a phenomenon that seems to have gripped the world. No. It seems unlikely that Sylvie had duped everybody and arranged a secret rendezvous.

They walk up the steep lane which is only lit by one dim street light. There are no other lanes turning off before they reach the Bowers' family home. They walk a bit further, compulsively, as if suddenly a hitherto hidden place would open up and reveal a cowering girl, but they all know that that isn't going to happen. It is only to satisfy the poor mother's drive to look into every nook and cranny, to leave no stone unturned. They have to be patient. There are no more street lights; thick darkness has descended, filling the spaces between houses. It is unlikely that Sylvie would have walked any further following the uphill path to the Moor. They are resigned to end their hopeless endeavour. They won't find Sylvie tonight.

As they amble slowly back down the lane, Sergeant Penhaligon bends down, out of habit or instinct, and picks up two pieces of shiny paper. They turn out to be empty sweet wrappers. His immediate reaction is to stash them in his trouser pocket until he finds a bin. As he looks at his find with faint interest, he deciphers two French words. Sylvie's mother steps closer, peers at what he is holding and cries out: 'Sylvie love *bonbon aux fruits ragalad.*'

A rapid exchange of words between Jeanne and Bernadette in French reveals that this type of sweet is Sylvie's favourite. Apparently, she brought three whole bags full with her from France.

Nobody has the heart to point out that these sweet wrappers could have been dropped long before Sylvie disappeared. Yes, they might be rare and French, but there had been tourists before Sylvie's arrival. Or, Sylvie might have shared her treasured sweets with somebody less concerned with keeping the environment tidy than the conscientious Charlotte. Sergeant Penhaligon puts the wrappers into his breast pocket, wishing he had a forensic bag on him. Those two sweet wrappers might, at a later stage, be worth handing over to the forensic team. One never knows…

'Bernadette, can I ask you a question?' Kathleen probes hesitantly before they separate to go to their different places to sleep. She doesn't want to make things worse for the poor woman, but a thought has plagued her since that first phone call to France: 'That morning, when I rang you in Morlaix?'

Bernadette nods almost imperceptively, a faint acknowledgement that she has heard her question and is willing to answer.

'Why did you say on the phone: Je savais?'

No answer. Bernadette's mind seems far away as if it has gone blank, and she remains silent.

'Do you remember?' Kathleen tries again to gently jog her memory. 'It sounded to me as if you had expected something to happen.'

'Oui, je me souviens.' Kathleen suspects, that Bernadette hasn't quite followed her train of thought.

'Why did you say: Je savais?' Kathleen looks at the petite figure with all the empathy she can muster and whispers: 'What did you know?'

Bernadette remains as if rooted to the spot, lost and silent.

# CHAPTER EIGHT

When Sylvie has neither returned nor been found after a week of searching, the community groups disband and distribute posters of the girl instead, whilst smaller teams of policemen and - women combe the moorland hills and forests further away over and over again, widening the search area with every day. Sylvie's face appears on village hall windows, notice boards in church porches, in bus shelters next to the bus timetables, on pub, tearoom and restaurant counters, and on the walls of every Tourist Information centre and libraries in the villages all over Exmoor. They take them even to the towns along the coast of West Somerset, North Devon and North Cornwall, all around the Bristol Channel and Atlantic coast. Some well-known retirees with past experience of working in the Media call in favours from old employers to broadcast appeals to the public, begging people to look out for anything out of the ordinary they might find on their rambles, walking their dogs or to farmers tending to their cattle or sheep. They urge everyone to report the slightest suspicion immediately to the police. Eventually, they can't think of anything more that can be done.

Bernadette's despair and occasional hysteria have turned into numb paralysis. She walks listlessly with the search teams. When they stop, she is seen in the company of the French policewoman ambling through the narrow Fore Street, looking into windows with unseeing eyes. Kathleen likes to keep tabs on her, popping in at the hotel or inviting her to her office, but Bernadette gets unsettled when she sees other people's children. An invitation to dinner at Kathleen's modest house is declined – nobody can think of enjoying food and company.

'I wish I could do something for Bernadette,' Jeanne, the French police woman, confides in the headmistress one evening in the hotel bar, after her charge has insisted on needing an early night.

'Don't we all?' Kathleen's sigh comes from the heart. They sip on a glass of cider, enjoying a little respite in each other's company.

'I wonder,' Jeanne muses, 'whether it would be worthwhile to deliver some posters further afield, in case Sylvie did run off to London.'

'Did she say to anyone that she might?' Kathleen says between sips.

'According to Sergeant Penhaligon, it came up in one of the first interviews,' Jeanne replies.

'But then, it's what teenagers want to experience, don't they,' Kathleen puts the empty glass down with a thud. '…until they realise that London is miles from here.'

'I just would like to try,' Jeanne sounds deflated and unsure and is fidgeting with frustration.

'Why not,' Kathleen says with sudden enthusiasm. 'If we run off some posters and leaflets at the school, you could show them to people at stations like Tiverton, Taunton, Taunton Coach Station, Bristol, Bath and all the way to London….just to set your mind at rest.'

'You know, that sounds absolutely the right thing to do,' Jeanne sighs with relief at the prospect of some activity. 'Bernadette is driving herself mad, just sitting around, waiting. This would give her something to concentrate on which might even lead to a result. At least we can say that we have tried.'

The plan is submitted to Bernadette the following morning over breakfast, which for her, consists of three cups of black coffee.

Bernadette listens attentively and takes to the suggestion with a kind of desperate zeal. To Jeanne's surprise, her charge goes to the Tantiviy opposite the hotel, the only shop in town which sells stationery. When she has found and bought all the materials she needs, she settles on a long table in the hotel's empty function room and begins to design leaflets and posters; Jeanne checks the wording and spelling. By late afternoon, they walk together to the school and submit their work to the school secretary, who has strict orders to print them off the same afternoon.

The following morning, Ant -standing in for Kathleen, who is expected at the school - drives the two women to Taunton station to begin their mission. Dawn has just broken and they hope to catch as many early commuters as possible. Bernadette is clasping a batch of print-outs to her chest showing Sylvie's face. Kathleen has kindly arranged that they can stay for a few nights with Annabelle, a friend from university, who lives in Central London: 'She is a doctor at St Thomas's;' Kathleen had explained before their departure, 'you won't be seeing much of her. She will give you a key, so you can come and go as you please.' It will be convenient for all concerned; moreover, Kathleen will know where to reach them.

When they have left, Kathleen pictures them in her mind: a sad little team huddling on drafty platforms, pavements and corners, distributing their leaflets and pointing to Sylvie's picture in the hope that somebody might recognise the French girl and say that they have seen her recently.

After the first day, they have given away too many leaflets and need more supplies. The school secretary Jenny triples the number of prints and laminates the new posters before rushing them personally to Taunton station, before the pair move on towards London the following day. For tonight, Sergeant Penhaligon has organised a B&B near the station for the night, so that they can have an early start. It is a harrowing assignment the two women have given themselves, a tight-lipped Jenny reports back to the headmistress.

Once in London, the entire enterprise turns out to be soul-destroying: to stand in the middle of crowds of people hurrying past, who shake their heads, often absent-mindedly, one after the other, when they are asked whether they have seen this young French girl. The pain in Bernadette's heart grows more unbearable by the hour, and they decide on the third day, that they should return to the relative calm and familiarity of the little West Country town which calls itself proudly the Gateway to Exmoor.

Deep lines of sorrow have etched themselves into Bernadette's wan face and around her pinched mouth. After a further three days, she has a call from Bertrand's father, who can't look after the boy any longer. It is a miracle that he agreed in the first place, considering that is usually not on speaking terms with his son's mother, and that Sylvie is not his daughter. Moreover, if Bernadette doesn't go back to work soon, she won't be able to pay her household bills, and her customers will have found someone else to clean for them.

Nobody dares to say so, but Bernadette's departure will be a relief for Sergeant Penhaligon and his team who seem to have reached a dead end. Someone from the Somerset police is assigned to take Jeanne and Bernadette back to Plymouth, so they can catch the Roscoff ferry. There is nothing else left, but to send her back with the heartfelt promise to keep on looking and to keep her informed - if only to say that nothing new has been found.

'Hopefully…' the young policeman, who is driving them, is trying to break the heavy silence, but Jeanne, who sits behind him, sends him a warning look via the rear view mirror. Nothing anybody says will console Sylvie's mother on her journey home without her child. For most of the way, they watch the windscreen wipers trying to cope with a sudden downpour of summer rain. Bernadette asks for the heating to be switched on to ease the permanent frost in her bones.

The following morning after Bernadette's departure, and the last day of school before the summer holidays, a boy is brought to the Headmistress's office by his mother. Kathleen listens and calls the police.

'Sergeant Penhaligon, there might be a new lead on the Karim case. Could you please, send someone to take a statement?'

# CHAPTER NINE

It is Sergeant Penhaligon himself, who turns up at the school half an hour later. This case weighs heavily on his mind, not least, because his daughter from his first marriage is the same age as Sylvie and will soon embark on an exchange trip to Germany. He feels frustrated by too many suppositions and no concrete evidence of any kind in the case, and he bemoans the fact that there has been no real breakthrough so far. The police team have no more an idea where Sylvie might be than they had when they were first called to look for her. He hopes that this call out is not another blind alley.

The mother of the schoolboy sits in the headmistress's office next to her son, on the two-seater sofa to be interviewed. On the request of the pair, the Headmistress remains seated at her desk going through paperwork, with one ear discreetly tuned into the proceedings. Sergeant Penhaligon sits down on a chair opposite the sofa and begins by looking sternly at his young interviewee: 'So, young man, let's start with your name.'

'Peter Shelley,' the boy replies hoarsely.

'…age, address, telephone numbers-yours, your parents' and any mobile you may have.' Sergeant Penhaligon aims to sound brisk and business-like so that there is no doubt in the youngster's mind that giving a statement to the police is a serious matter. The boy is encouraged to speak up and to give precise information, which, after a few attempts, he manages.

'Now what is it, you haven't told us last time.' The Sergeant looks straight at him, narrowing his eyes with barely hidden disapproval. The boy's face turns bright red, and his eyes are fixed onto the low coffee table glass top between them. His mother's elbow nudges his arm unceremoniously.

'Sylvie and I were friends when I was over there on exchange.' He stops, while his pink blushes turn bright red.

'Was she your girlfriend? Is that what you mean?' the Sergeant asks matter-of-factly making copious notes. When he looks up, he just catches the mother's furious glance at her son.

'Sort of...'Peter stutters.

'You never told me!' the mother scoffs, but everybody ignores her.

'What do you mean by sort of?' Penhaligon looks over the rim of his reading glasses, impatient, but inwardly amused.

'Let me put it another way, Peter: How close were you and Sylvie Karim?'

'Is that really necessary?' the mother hisses with outrage. She had not expected this turn of events. If looks could kill..., the Sergeant thinks.

'We need to establish whether there was a close relationship between the witness and the victim.'

'I wouldn't have encouraged him to come forward if I had known that all you are interested in is raking up dirt,' snaps Mrs Shelley. 'I think I better take him home.'

'That is your prerogative, but then we shall have to continue the interview at your place or at the Police Station in Taunton,' Sergeant Penhaligon replies coldly. She strikes him as a woman who would hate her neighbours to witness a police officer to arrive at her door.

Kathleen has got up from her desk, walks over to the group and suggests: 'Mrs Shelley, maybe you would like to come with me. We can have a chat over a cup of coffee in the canteen?'

Peter's mother is confused, but relents and accepts. She gets up and follows the Headmistress who kindly holds the door open for her. Before the door shuts behind them, Mrs Shelley turns to her son and reminds him angrily: 'Whatever it is, tell the truth and don't bring shame on us!'

As soon as the mother has left the room, the boy relaxes and Sergeant Penhaligon adopts a kindlier tone.

'So, you and Sylvie were friends, maybe even in love during your exchange visit in France.' He looks up and sees Peter blushing again. 'You must have stayed in touch in between the two visits; did you?'

Peter shakes his head: 'I don't have a mobile. My parents don't let me have one, and Sylvie never rang on the landline.'

'Did you have her mobile number?'

Peter shakes his head.

'Or a land line number?'

'They didn't have a telephone at home. They couldn't afford one on top of Sylvie's and her mother's mobiles.' It doesn't make sense to the Sergeant, considering that fancy mobiles are vastly more expensive. He sighs.

'You could have written her a letter or a postcard, couldn't you?' Peter looks baffled, as if he had never heard of such things. Not something young people do these days, the Sergeant thinks. No more romance and fluttering hearts when a certain envelope arrives. More's the pity! Peter stays silent.

'Did that – let's call it your friendship - resume when Sylvie came over?'

53

'No… she avoided me.' Sergeant Penhaligon listens up and wonders whether the boy realises that he has just provided a motive - against himself. 'Were you angry with her?'

'Not angry,' Peter whispers, his eyes filling with tears.

'…but disappointed and sad?'

'Yes,' Peter admits in a whisper.

'Did Sylvie find another boyfriend while she was here?' The Sergeant hates rubbing it in, but he needs to get to the bottom of this. 'Did she meet someone in town; maybe someone older? Or someone from the French group?'

'I don't know. I don't think so. I hardly saw her. She was always with Charlotte, but they didn't like each other much either.'

'Who is your exchange friend?'

'Olivier.'

'Does he know that you have a crush on Sylvie?'

'We didn't talk about her, but he kept teasing me whenever she came near us.'

'Did he like Sylvie?'

'I don't think so. I haven't asked him.' Peter says miserably. Isn't life and love complicated when you are a teenager, Penhaligon secretly commiserates; nothing seems to have changed in that respect from when he was courting.

'So what was it, you wanted to tell me today? Something you think might help us to find Sylvie?' Sergeant Penhaligon sits up straight, puts his biro on the table and looks straight into Peter's face.

'When we were talking in Morlaix,' Peter sighs, as if getting rid of a heavy burden, 'Sylvie told me….told me,' he splutters and stops. Penhaligon waits patiently.

'I am listening,' he encourages him.

'She said she missed her dad, and that she wanted to be with him rather than her mother. She was so tired doing all this housework and looking after her brother and doing school work as well.'

'Is she in contact with her father?'

'She was trying to find him on Facebook and Instagram.'

'Did she?

'I don't know, but she found some papers in her mother's belongings which gave her an address in Paris. He is called Abdullah Karim.'

'That doesn't sound entirely French. Do you know where her Dad came from?'

Peter shakes his head and shrugs his shoulders for good measure.

'So, you think Sylvie might have contacted him?'

'I don't know. She did mention though, that she could meet him in Paris or in London when she came over.'

'…just to meet him or to go home with him?' Was this turning into a case of child abduction? He must find out, what the custody arrangements were.

Peter shakes his head again, deflated and defeated.

'Interesting,' Sergeant Penhaligon is more upbeat than Peter. He can see a chink of light. 'Do you think she was likely to arrange a meeting with her father without telling her mother?'

'I warned her,' Peter adds hastily, 'that London was miles away from Dulverton.'

'Very wise,' the policeman agrees kindly. He has brought up his children in the area, and has always found it a blessing to be far removed from inner city life; he would hate to be a policeman on the streets of London, where communities tend to be more secretive, unhelpful and hostile than their counterparts in the West Country.

'Was there anything else you wanted to talk about?'

'No, that was it.' Peter's sigh of relief is like a large bolder falling from his conscience.

'Here is my card, Peter. If you remember anything else, give me a call. You have done well to come forward. It takes guts to do that. Thank you for your help.' The boy can't believe it's all over; that he has done well and got even praise for his courage. He allows himself a tentative smile.

The door opens to a narrow gap and a head of grey hair appears: 'Can we come back, Sergeant Penhaligon?' Kathleen asks with a broad smile aimed at both of them. The door opens wider, and the headmistress and Peter's flustered mother, looking anxiously at her son, appear.

'Yes, we have finished, and Peter was very helpful,' the Sergeant repeats to everyone's relief. He begins to pack up.

'You can be very proud of your boy,' he says shaking Mrs Shelley's plump hand; then he tips his cap to the boy and gives a friendly wave to them all.

# CHAPTER TEN

'It's decision time,' Ant says to Kathleen, as they sit round her kitchen table, sipping tea. Kathleen has gone over to drinking herbal teas to soothe her nervous stomach. Ant knows she should join her, but has convinced herself, that she needs caffeine to see her through the day. Poor Kathleen hasn't got a choice: all this business with the French girl's disappearance combined with the daily demands of being at the helm of a school have taken their toll on her digestive system, which means that, according to the local doctor, she has to watch what she is eating and drinking. It's annoying and inconvenient, because she really likes to treat herself to cakes and the odd glass of wine or Prosecco, or even a gin and tonic to de-stress. Kathleen sighs.

'What? Sorry, Ant, I got distracted for a moment.'

Ant grins: 'Sorry, to be so boring. I was talking about the pigs, remember? I can't keep them all, however much I want to. I really need to make a decision which way I want to take the farm.'

Kathleen laughs, the first time in days: 'I just pictured you, overrun by boars, sows and piglets, on a protest march up and down the enclosure, a freedom banner stretched across the gate, you the only human being in the middle, swamped by piggy-bodies.' Still laughing, she takes a sip from her camomile tea and almost chokes. Ant gets up and wallops her on the back until she stops coughing. As she sits down again, Ant pulls a face: 'Do you often have these flights of fancy?'

'Not really; only when I am in your illustrious company!' Kathleen croaks.

'Is that a compliment or a hint that I am driving you mad?' Ant bats back.

'A bit of both,' she admits. It's good to laugh, but Kathleen feels suddenly guilty: 'There we are, having fun and that poor woman in Morlaix…'

'I know.' The thought is never far away from Ant's mind either.

'Have you heard from Bernadette?' Ant asks.

'Not much. Sometimes I put a call through, and sometimes she sends an e-mail to the school computer, just asking whether there is any news, but of course, there never is.'

'Dreadful! How is she coping with her son?' Ant enquires.

'She mentioned that he has transferred to a sort of school for behaviourally disturbed children,' Kathleen replies.

'Probably the best place for him. At least she can go out to work without having to worry about what he gets up to.' Kathleen isn't sure whether she agrees with Ant. Children feel so easily abandoned, even if they pretend they don't. Often, the consequence is that they fill the void in their hearts with undesirable activities and acquaintances. Maybe it is simply the best solution for Bertrand. From what they had heard, Bernadette finds it hard to cope as a single mother and has in the past put far too much responsibility onto her daughter's young shoulders.

'You might be right,' Kathleen agrees, 'I guess it's less stressful for her if Bertrand is away, but ever so lonely. Imagine she used to have two children, now she comes home to an empty flat.'

'They can have the school holidays together,' Ant points out.

'That was exactly what we talked about during our last conversation,' Kathleen admits. 'Bernadette bemoaned the fact that every time she sees Bertrand, he seems more distant and estranged from her than the last time.' Kathleen absent-mindedly stirs sugar into her tea: 'Oops! I don't even like sugar!' She exclaims and pushes the sugar bowl to the middle of the table.

'That's nothing out of the ordinary,' Ant replies, grinning across the sugar bowl. 'Most teenagers want to get away from their parents. It's called *growing up* and *spreading your wings.*' Ant, who never had children, has formed her opinions through observing fellow citizens, but feels out of her depth to say more. At least, Kathleen, dealing with children and their parents on a daily basis, has more grounds to trust in her conclusions.

'…maybe you can help her work out a so called 'cool' programme for the weekends when he does come home,' suggests the ever practical Ant.

Kathleen shrugs her shoulders: 'I wonder whether Bernadette has the strength and patience at the moment; she is exhausted most of the time because she tries so hard to make ends meet. She has to contribute to these new school fees'.

'You should keep trying. She can only learn from someone like you. It could make a great deal of difference to her healing – to improve her relationship with her son, however slowly.'

Kathleen nods, pinning a loose strand of grey hair back up into her bun: '…you're right, Ant. That's probably the role I am supposed to play.' Her face lights up with the realisation of this new responsibility, and then, typically Kathleen, she launches immediately into making plans: 'I could even ask her to come over for a holiday.' A short moment of reflection results in a flood of ideas: 'If he fancied, Bertrand could help you out on the farm…he might take to animals.' Ant frowns. She can't honestly imagine that a wayward boy like Bertrand would be impressed by a holiday on a pig farm; nor does she think that Bernadette would want to return to the place where her daughter disappeared. She says as much to Kathleen.

'We might have to throw in a couple of days sightseeing in London to lure him,' Kathleen suggests unperturbed. She is like me, Ant thinks and smiles: once we have the bit between our teeth, we run with it. 'Good thinking,' Ant encourages her. Both fall silent for a while.

'Has anybody tried to contact Mr Karim?' Kathleen perks up.

'I don't know. Why do you ask?' Ant is surprised by the change of topic.

'Young Peter mentioned that Sylvie wanted to make contact with her father.' It is news to Ant. 'You didn't know,' Kathleen's eyes widen. 'Didn't Sergeant Penhaligon tell you?'

Ant shakes her head: 'I am not supposed to know,' she whispers, 'I am not on his team.' She shrugs her shoulders while speaking.

'So?' Kathleen drawls out the syllable in disapproval.

'I did wonder whether, with a name like *Karim,* her father was born in France.'

'We must find him,' Kathleen stands up suddenly, almost losing her balance. She gulps down a mouthful of cold herb tea, which predictably goes down the wrong way again.

'Shall I hit you on the back?' Ant offers, but Kathleen shakes her head, splutters a few more times and repeats in a shaky voice: 'We must speak to him!'

'I was afraid you might say that,' Ant jokes, 'but I would have thought that Sergeant Penhaligon has made enquiries by now.'

'We might be on to something, Ant,' Kathleen ignores her comment, growls stubbornly, like a dog with a bone. 'At least,

Mr Karim should be ruled out as a suspect.' Ant is quite astonished at Kathleen's fervour.

'He would not be the first father who kidnapped his child.' It is a dramatic end to the argument.

'Taunton police might have checked already,' Ant warns and puts a soothing hand on her friend's arm.

Kathleen walks out into the landing and grabs her navy blue blazer from the hook on the wall above the telephone.

'I promise, I'll check,' and, adopting a totally different tone, Ant returns to her previous pressing problem: '... and now back to my very personal dilemma: what do I do with so many pigs?'

'I must go,' Kathleen announces abruptly, her thoughts definitely already somewhere else. Suddenly, she looks Ant with a serious face, as if she had just heard about Ant's problem for the first time before she speaks: 'As far as I know, farmers do two things: market or abattoir.' Kathleen half expects an angry outcry and disappears with unexpected agility through the door.

'I hate both,' Ant winces, listening as the front door slams into the lock.

# CHAPTER ELEVEN

Zac,' Ant hasn't heard his voice since they worked together on the Turner case, which had been close to all their hearts as the victim had been one of their own: the pathologist Lucinda Sheridan. Ant still misses her. Lucinda had been a good friend bringing a great sense of humour and female solidarity to their relationship.

'How are you, Ant?' Zac's distinctive London accent has almost disappeared, ironed out. Pity! Ant pictures him for a moment, fresh faced, handsome, tall, athletic, lovely smile.

'Fine…'

'And how are the pigs doing?'

'Wild and greedy as always!' she replies with undisguised pride.

'You love them really, don't you?' he teases.

'Yeah, most of the time…'

'I reckon you didn't ring me about the pigs, Ant. How can I help you?'

Ant gives a quick outline of the new case, Sylvie Karim's disappearance and Kathleen's idea that there might be a remote possibility that the girl has been abducted by her father, taken to Paris or wherever he might be living now ….It's a long shot, I know, but we are at the eliminating stage.'

'Of course, you need to check everything. Did he know his daughter was going to England on exchange?'

'Not sure. He hasn't been in contact with his ex-wife for years, but Sylvie mentioned to someone in the exchange group that she would prefer to live with her father rather than her mother. How much that was wishful thinking rather than a plan, I have no idea.'

'Have you submitted this to your local police,' Zac queries.

'It's quicker, if you do it… The wheels are turning a bit slower down here,' she adds apologetically. 'It's not meant as a criticism; they are all snowed under – particularly with eradicating the County Lines establishing themselves down here'.

'Good job!' Zac mutters and seems to be typing already things into his computer.

Of course, she will keep the Taunton team in the loop, she promises. Conventional practices have never been Ant's strong point, and Zac is one of the few who understands and appreciates the more unorthodox way she works and gets results. Bex is another one. She shakes her head as if to disperse any thought of Bex.

'Do you mind, Zac?' she hopes, she isn't stretching his loyalties.

'…of course not,' he reassures her with a happy chuckle, 'I just don't want to tread on anybody's toes.'

'I'll be extremely diplomatic if you find something; and I'll take the blame if we get a ticking off!'

'You haven't changed, have you, Ant,' his laughter now booms through the telephone. She can just imagine his face splitting into creases of merriment from one ear to the other.

They exchange details of Sylvie's case, the answers she is seeking and a few hints where she thinks he should look.

Even Ant is impressed when he rings the following day with news: 'Mr Karim is called Abdullah Karim, born in Algiers in 1985. His father's name is Muhammed Abas Abdullah Karim and his mother is called Hafsa. That's how far I got with birth and marriage certificate. I didn't have time for more.'

'Sylvie's mother, Bernadette, mentioned that she and her young husband used to live in one of those ugly high-rise buildings on the northern fringes of Paris until the baby arrived, and everything fell apart.'

'What do you mean?'

'Well, they divorced.'

'North of Paris: that's where the French authorities house most of their economic migrants and asylum seekers.' She can imagine Zac shaking his head in disgust. 'I'll see what more I can find out,' he promises hastily, obviously in a hurry, but she can't let him hang up with having asked:

'How is the divine Melanie?' Ant enquires before he can end the call.

He chuckles. He is like a blushing schoolboy when his young wife is mentioned: 'She is fine and highly pregnant; enjoying married life – being married to me.'

'That's what I like to hear – married bliss. Hold on to it!' Ant jokes. There is a little pause when she hopes he doesn't mention the past, but it seems to have crossed his mind, too:

'Have you heard from Bex?' he asks, hesitantly. Bex used to be his boss.

'No. Not a dickie-bird since the Turner case. He must be all right; busy being retired,' she says breezily trying to distract him from the topic.

'He looks…' Zac is searching for the word and chooses one eventually: '…peculiar.'

'You mean scruffier than usual?' Ant is nonplussed. Peculiar is not a word she would ever choose for DI Benjamin E. Cox; her erstwhile partner in more than one sense.

'You'll see when you meet him.' Zac chuckles and leaves it at that. 'I'll ring when I have more results,' he says. He is definitely in a hurry now.

'Thanks Zac, and love to Melanie,' Ant just manages to squeeze in before he hangs up.

# CHAPTER TWELVE

'I just received news from Paris about Mr Karim, Ant. Are you still interested?' Zac sounds breathless on the messaging service. She has just come in from stacking neatly a delivery of straw in the shed, she calls The Barn. She and the pigs will be alright now for the next few months.

Ant rings Zac back immediately. While she waits for the phone to be picked up, she shudders, looking out at and hearing the foul autumn rains bashing at her kitchen window.

'Of course I am still interested, Zac. How are Melanie and the tadpole?'

He bursts out laughing: 'Is that what you call him or her? Blooming together the last time I saw them.'

'When is she due?'

'Not long to go now: a couple of weeks.' And then he confesses: 'Ant, I am so much more stressed about becoming a father than I have ever been at work. Is that normal?' It explains why he speaks so fast, as if somebody had given him only a limited supply of oxygen.

'Of course it's normal. I would worry if you weren't,' she tries to calm him diplomatically. She has never been in that situation. Becoming parents must be such a dramatic event between overwhelming happiness and constant undermining self-doubt.

'So, what was it you wanted to tell me?' Ant reminds him gently.

'Oh yes, of course; I almost forgot. Does having children make you lose brain cells?' he deviates again.

Ant giggles: 'I wouldn't know, but I am sure, it's not as bad as it feels right now. You'll get used to it.' She waits, and the silence feels as if he has fallen asleep at the other end.

'Oh yes,' he suddenly perks up, 'Mr Karim. He has left Paris ten years ago. According to old neighbours, he moved back to Algiers to get married again.'

'No point in going to Paris then,' Ant concludes. Not that she had any intention to do so.

'No, but Algiers might be interesting,' Zac points out. 'If Mr Karim has settled with another wife, he could have a motive for luring Sylvie to live with him.'

'Hm,' is all, Ant can say; she has no intention to go there either. '...but thanks for letting me know, Zac. And give my love to Melanie. I shall be thinking of you both! Let me know when young Miss or Master Weymouth has made an appearance.'

'...shall do, Ant!' He seems happy to return to thoughts of his impending fatherhood.


Ant wants to ring Kathleen, but her friend beats her to it: 'Just checking you're okay,' Kathleen enquires, 'and of course, '... is there any news?'

'No, nothing after the first forensic report,' Ant says regretfully, 'but we have established that Sylvie's father has not lived in Paris for the last ten years. He remarried in Algiers where he was born.'

'You started investigating him?'

'How can I ignore your telling off?'

'I didn't tell you off,' Kathleen replies, pretending to be outraged..

'Not in so many words, but I got the message.' There is silence at the other end until Ant can't help laughing about the silliness of the situation: '…and I have a result.'

'Have you?' Kathleen sounds incredulous and terribly excited..

'Yes, indeed. A colleague of mine has unearthed Sylvie's father in Algiers.'

'So enquiries move to Algiers now,' Kathleen concludes.

'Well, not officially, but we could do our bit to establish whether or not he has anything to do with his daughter's disappearance.'

'What do you mean?' Kathleen's breaths are quickening.

'…as a peace offering…we could both pay him a visit -'

'Isn't that Sergeant Penhaligon's domain?'

'He won't mind me taking on one of the lines of enquiry, if I ask him nicely. He is probably glad if he doesn't have to delegate someone to do it on his behalf; it's an unnecessary expense with no guarantee that anything will come off it.'

'Couldn't he ask the Algerian police to find Sylvie's dad?'

'He could, but how long would it take to get an answer from them, and could it be trusted? I have no contacts anywhere near to verify any findings.'

'So when do you think you will go?'

'You mean *when are we going*?'

'I can't really leave the school during term time.'

'I thought during your next school holiday. We can dress it up as a private short break.'

'That would be Christmas,' Kathleen muses

'Oh, sorry; your family...' That sort of thing doesn't enter into Ant's consciousness, particularly when she is dealing with a case..

'No, not family, but I must catch up on a lot of paper work. By the time Christmas comes, I had enough of it with all the Nativity plays, staff dinners and pre-Christmas invitations.'

'There you are,' Ant says cheerfully; 'you will be in need of a break. How long are your holidays?'

'Two weeks until the 6th of January.'

'Perfect: you can work until the first; we leave on the second and come back on the fourth or fifth. Just imagine all that sunshine...' Ant knows her offer is irresistible. However, it is met with silence. 'Think it over. It's my treat, and I might need you as an interpreter.' There follows a long pause, in which both sides seem to weigh up the pros and cons, until Kathleen mumbles hesitantly, as if trying to convince herself: 'It's something we could do for Bernadette, isn't it?' Kathleen seems to have found a good justification to be so profligate.

'Absolutely, even if it doesn't produce a new line of enquiry, at least we can eliminate the possibility that Sylvie was abducted by her father, willing or otherwise.'

'Done,' Kathleen sounds suddenly enthusiastic. 'Are you going to make the arrangements?'

'Of course, you just carry on with your Nativity plays, and I prepare our visit to Mr. Karim.'


The following morning, Ant is woken before dawn. The phone rings downstairs. Nobody she knows would ring that early. Boy is catapulting himself off her duvet in panic when she throws it back all over him to disentangle herself and get out of bed. She can't find her slippers and rushes barefoot out of the room and down the stairs. The telephone has gone already to answerphone mode. Ant has to wait till the caller finishes with the message. Before she can dial 1571, the phone rings again. Ant picks up the receiver instantaneously, as if her life depended on the call: The first thing she hears is a great commotion in the background.

'Hallo,' Ant says, holding her breath in suspense.

'Ant, I am so sorry to wake you up so early. I don't think my message recorded. She has arrived!' His voice makes a somersault with excitement.

For a moment, sleepy Ant is bewildered: she knows that voice, but she can't place it. Who has arrived and where? It's 5.30 a.m., too early to gather a clear thought. For one moment a ray of hope shoots through her brain: Sylvie has returned, but it is extinguished within seconds when she hears: 'Ant, it is Zac. She has arrived... our daughter!' and before Ant can congratulate him, the words tumble out of him: '...and we called her Caroline Antonia.'

'Stop shouting, Zac, I can hear you well enough.'

'Sorry, Ant,' he stutters, but Ant interrupts him: 'Stop apologising, Zac! I did ask you to ring me as soon as your baby is born. Is that what has happened? ' He giggles like an overexcited schoolboy, and can't help shouting again in triumph: 'Yes! We have a daughter!'

'Congratulations to you and Melanie,' Ant says warmly, carried along by his joyfulness. 'Now tell me again that last bit about your baby's name!' He obliges: 'Caroline Antonia.' Ant has to choke back the tears.

'The Antonia is after you,' Zac explains unnecessarily. '... and we would like you to be her godmother...we would love that!'

It doesn't happen often, but Ant bursts into tears of happiness: 'What an honour, Zac!' is all she can bring herself to say without blubbing.

'So you will do it?'

'Of course, I will.' It will be the only family she has ever had. 'Of course I will, I'll be delighted!' It's a strange feeling, that feeling of a family bond. In a tiny way, she has it with the pigs and Boy, but being asked by fellow human beings to join their tribe, to play a role in their family is rather special.

'Zac, I am so happy for you and Melanie. You will make wonderful parents.

'We'll have to see about that,' he chuckles. 'Must go, baby's crying!' She can imagine the spring in his step, as he rushes back to the maternity ward.

# CHAPTER THIRTEEN

'Oh my word, wasn't it horrible weather all week,' Kathleen shivers when she arrives at Ant's farm in her little Renault Clio, shaking the raindrops off her ample mackintosh and wide-brimmed hat.

'It's January,' Ant reminds her. At least it's not snowing which could close the airport.' It's the 2$^{nd}$ January, the day of their departure, and Ant is still rushing around to organise things for Felix who will be here any moment to take over the running of the farm. The pigs have been fed, watered and told that Felix would be once again looking after them for a couple of days – not long at all -, but they didn't seem too bothered, munching happily through the banana treat, her barely veiled bribe.

'Can you hold on to these for a moment,' Ant hands her a wodge of papers which, on closer inspection, consists of her passport, flight tickets, an old police notebook and various photocopies of first reports on the Karim case, plus her rucksack bulging with what Kathleen fears, are Ant's casual changes of clothing.

'Is that all you are taking?' Kathleen asks, raising her eyebrows.

'Yep,' Ant replies with a tinge of defiance. 'Why?'

'Shall I put it all on the back seat,' Kathleen diverts diplomatically to avoid a confrontation.

'Rucksack in the back, the rest on the passenger seat,' directs Ant. She intends to use the time in the car to go over some details.

Kathleen opens the car boot briefly to retrieve bottled water from a Shopping for Life bag. 'We might need these during the journey. It will save us stopping at service stations.' Before she can shut the boot again, Ant bursts into a fit of hilarity until she almost chokes: 'How long are you going for?' she asks eventually, pointing to the boot full of Louis Viton luggage.

'I was under the impression, that only a part of the trip is meant to be work related; I expect fun and adventure from the rest, and I want to be dressed appropriately for each occasion,' Kathleen mutters defensively.' Better not to refer to luggage again, Ant decides; after all, they don't want to begin the trip with an argument.

'I have done a little research on Algiers,' Kathleen announces and waves a pink plastic folder in the shape of an A4 envelope.

'Very fetching colour,' Ant grins: 'Very organised,' she adds quickly, so that there can be no misunderstanding.

'Unlike you,' Kathleen counters. They walk slowly back to the house. They are still waiting for the arrival of the man to take over the farm for the few days they will be away. Ant remains silent, while Kathleen babbles on: 'I can't bear to leave things to chance; I need to know where I am going, what I am doing when, particularly in a foreign country, somewhere where I have never been before.' Ant nods in agreement. Encouraged, Kathleen carries on with her self-justification: 'Being meticulously prepared has become an affliction. But if I,' she puts great emphasis on the word *I*, 'am not organised, the whole school will fall apart. Sorry. I hope you don't mind.' Ant has only half listened, ticking off in her mind a silent list of things to do with the farm. She has only heard the last bit. 'Of course, not,' she reassures her absent-mindedly. 'I look forward to you being my tourist guide.'

Kathleen is still on the same subject: 'The French have a word for it,'

'…for what?' Ant is a bit lost.

'You know, me being super organised; a bit over the top.'

'Have they really…' Ant replies laconically.

'Yes, they do. They call it: *deformation professionellle.*'

'That sounds like a pretty accurate description,' Ant has finally caught up with her friend's train of thought. She can think of quite a few professional obsessions people among her previous colleagues had acquired over the course of their careers. Even she tends to be meticulously organised when working on a case, Pity, it never transferred easily to her private life. Even now, her kitchen table is constantly strewn with forms to fill in and letters to reply to. Paperwork is the bane of her new life. However, ask her to do a forensic sweep, and she is at least as obsessionally thorough as Kathleen.

There is a knock on the door.

'That will be Felix,' Ant remarks with relief and shouts:

'the door's open, Felix.'

Kathleen gasps when a mass of red curls pops round the corner, together with a pair of startlingly green eyes in a face bathed in a huge smile; finally, the entire athletic figure of a man in his prime stands under the door frame. 'Sorry, I am a bit late,' Felix apologise standing loosely on the threshold. 'Shall I do the pigs first?' he asks, but Ant shakes her head.

'I have done them. They know you are coming; and Boy is somewhere around, having already eaten both breakfast and what was meant for dinner.,' Ant tells him. Kathleen looks puzzled from one to the other. Felix notices and laughs. He is used to Ant anthropomorphising her animal: 'Your friend is mad,' he jokes holding Kathleen's gaze, but nodding sideways towards Ant. Kathleen hopes that nobody notices that a crimson red is creeping up from her throat. Ant introduces them hurriedly to each other before announcing:

'I think we better make tracks,' and gathers up her Parka jacket.

'Have you got everything?' Kathleen whispers with concern in her voice. She still can't believe that Ant is only taking enough for, what her friend would consider a stroll in the local woods.

'I can always borrow something from you,' Ant whispers back, smirking. 'As long as I have my passport, flight tickets and hotel booking, I shall be fine,' Ant laughs to reassure her. 'I have always travelled light.' By now, Kathleen has gone pink in the face. Luckily, Felix has just turned and is already stomping uphill to say 'hello' to the Girls.

'We must go,' Ant says and slings her jacket over her shoulder.

'Don't you have to lock?' Kathleen mutters.

'No. Felix will do that before he leaves. He's got a key.' As they approach the car, they hear a cheery: 'Have a good journey,' from high above and see two arms waving through the treetops. They give a friendly wave back, and as soon as they have closed the car doors and are out of earshot, Kathleen hisses: 'Goodness me, where did you find him?'

'You mean Felix? He is a local farmer's son. What did you expect?' Ant grins, 'Not all farmers are old, wrinkly and toothless.'

'I certainly did not expect an Adonis,' Kathleen splutters.

'Don't get your hopes up,' Ant cautions, highly amused.

'Why?' Kathleen looks at Ant with suspicion. This is followed by a realisation: 'No-ooo!' It's a long drawn-out moan of disappointment, 'don't tell me: he is either spoken for or gay.' As Ant nods at the latter, Kathleen bursts out: 'It's not fair. It's always the nicest and best looking guys. The story of my life! What a waste!'

'Quite,' Ant commiserates. They look at each other with resignation and laugh.

# CHAPTER FOURTEEN

'Do you mind listening to a bit of music?' Kathleen asks fifteen minutes into their journey on their way to Taunton.

'It's your car. Please yourself.' Ant has plans to read once again through her notebook and the papers relevant to the task before her: to interview Sylvie's Dad. At the other end of town, they reach the A303. It will be a long stretch from there to Gatwick. Ant whistles occasionally along to a tune she recognises, but for most of the journey, she is engrossed in reading and nulling over the case of the missing French girl.

Once they have reached the airport and parked the car among thousands of others, they battle through the crowds in the departure hall, check in Kathleen's oversized suitcase and pass through elaborate security checks; they have just enough time for a quick cup of coffee before they are called to the gate for the flight to Algiers. Not many people are waiting with them in the lounge, which suits them fine.

'It will probably be a small aeroplane,' Kathleen speculates.

'It must be murder in those jumbo jets with hundreds of passengers squashed together,' Ant remarks light-heartedly until she sees Kathleen's horrified face.

'Sorry, it wasn't the comment to make under the circumstances,' she apologises sheepishly.

She must be more careful. Black humour is obviously something that stays with you. The murder squads have often a peculiar, dark sense of humour which nobody else finds funny. In truth, her one and only flight experience was a trip to New York in the company of several burley colleagues from the Met who had considered this an extravagant jolly rather than a professional and educational visit. Obviously, her colleagues, an all-male group, had resented her calling them to duty from what they perceived as a well-earned sight-seeing holiday; she had totally blotted her copy book when she objected to their offensive and sexually explicit contributions in mock/practice interrogations. 'This is what you have to expect from dumb criminals,' they had defended themselves but she knew as well as they did, that they only exploited the situation and were enjoying their little power game. Ant shakes her head to blow those particular cobwebs away.

They are called to board the plane and find their seats. 'I have travelled on one of those double-decker planes once,' Kathleen reminisces, 'when I visited my brother in Australia during his gap year. However lovely and helpful the air hostesses were, it reminded me of a cattle truck. It was exhausting for all concerned.'

Ant closes her notebook into which she has written a number of questions which she intends to put to Sylvie's father - if they can locate him, that is. The light coming through the oval window is dull in spite of the plane having already left a thick ceiling of grey clouds below. Even flying south doesn't improve upon the milky, cold sunshine. As they had an early start, they both feel sleepy and fall into a doze for most of the three hours until the captain's voice announces over the loudspeaker that they would be landing in Algiers in about fifteen minutes.


Houari Boumediene Airport is surprisingly modern, large and even more crowded than Gatwick.

'Goodness, there are three terminals and the entire town's population seems gathered, too.'

Inside one of the buildings, they follow the passengers of their BA flight in the hope that they will lead them to passport control and the luggage carousels. There is hardly any scrutiny of the passports, and soon they reach the luggage hall.. Ant jokes about Kathleen's suitcase having flown to Japan, but eventually –after a wait of no longer than it would have taken at any of the London airports – it arrives intact. 'Don't yank it; it's heavy,' Ant hisses, 'you'll do yourself a mischief,' but too late: Kathleen has already lifted it from the conveyor belt with a barely supressed yelp. She has probably pulled a muscle. Ant shakes her head.

It is past midday in Algiers. Surprisingly, there is no time difference between England and Algiers. Ant and Kathleen are surrounded by colourful, noisy groups of families - from babies in their mothers' arms, to toddlers and children chasing each other through the legs of the adults; right through to the older generations, men with white beards dressed in white cloaks over cotton shirts and black trousers; most women are wrapped from head to toe in traditional white gowns over white, baggy trousers which are gathered at the ankles; they are clearly at the airport to welcome their very own visitors with great excitement. Kathleen leads the way through the mayhem like a haughty battleship commander. Everybody steps aside respectfully to let her pass. Ant follows obediently, feeling like a faithful servant. They breathe a sigh of relief when they reach the exit door and step outside into cool, fresh air. The sun is a little warmer than in England; the mid-teens temperature feels the same as a cool summer's day at home. It is not raining and not likely to, the pilot had said. Kathleen puts her heavy suitcase down onto the pavement.

'Now, there is a regular bus into town…' Ant suggests, but Kathleen interrupts: 'How far out are we from the town?'

'About ten miles,' Ant has looked it up when she had booked the flights. She is amused by Kathleen's wide-eyed silent plea, begging her not to make her walk ten miles, never mind dragging along her luggage. 'All right, we'll take a taxi to the hotel.' Kathleen sighs with relief. They join a queue, but are suddenly ushered to the front of it and whisked straight into a cab, followed by a few furious outcries.

'Hotel?' the driver asks with a huge, smile revealing a row of perfect white teeth. His hopes of a good tip are immediately confirmed when Ant directs him to the El Aurassi Hotel. During the drive there he makes little detours to point out the sights of Algiers, various museums, a couple of public gardens and the old town on the hill, the famous *Kasbah* - all little tasters to lure them into asking him to be their tourist guide for their stay. Finally, they arrive at a gleaming white, ultra-modern hotel complex.

'Oh,' the disappointment in Kathleen's voice is palpable. The ultra-modern hotel façade is covered in balconies all along its front, which look like hewn out of dazzlingly white marble.

'We'll be safe here,' Ant explains. She doesn't like these modern hotels either and would have preferred to rent an old-fashioned Moorish family town house with an inner courtyard filled with scented flowers palm and banana trees, but she has been advised to stay in the tourist district which is better protected than the old quarters of the city. Of course, she feels responsible for her friend's safety. They really don't know what will await them. Their search for Sylvie's father could provoke all sorts of reactions, and they have absolutely no contacts they could call for help if things went wrong. As they disembark from the taxi, the driver offers, almost insists with his dazzling smile, that he will pick them up the following morning from the hotel to show them the best sights of Algiers: 'Only twenty minutes in car from hotel,' he says in broken English with a strong French-Algerian accent.

When Ant shakes her head, he looks hopefully at Kathleen and changes his tactic: 'Ah, you want beach?' Kathleen groans inwardly and declines, but he takes it for encouragement: 'Only 'alf 'our!' Kathleen remains silent, looking past him. She hates to disappoint people. When Ant finally pays him for the journey from the airport, including a rather more modest tip than expected, he quickly returns, unsmilingly, to the driver's door, slams it shut and drives off with a furious roar of the engine.

'...the cheek of him!' Ant shakes her head.

'That was rather mean. You have totally put him off us,' Kathleen complains. 'What if we meet him tomorrow again?'

Ant rolls her eyes: 'It wasn't mean, I know how much the journey should have cost; he vastly overcharged. And furthermore,' she pauses with a grin, 'the *Kasbah* and many of the tourist attractions are not twenty miles away; they are just round the corner, well, about two miles from our hotel - within walking distance!' Kathleen remains silent at the prospect of trying it out.

'Anyway,' Ant gloats, 'things are looking up: we have hardly arrived here and you have already an admirer.'

'Nonsense,' Kathleen blushes and counters: 'He might as much have been after you. They like feisty women.'

'Your voluptuous figure is far more attractive to exotic men like him than scrawny me,' Ant teases with glee. She is suddenly in high spirits. 'Come on. Let's see where we are going to sleep tonight.' A hotel porter relieves them of their luggage and leads them to the reception desk.

'...and then lunch; I am starving.' Ant agrees. Food is not really her priority on this trip, but it will give her a chance to finalise her list of things to do for the next three days. Good, old

Zac in London had come up with an address for Mr Karim's whereabouts, just before their departure.

'Sorry, Ant,' he had breathed heavily into the phone, as if he had been on a run. 'I almost forgot.' She had heard him supressing a yawn through the phone line.

'Sleepless nights,' Ant had guessed.

'Tell me about it!' he had groaned, and then launched into giving her all the details he had managed to find out about Abdullah Karin, the French girl's father. It was so kind of him! Now, being installed at the El Aurassi in Algiers, it is only a matter of finding the man in the tangle of narrow roads they have seen from the taxi.

Their room is on the second floor. The view over the Mediterranean coastline and the town's port compensates for the globally repetitive modern glass and chrome interior of the hotel. Ant sits down on one of the twin beds and hops up and down on the mattress.

'That will do. It's actually really comfortable.' she announces lying down and stretching her legs`. Kathleen shakes her head. Just like a kid, she thinks.

'I hope, there is a bar,' Ant hears Kathleen mumble.

'Oops! I haven't thought of that: It's a Muslim country.'

Kathleen's face darkens as if a black cloud had descended. A Kathleen eclipse, Ant thinks and proposes: 'Let's go and find out.'

'It's not funny,' Kathleen moans.

'Let's go down and eat.'

Ant jumps up, grabs her notebook with attached pen and leaves the room closely followed by her slightly dejected friend. On the way down in the lift, Ant muses that this hotel could be anywhere in the world; there is nothing particularly Algerian about it.

The dining room is vast, luxurious and equally characterless, but they find a lovely corner where they can tuck themselves away. Hot meals, the menu card on the table announces, are available all day long, and to Kathleen's delight there is a wine list, too.

'I am feeling a sneezing fit coming on,' Kathleen says suddenly and rummages around her dress pocket for a tissue. No luck! She takes a paper napkin instead and covers up a minor explosion within. When the sneezes have subsided, she grabs a small vase with blue flowers standing in the middle of their table. Before she can put the vase down on the empty neighbouring table, a tall, most distinguished looking man comes along and takes them from her hand. Another sneeze overtakes her, and she has just enough time to reach for Ant's paper napkin to avoid sneezing all over the marble top. The waiter's smile is polite, but – as his curling lip reveals - disapproving.

'They are Algerian lilies,' he explains haughtily with a French accent, 'Algeria's national flower.'

'Trust me to be allergic to it,' Kathleen quips and doesn't dare to look at either Ant or the waiter. The latter is definitely not amused, and Ant puts one hand over her eyes to stop herself from laughing.

'The blue is really stunning,' Ant tries to recover the situation, 'but unfortunately my friend suffers from hay-fever.' She hopes he understands the word *hay-fever* as she has no idea what it is in French, but her words are drowned out by another ferocious sneeze into the serviette. With a tango-twirl and a shrug of the shoulders, the waiter removes the flowers as if these tourists didn't deserve them.

'I am not sure, we made a friend there,' Ant remarks and turns her attention back to the menu.

'And I still haven't ordered a glass of wine,' Kathleen wails into her serviette.

'He might be back for our order soon,' Ant chuckles, 'if he dares.'

The menu is tempting. Ignoring all the European dishes and American hamburger combinations, they opt for local cuisine: lamb tagine with couscous and a side dish of chickpeas.

'And a glass of red wine,' Kathleen is desperate to dull the embarrassment. The waiter doesn't bat an eyelid.

'I'll join you. Anything you prefer?' Ant asks.

'I can't see many local wines listed.'

'It might be safer to stick to something we know,' Ant suggests and they both opt for an Italian Papavero.

When the stew-pot with a dome-shaped lid is brought, they can smell aromatic spices before the waiter has reaches the table – according to the menu it contains cinnamon, coriander, ginger, turmeric, garlic, cayenne pepper, and with it, a bowl of steaming lemon and pomegranate couscous. The lamb cubes are so succulent that they melt on the tongue. A bowl of Greek yoghurt surrounded by lemon wedges is a surprise tasting heavenly combined with the meat, as does the chickpea puree, which they doubt they will be able to finish.

They enjoy the meal enormously and drag it out until the waiter returns and sternly asks whether they have chosen a desert.

'I think his shift is finished,' Kathleen whispers as she looks longingly at the long list of sweets, but decides that she has eaten enough for the moment.

'We'll have a sweet tonight,' she says with an apologetic smile to the waiter. They get ready to leave the table, while he is already clearing away the crockery and cutlery. To their relief, the table cloth is still pristine; at least, they haven't disgraced themselves even more.

Back upstairs in the room, Ant shows Kathleen the details for Mr Karim Zac had phoned through a couple of days ago: born in 1985 in Algiers, resident in the north of Paris where he had met a young French woman called Bernadette; where they had fallen in love and had produced a baby girl, whom they named Sylvie. Ant has no idea, how much Mr Karim had been involved in his daughter's upbringing; how much he had wanted to be involved; or whether he had fled back to Algeria to escape his parental responsibilities. Ant has not come to Algiers to be judgemental but she has to find out what Sylvie's father is like, and whether there is a chance that he might have lured her to live with him. Wouldn't it be wonderful if Sylvie opened the door to them? In any case, it is better not to announce her visit, Ant decides. If he does know where his daughter is, he will go into hiding; if not, her disappearance will come as a shock to him; or maybe, he won't care. Ant has no idea, how he will react.

# CHAPTER FIFTTEEN

Ant stretches and yawns and has to close her eyes again against the bright Algerian morning sun.

'What time is it?' Kathleen mumbles still half asleep.

'You can sleep a little longer, while I am having a shower.' Ant pulls the feather-light duvet over her friend. Kathleen sighs with pleasure and turns over. Ant pads on tiptoes to the en-suite bathroom and enjoys the stream of warm water running from the shower through her hair and down her body; it's refreshing without making her shiver; last night's shower had been more about rinsing off the traveller's dust and sweat; this morning it feels like pure luxury. She is dawdling, filling the time, which she usually devotes to the pigs, with pampering herself... It's a strange feeling to be at a loose end. Relaxing is not her strong point.

'Come on, lazy bones. We are on a mission.' Ant pulls the duvet from Kathleen, who protests with a heartfelt groan.

'Breakfast,' Ant lures her, standing at the foot of the luxurious bedstead with the thick mattress and silky bedclothes. Only a few modern art reproductions grace the walls - stripes in the colours of the rainbow – and liven up the beige background.

Kathleen's morning ablutions are astonishingly quick and efficient and soon the women make their way down to the breakfast room. Obviously, the headmistress is used to an efficient morning drill.

'I wonder what Algerians eat for breakfast.' Kathleen mutters. 'I'll treat myself to a coffee. If I start a school day with coffee, I usually get heartburn...but I might risk it today.'

It wasn't a big surprise that a European buffet was awaiting them, a long table with baskets and plates full of French baguettes, croissants, jams, and small pots of honey; and for the benefit of British tourist, there are even trays keeping the ever present Full English Breakfast warm.

They both stand in front of it all, and suddenly don't fancy it.

'Can I help you,' a young man wearing a white apron reaching to his knees, asks; they presume that he is part of the kitchen staff. Luckily, the waiter from last night is nowhere to be seen.

'What would a typical Algerian breakfast consist of?' Kathleen asks in French.

The waiter's face brightens in surprise, and he says without hesitation: '*Chakchouka*'.

'And what is *Chakchouka*?' Ant enquires.

'Fried eggs with red, yellow and green pepper, garlic and tomatoes.'

'Fancy it?' Ant looks at Kathleen who nods keenly, eyes sparkling.

'Two *Chakchoukas* please; and we shall sit over there by the window.' Ant notices with relief that it was still free of Algerian lilies. Even the waiter seems delighted at their choice, clearly surprised that they are trying something new, something local.

The *Chakchoukas* arrive in a huge pan for the two of them; the waiter spoons them on two plates and wishes the ladies: 'Bon appétit.'

They tuck in, never thinking that they would have seconds, but they do, rounding off the breakfast with strong black, heavily sweetened coffee flavoured with cardamom pods.

Kathleen wipes little flakes of red tomato, golden olive oil and a tiny speck of egg yolk from the corners of her mouth with her napkin and declares: 'I am ready to take on the world!'

'That won't be necessary,' Ant grins. All we have to do is find Mr Karim and ask him a few questions. After that we are free to turn into tourists.'

'How far did you say it was?' Kathleen asks and answers the question herself: 'Two miles?' Nothing will deprive her of her holiday mood.


Three quarters of an hour later, they arrive at the foot of the *Kasbah*, tourist attraction and World Culture Heritage site. Kathleen reads, ever the teacher, from the guide book. ' According to this, Algeria was much  colonised and occupied  - from the native Berbers, to the Numidians, Romans, Christians, the Ottoman Muslims (when Turkish was the country's official language);  and latterly by the French. It was known as The Bread Basket of North Africa, so everybody wanted a share in it.' Kathleen takes a deep breath before continuing.

'*Kasbah* has already been known to the Romans as a town called Iscarium. First it was a citadel, a fortress. When the Ottomans came, they added splendid Mosques, palaces and houses for the community. During the three hundred years they ruled, the Ottomans developed the *Kasbah* into a thriving city of craftsmen, tradesmen and servants; a sprawling, walled town with a splendid view over the Mediterranean Sea.'

'Are you listening?' Kathleen stops reading. Ant only nods absent-mindedly. She is guessing that Mr Karim lives somewhere along these dusty lanes.

'It was magnificent at one time,' Kathleen is clearly enthralled by the diversity of influences in Algeria's past. 'Look at it now,' she exclaims, pointing at the huddle of derelict buildings. Where has all the splendour gone? Kathleen looks at Ant who seems to be elsewhere with her thoughts. Kathleen is giving up and changes the topic: 'So where does Mr Karim live?' Ant points to the top of the *Kasbah*, earning herself a stare of incredulity from Kathleen. She is not wearing the right shoes for this sort of trek and soon begins to limp.

'This is a great place to hide' she says out loud and points to the maze of narrow lanes, tumble-down houses or cave-like dwellings,' Ant stops and nods. They are both out of breath.

'The French had no end of trouble during Algeria's Independence War, trying to dislodge the National Liberation Front fighters from here. They even kept their Headquarters at the top – brazen, I call that.'

'…and?' It's the first sign of interest Ant shows in the history of the Kasbah.

'The Algerians won,' Kathleen says triumphantly. Yeah, Ant thinks by herself, and look at it now. She is only interested in one thing: to find Sylvie's father.

Ant pulls out her notebook and leafs through it until she comes to the page where she has written down the address. She looks around herself for orientation: There are elderly men standing around with no discernible purpose apart from chatting to each other. 'We need a guide,' she pronounces and walks up to the group.

The men wear cotton shirts and black trousers shiny from use or frequent washing; a few are wrapped in traditional white cloaks. As the women approach, the men step back a little and stare at them with curiosity. Kathleen asks in her best French for directions to Mr Karim's home. They are willing to help; everybody has something to say, all at the same time; they interrupt each other with determined head-shaking while their voices rise steadily to a deafening crescendo. Ant and Kathleen watch and wait until everybody has calmed down. Finally, out of the general hubbub, one man, middle-aged, short, stout with a round protruding belly and a brown, wrinkled face is pushed forward and declared a tourist guide: he would find M. Karim for the foreign ladies. Ant and Kathleen can only hope they are right.

'Tour of *Kasbah*?' he asks hopefully. 'No, only this address,' the tourists insist and Ant points to the page in her notebook. He can't understand why they can't accept both. For a moment, the guide looks unsure whether he wants to accept this peculiar assignment but to their relief, he begins the steep climb on the dusty lane. Kathleen hopes it's not too far, as her feet are already aching from just coming to this point. They walk past dilapidated mud-brick houses, alternating with tall buildings which glow in the brilliant sunshine. People wrapped from head to toe in billowing white cloths scuttle in and out of small doorways. Eventually, they meet a group of veiled women, they had seen from below High up in the distance a couple of veiled women they had seen from below, some carrying items in baskets on their heads or against their hips, chattering animatedly while walking. They inspect Ant and Kathleen with beady eyes, as they pass each other. The Westerners smile in greeting, but the Kasbah women turn their backs and continue with their natter. Kathleen begins to huff and puff .Pieces of laundry flutter in the hot wind like sails within low mud walls next to small hovels. Do people really live there? The billowing winds are echoing centuries old poverty .

And suddenly, they get a first glimpse of the glorious splendour of the Kasbah, a magnificent mosque. Kathleen stands and admires, but Ant gestures that they have to push on -duty first.

'What sort of people live here?' Ant asks the guide.

'Poor people, Imams and...' he pauses dramatically, 'criminals.'

'Charming,' Kathleen mutters, and hopes, Mr Karim is not one of them.

'What's your name?' she asks politely.

'Khalil,' he says with a smile.

'Khalil, do you live here?' Ant wants to know.

He shakes his head, the question not worthy of an answer. It should be evident that it is not honourable to live here. He is only visiting old mates.

'Do you know some of the people who live here?' Ant asks in hope.

'A few,' he mutters.

'We are looking for a Mr Abdullah Karim and his family,' Ant persists; 'This is his address.' She shows him her notebook again.

'You police?' The tourists shake their heads vigorously. He ponders the request. 'I take you,' he says eventually, unsure whether he is doing the right thin---

They have to climb to the very top to the *Higher Kasbah* quarters, where the houses suddenly look better cared for, tidier; some of them are still undergoing renovation. Obviously, the Cultural Heritage Fund's monies have arrived to preserve this ancient treasure. Several Mosques are gleaming and sparkling in the bright sunshine, representing a safe haven for all.

'Beautiful!' Kathleen gasps, but the guide is in a hurry to finish this strange mission. He stops at a wooden door, the entrance to a three storey house. He knocks. They can hear voices inside, as if people are debating whose duty it was to open the door. It takes a few more moments until someone - a veiled woman in a faded red gown - opens the door. Khalil speaks to her in a rapid exchange of Arabic; she shakes her head. Ant deducts that the Karims don't live here any longer. Just as the young woman is about to close the door, Ant sticks her foot into the narrow gap: 'Sorry, do you speak English?' The girl sends her a dark, almost hostile look.

'Khalil, could you please ask the lady where the Karims have gone? We really need to find them.' The guide repeats the question in Arabic, but is answered with an angry shrugs of the shoulders and a brief torrent of words.

'Outside *Kasbah*,' he translates, 'district Uizdad, near Le Jardin D'Essai Hamma. But she is not sure.'

Kathleen says something in a soft voice in French, which seems to calm the tempers and elicits a reply also in French. Kathleen seems to thank the woman over and over again.

As they walk away, Kathleen translates triumphantly: 'The Karims have moved just outside the *Kasbah* and work in one of the hotels in the tourist district. We should be able to find them now.'

As they trudge downhill, Kathleen winces, noticing every stone through her deck shoes feeling a bit foolish like one of those people who climb mountains in flip flops.

'Shall I ask him to give you a piggy-back?' Ant whispers to lighten the mood. 'It's not funny,' Kathleen whispers back. Their guide has no idea why these English women behind him burst into fits of laughter.

Ant pays Khalil more than she had planned, but he has earned a generous tip with his patience, forbearance and putting up with their strange requests.

'Taxi,' Kathleen shouts, before Ant can suggest they should walk back to the hotel.

# CHAPTER SIXTEEN

Algiers evenings in January are pleasant, certainly milder than in England. Refreshed from a light meal and an afternoon nap, they go downstairs and order a coffee to be drunk on the hotel's patio. It's a lovely spot, although they can hear some of the traffic of the nearby main road. Here they are sheltered by flowering poinsettia hedges, palm trees and colourful exotic flower borders featuring frequently the Algerian national flower, iris tectorum. The air is filled with a minty scent. Kathleen looks in the borders next to their little round table and the rattan chairs they are sitting on.

'What are you looking for?' Ant enquires.

'I thought I could smell mint.'

'Maybe, but I guess it's the Eucalyptus tree over there.'

'Trust you to spot it within seconds.' Kathleen admires Ant's ability to sift and scan a space within seconds.

'It's called awareness; professional obsession more like your *deformation professionellle,*' Ant corrects her; 'It can be a real pain, never being able to just enjoy a place; always automatically scanning the surroundings for minute details, things which might stand out, which shouldn't be there. It's a bit like you being organised at all times.' Ant gets up. 'Are you ready?'

They get in one of the taxis which queue to the right of the main hotel entrance, close to the eucalyptus trees.

'So, where are we going?' Kathleen asks.

'Not far,' Ant explains. It's somewhere near that lovely park we passed on our way from the airport.'

''You mean Le Jardin d'Essai duHamma?' Kathleen grins smugly, 'the Research Garden of Hamma?'

'Yes, clever clogs.' Kathleen thumps the guidebook like a trusty old friend.

'It used to be a swamp,' Kathleen launches into reciting an abbreviated version of what the guidebook says: 'before some enthusiasts drained it in the early nineteenth century and turned it into the Government's agricultural research centre. Later on, botanists took over and, according to the pictures here, it has magnificent lakes with stunning vistas. It looks here like a mini Versailles if you can call nearly 200 hectares *mini*.'

'Oh, spare me the details,' Ant groans, burying her head in her palms from where giggles emerges. 'Let's first concentrate on our visit to Mr. Karim.'

'I know; I just wish I could be of more help'.

'You are a great help with your French, and to be honest, I did promise you a nice trip. I admit that so far, it was mainly work-related. Tell you what: tomorrow is sightseeing day.'

The taxi drops them right outside Mr Karim's house. As they approach to knock on the door, Ant's heart thumps. This could be a total waste of time, or it could be a breakthrough. They are greeted by a pleasant front garden, laid to lawn featuring a clump of palm trees. An elderly woman comes to the door, listens before calling into the back of the house: 'Gazala,' followed by a rapid stream of Arabic.

A young woman, dressed in one of the white billowing garments - a pretty little white cloth with lace borders covering mouth and nose - appears next to the old woman. Kathleen launches into repeating what she has asked before: Is this the residence of Mr Abdullah Karim, and is he is in? The young woman shakes her head, and all Ant can understand from her stream of words is something about *travail* which, she knows, means work, and *ce soir*, meaning: this evening.

'Ask her whether he speaks English.' Kathleen does so and Ant understands the answer: *Oui.*

'Ask whether Sylvie is here,' Ant probes.

Kathleen looks uncertain whether she should dare: 'Do you think that's wise?' she whispers.

'Let's see.'

Kathleen does as she is told and asks with a warm smile whether Sylvie, their French relative, lives here, too - or is maybe visiting.

The women keep interrupting each other, as if discussing the matter amongst themselves; then they tell Kathleen: 'No, she doesn't; and they haven't seen her for years; actually, since their family have left France.' The Karim's sound mystified, as if Sylvie is a far distant memory they rarely think about.

They establish that Abdullah Karim is manager of a small hotel nearby and that his shift ends late tonight. They might catch him though the following morning between ten and midday; his next shift begins at two in the afternoon which should give them enough time to speak to him. They arrange with the women that they will return by ten in the morning, to ask him a few simple questions about his daughter. They notice that neither of the women seems unduly perturbed nod nodding their agreement. A moment later, the old lady has turned her back on them and disappears along a narrow corridor.

'They didn't really want us in there, did they?' Kathleen comments drily. Ant is still staring at the shut door.

Ant and Kathleen return to the Karim's house at ten o'clock sharp the following morning. A man in his forties opens the door, taller than the average Algerian; he is lean and has thick, black hair neatly trimmed and brushed back. He wears an open-necked freshly laundered white shirt, tight jeans and brown leather sandals. His welcoming smile is warm and friendly suffused with curiosity. The visitors can see why Bernadette had fallen for him.

They introduce themselves without coming to the point immediately.

'You have come from England?' he asks directly and in perfect English.

'Yes,' Ant smiles back.

'Come in,' he waves them to enter and opens the blue door wide. They are ushered into a reception room which has oriental wall hangings and enormous floor cushions on which they are directed to sit. Agile Ant lowers her body nimbly onto the cushion and crosses her legs. Kathleen watches her uncomfortably; scanning the room for a chair, but there isn't one. Before Mr Karim can leave the room to fetch something more comfortable, they hear a muffled thud as Kathleen drops onto the cushions next to the surprised Ant. Mt Karim sits down opposite them.

'We were looking for you at the *Kasbah* yesterday,' Ant opens the conversation. He doesn't flinch, demonstrating the same friendly openness. Ant and Kathleen are both wriggling a little, trying to alleviate the discomfort of the unusual way of sitting. 'Lean against the cushions on the wall,' he suggests apologetically and explains. ' We don't have many foreign visitors…'

'Don't worry,' Kathleen tries to rescue the situation,' it's just that the cushions are almost too beautiful to lean against.'

Indeed, they are embroidered in striking prime colours, sparkling with little mirror inserts. The two visitors do as they are told.

'Why did you move from the Kasbah?' Ant enquires.

'Better job; better house,' he explains cheerfully and with pride.

'When was that?' Ant persists and earns herself a secret nudge into the waist from Kathleen. A shadow of suspicion creeps over Abdullah Karim's face.

'Are you the police?'

'Not exactly, but we are involved in an investigation in England, which led us to you.'

'…to me? A shadow of bewilderment crosses his face. His smile fades a little. 'How can I help?' he asks with slightly cooler politeness.

There is no point in beating about the bush. Ant takes a deep breath and begins the interview: 'We are wondering whether your daughter Sylvie has come to live with you.'

'No, she has not!' he says emphatically. 'Why?' He shifts uncomfortably on his cushion and looks anxiously from one to the other. 'Is she not with her mother in France?'

'No. She was on a school exchange visit in England and has disappeared,' Kathleen informs him. 'I am the headmistress of the English school.'

He looks bewildered. Her heart goes out to him. He nods slowly, as if something has become clearer in his mind.

'I was wondering why two English ladies were looking for me yesterday…So, where is Sylvie?' Mr Karim looks from one face to the other, sudden panic in his voice and hoarse with the shock.

'That's what we have come to find out. We are following up every possible lead... and you were one of them.'

'And you have a lead in Algiers?' There is wildness in his black, glittering eyes. The guests simply look at him, until he understands: 'Me?' he groans, incredulous; he also realises that he might be a suspect. He is understandably upset: 'She not here in Algiers,' his voice almost flips over with emotion and his English deteriorates with fear and anger. He rests his elbows on his thighs, folds his hands and supports his chin with them in an effort to compose himself.

'We just thought you might know where she is,' Ant explains. 'One of the English school children told us, that Sylvie might have planned to get in touch with you.'

'She wants to come here?' He is baffled and contemplates the enormity of this. 'She was unhappy with her mother?'

'You know teenagers,' Ant says vaguely. He looks straight into her eyes: 'I swear I did not hear from Sylvie for many years.'

'...why not?'

'You know, divorce and bad feeling. Bernadette want to stay in Paris, I wanted to go home to Algiers. Sylvie stayed with her mother.' After a short pause he adds: 'Algerians are not welcome in Motherland; life is not good for us.' He is calmer now, regretful; they are not sure whether that is because he had never felt at home in France or that his marriage had broken down.

Ant is not willing to get into discussing either. 'Would you mind if I had a look round your house?' she asks briskly. 'I won't disturb anything,' and then she adds - as if the thought had just occurred to her: 'And I shall need a DNA sample before I leave, if you don't mind, just for the purpose of elimination.' Kathleen is holding her breath expecting an outburst of temper.

Ant ignores her, and takes Abdullah Karim's shrug of defeat as a sign of consent: '*C'est nécessaire?*' he lapses into French; Ant understands and nods: 'You are very welcome to accompany me round your house, Mr Karim,' she invites him, but he shakes his head as she leaves the room.

'Is anybody else in the house?' Ant remembers the two women they had spoken to yesterday.

'*Non.*'

While Ant begins her tour of the rooms, Kathleen feels obliged to make polite conversation and possibly retrieve some of the initial goodwill of their host: 'Your English is excellent, Mr Karim,' she begins. He doesn't look at her, but mumbles something about it being necessary for his job in the hotel.

'How long did you live in France?'

'Five years.'

'Sylvie was very little then, when you left?'

'*Oui,*' he mutters unhappily staring at his clenched hands. It must be difficult to hear other people dredging up your flawed past; Kathleen feels with him.

The conversation comes to a halt, until he asks in a whisper: 'How is Bernadette?' Kathleen is surprised at the question, but happy to answer it: 'She came to England to help us look for Sylvie. She is naturally very upset and worried.'

'She works?'

'Yes; but it's hard as a single mother.'

'...she married?'

'Not as far as we know. Did you get married again?'

'Yes, and we have three children...two sons, one daughter.'

'Where are they now?'

'In school, and my wife and my mother go shopping.'

'I see.' Kathleen is fast running out of conversation topics and breathes a sigh of relief when Ant returns. She smiles at both of them kindly. 'That's all fine. Would you mind if I did the test now, Mr Karim?' she asks as she takes her packet of sterilised DNA swabs out of her rucksack. She un-wraps them, but before approaching him, she asks for his permission again.

Kathleen averted her eyes, while Ant is taking the humiliating DNA swab from Sylvie's father's mouth - a rare chance to collect a sample for examination, which they might need in the future...

'Thank you so much, Mr Karim,' Ant says when all is packed away securely in Ant's rucksack. Mr Karim has been cooperative and compliant, which will count in his favour, too. They couldn't ask for more. Ant smiles warmly at him and says: 'I am so sorry to inconvenience you like this, Mr Karim, but we must find your daughter. I wish I had come with better news.'

He looks to the floor, shoulders slumped forward. Suddenly, his head jerks up as if a thought had struck him: 'Shall I come to England and help looking?' he offers.

Ant shakes her head: 'It won't be necessary, Mr Karim. The police are doing all they can to find her. But thank you for offering.' He nods with resignation, as if he had expected that answer.

'If you want, we can keep you informed, but we'll have to tell your ex-wife if we do.'

'Yes, of course, I want to know, she is my daughter,' his voice vibrates with the sorrow of having neglected her for so long. These strangers have unexpectedly restored the link between the present and the past. From now on, he will always say that he has two sons and two daughters.

'And you will let us know if you hear from Sylvie?' Ant begs him.

'There is hope?' He looks at her pleadingly, but Ant can only shrug her shoulders.

'There is always hope, Mr Karim. Thousands of youngsters disappear every day all over the world.'

'Of course,' he says quietly with his hoarse voice.

Ant hands over her card with contact details. He turns it back to front in his hands and says: 'Thank you,' as if she had thrown him a life belt.

'Will you be all right on your own now?' Ant asks with concern.

His 'yes' is hardly audible.

'We'll be here another day. We are staying at the Hotel Aurassi. Give us a ring if you have a question or remember anything else that might be helpful.'

Their good-bye is subdued, less cheerful than their friendly welcome has been. Sylvie's father looks exhausted. He just stands outside his house, too upset to wave off the English visitors.

# CHAPTER SEVENTEEN

'Did you find anything in the house?' Kathleen asks as they walk away to flag down a taxi in the main street.

'There is no indication, that Sylvie has ever been here,' Ant replies. There are only three bedrooms: one with a double bed, one a single, I presume, for the old lady, and three beds in another room, probably for the children.'

'He didn't strike me as a vengeful husband either. He seems quite happy with his new life,' Kathleen comments.

Ant remains silent. She knows how devious people can be. It's easy to trust a person, to be taken in by protestations of innocence, only to find out later, that he or she had been first class actor. Ant reserves judgement for the moment and hopes to check when Mr Karim has last been on holiday abroad.

When they reach the busy High Street, they flag down a taxi and begin with their promised sightseeing tour.

'The Research Garden first,' Ant snuggles into the comfortable seat of the car. 'Let's forget about the case for a few hours and have a good time.' Kathleen is delighted. Of course, she wants to find Sylvie as much as Ant and Bernadette, and everybody else in Dulverton, but they both need a break.

'Destination?' the driver asks a little impatiently in French with the heavily rolling letter 'R', so typical of Arabic and most other languages spoken around the Mediterranean rim. Even Ant's poor school French stretches to that, and the answer, which Kathleen has mentioned so often that Ant dares to repeat it: 'Le Jardin d'Emploi du Hamm.' To the amusement of the driver, both women seem to congratulate each other for some unknown reason. He likes cheerful passengers.

'Oh, there it is,' Ant cries out.

'What?'

'...the hotel where Mr Karim works. Please, driver, stop; I won't be long. I need to find out something important.' Ant jumps out of the car, into the hotel, and comes back not long after: 'They'll check,' she says breathlessly but with triumph in her voice, 'they'll give me a call tonight.' A grin of satisfaction spreads all over Ant's face. 'It's called being smug,' she hears Kathleen mumble before she quickly buries her nose again in the tourist guide. As nothing more is said, Ant confirms to the driver: 'Jardin d'emploi du Hamam - here we come.' Strangely, she, too, is really looking forward to a few hours of unbridled idleness and leisurely strolls around a fabulous garden


'How beautiful was that!' Kathleen almost swoons in the back of yet another taxi.

Ant has decided that Kathleen is not the walking kind of tourist, so to avoid any more blisters and complaints, she has given in to doing their sightseeing the easy way: by being chauffeured everywhere. Originally, the Museum of Popular Arts and Traditions at the Kasbah was on Kathleen's list of things to see but they had hardly been able to tear themselves away from the Gardens and now there was not enough time to visit everything. , Ant also suspects, that the memory of their first climb and descent of the *Kasbah* has helped to make up Kathleen's mind to forego it. 'I could murder a coffee and something to eat,' Kathleen declares, 'let's go to the market!'

It seems a long way to get there, even by car; they suspect that the driver makes a profitable detour. Ant doesn't care and sinks into pleasant reminiscences of the Garden they have visited. She had expected to be bored, and was instead charmed. It was everything the picture in the guide book had promised: lush, exotic planting, tall palms, magnificent lakes to walk along and long-stretching views towards Algiers town centre in one direction and the Mediterranean in the other. Above all, the sun was shining gloriously, deepening the colours and emphasizing the Garden's beauty - more than they could ever have imagined.

'Market,' the driver announces with an excited cry. He seems pleased with Kathleen's tip and helps her gallantly to disembark. Ant waits for a couple of seconds for a similar treatment, but realises quickly, that it won't be forthcoming and that she has to clamber out under her own steam.

'Hold on to your wallet and credit cards,' Ant warns her friend, a little disgruntled, before they join the throng. They are immediately swallowed up in the narrow lane between stalls by masses of mainly female shoppers, dressed in their traditional white, hooded *Djellabas* 'Those cloaks look as if they are made of wool,' Ant whispers, nodding towards the women walking right in front of them.

'I think they are,' Kathleen whispers back, 'it's original Berber clothing – protecting against summer sun, desert winds and the cold rains of winter.'

'You show off!' Ant laughs good-humouredly, but is secretly pleased that her friend has taken the trouble to read up beforehand to fill in their gaps of ignorance. Watch out, someone might offer you a job.'

They amble along behind a noisy crowd; the colours of the wares on display are dazzling in the late afternoon sun. Ant and Kathleen begin to feel hot, their clothes clinging to their skin and beads of perspiration appear on their foreheads. The noise of thousands of people speaking loudly, stallholders offering their wares and customers haggling with them, make even Ant and Kathleen's briefest conversation difficult. Several times they have to hop out of the way of carts, bicycles, mopeds and carts which, regardless of the mayhem, try to squeeze through, the drivers impatiently hooting, gesticulating and shouting.

The chaos is tiring. Ant and Kathleen collapse onto chairs outside a stall, a small, round metal table, rusty in places, between two rickety chairs. Ant orders a cup of mint tea while Kathleen opts for the black coffee she has craved. 'We can't go wrong with that,' Ant says, watching to make sure that the stallholder boils the water thoroughly.

'Sorry being such a drag,' Kathleen apologises, as she leans back onto the far too narrow support for her broad back. 'I know I should lose weight...' she sighs. Ant is a little taken aback by her self-flagellation and puts quickly a reassuring hand on her friend's shoulder: 'Kathleen, you are fine as you are. .. And moreover, I have never told you that: you are a lovely woman, and...you have a lovely accent.'

Kathleen's face brightens: 'Pure Irish, I have you know,' she declares proudly. 'After all those years in England, it hasn't faded.'

'Tell me about your family!' Ant asks and leans forward in expectation.

Kathleen clears her throat and launches happily into reminiscences: 'I grew up on a farm in Cork with my Ma and Da, Eileen and Jonny, and three brothers, Ryan, Donal and Patrick, and my sister Marie.'

'Are you in regular contact with them?'

Kathleen sighs:' Not as much as I should be. My Da is in his eighties now. Since Ma died, he has lost his zest for life. He misses her...'

'When did she die – recently?'

'Oh no… She died of cancer about fifteen years ago. My brothers Ryan and Donal took over the farm. The youngest, Patrick, became a doctor. He studied in London, but came back to practise in Cork town. Marie got married to another farmer and has three children; they are a great joy for Da!'

'And why did you come to England?'

'…Lurve!' Kathleen imitates Paul McCartney's intonation.

'Tell all!' Ant insists and leans even further over the little metal table.

'My youngest brother had a girlfriend at university, and when I visited him in London. They wanted to take me out, but didn't want me to be a gooseberry; so they brought a guy called Karl along. Well, one thing led to another – my first love, so to speak – and I decided foolishly to take a teaching job in Tower Hamlets. Coming from Cork, this was a shocking adjustment to make, and the boyfriend Karl didn't last very long either. I have been in England ever since.'

'Did you never think of going back?'

'At first I was too embarrassed to admit to have failed, but I did, consider moving back to somewhere in Ireland just before I was offered the job in Dulverton; since then, I changed my mind. Exmoor is as beautiful as Ireland, just in a different way. And then, life in Ireland has changed, too. As a spinster, I would just end up as the maiden aunt to my nieces and nephews.' Kathleen sniffs and takes out a tissue from her handbag to blow her nose. 'They all have their lives; they don't need me there.'

'And you?' Kathleen asks Ant, while she stuffs the tissue back into the bag. When it is done, she looks expectantly at her friend, raising her eyebrows in anticipation of an answer. She doesn't really know much about Ant. Ant just stares at the table top,

107

obviously taken aback; 'There is not much to tell,' she dismisses the enquiry.

'Oh, come on, Ant. That's not fair! Start with your birth! ' Kathleen protests so loudly that the stall owner looks over to them.

Ant stiffens, and for a moment, Kathleen thinks, she is getting up to leave, but then she hears a quite unwilling mutter: 'My father was rather peripatetic. I hardly knew him. I don't even know whether he is still alive. I grew up with my mother, who seemed besotted by my father in spite of his infrequent appearances. She fell totally apart and into depression, when he stopped coming altogether. I looked after her for the rest of my adolescence. No siblings, no relatives I know of. There came a point when she didn't even want me around, so she was admitted to a psychiatric institution where she died soon afterwards. I went off to university, and after that, my work as a forensic scientist took over my life.'

'That's sad, Ant,' Kathleen commiserates. It's her turn to pat her friend's hand.

'Not really. I am happy.'

'No boyfriend at all?'

'No. My father put me off relationships.' She doesn't mention Bex, who came closest to being one. 'Feeling refreshed?' Ant changes the topic breezily.

'Is that all I am getting?' Kathleen protests as she struggles up from the small metal chair while Ant is already walking away. She quickly grabs her handbag, leaves a tip on the saucer, gives a cheery wave to the stall holder and rushes after her friend. When she has caught up with her, Ant comes out unexpectedly with the question that seems to still bother her: 'Why did your relationship with Karl not work out?'

'He discovered that he was gay,' she answers drily – 'and yours?' So she had guessed that there must have been somebody at some time…

When she looks at Ant's tight lips and nervous eyes like those of a trapped animal, she realises that there is no point in pressing her now.

'Let's head back to the gift stalls,' Kathleen suggests.

'…anything in particular?' Ant asks, palpably relived to have escaped further interrogation about her private life.

Kathleen is looking for souvenirs for the school children at home.

Ant thinks of souvenirs as unnecessary dust-catchers, but keeps quiet trotting patiently beside Kathleen, who now inspects each and every stall. Ant is itching to review the case and to send a report to Sergeant Penhaligon ahead of their return (preferably today before he leaves the Police Station in Taunton for the day), and a message to Zac in London. Just when Ant is giving up all hope of ever getting back to the hotel, Kathleen decides to buy a Berber runner for her bedroom, several Touareg bracelets, small hand-stitched purses, a couple of hand-painted wooden boxes and an *arghul*, a kind of recorder which the stall holder's son played with abandon as they approached.

'The children will love these things – colourful and from another country,' Kathleen smiles happily at Ant.

'Lovely,' Ant comments politely and is glad when Kathleen goes to pay the very happy stall holder. She even gets to shake the hand of the young musician, clearly the pride and joy of his father. Ant looks back and nudges Kathleen: the man is bowing to the two foreign ladies who made his day.

Weighed down with souvenirs and presents, they make for the exit of the market and the taxi rank.

'That was a good day's work,' Kathleen proclaims, 'but I could murder a glass of wine.' Just as well that they reside in a western style hotel with all the comforts to soothe their exhausted senses and aching limbs.

'Hot bath,' Kathleen gasps. It will give Ant time to file her e-mail reports to England before they go down for dinner. It seems hardly possible, that their trip is already coming to an end.


Flying back to England the following morning, they both agree, that Algeria is a fascinating country, undoubtedly a place where Africa, the Arab World and Europe still meet as they have done for centuries.

Ant opens an envelope the hotel receptionist had handed her before their departure: Mr Karim's boss confirms that his employee has not taken time off for the last two years.

# CHAPTER EIGHTEEN

It's one of those dull, dreary end-of-January days on Exmoor, when daylight never breaks through and dawn and dusk stretch over hours to meet somewhere around midday. The windows are speckled with glittering raindrops, clinging on and eventually falling to the already sodden ground. More rain is hanging in the air and the temperature has dropped to somewhere between chilly and uncomfortable, but not enough to make way for frost.

'Come on Hooch! If we wait for sunshine, we shall wait forever. Let's go!' Annette Rice from Bury village tells her red haired Irish setter, who jumps up from his dog basket, where he has lazed the morning away; sluggishness is immediately replaced by pent-up energy and great excitement. Hooch runs to the entrance, flips his lead from a hook next to the door – he is tall enough to reach it without stretching, supporting himself with front paws on the wall – and carries it back triumphantly to his mistress. He knows the drill: keep lead in mouth; sit still on haunches; wait for mistress to take the lead from him; bark with joy and run out when she opens the door, laughing.

'Good boy!' she says outside and puts him on the leash, just in case a rare car comes along the narrow lane. Hooch knows that she will let him roam free, when they have reached the steep, scrubby incline which leads to the top of Haddon Hill. Once up there, he will be allowed to wander and explore freely, as long as he stays in view of his mistress and leaves the Exmoor ponies in peace, if they can be seen at all; the other 'no, no' is, to rush up to other dogs should they meet any and no barking or growling at them. They probably won't meet any today in this appalling weather.

It has stopped raining by the time they reach the top, but fog and mist still cling to the silhouette of the hill like a grey tulle skirt. It feels as if they are walking above the clouds. Annette shudders a little; inter is not her favourite time of year, but luckily, she has Hooch who forces her to go out even in the foulest of weathers. Annette knows it's good for her. She pulls the hood over her head of brown, straggly hair and trudges along the muddy lane, almost liquid mud squelching under the soles of her green Wellington boots. Her thoughts wander to what she would eat for dinner. There isn't anybody she needs to cook for, but as she is somebody who likes to eat, she usually ends up producing something she fancies: a steak or a stew or some fry-up, her bad conscience assuaged by fruit for desert. She has long given up listening to people's advice. They always seem to know better, but since the big change in her life – divorce a few years ago, followed by a not altogether surprising period of depression, and moving from Hampshire to the West Country and the tiny village of Bury at the foot of Haddon Hill – she has promised herself that from now on, she will only follow her own instincts and do what she likes: nothing out of the ordinary; mainly a calm, peaceful life, close to nature and an occasional modest treat for herself and Hooch, her fury companion. It has all worked out well, and as far as she is concerned, the past has lost its hold on her; she might be leading am uneventful life, but she is moderately happy. No more highs and no more lows, since she has discovered that she is not half as bad, useless and stupid as she had been made to believe by the man who had professed to love her. She smiles to herself, and a feeling of contentment drowns every unpleasant memory.

Suddenly she realises that Hooch has gone out of sight, probably into the bushes. It's hard to see any detail in this misty, grey moor landscape, never mind an animal with auburn fur flitting about like a thin arrow or sniffing the bushes and trees to ascertain who else has left their scent recently.

'Hooch; Hooooooch!' she shouts loudly, a little disgruntled. There is no one else around she could ask whether they have seen him. 'Come on Hooch! Be a good dog! Let's move on!' I hope he doesn't bring an injured bird or a sick rabbit or something else ghastly to drop at her feet, she thinks and shivers. 'Hooch!' she shouts with urgency now. She stands still and looks around her; not much to see in the grey, moisture-laden, chilly air. She is beginning to feel uneasy. Hooch is usually obedient. Something must have really captured his curiosity. 'Hooch!' she shouts in her angry voice steeped in disapproval. That should work! She hears crackling several steps ahead of her in the undergrowth on the right hand side. 'Hooch?' she calls, hopeful. More rustling, and finally a big red-haired head with long fury ears appears. 'There you are, you naughty boy,' she scolds him with relief. 'What have you got there?' He holds something in his mouth and won't let it go. It looks like a stick with lichen on it. Sticks are not good; they can pierce the insides of a dog's mouth or the throat. 'Come here; let me see what you find so fascinating.' She has to make a few steps forward towards Hooch. Usually he would deposit his find at her feet and then excitedly wait for her to pick it up and throw it to be retrieved again and again. It's his favourite game. Oddly, this time, he keeps his distance. She grabs the stick from his mouth, but he won't let go; he isn't going to give it up that easily. He even growls. Suddenly her hand withdraws in revulsion. The stick doesn't feel like wood at all. Rain drops fall from her hood over her forehead and into her eyes. She wipes them away with the back of her hand. Hooch still wants a tussle over his stick, standing over it; waiting for his mistress to make a move. Hooch senses that this time he has found something really special and suspects that if his mistress gets hold of it, she won't return it. 'Let me have it, Hooch,' she says predictably, now in her strict voice, but he holds on to it and growls again. What the hell is it? Annette thinks with a sick feeling in her stomach. She doesn't really want it; she will discard it as soon as he lets go. Hooch is sitting down, delighted that his mistress seems to find his stick so intriguing. He is still up for a tussle. But why does she stand there motionless with a strange expression on her face, he has never seen before?

It suddenly dawns on Annette what she is looking at. 'Drop it, Hooch! Drop it!'' she screams. He doesn't like her screaming and is definitely not going to give up his find...

She pulls out her mobile phone from the inside, zipped-up pocket of her rain jacket and dials. Luckily there is a mobile signal on Haddon Hill; there wouldn't be one in many of the villages below.

'Police,' she says, staring with horror at her dog still with this horrible stick in his mouth. The hood has slipped from her head; rain drops drip from her hair onto her face where they mingle with her tears and run down her cheeks.


The police take a while to find her. Luckily a car was just patrolling the villages. Usually, they have to come all the way from Taunton. A policewoman offers her a cup of tea from a flask, puts a blanket over her shoulders and offers her a seat in the car. She declines; she rather stays with Hooch, who is totally confused by the arrival of more people. All he wants now is to carry on with his walk, but even his mistress is behaving strangely; she seems to be rooted to the spot. Annette can't feel the penetrating, wet cold anymore. She is stunned and feels numb. Several policemen and one other policewoman cordon off a huge area, in the middle of which Annette stands with her cup of tea, the bewildered Hooch by her side. He keeps growling menacingly at the police officer who walks past, who has taken 'the stick' away from him and made it disappear somewhere in the car with the flashing lights.

'I can't believe it,' Annette sobs.

'You are in shock. Everybody would be.'

'What happens now?' Annette is not really interested; she just wants to get away, go home and have a hot shower, but she has been told that she will be taken shortly to Taunton Police Headquarters to be questioned. It is Hooch's feeding time soon. Will she have time to quickly rush home and put something in his feeding bowls, at least for the night? Or will she still be away in the morning?

'Don't worry,' the police woman, who is called Jodie, reassures her.

'There is nobody else at home,' Annette struggles to explain.

'Hooch can come with you, if he is well behaved. I am sure we can find him a few dog biscuits.' Thank goodness! That's one less problem for Annette.

The policeman, who introduces himself as Sergeant Penhaligon, finally gives the signal that Annette and Hooch can be taken away from the gruesome scene, Hooch has discovered. It is now pouring with rain again, hard drops, almost like hail, and Annette does not envy the men and women who have to stay to secure the scene of a crime and dig out the remains of the body in the thicket where Hooch found a thin arm.


Annette has never been in a police interview room before. She is not only numb with shock at Hoch's find, but feels cold, nauseous and slightly afraid of the unknown. Reason tells her that she has nothing to fear, but she can't help feeling uneasy. She can't think that she has done anything wrong. Hooch seems more at ease. He has already wolfed down several of the promised dog biscuits and has settled on her feet; he seems to need as much reassurance as she does.

Suddenly, the door of the interview room opens and Sergeant Penhaligon and two female officers enter the drab, sparsely furnished room with the whitewashed walls. There is hardly any natural light coming in apart from a narrow window at the top of one wall. It's one of those rooms where one automatically reaches for the light switch on entering. Nobody will be able to escape from here; for a moment, Annette feels the urge to escape herself and leave it all behind. The Sergeant is in such a hurry, that he almost slams the door in the face of the person behind him, one of his female colleagues. 'Sorry,' he mutters turning round to hold the door open. They both sit down opposite Annette at the large, oblong, functional table with an easy to wipe down surface. He puts an A4 envelope on it, which is, Annette notices, already half opened. The officers grab a writing pad and pen each from the middle.

Annette looks at the Sergeant with apprehension. 'Nothing to fear,' she keeps telling herself inwardly. At least something is happening which will ultimately sort things out and will make her feel less anxious, less inexplicably guilty.

'Mrs Rice, I am Sergeant Penhaligon, and these are my colleagues Rita Learner an,' he points at the officer standing by the door, 'Patricia Hamilton.' He fiddles around with a machine on his left side of the table. Finally it is set up and he turns to her:

'So, Mrs Rice, I am going to switch on the tape recorder – you don't mind, do you?'

Annette shakes her head. What a silly question…What would happen, if she said 'no'?

'Please, confirm your name, date of birth, address, a telephone number, e-mail address, so that we can stay in touch with you during this investigation.'

Annette reels off her personal details, while the Sergeant writes i down every word she says, in spite of the tape recording.

'Would you mind speaking up a little, Mrs. Rice?' Sergeant Penhaligon encourages her with a professional smile.

Annette clears her throat and repeats her last sentence.

'Excellent! Now: would you mind telling us, what happened this afternoon, Mrs Rice?'

He nods encouragingly, and she begins:

'I took Hooch for a walk on Haddon Hill… around three o'clock. I thought I better go earlier than usual, before it gets dark. I want to give him a good work-out every day…'

'Hooch is your dog, an Irish setter?' Annette nods.

'Could you please, say it aloud for the record, please,' the Sergeant reminds her.

'Yes, of course,' she apologises. Her brain seems to have gone numb, too. 'Hooch is my dog, and he is an Irish Setter,' she apologises.


'Excellent. So you went to Haddon Hill from your house at Bury about 15.00 hours? How did you get to Haddon Hill?'

'I live at the bottom of the Hill, and all I have to do is walk out through the gate at the back of my garden and walk up the steep path to the top.'

'Do you keep Hooch on a lead?'

'No. it's a footpath, unsuitable for cars. Hooch can roam freely, but he usually stays close to me, so I can see him.'

'Is that what happened today, Mrs Rice?' The Sergeant has put on reading glasses and looks sternly over the rim at her.

'Yes… to start with…' she stutters, 'but when we reached the top path, he disappeared. I was thinking about something, and I forgot to watch him; I don't know for how long.'

'On your way up and along the top path, did you notice anything unusual; anything that caught your attention, because it was different to your usual walks?'

Annette thinks for a moment, trying desperately to find the remnants of a memory, but she can't even remember whether she has closed the garden gate. Life on Exmoor is usually so simple, uneventful and safe. She shakes her head.

'Please speak up, Mrs Rice.'

Annette clears her throat and obliges with a clear voice: 'No.'

'Was anybody else around, other dog walkers for example?'

'No,' she whispers and shakes her head again.

Sergeant Penhaligon says for the benefit of the tape recorder: 'Mrs Rice is shaking her head. Could you please, confirm that, Mrs Rice?'

There wasn't anybody else as far as I could see. It was such terrible weather.'

'Thank you. What happened next?' asks the police woman with the reassuring voice and kind eyes next to him.

'I called him.'

'Do you mean, you shouted your dog's name out loud?'

Annette nods, then remembers to speak up and whispers hoarsely: 'Yes.' A horrendous picture reappears in her head.

'Could you, please speak up for the recording?' It's the police woman who pleads with her this time sounding apologetic. Most people they interview lose their voice temporarily with the shock of it all.

'Yes, I shouted *Hooch* several times.'

'Thank you. Did he come immediately?'

'No. He is usually obedient, but I had to call him several times. In the end, I shouted because he might not have heard me over the wind and the rain.'

'What did you do when he didn't turn up?'

'I walked a little further on, and when I heard rustling nearby in the bushes, I knew it must be him, and I followed the sound; and when he emerged from the bushes, he came out with something in his mouth.' Annette sighs with the effort of being coherent and being heard.

'What was it he had in his mouth?'

'I couldn't see at first in this half-light and with rain in my eyes, but I did think it looked peculiar; not like a normal wooden stick. So I grabbed it; Hooch thought it was a game and pulled back; there was a little tussle over the stick, until I shouted at Hooch to drop it. He was very reluctant and growled, but eventually he did let go. That's when I saw that it was something else, and I called you.' Annette sits back in her chair, exhausted from her long speech.

'So you touched or handled the item your dog found, didn't you?'

'Yes, but I had no idea…, we often play on our walks,' Annette stutters.

'I know. Of course, you were not to know, but unfortunately, it makes at least taking your fingerprints necessary, just for elimination,' the Sergeant says regretfully and is relieved when she doesn't protest and says instead: 'That's all right.'

'Mrs Rice, did you in any way recognise what this 'stick' was? I am sorry having to ask this question.' Sergeant Penhaligon tries his best to be sympathetic; he is feeling the pain, too.

'It's an arm,' Annette can hardly bring herself to say it.

'Yes, it is indeed a human arm with bits of sleeve sticking to it. Did you recognise it or the fabric?'

'No!' Annette protests, eyes wide with horror.

'You are sure about that?' the Sergeant persists. 'You have never seen anybody wearing this type of garment?'

'Yes. I am sure!' Annette feels under attack and bursts into tears. She takes out a tissue from her trouser pocket and blows her nose.

'Have you heard of a French exchange student who went missing last June from Dulverton Middle School?'

'Yes,' Annette whispers, aghast, eyes wide and the corners of her mouth trembling with the realisation, 'it's not her, is it? Oh please, God, no!'

'Well, obviously, we have no formal identification yet, but we strongly suspect that Hooch has unearthed the body of Sylvie Karim.'

# CHAPTER NINETEEN

'What a lovely surprise,' exclaims Ant when she sees Kathleen get out of the car. She is just about to feed the pigs, but that can wait.' She suddenly stops and becomes aware of Kathleen's grim face. 'What's wrong?' She enquires.

Kathleen bursts into tears: 'They found Sylvie's body on Haddon Hill,' she sobs.

'Come on in, quickly! I'll make us a strong, sugary cup of tea and then you must tell me all about it!'

'You were just going to feed the pigs,' Kathleen points at the well-known, large tin plate on the kitchen table?'

'Never mind that; the pigs will have to wait,' Ant replies, puts the plate onto the floor by the front door and leads her sobbing friend by the arm to the wicker chair by the Raeburn. For good measure, she stuffs the cushion embroidered with a large pig in the middle, into her back and walks over to the kettle to boil water.

'Tell me what's happened,' she encourages her gently.

Kathleen takes a tissue from the box on the table, blows her nose and begins to relate the horrific events of the afternoon, ending with: 'Sergeant Penhaligon rang me, just as I was about to leave the school.' A little bell rings in Ant's mind, but she brushes it aside.

'How absolutely dreadful,' Ant exclaims, 'poor Bernadette...'and looking at Kathleen she probes: 'I presume someone has informed her and the French police?'

Kathleen shrugs her shoulders and Ant adds quickly: 'If not, I'll take care of it.' Kathleen nods in acknowledgment.

'Bernadette will have to come over again for identification before she can repatriate the body.' Ant's brain is working away, organising practicalities. It was always her salvation when confronted by tragedy: keep on working when everybody else is losing their head; concentrate on what must be done next; keep busy and focused… a habit people in mourning often misinterpret as dispassionate coldness. It wouldn't be helpful, if she and her colleagues fell apart, too, would it? She has never allowed herself to do that. They all wear a professional armour round their hearts, which leaves the brain unencumbered to fun 'It sounds so clinical,' Kathleen stares at Ant.

'I know, 'Ant whispers gently and hands her a mug of steaming, sugary tea.

'Sorry! That was the professional in me kicking in. You said she was found on Haddon Hill. That's not far from here.' Ant looks through the kitchen window vaguely in the direction of Haddon Hill. It's only about 4 miles away by car. 'Sylvie couldn't have walked that distance. Why would she; she probably didn't even know about Haddon Hill. She must have accepted a lift in somebody's car.'

'Who found her?'

'…a local woman who walked her dog.'

'…in this weather?'

'Dogs need to go out whatever the weather,' Kathleen mumbles.

'Yes of course. What a shock for the poor woman!'

Kathleen doesn't react and keeps staring into a void, red rimmed eyes staring at nothing.

'…that poor girl! It doesn't bear thinking about what she has gone through.'

All sorts of thoughts and questions tumble through Ant's head. She waits until Kathleen has finished blowing her nose again.

'Did the Sergeant give any details?'

'He only said that they found a body and that it looks like murder. The forensic team are working on the site.'

'Good. He is a good chap; he will do his best.'

'Ant,' Kathleen whispers.

'Yes? What is it?'

'Could you help them?'

'What do you mean?' Ant knows very well what Kathleen means, and the answer is unfortunately 'no'.

'Help with the investigation?'

'There is no need. Sergeant Penhaligon is in charge, and he and his team will get to the bottom of what has happened.' She hopes she sounds confident.

'I want the best for that poor girl and her mother…' Kathleen begins to cry again, big heart-wrenching sobs.

'Of course, you do…We all do! I tell you what: Let's wait for the first results, have a conversation with the Taunton team and then ask whether we can help. Help from outside is not always welcome or necessary; it often muddies the waters, and it's not my place to interfere. I retired from the service.'

Kathleen looks horrified: 'So, you won't do anything - with all your expertise and knowledge?' Ant realises that there is no calming her friend with platitudes. She walks over to her wicker chair and puts an arm round Kathleen's shoulders: 'I promise you one thing: If they get stuck or ask me for assistance, I won't say no. Is that good enough?

Kathleen nods in slow motion, looking desperately unhappy.

'I let you get on with the pigs,' she says eventually, totally deflated. 'Thank you for listening.' She gets up as if fighting gravity.

'Stay here, Kathleen. You are in no state to drive back. I shall do a short-cut with the animals, and when I come back, we can have dinner and another talk.'

'No, I must let you get on...' Kathleen sounds distant and walks to the door without looking back.

'Keep in touch and let me know what's happening,' Ant shouts after her, but she isn't sure whether Kathleen has heard her.

Ant returns to the kitchen and sits down in the wicker chair, puts her elbows on the arm rests, covers her face with her palms and groans: 'Oh God. When will people stop killing each other? When will I be ever free of that job?' It had never been the job itself that had enticed her for years to get up in the morning; it had been the relentless feeling of duty towards the distraught families of victims and the victims themselves; guilt that she and her colleagues hadn't managed to keep people safe, so doing them justice after death was the next only thing that was left to do. It had never been good enough, to give her a feeling of satisfaction. Maybe a grim feeling of achievement once they had caught the murderer, but it was never pure joy any of the team had felt, because none of it could bring back the person someone was grieving over.

Ant suspects that eventually she might have to get involved in Sylvie's case, but not yet; not without being asked.

At the end of the week, Ant receives the news via a telephone message from Sergeant Penhaligon himself that the investigation has come to a standstill and has ended in a cul-de-sac. They hadn't been able to find any traces to identify the murderer. Everything, he assures her, apologetically with a kind of desperation in his voice, has been done, but it has neither led to new lines of enquiry nor to a suspect. The only things that could be established were the identity of the victim, Sylvie Karim, and the method of murder: Sylvie was strangled by somebody's big, gloved hands.

'Ant, will you help us now?' Kathleen pleads through the telephone. Bernadette is coming over to make the identification; she will be staying with me. I beg you,' she implores her and adds: '… and the Sergeant seems relieved at the thought of you getting involved.'

When she does ring Sergeant Penhaligon, he is not half as enthusiastic about her involvement as Kathleen had described.

'You can come and have a look at the lab results but to be honest with you, I don't hold out much hope. All we know so far is that the French girl is dead, that she has been murdered and buried on Haddon Hill, but we have no idea why and by whom.'

'These things take time,' Ant consoles him. Haste threatens thoroughness and stymies logical thinking; emotions must be banned. 'I'll leave you to it then,' Ant says; 'I do understand. Just keep in mind that if you do need assistance, you can phone me any time.'

'Will do,' he says dejectedly. He feels almost guilty that he hasn't come up with more results. What is he going to tell poor Bernadette? At least Ant understands his predicament.

# CHAPTER TWENTY

Bernadette, Sylvie's mother, comes over the following Friday. It is time for another media campaign and Bernadette's presence is invaluable. She arrives unaccompanied but is picked up from the ferry port by Sergeant Penhaligon himself. As she climbs in his car and throws her rain coat unto the backseat, he thinks that she looks less miserable, less unkempt; her face is a little fuller and her blonde bobbed hair is freshly washed, cut and styled; the shadows under her large eyes, the colour of grey slate, have lost their red rims. He also notices that the clothes she is wearing – a soft, dark blue lambs-wool V-neck pullover over a crisp, white blouse and a rather elegant navy skirt covering her knees - underlines her slight figure and makes her look rather attractive. As it is still early afternoon, Bernadette decides to accompany him straight to the morgue to get the identification over and done with. She has no idea how she is going to feel, seeing her beloved daughter laid out on a slab, head to toe draped in a white cloth which covers goodness knows what, horrific injuries and signs of decomposition. She has braced herself for weeks for this moment and all through the ferry journey across rough waters, knowing that it was inevitable; she is more than ready, eager even, to put it behind her and to take her daughter's body home. She hopes that the sight will not stay with her and give rise to endless nightmares for years to come. After this visit Bernadette wants to remember the sweet little girl with the brown skin, huge smile, mischief sparkling in her eyes and a mouth blessed with full lips, pouting coquettishly quite early on early on; and the same mouth, later, in her teenage years, frequently in a sulk. Maybe she might wish to remember the latter less so.

Sergeant Penhaligon's voice is gentle, and the presence of the pathologist is reassuring. Yes, she does recognise her daughter, but, although they have arranged Sylvie's body to make it look less disjointed than they had found her, and her mother had expected to see, she is shocked that she can't relate to what they show her: her child looks remote, unfamiliar and soulless. These could be the bones of anybody. Sylvie's spirit has left her body long ago. Bernadette stands there, staring blindly, numb, her thoughts frozen. Eventually – was it a long time or just a few minutes –she nods, turns away and walks out in a trance, hunched as if a dagger had been thrust into her heart. Bernadette has already learnt to live without her daughter whose remains are just an unreal shell on the slab.

Back in the car, she suddenly sobs violently, as if the dam of her pain had been breached. There is a big box of tissues on the dashboard, which she puts on her lap and holds on to. After she has blown her nose several times, wiped her tears away, she is calmer. Sergeant Penhaligon has been waiting patiently to explain: 'I shall take you to Antonia Bell, who has kindly agreed to help us with our investigation.' Indeed he had a change of mind and had rung Ant back, while Bernadette was on her way to England. Ant, the retired CSI or SOCO in old terms, with credentials most of her former colleagues could only dream of, could only be an asset to his endeavours. It can't do any harm to seek a second opinion, particularly one underpinned by so much experience. 'Hunches' were mentioned, but he wasn't too keen on those. As his team's efforts had hit the buffers, an injection of fresh ideas, energy and someone's vast experience in murder cases might be just the thing to energise the investigation. Even he feels refreshed at the thought. He is so glad now that he rang her last night, and that, to his relief, she had accepted his invitation. He even found a message of thanks from the nice Headmistress on his answer phone early in the morning.

'I know Ant,' Bernadette remembers Ant fondly.

'She is a retired forensic scientist and has agreed to assist us in the hunt for your daughter's killer.'

'Good! Ant is friend of Kathleen,' Bernadette states another important fact simply. She is happy with the new arrangement. 'She has a farm. She is busy…'

'She will make arrangements,' Penhaligon explains. 'No need to worry, Mrs Karim.'.

''You are all so kind,' Bernadette murmurs.

It is like a reunion of friends when they arrive in Dulverton. Ant has cooked a nice meal of pre-packed Duck à l'Orange, boiled some new potatoes and has prepared a mixed salad for starters. Dessert would have to be a doughnut and coffee. Of course, she has also invited Kathleen.

Ant enquires about Bertrand. The news is good: the shock of losing his sister, whom, when alive, he had considered a pest, had concentrated his mind and brought about much change in his behaviour. He was even allowed to re-join his old school, repeating a year to catch up with what he has missed during his - what he and his mother now call - wayward period. He didn't mind now that his mother was watching him like a hawk and accepts that she means well. They only have each other now, and he wanted her to be proud of him. Bernadette herself has cut down on the hours she is working, realising that money is no substitute for time lavished on her child. They do simple things together, like going for walks, watching seabirds on the pink cliffs of Morlaix and spend time at the beach. A slower pace of life makes her feel less haunted and more confident about her and Bertrand's future. She will tell her English friends about the changes she has made and she is proud of. Sylvie would have liked them, too.

'How long can you stay?' Ant asks, and is relieved when Bernadette says that she has taken two weeks annual leave. Bernadette's presence will be useful to stir people's memories. The French girl has been murdered in their midst; she must not be forgotten, will be the investigation team's mantra. The murderer is still among us and must be brought to book. Ant is ready to throw everything she has got at it; every ounce of her being, senses, professional training, experience and time.

'Who is looking after Bertrand?' Kathleen asks.

'He is with his father. They are getting on better now that Bertrand behaves himself.' She smiles with silent pride.

'Excellent.' Ant is glad that there is not much chance of Bernadette having to rush back to France. 'Let's make a plan,' Ant suggests after dinner, and Kathleen agrees whole-heartedly.


Work begins the following morning. They first check with Taunton Police Station, that there are no more interviews outstanding and leave the message that they were making the most of Bernadette's presence, involving her in a renewed publicity campaign.

They book her first into a small but very wide-reaching local radio station, which serves and reaches at least ten local communities. They are hoping against hope that somebody might come forward, somebody who might have seen something out of the ordinary in June last year, on Haddon Hill or in Dulverton, on the day Sylvie disappeared, someone who hasn't reported a tiny nugget of something they noticed, something which caught their attention, a nugget of information which could make all the difference to the investigation. Ant composes a follow-up article of the case and distributes it among the local weeklies and monthly newspapers and magazines reporting on and featuring Exmoor life. After that, they bombard the national newspapers in

London with the latest news in the enquiries into the death of the French exchange student Sylvie Karim. It must strike fear into the heart of every parent where ever in the country. Bernadette is happy to watch the 'twitter and tweet' accounts and writes daily on her Facebook page. She is surprised by the interest and positive responses of the public and the willingness of people to help. Many readers all over the country seem to put themselves into the shoes of that poor French mother, whose daughter didn't return; a nightmare scenario for every parent whose child goes on a school trip.

'Next, bigger local radio stations,' Ant presses on, and they are thrilled to be invited to several interviews between Bristol and Plymouth. The highlight of them all - and they hope the one with the biggest audience - is a five minute interview in the BBC Spotlight studio in Plymouth, in which Bernadette pleads tearfully, but with great dignity, for anybody to come forward if they have any information which could help to unmask the murderer.

'Pity, the BBC have axed the Crime Watch programme,' Ant mutters, but then they have a call from Salford that there would be interest in producing a television appeal on behalf of the bereaved family.

'Grab it!' Kathleen whispers to Ant, who is still on the phone.

'They'll send a team down to Exmoor, so we don't have to come to them.' Ant reports back with a big grin.

'Even better - when?'

'...tomorrow.'

'Is that all right with you, Bernadette?' Ant asks, a little overtaken by her own boldness.

Bernadette nods eagerly: 'Of course!' anything to find out who murdered her child.

The television team arrives at lunch time, and as it is a reasonably sunny day, they make the most of the beauty of the rural location: first a few pictures of Ant's farm and, to butter up the viewers, a couple of shots of the adorable gambolling, shrieking most recent piglet arrivals and their mothers: Iolanthe, Persephone and Agatha stand there like the stars of the show, chewing languidly through the heap of unexpected treats, posing as if they were old hands at being filmed. Next the crew present Bernadette sitting in Ant's country kitchen, giving a brief and sorrowful account of her daughter coming on exchange to this lovely little town; her inexplicable disappearance on the way home from school and the discovery of her body after months of lying in a shallow grave on Haddon Hill. They insert as background a photograph of Sylvie as a little girl and Sylvie as a teenager. From the farm, the television crew moves on to Dulverton and the school Sylvie disappeared from and the narrow lane leading up to her host family's home. Members of the Bowers' family are asked to express in a few words their anguish, shock and pain, which, they say, is obviously nothing compared to what Sylvie's mother must be going through. Charlotte is a particular hit with the film crew, with her old-fashioned plaits and a heartfelt tribute to her French friend with an emotional tremor in her voice. There follows a little feature of the bustling main street of the town: people coming out of the little supermarket; popping into the butcher's, the newsagent's where most tourists buy their souvenirs, the pharmacy, the post office and one of the lovely gift shops – the crew think they are giving tourism a discreet helping hand; they might as well, now that they are here, as someone puts it. Finally, the entire convoy decamps on Haddon Hill, taking shots of stubby, dark-green heather - which turns the hillside purple around August time - interspersed with taller, prickly gorse bushes, which are about to burst into small, golden coloured flowers; a gorgeous view over

Wimbleball Lake, and a vague picture of a round patch where Sylvie had lain all those months, end the sequence.

The producer of the documentary thinks it best that one of the police officers should make a final appeal, recapping the vital details the viewers should remember, look out for and report; a few more pictures of the distraught Bernadette to pull on heartstrings and a reminder that the murderer is still at large; someone who treats women badly; someone with a predilection for young girls; someone vile and predatory.

'Can we invite you to something to eat,' Kathleen suggests to the BBC team, a vivacious female presenter, two cameramen and a host of male and female technicians and members of the production team.

'Nice thought,' the presenter says. 'Thank you for the offer, but we better make tracks. It will be quite a few hours to get back to the editing studio.'

'And we have another assignment early tomorrow morning,' one of the cameramen chips in.

'…pity! We can't tell you how grateful we are,' says Ant and shakes everybody's hand. A bewildered Bernadette follows her example, trying to convey her enormous gratitude in one handshake: 'Thank you so much,' says Bernadette to no-one in particular in her charming French accent.

'And we hope,' replies the producer, 'that it will stir viewers' hearts when it is broadcast.'

'Any idea when that will be?' Ant asks, ever the pragmatist.

'Probably quite soon; editing tomorrow; before the weekend, I would have thought. Someone will let you know.' With that promise, they pack up their impressive and weighty gear, stow it in the transmission van, turn around once more to wave, climb into it and drive off.

132

All the people left behind, can do now, is to wait

'I shall go home,' Bernadette decides the next morning.

'You are very welcome to stay,' Ant insists.

The two women smile at each other with the mutual understanding of kindred spirits.

'I must go back to Bertrand. He is very good now, but I am afraid a little, too. He must not 'have bad company.'

'I know. I'll take you back to Plymouth,' says Ant calmly, 'There is nothing much you can do here. We'll keep you informed, as soon as something happens. And thank you for your help, Bernadette.'

'Thank you for taking the trouble. You and Kathleen are good friends.'

They have an early night in view of a long day's travelling.

The next morning, they hug before Bernadette boards the ship. This time it is a much greater wrench to let her go. 'Bernadette,' Ant says, holding back a tear, 'Kathleen and I will miss you. Please, remember that you will always be welcome – use my place as your home from home. Any time you want to come over, just hop on the ferry!

As soon as Ant gets back to her farm, she makes a call, she should possibly have made much earlier.

# CHAPTER TWENTY-ONE

Ant has just come into the cottage from feeding the animals high up on the slippery hill. When she hears the telephone, ring she kicks off her Wellington boots by the door and pads on thick socks into the kitchen.

'Hello?' she says, still out of breath.

'Ant, you left a message. What's up?' He sounds happy. She doesn't want to know the reason.

'How is retirement? Does it suit you?' she needles him.

Bex clears his voice as if his vocal cords were suddenly covered in sand. Before he can get out a word, Ant answers herself: 'Bored stiff, I imagine. Just as well, I have something interesting for you to do.'

'I don't need an occupational therapist.' He scoffs, 'I am perfectly capable of entertaining myself.'

'Bex, don't contradict. I know you. You are not the ideal candidate for endless leisure.' She hears a throaty chuckle.

Indeed, she does know him well. They knew each other for years before they became lovers. Undoubtedly it was awkward, as he used to be the Senior Investigating Officer on many cases she was called to in her role as a SOCO, which would now be called CSI or Crime Scene Investigator. She would always be called to the scene where a crime had been committed. She had been passionate about her work, however horrible the circumstances, always keeping in mind, that a difficult day at her place of work was always a disastrous day in somebody else's life – so no need to feel hard done by. She had always felt a deep sense of obligation to the victims and their families to get to the bottom of what had happened. If a crime had been committed, it was her duty to find enough scientific proof, so that the perpetrator could be brought to justice. She had been good at it! There was only ever one case, where she had to conclude that the whole tragedy had been an unlucky accident.

'So, why did you ring me, Ant?' Bex, short for Benjamin Edward Cox, sounds touchingly hopeful and keen.

'Remember the French exchange student who went missing?'

'Yeah; any progress on this?'

'No,' her voice trails off. 'The body has been found though.'

'Remind me, why are you so involved in this case? You are retired, too.'

'The Headmistress of the local school is my friend.'

'I am sure that the local police will do their best to piece it together.'

He knows full well, why I am ringing, she thinks; he likes to keep me in suspense. 'Look, if you are not interested...' It's a game they play.

'Tell me what has happened so far.'

'The local police are pretty good, but they are stuck. They know the identity of the victim and how she died, but they have no idea where to look for the murderer.'

'Kathleen Fitzgerald is the Headmistress, I presume?'

So he has followed the case – probably read about it in the national press or even listened to one of their appeals. Why else would he know Kathleen's name. Maybe Zac, his successor, has discussed the case with his former boss, or told him about Ant and Kathleen's trip to Algiers.

'Any new leads?' he asks full of excitement. That's the Bex she knows.

'Very few and not very promising ones.'

'Like what?' he enquires.

'A dysfunctional family; a father who lives in Algeria...'

'That's not a crime...'he interrupts.

'Kathleen and I have eliminated him as a suspect...' Ant continues unperturbed.

'Have you?' he speaks with a hint of sarcasm.

'Yes, I have interviewed Sylvie's father and have made enquiries about him.'

'...in Algeria?' he can't believe it. Ant never liked travelling abroad.

'Yes, I went because I thought it was an important lead: one of the English boys in the exchange group had been in love with Sylvie, and she had confided in him, that she would rather live with her father than with her mother in France. The girl was also terribly moody all week before her disappearance, and we thought, she might have somehow arranged to meet her father either in London, or Paris, or Algiers – unlikely though it sounded.'

'Tell me about a teenager who isn't moody!' Bex sighs; she had almost forgotten that he has a daughter. There is a pause.

'Have you seen a forensic report?' Bex asks eventually.

'I have been promised that I can have a look at it as soon as it is available.'

'I think, you should do your own forensic sweep,' he says with conviction. It almost sounds like an order.

She swallows hard: 'You really think so...?' She hadn't thought that that would be acceptable – desirable maybe, but was it ethical? 'Won't it be considered as blatant interference?' she asks hesitantly.

'Absolutely: necessary interference. Just try not to tread on people's toes too much. Keep it quiet for the time being,' he confirms. She can picture his jaw clenched determinedly. 'Give me a call when you have done it, and got the results. In the meantime I'll speak to Sergeant Penhaligon.'

'So you are in?' she holds her breath. Of course, he is. He wouldn't let a murder case like that slip through his fingers. 'Great,' she says and sighs with relief. The old team – if they can't crack it, nobody can!

She can hear an enormous sigh at the other end of the line. Bex seems glad, too, to be released from retirement.

When she puts the receiver down, she stretches both her arms into the air, makes a victory sign and allows herself a triumphant 'YES!'

Ant imagines Bex feeling equally relieved that there will be a chink in his endlessly monotonous days. He was never any good with hobbies, only his job. He will love to make use of his professional expertise which he must still have at his fingertips, and she wonders whether he is still living in that dreadful flat with the impersonal black leather sofa, bare, polished floorboards and office type blinds instead of curtains at the windows.

They had been very happy for a while, although she knew that there was no prospect of ever making it permanent. Bex had been married for years, and when his wife developed Multiple Sclerosis, Bex had felt duty-bound to stay with her and had broken off his affair with Ant. She never told him that she had just discovered that she was pregnant. She still remembers the mixture of hurt and relief when she had agreed to end their relationship. He had appeared strangely baffled by her willingness to split. After a lot of soul searching and agonising vacillation, she had decided that a baby would not be compatible with the love of her life, her job.

From then on, she had tried to keep out of his way, privately and professionally. It couldn't always be avoided, but they had always been civil to each other and had eventually found a neutral way of communication based on combined professional expertise, punctuated occasionally by harmless banter. Does she still love him? Particularly now that she knows that his wife has died a couple of years ago? Bex had told her on his last visit after they had solved the mystery of Lucinda's disappearance.

She is glad that Bex has agreed to help. For once, she will do as he said. He is absolutely right. She makes a big cross through tomorrow's date on her Exmoor wall calendar and writes: SECOND FORENSIC SWEEP ON HADDON HILL.

# CHAPTER TWENTY-TWO

The following morning, Ant wakes up with sunshine filtering through her bedroom curtains. She has no idea what time it is, but she is immediately ready to jump out of bed, energised by anticipation and an inner drive. Strangely, something is weighing her down, pressing across her legs, and the energy she feels spreading throughout her body is not reaching her feet. She pulls herself up to a sitting position. She wants to inspect why the lower half of her body is so inert. It becomes clear that something is pinning her legs down below the knees, something that wasn't there before she fell asleep as if something had fallen from the ceiling onto her bed overnight. Surely, she couldn't have had a stroke, could she?

'What is that…?' She reaches out for it, eyes still unfocused from sleep. It looks like a plump cushion, white with a very strong black pattern. It unfurls, stretches four legs and then raises itself ever so languidly to sit up on its haunches, staring at the other creature in the bed. The black and white tuxedo pattern gives it an air of grandeur. 'What are you doing here, cat?' Ant mutters and stares back. 'How on earth did you get in?' but she knows the answer: any agile feline can climb up the tree outside and jump into the tiny window to the right of her bed, high up just underneath the ceiling, which she keeps open for fresh air. No human body could squeeze through it, nor could anyone climb the knarred old tree outside and balance along the brittle branches which reach nearly into Ant's bedroom. She must have been fast asleep that she hadn't woken up when the creature had made his or her enormous leap from up there onto her bed. 'You are a clever cat!' They look at each other, waiting for the other to make a move. Considering the degree of numbness in her feet, he

– she has given his nether-regions a quick check - must have slept on her duvet for quite a few hours.

'So, you think, you can move in here, young man? I have news for you. I am getting up, feed the pigs, grab a sandwich and off I go to do a forensic sweep.'

Why do I talk to a cat, I have never seen before? She shakes her head in mock-disbelief. After all, she does speak to her pigs, too –and they have all names. She brushes the thought away. Sometimes, she thinks, I communicate better with animals than humans. She sighs and goes downstairs. The cat follows her, as if this has been his daily drill for years.

'What?' she looks at him. He is sitting prettily in expectation of breakfast.

'I am only geared up for pigs, not cats,' she mutters defensively, but then she relents, goes to the fridge and cuts up the remnants of the chicken breast she hadn't managed to eat last night. 'That's a one off,' she wags her finger in warning, but is aware, that it might be more hopeful thinking than what is bound to happen. She fills an old, but clean cereal bowl with water, which he duly ignores. There are much tastier puddles outside. 'Suit yourself,' she mumbles and turns away while he tucks heartily into the chicken.

'I might as well,' she tells him while he is wolfing it down, and prepares a cheese sandwich with pickle for herself. To her surprise, it is enjoyable to have company for breakfast.

'Right – you: out! I need to feed the Girls, and then it's off to work.' He does not need telling twice: he sits already by the door and rushes out like a black and white arrow.


Before she finally leaves for Haddon Hill, she checks the professional equipment she has never had the heart to discard: a

140

scalpel blade to scrape things off; long cotton bud sticks on plastic screw handles for swabs of any stains  - dry ones, wet ones, and the tubes they are stored in; vials for liquids; labels; pens; her camera; a large paper bag sewn at the bottom should she find anything large which could be useful as evidence; two blue and black forensic suits and a change of her own clothes, in case she gets filthy and needs to change before getting back into her car. Better to take the whole gear with her than regretting not to. She is getting excited: traces and tiny fragments of evidence can so easily be overlooked at the first forensic sweep, but they should be picked up the second time round - there is no excuse to overlook anything this time! Yes, Ant is excited rather than nervous: she knows this is what she is good at.

Even though the body has been removed several weeks ago, there could still be enough clues to what might have happened. The Taunton team might have done a superb job, but it didn't yield much and they need new leads, an injection of concrete evidence. She can't wait to search for it.

She puts it all in her old, battered Land Rover, which she only bought at the beginning of her life as a pig farmer, in case she needed to take animals to the vet or, perish the thought, to market. As she drives off, the sun struggles against grey clouds and early morning mist, but eventually breaks through gloriously. The air is fresh, gradually warming under a suddenly blue sky. It's a bonus if a forensic sweep is not accompanied by driving rain, hail or anything else unpleasant in the weather repertoire. Sounds, sights and smells could be easily adulterated in filthy conditions to what they really are, and it does make it easier to be thorough and totally focused throughout the sweep; Ant will call herself lucky if she is not driven indoors by inclement weather today. A bit of luck at the start would be welcome.

Ant drives the long way round to Haddon Hill and turns left up the Upton to Bampton Road up to the gate which leads into the Haddon Hill Nature Reserve. The hill turns purple with heather in August and is home to families of wild, hardy Exmoor ponies, deer, rabbits, and a variety of birds, even birds of prey, and a multitude of insects and butterflies hovering over the natural Moor landscape. When she arrives, there are no cars around; the dog walkers usually arrive about lunchtime or in the afternoon. As Ant gets out of the Land Rover, the wind blows her Parka hood from her head. The Hill stands well over a thousand feet high. Ant grabs her bag with the tools of her trade, locks up the car and begins to walk away to a sign-posted path which leads straight downhill just as suggested by the Taunton team. The path turns soon left, and as she follows it, the most beautiful view over the green meadows and hills surrounding Wimbleball Lake opens up. Little sailing boats float on the water in spite of a chilly breeze, sailors making the most of the favourable conditions.

She continues to walk along the path which is framed by gorse in bloom, little golden helmets on unexpected prickly branches. She can spot a few of the Exmoor ponies up top in the distance, who graze here in all seasons come rain or shine, hail or snow. The gorse and stubby heather bushes look as tough, prickly and wild as the shaggy ponies.

After a few hundred yards of a downward slope, the vegetation loses its moor appearance, and dense scrub, bushes and tall trees take over. This should - so the earlier report says - lead her shortly to where Sylvie had lain for month. Ant soon finds yellow and black cordon tapes which look bedraggled and limp with damp but are still holding up around the area. Ant is looking around for tyre marks before she leaves the unmade, stony lane, which only rangers and foresters use for access. Unsurprisingly, she can only see a few tyre tracks in the mud which are fresh and indicate that a huge tractor or agricultural machine has come this way recently. Too many months have passed since Sylvie's disappearance to hope that evidence of the murderer's car might still be found – if, in fact, the murderer has used one to move the body.

Ant makes a mental note to check out any other access routes to this spot. For now, she will restrict herself to the crime scene.

She is leaving the path towards the left and is fighting her way through thick bushes, cautiously and gently, aware not to disturb, alter or displace anything with her feet, arms or body. Tall trees block out the sun overhead. Suddenly, Ant comes across a shallow indent in the ground where soil has been disturbed and displaced. It lies in deep shade - a dark, sad lonely place!

No time for feelings, Ant tells herself and changes quickly into her forensic suit, the shapeless, all-in-one outfit worn for murder and rape cases; she even puts on the face mask and the hair net to avoid any contamination of the site. The first thing she does is to take photographs of the ground and its surroundings. She also has to take a photo of her shoes, particularly their soles, to eliminate them should she find others which are not hers. Rough grass, leading into the scrub, is trampled down and curiously, has not yet had the time to re-grow light green stalks. The rain of the last few weeks is bound to have shifted, altered or buried things, and the recent public interest in the site after Sylvie had been found, hadn't helped to preserve the crime scene, or what was left of it, either. She will have to be pedantically observant and eagle-eyed. Ever so slowly, she squeezes herself through low hanging branches of bushes, looking out for anything that seems unnatural, taking a photograph here and there. Some twigs on her right bend strangely downwards, and as her rubber-gloved hands hold them up gently, she can see that quite a few have been broken off violently, all along at the same height of about five foot ten inches. The bushes on the other side are unscathed although the gap between the two sides is only the width of Ant. Somebody very tall must have pushed through those branches and broken them off with tremendous force; or someone could have carried something on his or her shoulder along the path, something heavy and unyielding enough to snapped off a whole horizontal line of branches. To be sure, she checks the ground but it is smooth; no signs of anything heavy having been dragged along here. Ant takes photographs and writes her observations into the notebook. Ant concludes that Sylvie had most likely been killed elsewhere, transported in a car and carried to her grave on Haddon Hill.

The narrow path ends in a small, round clearing, where the soil around Sylvie's shallow grave was greatly disturbed by the team retrieving the body. All they left behind is a hollow, loosely covered over with soil. Ant takes more photographs and then kneels just beside the hollow. She scrutinises every inch of the almost circular patch surrounded by dense shrubbery and shielded by the umbrella-like crowns of trees. As expected, there were flies buzzling around where the body had lain, and as she looks closer, she can see maggots wriggling. It always puzzles her, how these creatures multiply so rapidly and survive even long after the host material has been removed. There had been one case, she remembers, where she and her colleagues had found maggots, larvae and flies two years after the corpse had been removed. Ant is trying to spot any droplets of dried blood, but knows that it will be difficult on such dark soil. She scours the patch for something unusual, something unexpected. She can't see anything. She stands upright and takes several more photographs of the patch for comparison on. Sometimes a picture reveals something that the eyes in daylight can't spot. She decides to pack up, return to the car, get out of her uniform, stash her samples safely away to avoid contamination, and then she would try and find access from the Wimbleball Lake side of the hill.

144

It takes her twenty minutes to drive all the way back to approach the hill from the other side. She uses the access gate for the dam maintenance vehicles. It is a steep narrow road just a wide enough space for one vehicle at a time. She can't see anybody who might stop her. She has brought her old identification card with her, just in case. Suddenly the road ends in a wide cul-de-sac for vehicles to turn round. This is certainly not the route the rangers take. Only a steep, unmade footpath leads upwards from here. Ant slips quickly into her second suit, grabs her toolkit and begins the climb. Soon she has to admit to herself, that it is unlikely that the murderer would have used this route to drag a body up the steep incline on a hillside bare of vegetation and in full view of anyone below. All the way up, the ground is loose and makes even the athletic Ant slide backwards a couple of times. Considering that it was probably night time when Sylvie's body was brought to Haddon Hill, this way would have been foolish and nigh on impossible. This begins to look, as if the murderer has not acted on impulse, but has rather been more informed and prepared than she had previously suspected. He or she certainly knew the area.

'Go to the top,' Ant drives herself on, until she is almost at the top. The growth of greenery thickens and she can haul herself up holding on to branches. She takes a few minutes to get her breath back and to orientate herself. She decides that Sylvie's grave should in her estimation be left of where the climb has led her. It doesn't take her long to stumble upon more soggy, black and yellow cordon tape, indicating that she has reached the crime scene. Ant takes a photograph from this side and squeezes through the almost impenetrable vegetation. Nothing is out of place, no broken branches, nor any sign of trampling by heavy footsteps. Nobody has come this way for a long time, never mind someone dragging a body. As she looks around, afternoon sunshine filters through a gap in the shrubbery and blinds her for a moment. As she blinks and squints, something grabs her attention: something on the floor is glinting. She picks it up and cradles it in her still gloved palms. It looks like a stud earring with a diamond splinter. Did Sylvie wear stud earrings? Nobody has mentioned any so far. It could be somebody else's of course, but how likely is that? Ant turns the thing round between her fingers. She puts it on the ground again where she has found it and photographs it several times from various angles. Then she puts it in one of the evidence bags she has brought along, seals and labels it and stashes it securely into the zip pocket of her kit bag. Instinct and experience tell her to scrape some soil samples from all around the patch into vials, too. One never knows what secrets they keep. With some luck, one of the soil samples reveals a drop or spatter of blood or other bodily fluids, invaluable to pinpoint DNA – confirming Sylvie's or, even better, somebody else's DNA - the DNA of a person of interest, who might or might not be able to explain how their DNA got there. Ant sighs: she will always be hopeful, even under the most dire circumstances.

It takes Ant a while, to label everything correctly: Her initials, location, today's date, time and case number. Just as she puts the last vial into her kit case, she notices something strange and incongruous hanging from one of those broken branches. At first, Ant thinks, her eyes are deceiving her, but it is something that doesn't look as if it would normally grow on a bush. She goes closer. It is thin, blue and it has three strands woven together at the ends, the reason why it got entangled having been scraped against a branch. Ant smiles: She is not sure what she is looking at, but is storing it carefully in another vial. She smiles: she ca recognises a piece of evidence if she sees one.

Not bad for one day, she thinks, peeling off her uniform, bagging it up, too, and placing it with everything else. As she makes her way back downhill to where she has left the car, the wind comes up, making her ponytail swing. She can't wait to get home, to feed the pigs, to have a hot bath, a warm soup and to put her feet up next to the Raeburn. I wonder whether that cat is still there, she smiles.

She has hardly parked the car outside her farmhouse, when she sees him, coming towards her, welcoming her with a loud purr. 'So, you haven't left yet,' she bends down to stroke him; he rolls over and accepts the affectionate gesture- however undignified for a stray. He strolls next to her to the door, as if this had always been his home. Ant shakes her head and puts the key in the lock. 'Come on then, Boy. Dinner,' she says rather moved by his unexpected, probably partisan loyalty. He is in the door quicker than his new mistress.

# CHAPTER TWENTY-THREE

'How did it go,' Bex asks calling her unexpectedly just as she is walking into the kitchen after a refreshing shower with dripping wet hair.

'I tried to ring you all afternoon,' he sulks. 'Why don't you take your mobile with you?'

'I haven't got a signal down here.'

'Oh come on! In which century do you live?' She doesn't comment.

'So, how did it go?'

'Not bad,' she keeps him in suspense.

'Is that all I am getting? Do you still want me to help?'

'Of course, I do, but I only did the sweep today. I'll hand it all in at the Sergeant's office tomorrow, collect their first forensic report, take it home and read about their findings. Then I will put their findings and mine together, compare the two, and with some luck…'

'Pick me up tomorrow at two from Taunton station. We need to put our heads together,' he says and, leaving no room for contradiction, he puts the phone down.

Is it consternation or a little frisson which sweeps down Ant's spine?


She can't believe her eyes, when she sees him coming towards her on the platform at Taunton Station. For once, the train is on time, and she has to rush into the station where compartment doors have just opened. He is still tall and sturdy, but less hunched, his beer belly has disappeared, and he looks trim, almost sporty. He has exchanged his usually crumpled attire for a beautifully cut light grey suit, a white shirt and a bold pink tie. She has never seen him dressed this smart, and the biggest surprise is a thick beard, neatly trimmed short, whilst his grey hair is as thick as ever and slightly falling over his ears to hide hearing aids. He comes towards her with determined strides and a happy grin. She wonders whether the happiness has anything to do with seeing her again or more with having a break from the grindingly dull routine of being retired. Not that she is ever bored...

'I see, you have come dressed to help with the pigs,' she teases him,' she greets him. For a moment she regrets, not having put on something smarter than her tidy jeans, a freshly washed pullover and her usual hooded jacket.

'You look handsome,' she teases him and he chuckles before kissing her on each cheek: 'Any new developments since we last spoke?' Goodness, he really is keen. She shakes her head. 'Any results from police headquarters?' he gets straight to the point, while inwardly acknowledging with amusement that she is still looking at him, trying to digest his changed appearance.

'Not yet,' she replies, trying to pull herself together. I thought you might be interested in hearing them directly from the horse's mouth.'

He sends her a funny look: 'how quaint: the vocabulary of a woman of the soil.'

She pulls a face at him and marches ahead. He catches up with her quickly.

'Did you bring the pieces of evidence you found yesterday?' he is serious now.

149

She nods: 'I've handed them in before I picked you up. It's already off to the lab.'

'Excellent,' he is impressed.

She leads him back to her car, almost in silence: 'You are well?' he enquires, but she knows that he is only faintly interested in an answer; his thoughts are already focused on the nitty-gritty of the case. As they drive to the Police Station, she fills him in on her observations during the forensic sweep, in particular what she has found – not a lot, but potentially important items.

As soon as they arrive at the imposing police building, the receptionist, a bright young uniformed police woman hands over a thick file, which is labelled FORENSIC REPORT, SYLVIE KARIM

'Sergeant Penhaligon thought you might want to read through this before your meeting. He apologises, he is out on a call, but he will be back soon.' She leads them to a sparsely , furnished reading room, puts the bulging file on the standard plywood table and invites them to sit down on the two visitors' chairs. Ant takes her own report out of her rucksack and puts it in front of Bex.

'Thanks. I'll read yours first,' he decides.

'I'll go through the police file then.' Ant has read it already once online, but now she can compare it with what she has seen and found. She can't wait to see the second report, the one the Lab will hopefully have ready within a couple of days.

They read in silence. When Bex has finished, he looks at Ant: 'Good work! ...still brilliant,' he grin as if a little embarrassed. Ant wrinkles her forehead:  Bex being complimentary? That doesn't happen often. As nothing else is said, she replies simply: 'You never lose your skills, do you?' He looks at her with something like admiration to reassure her that they are still on the same wave-length, as they have always been; it's the foundation of their cooperation.

'There is something about blue, hairy fibres in the pathologist's report, just like the ones I found handing on the bushes,' Ant points out. He found a tiny strand around Sylvie's wrists.'

Bex looks up sharply: 'That means that she was bound a gagged.' He shakes his head in disgust.

'But blue is an odd colour for a rope or a string, isn't it?'

'The lab thinks its Polypropylene, the cheap, hairy stuff.'

'Degradable,' Ant guesses. Bex nods: 'Not a bad choice for a murder. It will decompose in soil.'

After half an hour, Sergeant Penhaligon enters the box-like reading room, moves the third chair from the corner by the small window and joins his guests.

'Nice to meet you, Sir,' he greets Benjamin Edward Cox enthusiastically. 'Your fame has even spread down to us in the West Country.'

'Well, I am retired now,' Bex mutters, a little embarrassed. Why are we both so awkward in accepting compliments, Ant thinks.

'Even more reason to appreciate your input!' The Sergeant sounds sincere and not a little star-struck. 'Life is not half as exciting down here as it is in the Big Smoke.'

Bex is about to say something, but then changes his mind. Sergeant Penhaligon gets the drift: 'Did you have a chance to look at the report?'

''Yes, we did, and, as you know, Miss Bell has added her findings from yesterday's forensic sweep of the crime scene. It's all with the Lab already.''

'Excellent! ...anything of note?'

'Yes, I found the stud from her belly-button piercing.' Ant reports briskly. She has just read in the report, that Sylvie had a pierced belly button - rather than pierced ear lobes - from where the stud must have fallen out.

'Did you really? Where was it?' He seems a little incredulous and maybe annoyed that it was overlooked by his officers.

'I think it was buried with her and simply fell off when the body was lifted out of the grave. I found it right next to the hollow in the soil.'

'Thank God for that! Anything else you can add?' Penhaligon is keen to brush over his team's failings.

'Yes, I saw a lot of dead wood on healthy bushes along the path leading to the grave; dead, snapped off branches and twigs, as if someone or something has brushed past them rather forcefully. Oddly, only on the right hand side... and even more interestingly, on one of those bushes with several broken twigs hung a couple of strands of blue fibres.'

'The pathologist found some of those on the body; deeply buried in grooves around the victim's wrists and ankles.' The Sergeant remembers, too. 'Someone has used brute force to truss her up. It doesn't bear thinking about...'

There is silence; everyone is trying to digest and banish this horrible scene from their minds, to concentrate on forging ahead.

'Could the fibres be from a blanket she might have been wrapped in?' Bex wants to know.     Ant shakes her head: 'Unlikely.  Blankets are not made from that sort of scratchy fibre.'

Bex recaps: '...so, you think, the murderer did not drag the body over the ground to the grave; he carried it slumped over his right shoulder? He snapped the branches off while he was carrying her through. From that assumption, it's unlikely that the *he* is a *she* unless she is an Olympic weight-lifter.

'Even a male perpetrator must have been pretty fit,' Bex interjects. 'Dead, rigid bodies tend to be much heavier than live ones.'

Sergeant Penhaligon looks impressed. His two guests have made more progress in an hour than his entire team had managed over all these months. Lack of experience maybe, but things will have to change.. This sort of thing doesn't usually happen in these parts of the country. Well, it has now, and he is grateful for Ant and Bex's support.

'To come back to the blue fibres on the body,' the Sergeant is keen to play his part, 'the lab examined them and thought they were Polypropylene.'

'Yes, I read that,' Ant confirms. 'That means that it's not likely to be from a blanket; these fibres are far more durable and scratchy. To me they look like rope or string.'

'Isn't rope usually made of jute or hemp, something more natural than Polypropylene?' Penhaligon asks.

'Not nowadays.' Ant answers; 'the natural fibres are too expensive, so the manufacturers produce things like Polyester, Nylon or that horrible stuff you found.'

They stay silent for a moment, each lost with their own, terrible conclusions.

'I also took soil samples from the scene, just in case, there was something clinging to it that wouldn't have been there before the murder,' Ant says quietly.

'How will you know what was there and what has been added?' The Sergeant is baffled. Obviously, scientific developments have escaped him. He looks really embarrassed, when Ant explains, that nowadays, most things can be given a timeframe with the help of various sciences like chemistry, biology and geology to name but a few: 'Let's wait and see,' Ant smiles at him reassuringly.

'I shall ring the lab to give our samples priority.' Penhaligon is glad that at least there is one thing he can do immediately.

'And let us know the results as soon as you get them,' Bex urges.

'I will,' he promises. 'Where can I reach you?' Penhaligon looks quizzically from Ant to Bex and back.

'I shall stay down here for a few days. ' Bex's answer is vague, but then Ant interrupts:

'Bex will stay with me.' It's a surprise to her as well. 'Send everything to my e-mail or ring.'

'Ant will know where I am,' Bex adds quickly, in case she regrets her generous offer.

'Any mobile number – just in case, there is a signal,' the Sergeant asks.

Bex laughs: 'Yes, I have heard of the problems.'

All three are happy with the meeting, reassured of each other's cooperation.


'Where are you going to stay?' Ant asks with an impish grin, as he climbs into her Land Rover. Pity about his suit, she thinks and makes a promise to herself that she would clean at least the passenger seat sometime soon.

'Your guess is as good as mine,' he replies cheekily.

'Will the guest bedroom and self-service do?' she jokes with a ironic intonation, as she starts the Landrover, swings out of the parking lot and almost collides with a car, that she has overlooked in the mirror.

'Don't kill us. We have a case to solve,' he jokes to hide his shock.

'...and a murderer to catch!' she agrees with contrition, 'Sorry, Bex!'


'Since when do you have a cat?' Bex sighs as they drive the car up to the house and walk to the garden gate. He is not particularly fond of animals. The stray is sitting there as if he owned the place.. 'I thought your pigs were weird enough...'

'You don't have to stay, if you don't like animals,' she snaps, but then gestures for both of them to go through.

'That needs oiling,' Bex comments laconically as the gate hinges whine.

'Are you offering?' she teases him, quick as a flash. 'There is a lot to do and to repair if you are willing...'

'What's the cat's name?' he ignores her allusion.

She hasn't thought of one yet.

'Boy,' she blurts out without thinking.

Beck chuckles: 'Very inventive, 'I guess, in contrast to the piggy Girls.'

They have reached her front door; she unlocks it and without another word, she storms inside leaving Bex and Boy on the threshold.

'Are we allowed in?' Bex hears himself asking the cat. Together, they take a chance.

'After you, young man,' he says mockingly and follows him in.

# CHAPTER TWENTY-FOUR

Bex ambles down the stairs on his first morning at the farm, yawning, still in light-blue pyjamas with a cheery red strip along the collar, when he hears Ant coming noisily in, making an awful din with something.

'Good morning Sleeping Beauty,' she grins when he is on the last step. I didn't disturb you, I hope.

'I overslept. No London buses, no horns, no sirens, no aeroplanes overhead,' he says apologetically and runs his fingers through his hair.

'Well, the pigs were in good form, grunting and snuffling and shrieking; the birds who stayed behind rather than fly to South Africa, have been singing their little hearts out; and the farmers are out in force with their noisy machinery…but they are different sounds,' she concedes, 'and the fresh air knocks the grockles for six in the first couple of days.'

'What time is it?' he yawns again, this time putting a hand in front of his mouth.

'Eight.' She is holding various feeding bowls in her hand and one large tin plate tucked under one arm, which she drops into the Belfast sink and begins to scrub under running water.

'Why didn't you wake me earlier?'

'Why should I? I am sure you don't want to help with the pigs at dawn.'

Bex takes a deep breath and mutters into his finely trimmed beard: 'Maybe not.'

'Breakfast?' she offers. 'I am afraid it's probably not what you are used to, but there is bread in the breadbin, butter in the fridge, and some honey and jam in that larder cupboard over there.' She points to the one next to him.

'Don't worry. Coffee will do.'

'I could do with one, too. The Instant is by the kettle.'

'No percolator?' he asks, looking around.

'And no Starbucks in the village either;' she looks at him with a mixture of amusement and irony, bracing herself for his response, but he only shuffles over to the half-filled kettle, switches it on, grabs two mugs standing upside-down on the draining board and puts two teaspoons full of instant powder into each of them. As soon as the water boils, he pours it into the mugs. He spills a little onto the working surface and – to Ant's astonishment -wipes it off immediately with a dishcloth. Bex house-trained? That's news to her. His excuse had always been that he was catching criminals instead. He looks at her and wonders why she smiles.

'I'll have a quick shower,' he says briskly, 'and when you are ready, we'll have a kitchen table conference, if that's all right with you,' takes his cup and heads for the stairs.

After tidying herself up with a hand-wash, pinning loose hair strands back and exchanging her thick, smelly pullover for a long-sleeved checkered fleece shirt – the jeans would just have to do as her second pair is in the wash - Ant does something she hasn't done in a long time: she prepares a tray of breakfast sandwiches, puts another two mugs ready for more coffee and places the sugar bowl and milk jug on the table. She adds her notebook, a pile of scrap paper and two pens, dries the pigs' bowls and plate and puts them outside the front door, ready for the evening feed.

By the time she has done all that, Bex reappears downstairs, his grey hair dark with damp, clinging to his skull, revealing the pair of hearing aids. She points to where she wants him to sit.

'Coffee?' she offers. He nods and gives a little whistle when he sees the plate of sandwiches.

'Tuck in,' she encourages him, and he does so heartily. She reaches for the kitchen roll and tears off a couple of sheets, in case he wants to wipe greasy fingers. Both wriggle a little on their seats, embarrassed to be caught in this homely scene.

'You have become rather domesticated?' he comments with approval, biting heartily into another sandwich.

'So have you, I presume.'

'Yes; I had to learn quickly when Sue fell ill,' he explains. Ant knows that he is talking about his late wife. She feels awkward and stares at her plate.

Both fall into their own thoughts, remembering the highs and lows of their illicit and ill-fated past relationship. After munching a second sandwich, Bex wipes his fingers on the improvised paper napkin, then his mouth and takes a gulp from the coffee mug. Bex notices the stationary and takes pen and paper. He goes upstairs and comes back wearing reading glasses. Hearing aids and glasses – how times have changed. At least he doesn't look scruffy as he usedto. She sneaks an admiring glance across the table. Should she make more of an effort, too? Rearing pigs is no less dirty than examining a murder scene. It's a way of life where standards slide easily.

'Sylvie Karim,' she begins, 'the victim, lived in Morlaix in Northern France with her mother Bernadette and a younger brother, Bertrand. She came to Dulverton on a school exchange visit. Last spring, the English children had visited the French school first. Charlotte Bowers was allocated to stay with Sylvie

Karim and her family. A few weeks later, the French children came over to stay with the English host families. Charlotte's parents are Ken and Christine Bowers.

'Was there anything remarkable about the visit in France?' Bex wants to know.

'One of the English boys fell in love with Sylvie and got quite close to her. A bit of kissing and fumbling, but I don't think it went as far as having sex. She confided in him, that she was unhappy at home, and that she would rather live with her father. He relished his role as a confidant, but just before the departure, she drops him. Of course, he is totally confused, but that is all he admits to.'

'Did he mention any particular reasons, why she would suddenly ditch hi?'

'None he could think of. He suspects another boyfriend, but he has no proof. She seemed to have kept herself to herself throughout her visit in England.'

'What about her family...' Bex moves on.

'...mother and father got divorced years ago. The father has a new family in Algiers. Mother tries her best to keep their heads above water. Her young son Bertrand is a handful, but his father, a different one to the Algerian, lives nearby and occasionally helps out. As far as I can establish, there was no abuse as such, but Sylvie was given rather a lot of responsibilities for someone so young: she was solely in charge of her wayward younger brother, while her mother was rushing from one cleaning job to another.' Ant pauses before speaking again: 'Mind you, Bernadette Karim, the mother, is a lovely woman. She is doing the best she can.' Ant describes briefly how she and Kathleen had first got in contact with Sylvie's mother in the early days, when the girl had first disappeared followed by a potted

160

description of Bernadette's subsequent visit to join the search for her daughter.

'What do we know about Sylvie's father?'

'Mr Karim lived in Paris as a young man, where he met Sylvie's mother; however, they split up when Sylvie was about three. He stayed a few more years in Paris, but eventually moved back to Algiers to have a new family.'

'Is that the chap you visited?'

'Yes, Kathleen and I went on a short break in January and visited his house in Algiers.

'That was… brave,' Bex pauses as if he had meant to say 'foolish' instead.

'So, what was the result?'

'Mr Karim had no idea that his daughter had disappeared. In fact, he hasn't seen her for years – since he split up with her mother.'

'And did you believe him?'

Ant nods: 'The hotel, where he is employed as the manager, confirmed that he hasn't taken a holiday for several years. He was described as ambitious, hardworking, popular and family-orientated. He lives with his family close to his work.'

'Okay, we won't rule him out just yet, but for the time being, we give him the benefit of the doubt,' Bex makes notes and puts the sheet aside on a little pile.

'Was the mother in France, at the time of Sylvie's disappearance?'

'Yes, we caught her on her mobile the day after the disappearance. She was just about to go to one of her cleaning jobs. We had hoped that the French police would have informed her by then… so our call came as a shock.'

'Poor woman,' Bex mutters.

'How old was Sylvie?'

'Fourteen: a year older than Charlotte. She had to re-sit a year at school because she couldn't cope with home-life and school work all at once.' They sit in silence for a moment, imagining Sylvie's childhood. Bex picks up another sheet from the pile of scrap paper.

'Has young Romeo been interviewed?'

'Peter Shelley? Yes, he is a nice boy; the innocent, romantic, naive type. His mother brought him in. He is quite frightened of her.'

'I wish more mothers were like that,' Bex proclaims irritably: 'I never understand why so many parents have no idea what their kids get up to…. running around with knives in their pockets; taking or dealing in drugs; – and the parents know nothing about it? Come on; really?' Bex's voice rises in volume. It's obviously a residue bugbear from his London life. Ant keeps quiet; in her opinion, every individual case is different, but of course, she, too, blames the parents rather than the children. Country folk seem to be closer to their children and alert to any signs of their youngsters going of the rails.

'Quite,' she remains impartial. Strange to hear Bex talk like this He has never expressed his observations that freely. Maybe in retirement, he feels more at liberty to voice his take on society?

As if he had read her thoughts, he apologises: 'I am getting old, grumpy and critical. I didn't have time to even think about things like that when I was working.'

162

'No problem,' Ant smiles, remaining impartial. Bex shakes his head: 'There we are, singing the praises of country life and the decency of country folks, in the middle of discussing a murder that happened right here.' Bex clears his throat and suggests: 'We might have to speak to young Romeo again. When Ant nods, he writes it on his list of things to do.

'It's odd that Sylvie totally ignored the boy, when she came over. Something must have happened in France or shortly after their departure; he wouldn't tell in the interview.'

'He wouldn't be the first young man to be overcome by jealousy and to have lashed out,' Bex speculates.

Ant shakes her head: 'He struck me as more sad and baffled than jealous. I think, Sylvie was his first love, and she simply got tired of his attentions.'

'Women,' Bex shakes his head, followed by a sharp, heartfelt: 'Ha.'

Ant doesn't even look up before she warns: 'Watch it!'

'He was spurned'. Bex sounds as if he defends the boy. 'He could have lost his temper. You know what we males are like when we are smitten.' She looks at him whether he is serious, but he looks at his notes. She laughs: 'No, tell me!' He ignores the request and doesn't elaborate.

'Okay,' Ant stops the banter and agrees that Bex should interview young Peter and his dreadful mother again; 'maybe you get more out of him; man-to-man.' Ant winks at him.

'Has Sylvie's mother got a boyfriend?'

'Bernadette? I am not really sure. All I know is that her son Bertrand is by a different father, but Bernadette was never married to him. He sounds a bit like an unenthusiastic father, but he agreed to look after Bertrand while Bernadette was in England for the search, and a second time for the identification. To be honest, I doubt Bernadette has time for a boyfriend,' 'Should we organise more appeals to the public?'

'Not just yet; once we have concrete lines to follow up, we can involve the public to answer one specific question.'

Bex looks at her expectantly: 'Any forensic results yet?' This is the most difficult part.

Ant is cagey: 'The Met's Labs are obviously working at lightning speed; ours are not quite up to that standard.'

'Can't you put a bit of puff behind them?'

'I scan and swab crime scenes. I have no power over how long the Lab procedures take,' she reminds him.

'They will come through soon, won't they?' Bex pleads.

'I have no idea, but I hope so, too.'

'Shall we get on to the first autopsy report – however sparse?' Ant nods.

'The autopsy predictably cannot guarantee definitively any cause of death, but  they pathologist is as certain as he can be, that Sylvie was bound, gagged, raped and strangled in a yet unknown location. There were no signs of a struggle anywhere near the burial site. She was already dead when she was transported to and dumped on Haddon Hill. She was possibly carried from a car to the grave side as branches and twigs were broken off on one side of the path leading up to it, suggesting that she was carried slumped over someone's right shoulder, a very fit person of medium height, around six foot tall.' They look at each other: It's not likely to be a thirteen year old weedy boy like Peter, is it?' Ant says eventually.

Ant and Bex steel themselves for the next bit, their faces grim with horror: 'Let's get it over and done with,' Ant whispers 'The pathologist found a tiny fragment of cloth down Sylvie's oesophagus, which means, the bastard not only bound her by the ankles and wrists, but he also stuffed a cloth down her throat; poor Sylvie must have bitten a tiny piece off in her desperate attempt to expel whatever blocked her throat, fighting for breath and her life.' The cruelty of it!

'As if that wasn't enough, he finally put his hands round her throat and strangled her.'

'… and how do we know this?' Bex wants a reminder.

'The pathologist found that the Hyoid bone in the throat was broken, a clear indication of strangulation.'

'Unimaginable terror and suffering,' Bex has witnessed many horrific scenes in his career, but the fact, that one human being can be so cruel to another still feels like a punch in the solar plexus.

'He is a monster, Ant. t's time to stop him in his tracks,' he says with passion and Ant nods in agreement.

She clears her throat: 'We mustn't forget the fact that I found three strands of rope-like fibre. We must find out who uses them and what for. There is not much else: There were no tyre marks, shoe sole prints, or fingerprints, which is not surprising after all this time that elapsed between Sylvie's disappearance and her discovery.'

'Can we say that this murder was premeditated?'

'I would say yes. The abductor might have picked his victim at random, but he must have had a car to cover the distances, to whisk her away, to get himself and the dead girl away from the murder scene, and finally, he brought tools to bury her.'

'What did the grave look like, Ant?'

165

'It looks like an untidy square under trees; with sharp edges and different types of soil hastily piled up on her body – various layers of soil mixed with top soil; no attempt at digging her in deep.

'That sounds like something hasn't gone according to plan. He might have run out of time.'

'Did you say you found a belly button stud?' Did they find anything on it - like a finger print, a drop of dry blood or bodily fluids; something to identify the murderer?'

'We don't know yet. But it's very unlikely after all this time.'

Push for Ant's forensic report, Bex adds to his list.

'I might go for a stroll up there in the next couple of days, just to have a look round,' Bex announces and points to the window and a faint shadow of the peak of Haddon Hill. He is not hopeful to find anything new; he has never known Ant to overlook a vital clue. But one never knows. Had they found the body earlier, there might have been traces. Everything of any value and importance has already deteriorated, disintegrated and disappeared,

'I wonder why the body wasn't found earlier if it was such a haphazard burial.' Ant wonders.

Bex shrugs his shoulders: '…because it was deep in the under-growth, under trees, halfway down a steep hill where people usually don't go; dogs tend not to stray too far from their owners.'

'…and of course, the local vegetation was at its most vigorous, romping ahead to summer, hiding everything close to the ground.

'Even the Exmoor ponies will have kept well away from a decomposing body. All, they are interested in, is fresh

166

grass…and of course, the hillside was impenetrable in June and over the summer months.'

Ant shuffles her pile of paper, putting the list of things to do on top, then she looks straight at Bex's face and summarises: 'So, we are looking basically for a sociopath, a psychopath and a sexual predator who kills young women on a whim and leaves hardly any traces. Poor Sylvie just crossed his path. If she hadn't, he would have murdered somebody else.'

'…any indication of approximate date and time of death? What does the autopsy report say?'

Ant leafs through the report until she finds the relevant page: 'It says here,' she reads, 'that considering weather reports and temperature recordings on the day, and after examination of the various types of flies and maggots in and around Sylvie's corpse, they estimated that she died on or close to the day of her disappearance; most likely, that evening'

'So he got rid of her quickly and left the area,' Bex concludes, 'which would indicate that he was not a local, but someone passing through.

'Which makes it difficult to find him,' Ant sigh.

Just as Ant gets up stiffly to pack her notes away, the phone rings.

'Yes?' she says distractedly.

Then 'Okay. Will you check again?' Ant listens to the answer before replying: 'Yes, please.'…and then she ends the call with: 'Thanks for letting me know.

Bex can hardly wait for her to return to the table: 'What was that about?' he asks, holding his breath.

'That was the Lab. They found a concentration of nitrate, urea, salt and potassium in my soil samples from around the grave' Ant's eyes are glittering with elation.

Bex interrupts: 'That combination means urine, doesn't it?' Ant nods. She can't trust herself to speak.

'The bastard obviously couldn't help himself to urinate on Sylvie's grave.' Bex shouts in triumph. 'That means…'

Ant has tears in her eyes when she whispers: 'We have his DNA.'

'They always think, they are invincible, until they make a fundamental mistake,' Ant can't believe her luck that it has happened this time as well.

The usual doubts creep in as Bex asks: 'It's definitely a sample from a rogue male?'

'Yes, they have gone through the process: they have already eliminated the victim; it's not from an animal and unlikely to have been produced by another person at such a remote and awkward spot.' Ant's voice quivers with emotion and excitement: 'Bex, if they are right, we have the murderer's DNA,' she says again, as if she can't believe it herself. 'They are sending the results to Penhaligon so they can try to find a match on the Police Data Base.

# CHAPTER TWENTY-FIVE

Impatience drives them the following morning to ring Sergeant Penhaligon.

'Has any name come up?' Bex asks while Ant takes a plate full of Blueberry Muffins out of the fridge

'Not yet. We are working on it, and you will be the first people we'll ring, if we can find a match,' the Sergeant promises.' Ant can see the disappointment in Bex's face and can guess the answer. She reaches for a muffin and bites heartily into it. 'Want some?' He shakes his head: 'If we are unlucky, he hasn't got a criminal record,' Bex sounds glum.

'He just hasn't been caught before.' Ant is much more upbeat. 'Don't be defeatist,' Ant tries to cheer him up; 'have a muffin!' She pushes the plate across the table.

'What do we do next?' she stuffs her last piece of muffin into her mouth, holding his gaze. He knows that sharp look of restlessness, accompanied by her body tense like a coiled spring. He knows Ant is up to something.

'Sorry. There is nothing much we can do right now,' he says.

'Let's start with the interviews at the school,' Ant suggests, ' They could yield something useful.'

'Didn't we say that young Peter was out of the frame?' Bex reminds her.

Ant doesn't answer and rushes to the phone to let the school know.

'Kathleen will organise it,' Ant reports back five minutes later. 'She is glad that something is happening. She still blames herself for some illogical reason.'

Bex looks non-plussed: 'It's nonsense! How could she have prevented the girl being abducted?'

'I know,' Ant agrees. I have told her a million times. Maybe you can get through to her when we see her today.'

'…what time?'

'…in half an hour.'

Bex laughs: 'You two work quickly.' Ant just shrugs her shoulders. 'Remember to be as unobtrusive as you can. People here live closely together and are easily upset when their reputation is at stake. Anything out of the ordinary and the whole town will know within the hour.'

'Charming,' Bex mutters.

'It's called community life. Of course, it includes gossip, which can sometimes be enormously useful to us.'

'Message received.' A smile plays round his lips.

'I mean it, Bex. I have to live here long after the case is solved.'

Ant grabs her rucksack, stuffs it full of notebooks, pens, scrap paper, and lastly her old-fashioned Dictaphone, she uses as a tape recorder… time to go. They rush to the car.


Kathleen is already waiting by the school entrance. 'Thank you for coming,' she says to Ant giving her a warm hug, wrapping part of her into her large cardigan. 'You must be Bex,' she greets him with a welcoming smile. There is something odd about the

170

way they look at each other… as if they knew one another from somewhere…I am imagining things, Ant scolds herself.

'Kathleen meet Bex,' Ant makes the introduction and watches them with a mixture of amusement and fascination, while twirling the end of her long ponytail round her forefinger. Bex would deduct, that she is impatient, but he is not looking her way. He is captivated by the Headmistress.

'Let's go in,' Ant reminds everyone that they have come for a purpose. Kathleen gets the hint immediately: 'Of course; sorry. Come with me.' She walks ahead crosses the foyer, turns left and opens the door to a rather sumptuous office. 'Make yourself comfortable. This is a situation where Bex would whistle normally, but he doesn't. The first thing Ant notices, is a vase on Kathleen's impressive oak desk with a beautiful bunch of bright red tulips and cheerfully yellow daffodils.

'Would you like tea or coffee?'

'There's no need,' Ant says, more brusquely than she had intended, impatient to make a start, but Kathleen insists on quickly nipping over to the school secretary to make a pot of coffee for them. As Kathleen leaves the room, Bex's eyes follow her until she disappears.

'What a nice woman,' Ant hears him mutter.


They decide that they wouldn't single out young Peter to be interviewed first. Instead the Headmistress announces at lunch time, when everybody is gathered in the canteen, that Senior Inspector of Police, SIO Cox and Miss Bell, a Police Scientist - otherwise known also as *the lady with Magnum, he piglet* - want to speak to everybody who has information about the French girl who has disappeared last year. Senior Investigation Officer Cox is working hard on Sylvie's case, the pupils are told, and needs all the help they can give. The last word is left to the Detective: 'We often remember many more details when asked a second or third time, simply because the first time round we were all still in shock and might have forgot to mention some things that didn't seem important then. So here is your chance to catch up, to tell us more, to fill in those gaps – even the tiniest bit of information might be terribly important to our investigation.' The children seem much taken with the Detective, several nod and everybody gives him a heartfelt round of applause. They look hopefully to Miss Bell, but she doesn't seem to have her piglets with her today. Before the children get up to put their chairs in neat rows by the wall, Kathleen announces that Miss Bell and Inspector Cox would be available all afternoon, even after school, in Miss Fitzgerald's office. There are excited whispers in the playground after lunch; they can't believe that they are important in a real criminal case. Of course, they all want to help that poor woman, Sylvie's mother, to get to the truth.

Ant and Bex sink into the soft cushions Kathleen has put on the visitors' settee in her office. The wait begins for Ant and Bex, while Kathleen keeps buzzing in and out. More coffee is brought in by the school secretary.

They did not expect queues of pupils to appear, but they had hoped for at least one or two. They are disappointed when nobody turns up all afternoon. Frustration sets in: they keep checking the door and the corridor; they leaf through the pages of their notebooks, reading listlessly through old notes and stare at empty pages where nothing has been added. Bex develops a twitch in one eyelid, and Ant is fighting not to fall asleep after her early start of the day.

'Bad luck,' says Kathleen, commiserating, when the school bell rings.

'We have to come again, but this time we have to call them in by name.'

'…tomorrow?' Kathleen enquires with a slightly anxious intonation. She doesn't mind being supportive, but too many disruptions of the school day are not good for the children's education and peace of mind.

'No,' Ant senses her friend's misgivings: 'We'll give you a rest for a couple of days and speak to another witness,' Bex nods: 'we need to interview Annette next, the woman whose dog found Sylvie's body…. she only lives another ten minutes' drive from here.'

Kathleen is happy with that; it will give her time, to calm the atmosphere. 'Thanks for your time, office and the coffee,' Ant is suddenly in a hurry to get away and Bex adds an apology: '…and your patience. See you soon.'

Kathleen watches them wistfully as they gather their things and leave through the main gate. .


'Sir?' says a little voice behind them. Ant and Bex turn round. A little, urchin-like girl with greasy, shoulder-length blond hair and lovely blue eyes stands there as if in awe of her own courage.

'What's your name?'

'Jilly.'

'Jilly…?'

'Jilly Smith.'

'How old are you, Jilly?' Bex enquires.

'Ten.'

'Shouldn't you be going home?' Bex sounds like a concerned father.

'I wanted to say something.'

'...what about, Jilly?' Ant is unsure whether this is the right place to hold an interview, however welcome.

'...the French Girl.' The adults listen up.

'Go ahead,' Ant encourages her paying her full attention.

'My sister Kirsty was on the exchange. When she came back from France she said that Sylvie and Peter had had a big row.'

'Which Peter was that?' Bex asks as if he didn't know.

'Peter Shelley.' The slight girl's voice is faltering when the Senior Detective addresses her.

'Do you know what they were rowing about?' Ant steps in quickly before Jilly clams up altogether.

'My sister says,' Jilly turns entirely to Ant, trying to ignore the intimidating detective, 'that they were very friendly to start with, but then they had a row before they went back on the ferry.'

'You lost me, Jilly. Who had a row with Peter: your sister or Sylvie?' Bex looks stern, narrowing his eyes. The girl shrinks a little more.

'My sister was always friends with Peter, but when they went to France, Sylvie became his girlfriend, and he ignored Kirsty. But before the English pupils got on the ferry to come home, the French girl and Peter had a blazing row. Everyone heard it,' the words gush out of her like a waterfall. Jilly looks at Ant for reassurance, trying to ignore the policeman whose eyes have narrowed again, which makes him look fierce.

'That's absolutely clear now. Well done, Jilly,' Ant throws her a big smile, bending down to be almost at level with the little

174

girl's face. An uncertain, watery smile plays around Jilly's mouth. She doesn't get praised very often and doesn't know how to respond. 'That is most helpful, Jilly. You can run along now' Ant says, righting herself up, expecting the child to turn and run off, but Jilly has more to say; she stays rooted to the spot, looking at something high up in the sky.

'…anything else, Jilly?' Ant is a little impatient. Sometimes interviewees grow into their role so comfortably that they don't want to relinquish it and carry on waffling.

'Yes Miss…' There is a long pause, as if the young girl is still debating inwardly, whether she should mention what's bothering her. The first words come out in a stutter before tumbling out: 'Sylvie wanted nothing to do with Peter, when she came to England, but Kirsty says, she saw Peter following her after school on the day she disappeared. Kirsty doesn't go to choir, and she was surprised to see the two together.'

'I can imagine,' Ant says feigning astonishment, 'Did they make up, you think?'

'Who?' Jilly is confused for a moment.

'Peter and Sylvie.'

'I don't think so: they shouted at each other. At least, that's what Kirsty said.'

'And how are Peter and your sister getting on now?'

'She dumped him.' It sounds funny from the mouth of a ten year old.

'That's most interesting, Jilly. Do you think your sister could confirm all that?'

'Don't say that I told you,' she begs hastily. 'She said not to tell anyone, but I think it is important.' She is clearly in a dilemma, but sticks out her chin and looks to Ant for reassurance.

'You are absolutely right, Jilly, and you did very well to come forward. Thank you. That was most helpful and very sensible behaviour for your age. Well done! And of course, we shall keep your secret! Scout's honour!'

Jilly smiles with relief, turns round and rushes off in the direction, they presume, of home.

Ant and Bex look at each other and almost say simultaneously: 'Peter and Kirsty next.'

They inform Kathleen that there will be a change of schedule, and that they would like to speak to both young people first thing in the morning.

'They could come in a bit earlier. I'll have to inform their parents and ask them to send their kids half an hour before school starts.' Kathleen suggests.

'Let's hope the Mums don't want to come along; it' always intimidating,' Ant mutters.

'I don't think their Mums will make it that early, but you never know.'

Ant can read it all over Bex's face: 'Bloody parents! They are either over-protective or not bothered, as if there was no middle way.

'I could sit in with you,' Kathleen suggests, as a sort of parent substitute.'

'By all means, but I am not sure whether they will tell us the whole truth, if the Headmistress is present,' Ant worries; 'I'll leave it to you.'

'Good. I'll be officially hovering on behalf of the parents.'

# CHAPTER TWENTY-SIX

'You are Kirsty Smith?' Ant asks, leaning back in the headmistress's swivel-chair, pretending to make notes. Bex is sitting on a chair in the corner by the window and watches the young witness come in. The early morning sunshine, which has flooded the office through the window until now, is slowly obscured by a bank of grey clouds. Ant goes to the door to switch on the light: 'We want to see each other, don't we,' she says conspiratorially to the young girl sitting opposite her, slumped into an ordinary chair without arm rests, probably borrowed from the assembly hall.. Usually, parents called by the headmistress sit on those. Kirsty doesn't look anything like her little sister Jilly; Kirsty has her mousy-brown, thin hair cut short in a classic chin-length bob on one side, whilst the other side of her head is shorn like a boy's number one at the barber's, close to the pink scalp; she is what can only be described as overweight, looking rather powerful and sadly ungainly, which is underlined by her ill-fitting school uniform: unbuttoned jacket, white shirt hanging partially out of the waistband of her skirt , which reveals round, fleshy knees. There is no charm about her thunderous, unsmiling face.

'Kirsty, you probably know that we are trying to find the person who has done harm to the French girl, who had come here on exchange to your school. You were a part of this exchange group, weren't you?'

Kirsty nods and asks matter-of-factly:   'You mean Sylvie, who got murdered?' She speaks in a thick West Country burr, much more so than her little sister did.

Ant nods and leans forward; 'Did you like her?' The only answer she gets is a shrug.

Ant coughs into her palm, surprised by the girl's feistiness. Kathleen had prepped her that Kirsty's trip had been sponsored by the school to spur her on to do better with her school work, particularly in French.

'Did you notice anything about Sylvie during her stay?' Ant persists.

'What?' Kirsty frowns with suspicion.

Ant remains patient: 'Did Sylvie, for example, mix with the group? Did she behave in England in the same way she had at home in Morlaix?' Kirsty stares at Ant as if she had spoken in Chinese, lips tightly pressed together like a clam's, but Ant carries on nonetheless: 'Did she get on with her exchange friend Charlotte – that sort of thing?' Ant leans towards the witness, trying to convey an impression of sympathy and understanding, a kind of girlie chat. Kirsty's features relax: 'She didn't mix much,' she volunteers, 'but Charlotte liked her. They were always together…until…' she stops and bites her lip.

'…until what?' Ant coaxes her.

'Until… Peter made friends with her.'

'Peter? Is that Peter Shelley?'

Kirsty nods staring at her knees.

'Did Peter make friends with Charlotte as well?' Ant asks to clarify the point.

'No,' Kirsty rejects the suggestion.

'So, what happened?' Ant is all ears; Kirsty has her undivided attention and likes it.

178

'They were always together and left Charlotte on her own or with us.'

'But they were most of the time with the group and your teachers, weren't they?

'No, they kept sneaking off, and my French friend Marie-Pierre and I saw them almost every evening in town when we went to buy ice-cream - just the two of them.'

'You mean you saw them in the evenings without Charlotte?' Ant is deeply concerned at the emerging picture.

'Aha,' Kirsty confirms.

'Where do you think, Charlotte was?'

Kirsty shrugs her shoulders: 'At home; probably babysitting Sylvie's brother.' It's a scenario, Kirsty seems familiar with.

Ant wonders whether Charlotte's parents knew. She exchanges a glance with Bex who seems equally appalled by the negligence of the adults in charge.

'Did Charlotte ever complain?'

'No. She never complains; she probably didn't want Sylvie to get into trouble,' Kirsty tries to be charitable to her poor, long-suffering classmate.

'Charlotte must have felt quite isolated,' Ant frowns. 'Didn't she tell anyone - if not the teachers, then one of her friends in the group?'

'Not to me,' Kirsty answers laconically.

Somebody should have picked that up, Ant thinks watched by a silent Kirsty, wriggling from a slump into a more upright position.

'So, let me recap that,' Ant continues: 'Sylvie hardly spoke to anybody in the group apart from Peter. Did she have any friends among the French children?'

'I don't think so. She was always with Peter.' Ant and her interviewee seem to be going in circles.

Ant takes a deep breath: 'And did that carry on when Sylvie came to England?'

'No, they had broken up before we travelled back. They had an almighty row.

'When was that?'

'…before we boarded the ferry to Plymouth.'

'Why?' Ant's question follows quickly.

Kirsty's face looks blank: 'You have to ask him that,' Ant grins faintly. Even Bex hides his face bending deeper over the paperwork on his knees. Kirsty's thinking is nothing if not logical?

'He must have been very upset,' Ant hazards a guess, trying to regain seriousness.

'Kirsty nods vigorously: 'Yeah! I saw him cry on the ferry, in a corner, away from everybody else; I went over and asked him whether he was all right. He made me promise not to tell anyone.'

'I am afraid, you will have to tell me now,' Ant says almost apologetically. 'So, what did he tell you?'

'That Sylvie had dumped him.' It seems such a big thing at their age, Ant muses; unfortunately, it's not news to us. Ant plays along and tries to look shocked: '…any reason for that?'

'She just didn't want him anymore. She didn't deserve him! She is a …' Kirsty just m stops herself from forgetting her

180

manners, leaving Ant to guess what she thinks of the French girl. One thing is clear: Kirsty is still, so many months later, outraged on Peter's behalf.

'Why do you think, Peter chose you to confided in, Kirsty?'

The girl blushes to the roots of her shorn hair, and her defiant look returns: '…because I was his girlfriend before we went to France,' she shouts, '…and a much better one than that…that,' Kirsty knows that she isn't allowed to say the word; 'I wish I had never gone!'

'You were Peter's girlfriend?' Ant feigns surprise and wonders whether Peter's mother had known. 'It must have been hurtful to see the two of them together during your visit to France,' Ant isn't prepared for the immediate outburst that follows: 'You are not pinning this on me! Me being jealous! I couldn't care less if he prefers that slut!' The word is out. Her hand flies to her mouth in shock that this time she has given her feelings away. 'I haven't done nothing,' Kirsty shouts and attempts to struggle hastily up from her chair.

The door opens and Kathleen's head appears in the gap: 'Everything all right?' she smiles innocently, as if she hadn't heard the commotion. She is obviously hovering outside, as she had promised, Ant thinks and feels grateful that her friend tolerates the enormous interruption of her working days without any fuss. 'I let you get on then,' Kathleen nods at all three of them, and shuts the door quietly.

She can't just let her go; they haven't even broached the subject of the French group coming over to Dulverton.

'Don't go, Kirsty. I am not trying to pin anything on you! I am just trying to imagine how hurt you must have been!' Ant sends a glance of commiseration across the desk when she sees tears welling up in Kirsty's eyes. Ant waits patiently until Kirsty has regained her composure, hands her a tissue from the box between them and allows her another few moments to blow her nose

'Did you and Peter resume your friendship after your return?' Ant asks cautiously.

'No,' she says simply, kneading the crumpled tissue between her hands. 'He keeps himself to himself. He sometimes waves to me, but that's all,' she mumbles miserably towards the floor. When they think, Kirsty has run out of things to say, she surprises them – even Bex looks in their direction: 'I don't think Peter looked forward to the French coming over.'

'What happened when they did?'

'Sylvie totally ignored him, and he looked miserable the whole time. He didn't even come to the excursion; he said he wasn't feeling well... and I had to look after his French partner Oliver.' Kirsty answers with passion and more outrage. She might be an awkward girl, Ant can't help thinking, but Kirsty is a good friend to have on your side.

'You mean Olivier?'

'Yeah, Olivier, or whatever... It means Oliver anyway,' she defends her sparse knowledge of French.

'Do you know Olivier's surname?'

Kirsty shakes her head.

'How do you feel about Peter now, Kirsty?' Ant tries to make the question sound unimportant, but Kirsty takes umbrage:

'I don't care. I just felt sorry for him,' she says huffily.

'No, what I mean is: is Peter a popular Boy; a good student? Has he changed in any way since the French group left?'

'He is nice; he never gets into trouble...she pauses before adding with a heavy sigh: 'but now you can never get near him.

His mother is always hovering!' Yes, that won't help. Ant hears Bex clearing his throat to hide a chuckle; just as she has trouble keeping a straight face.

'One last thing, Kirsty: Did you ever see Sylvie and Peter together, while the French group were over here?' Ant fixes her eyes on Kirsty's face.

Kirsty is silent as if turning something over in her mind, her thick eyebrows knitted together as she weighs up the benefits of telling the truth, fudging it or keeping quiet. Finally she makes up her mind and forces out the words: 'You know, the day when Sylvie disappeared?' she looks at Ant to make sure she follows her train of thought.

'Yes, the day when Sylvie went home without Charlotte,' Ant reassures the girl of her attention, 'what about it?'

'I don't do choir. My class teacher Miss Pope wanted to see me about some homework. When I finished, I went home. I live down Northmoor Road; it's the same way as to Charlotte's house, just a bit further on.' Kirsty looks Ant straight in the face to see whether she is still following her.

'Yes, go on,' Ant encourages her.

'When I went out of the school gate, I saw Charlotte running after Sylvie, trying to make her stay for choir, but Sylvie shouted something about her mother ringing from France.' She looks up again and Ant nods further encouragement.

'So, Charlotte goes back into school, and then suddenly, Peter appears? Was he behind you, Kirsty?'

'No; he was suddenly in front of me running after Sylvie.'

'Where did he spring from?' Ant seems baffled.

'He must have been hiding in the hedgerow.'

'…really?'

Kirsty can't imagine why that should be strange. They are wild hedgerows, wide and dense; she and her friends have often hidden in them when they were younger.

'Okay, Kirsty,' Ant takes up the description,' Peter staggers out of the hedgerow as if he has been hiding there, and then he followed Sylvie, right up to her host family's house..' Kirsty is pleased to notice that she has the undivided attention of both grown-ups.

Time for a dramatic delivery: 'He just followed her until they turned off to the right, up the hill to where Charlotte lives.'

'…and you, did you follow them?'

'Of course not,' she protests vehemently, but Ant sees a crimson flush creeping upwards from the girl's throat.

Ant raises her eyebrows in question, suggesting: 'Maybe slowly and at a distance?' Ant probes but Kirsty doesn't answer.

'Come on, Kirsty. You must have observed what happened next,' Bex interrupts from his corner looking at her over the rim of his glasses. It has the desired effect. Kirsty, who has almost totally forgotten about him being there, is in shock.

'He caught up with her,' she stutters; 'and I couldn't help hearing them shout at each other. I think they had another row.'

'Could you hear what they were rowing about?'

'No.'

'Just words, or did they fight physically, Kirsty? Did he pull her arm? Did thy push or hit each other?'

'No, no! Just shouting,' Kirsty is getting desperate to leave this room.

184

'…for how long?' Bex keeps on with the questions.

'I don't know, do I?' she is shouting. 'He suddenly turned round and came back down the hill again.'

'So, hold on, Kirsty: You saw him after the row had ended? He came towards you? Did you speak to him?''

'No. He looked angry, so I got out of his way. I don't think he even noticed me.'

'Strange. There is hardly any space for pedestrians, never mind two, and only on the one side of the road. Are you saying, Peter barged past you and didn't even acknowledge you? Ant makes sure they are talking about the same spot. 'What did you do then?'

'I went home.'

'Did you see anybody else?'

'No, and the next day, the French girl was gone,' Kirsty tries to recover some dramatic effect, but nobody seems impressed. She takes refuge in yawning, a big uninhibited yawn, to convey that the interview is beginning to bore her. No point in carrying on.

'Did you see Sylvie again as you went past the hill?' Kirsty shakes her head: 'She had let herself into the house by then, I think..'

'Okay then,' Ant gets up and stretches out a hand: 'Thank you, Kirsty. That was enormously helpful. You are a star! Sorry to keep you so long!' A shadow of a lopsided smile creeps across the girl's broad features, softening them, brushing boredom and anxiety aside, leaving a little glow in her eyes. She is obviously lapping up the praise. Ant flashes another big, warm smile of approval in Kirsty's direction and reaches to open the door, but Kirsty lingers, as if there is something else she wants to say. The girl, who couldn't wait to escape, now hesitates to leave, glowing with her new -won importance.

'Thank you again,' Ant encourages her to leave: 'If there is anything else you remember, tell Miss Fitzgerald to give me a ring...', but Kirsty has already changed her mind, opens the door and disappears fast down the corridor to join her class.

# CHAPTER TWENTY-SEVEN

'That was interesting!' Bex gets up from his chair to stretch his legs. 'Peter is next,' he grins, just at the moment when the door opens again. They assume that Kirsty has left something behind, and adjust their faces to serious mode, but it is Kathleen again popping her head round the corner:

'Any luck?' she asks bursting with curiosity.

'Possibly; I'll tell you later when we have finished here.' Ant is looking past her to the door to make sure that the boy isn't approaching just yet.

'It is Peter next, isn't it? Sorry, I overheard.' Her apology doesn't sound convincing. Ant grins knowing how eager Kathleen is to remain involved and to be regularly updated.

'He is sitting out here, waiting very patiently, aren't you, Peter,' Kathleen's head disappears for a moment to extract a confirmation from her pupil, who is sitting on an assembly hall chair in the corridor, staring bleakly at the wall opposite; only his swinging legs give away how nervous he is.

'You can send him in, Miss Fitzgerald,' Bex says loudly and with authority, addressing the boy outside as much as his headmistress.

They hear her say an encouraging: '…in you go, Peter; nothing to be afraid of, if you tell the truth!' Shortly afterwards, he appears in the door frame for another interview, forlorn and apprehensive. 'Be gentle with him,' Kathleen mouths to them and they nod in confirmation that they would. Another push from behind, and the boy stands far enough inside, so that Kathleen can close the door behind him.

Ant and Bex quickly swap places, Bex at the desk and Ant in the corner.

'Hello again, Peter,' Bex says from behind the desk, standing up and extending his hand in a friendly gesture. Peter is even ganglier than Bex remembers him from the last time. His blond shock of hair, neatly parted on the right hand side of his head, flops a little over his ears. Undoubtedly, his mother will take him to the barbers soon or wield scissors herself. Bex points to a chair opposite him. The boy sits down, his knees together and his toes pointing inwardly towards each other. Bex will lead the interview. He smiles jovially; no point in antagonising the young witness.

'Just a few more questions, which have come up recently, you can help us with, Peter,' Bex begins, adding as gently as he can: 'Now that we know that Sylvie has been murdered.' Peter's brown eyes dart around the room as if looking for an escape route. Bex looks over his reading glasses like a kindly grandfather. Peter nods silently.

Bex observes Peter's reaction and puts his first question to him: 'Can you tell me again about the day Sylvie disappeared?'

Peter nods again, but remains silent.

'You were in school that morning?' Bex coaxes him.

'Yes,' he whispers. They can hardly hear him.

'Did you speak to Sylvie at any time during that day – in class, in the playground, at lunch?'

Peter swallows hard before he manages to get a few words out: 'No, not really.'

'What does that mean, Peter? You either spoke to her, or you didn't.'

'I tried in the playground at break, but she walked off.' He swallows hard.

'Okay,' Bex says quietly and pauses to give him time to calm his nerves. 'That's fine.' Bex repeats, takes a deep breath and launches into his next question: 'Did you speak to Sylvie at any other time that day?'

Peter's face turns purple, and he has great trouble to catch his breath.

'Take your time before you answer,' Bex nods to indicate that he understands how difficult all that must be for him. It won't help to panic the boy into making things up.

It takes a few moments for Peter to compose himself; when he does speak, he stutters: 'I-I s-s-saw her a-a-a-after school.'

'Aren't you part of the choir?' Bex takes a chance on guessing.

'Yes, but I skipped it,' Peter admits, head bowed, as if he had committed a great sin. 'Don't tell my mum!' he pleads.

Bex doesn't reply. Like a police search dog, he follows the scent: 'So, where did you meet Sylvie?'

'Outside school; I waited for her.'

'…where exactly?'

'…outside the school gates.' Peter splutters and almost chokes coughing. Not good enough, Bex thinks and asks again: 'Peter, this is important: when Sylvie came out of the school gates, where were you?'

'Charlotte was there as well,' he attempts feebly to change the subject. 'She wanted her to stay in school.'

'We know that,' Bex interrupts him brutally. 'She didn't want Sylvie to walk home on her own, and if she had succeeded, the girl might not be dead now.' Peter shrinks into his chair. 'But, Peter, that is not what I have been asking; we are talking about what you did; where you were at that moment.' Peter stares at his knees, then looks up and sees Bex's stony face

'I was hiding in a hedge,' Peter bursts into tears, while Ant bows her head over her notebook trying to hide her grin; poor boy – or maybe not quite so innocent?

'Why?' Bex can't consider the boy's feelings.

'Because I wanted to speak to Sylvie,' he says miserably.

'Okay, Peter. We know that Charlotte ran after Sylvie, but Sylvie didn't want to go back to school, so Charlotte went back without her; is that correct?' Peter nods, more tears rolling down his cheeks.

'At which point did Sylvie notice that you were there?' Peter stares at the desk top and remains silent.

'Peter,' Bex sounds displeased, 'when did you jump out of the hedge and speak to Sylvie?'

'I waited for a bit, until she had walked on and Charlotte was out of sight.'

'Come on, Peter, this is dragging on unnecessarily!' Bex begins to sound cross.

'Sylvie went straight on and I followed her. She didn't see me.'

'…for how long?'

'…until she turned the corner up to Charlotte's house.'

'Was there anybody else before or behind you; I mean, did anybody see you coming out of the hedges and following Sylvie?'

190

Peter looks at Bex in horror at the thought and mutters: 'I don't think so.' He hopes, no one saw him, more like it, Bex thinks angrily. This is taking too much time. Why is that boy so reluctant? Is it really just embarrassment?

'When did Sylvie discover that you were following her?' Bex comes to the main point he needs to clear up: the row between Peter and Sylvie.

Peter mumbles something into his lap, but Bex is not having it: 'Come on, Peter, speak up. We need to get to the truth.' So far, it is a curious, almost ridiculous picture of a boy hiding in the bushes, but what followed? What happened after that? Nothing or something catastrophic?

'I put it to you that you ran after Sylvie, Peter; but what did you do when you drew level with her?'

'I didn't. When I was close, she turned back and saw me.'

'Now we are getting somewhere!' Bex exclaims. 'What did you say to her?'

'…nothing.'

'…really? …why not?'

'She shouted at me to leave her alone.'

'…and??' Bex persists.

'I didn't say anything. I lost courage.'

'Oh come on, Peter. Are you seriously telling me, that you let the chance pass to speak to her, to ask her to explain why she has broken up with you?'

Silence… Peter looks as if has been struck by lightning.

'So you didn't speak to her at all?' Bex reverts to his brisk interview mode.

'She shouted at me.'

'And what did you reply?'

'That I wanted to know why she didn't speak to me anymore.' The words tumble out of him in a chute of desperation.

'…anything else?' Bex asks curtly.

'…that I shouldn't follow her… that she would shout rape.'

'Did you touch her?' Bex's eyes narrow with suspicion.

'No, of course not,' he begins to cry again. Bex hands him a tissue from the box on Kathleen's desk, and, to keep up the momentum, asks again:

'Are you sure, you didn't touch her?'

Peter's denial nod is frantic.

'Can anybody confirm that? This is important, because, Peter, if you haven't got a witness who can vouch for you walking away from Sylvie while she was alive, you could be in deep trouble. So far, you are the last witness who saw her alive.'

Peter looks aghast. 'So, what happened after that?'?' Bex pushes him on:

'I asked her why she ignored me; what I had done wrong; why she had broken it off.'

'Yes, you mentioned that before,' Bex comments sarcastically.

'And what was her answer?' Bex looks at Peter expectantly.

He sighs deeply: 'She just shouted at me, that I should leave her alone; that she was finished with me; that I was boring and a looser.' Peter begins to sob again.

'That wasn't very nice, was it, Peter,' Bex can sense a breakthrough: 'That was rather hurtful, I would have thought.

Was that why you hit her?' Bex observes the young face as the teenager absorbs the hidden accusation.

Peter's sobbing stops at once; he looks shocked, eyes wide open, appalled at what Bex has just suggested; then he shouts in sudden desperation as if his heart would break: 'I didn't hit her! I loved her!'

Bex gives Peter a few minutes to compose himself. Eventually he speaks softly: 'I didn't say you did, Peter. I just asked if that's what happened. It wouldn't be the first time that a girl provoked a boy into losing his temper.'

'I would never do that,' Peter raises his voice in protest, almost hysterical, 'I am not like that.' It sounds pathetic, but true, Bex must admit.

'So what did really happen?'

'We had to make way for the post van, and then I ran back to the school.' Crying and subbing, Bex presumes.

'Did anybody see you returning to school?'

'The postman must have seen me; he waved and when I turned and walked back down, he nearly ran me over... but he stopped and let me cross the road at the bottom.' That sounds true, too, Ant thinks – Peter being so upset that he walks straight into the path of a car.

'Correct me if I got this wrong: you followed Sylvie along the hedges; she didn't see you;, crossed the road after she did, at some point, she turned to shout at you to leave her alone; you argued back;; then you retraced your steps; the post office van drove past; the postman waved to you both; you ran downhill where you met him again and he let you cross the road back to the pavement and then you walked back along the hedge to the school. Is that absolutely correct?' Even Ant looks bored.

Peter nods.

'Where did the postman's van go?'

'To the post office, I think.'

'It turned right. Is that correct?'

'Yes,' Peter whispers

'...and did anybody see you in school when you returned?'

'I don't know. I hid in the toilets until choir practice finished; then I got my coat and went home.'

'...And didn't tell your Mum,' Bex concludes, to which Peter hastily shakes his head.

'...and what do you think Sylvie did? Did you see her letting herself into the house?''

'I didn't look back. I don't know.'

Bex realises that this is probably all he will get out of Peter today. He points to the tissue box on the Headmistress's desk.

'Now listen, Peter: dry your eyes; maybe wash your face in the toilets, and then you can go back to your class.' The boy stares at him with incredulity, as if he had expected to be arrested. He looks at Ant in her corner, as if to ask whether this is true.

'Are you sure, you have told us everything?' Bex presses him one last time.

Peter nods eagerly. He can't believe that he is on the verge of escaping from this room.

Bex clears his voice. Peter looks at him in alarm.

'Do you have a questions, Peter?' Bex asks. At first, the boy is dumb-founded and can't think of anything, until he remembers something that has been playing havoc with his mind: 'Would Sylvie be still alive, if I had stayed with her?' he whispers.

You can see the pain in his eyes; Ant thinks and does her best to console him: 'We'll never know, Peter, but like in so many cases, she was unlucky, being in the wrong place at the wrong time.

'None of this seems to be your fault,' Bex agrees, more generous than he had intended to be, 'but if you remember anything else, give me a call – any time! This is the best thing we can do in her memory.' Peter nods. He will promise anything, if he can just leave. He is like a coiled spring, ready to storm out. Then he hears the words, he has so longed for: 'You may go now, Peter, and thank you for being honest.' Peter gets up shuffling towards the door as if his legs were filled with lead; and suddenly, quick as a flash, he is gone.

'This was either a brilliant performance or the boy really is innocent,' Bex mutters to himself.

# CHAPTER TWENTY-EIGHT

It's almost lunch time. Kathleen has taken Peter back to the classroom to gather his things while his classmates are still in the sports hall for their PE lesson. She offers him a meal, but he doesn't want it. She doesn't think that he is in a fit state to re-join lessons; she rings his mother to pick him up and briefly outlines the events of the afternoon. She then takes the boy to the school gate and hands him over to his mother, repeating her plea to be gentle with her still very emotional son.

'Are you feeling okay?' she asks Peter, while the mother is treading impatiently from one foot to the other: 'Get a move on,' she orders her son. Kathleen half expects her to give the boy a clout. Poor Peter seems to have shrunk since his mother has turned up. Goodness, she is such an intimidating harridan, Kathleen commiserates with her pupil in secret.

'You have done very well today,' she repeats, 'go home and try to forget all about it, and have an early night. The world will look much brighter in the morning.' She touches his shoulder for reassurance trying to avoid any impression of inappropriate familiarity. For Goodness sake, she thinks; why shouldn't I put an arm around a child that needs comfort? His mother isn't likely to provide it; all he will get from her is recriminations, I bet.

The Headmistress turns to Mrs Shelley: 'He is upset,' Kathleen addresses the insensitive mother, 'because they had to rake all over the day of Sylvie's disappearance again. It's even more devastating now that we know that the poor girl is dead.' Kathleen hopes she hasn't provoked any outrage and adds quickly: 'Thank you for coming to get Peter.' Thankfully, Mrs

Shelley for once doesn't know what to say; she gives Peter a nudge with her elbow and declares: 'Home, you!'

'Bye, Peter,' Kathleen says gently, smiling a little smile of compassion and waving him off with a hesitant move of the hand, only chest-high as if trying to hide it from the mother, 'see you tomorrow morning.'

Meanwhile, Ant and Bex are packing up, too, checking that they haven't left anything behind before leaving the office. They meet Kathleen just as she comes back into the foyer.

'Gosh, that was a marathon session,' Kathleen comments.

'Is Peter alright?' Bex asks.

'I hope so. Another grilling from his mother is not what he needs right now. I'll check on him tomorrow morning first thing.'

'It's horrible how a crime affects absolutely everybody who had the slightest connection with it– witness, bystanders, distant acquaintances, never mind the families involved like the Bowers. They will never forget this.'

'I don't know about you two,' Bex interrupts the brooding; it's his way of coping, Ant knows; 'but I feel peckish. Can I invite you both for a meal?'

'I must go home and see to the pigs,' Ant declines hastily and notices that Bex and Kathleen exchange a glance.

'…and I still have paperwork to finish, as some people, I will not name, have occupied my office all afternoon,' Kathleen teases.

'How about meeting tonight at seven at that little restaurant by the church?' Bex persists.

'Ugh,' Kathleen groans, 'that's rather pricey.'

'Just this once,' Bex pleads with the ladies.

'I might as well, otherwise I only eat rubbish,' Kathleen shakes her head at her own bad habits, 'you are on, Bex: seven o'clock on the dot at The Wine Cellar.' They look at Ant, who shakes her head: 'Not tonight,' she says apologetically. She can see the word 'spoilsport' written all over his face.

'See you tomorrow morning then,' Ant gives a quick wave and walks out into the school car park.


In fact, Ant sees Bex earlier than expected. She hadn't heard him coming back. She must have been exhausted and fallen asleep as soon as her head hit the pillow. As usual, her dreams are wild and can be classified as a nightmare. It's a frequent occurrence since the arson attack on her house well over a year ago. She has never told anybody about them; she is convinced that they will disappear eventually. She has had them before when she had still been working on particularly harrowing murder cases. She is fast asleep when suddenly she is rudely awakened by a sharp voice:

'Ant, what on earth are you doing?' It's Bex, stands in the upper landing outside his bedroom door in striped pyjamas, holding her tight. Weirdly, her arms are flailing around her. They are both standing perilously close to the staircase. At one point, she tries to bite him, but he just presses her head firmly against his chest. She frees herself and looks wildly around, totally disorientated; obviously thinking in her half sleep that he is an intruder.

'Ant, it is Bex!' He repositions his grip of her. The stairs are uncomfortably close; she could lose her balance and throw both of them headlong down. 'Ant, you are at home. You had a nightmare.' She stops thrashing about and looks at him in a daze.

As she slowly calms down and fully awakes, he releases her. 'Sorry,' she mutters and is about to stumble back to her room, when he offers:

'Let's go downstairs. I'll make you a cup of tea.' She lets him lead her by the shoulder down the stairs and presses her gently into the chair by the Raeburn. She sits there still in a trance, lethargic, confused

Bex takes the kettle to the sink, fills it with water, puts it back on its stand and switches it on. The noise of water slowly getting to the boiling point is soothing. He sees rinsed mugs from the night before on the draining board. 'Normal tea or camomile?' he enquires.

'Black,' she mumbles weakly.

Camomile might be more soothing, he thinks, but Ant will probably not even notice what she is drinking. He takes black teabags, puts them into the mugs and pours hot water over them. Better not to make it too strong, otherwise neither of us will sleep for the rest of the night; he retrieves the teabags after a couple of minutes, squeezes them out, adds a drop of milk from the fridge to his and ladles three teaspoons full of sugar from the bowl next to the kettle. At least that's how he remembers she takes her tea.

'Here you go,' he says gently and pulls a chair up to sit opposite her. They both take a sip, Bex observing Ant's motionless face.

'How often does this happen, Ant?' he whispers, looking concerned; almost shocked.

She has got hardly the strength to shrug her shoulders: 'Often… most nights.'

'I noticed on the first night I slept here, that you were abnormally frantic about locking the doors, windows and checking them over and over again. I thought then, that things were not right. I had seen it before in others. Post-Traumatic Stress syndrome is not unfamiliar in jobs like ours.' He looks at her reaction, but there is none. 'Has it got to do with the fire?' Last time, when they were close to solving the riddle of Lucinda Turner's disappearance, someone had tried to stop Ant by setting her house alight.

Ant nods with a little more vigour.

'Have you told anyone – a friend; a doctor?'

She shakes her head almost imperceptibly.

'How long has this been going on?'

She tries to speak, but has to clear her throat first; eventually she croaks: 'It started almost immediately after the fire.'

'And it still hasn't abated? That's a long time, Ant. I am surprised that you can function at all, with months of sleep deprivation!'

'It's getting worse. At first it was just the nightmares, now I seem to sleep-walk, too.'

'Apart from it ruining your health, it is downright dangerous, Ant.' He pauses and looks at her, taking her limp hand into his: 'I guess, you know what to do.' She nods, but doesn't speak. 'When will you do something about it?' he pushes for an answer.

'What?'

'Go to the doctor; get therapy,' there is an urgent, anxious quality to his suggestion. Either Ant is still trapped by the after-effects of the nightmare, or she really hasn't considered asking for help. Bex is at a loss how to approach this without being patronising. He feels that someone should take her in hand. But who? He would do no good at all and only make her hackles go up. She wouldn't allow it; she would accuse him of taking over

200

the reins of her life. Come to think of it, he is the last person who should even try to advise her.

'Do you remember Tim Grace?''

'…the Police psychiatrist?'

'Yes.'

'Isn't he retired?' Ant takes another sip from her tea which has gone cold. At least, she is listening.

'Yes. Now that I am retired, too, we sometimes meet up for a drink in London. He is a good bloke, and he remembers you. I am sure that he can come up with a suggestion to help you.'

'I am not going into therapy, if that is what you mean.'

Bex is shocked at her bluntness and retorts like with like: 'I don't think you have a choice, Ant. If you don't, you will be heading for an almighty mental breakdown.'

She stares stubbornly at the rim of her mug.

'Why don't you have a chat with him? You might not need therapy.' Bex suggests.

After a while she looks up, bewilderment in her fascinating green eyes.

'I can't bear it any more, Bex,' she whispers as if admitting to a humiliating defeat.

'Ant, it's not your fault. Someone tried to kill you; of course, there will be consequences.' He pauses, before suggesting: 'Shall I ring Tim, or do you want his card and do it when you are ready?'

She is breathing fast, in short burst and gasps as if she had run a marathon. Bex observes her with great concern.

'Which is it, Ant?'

'Both.'

'All right,' he says, 'I'll do my bit first thing in the morning; the rest is up to you. Now let's go back to bed! It's only three-thirty.'

'I think I shall stay up a bit longer,' Ant mumbles.

'Are you afraid it will start again?'

He can guess the answer. 'Tell you what,' he says, 'and don't take that the wrong way: why don't I sleep in your bed for the rest of the night. You can snuggle up. No hanky-panky; just to make you feel safe.' He looks at her almost with embarrassment. She knows it's a genuine offer of protection and compassion.

'Boy will ...' she begins, but a yawn stifles the rest of the sentence.

'Don't worry. I'll do battle with him. He can have my bed all to himself.'

'It's his bed, too,' she protests sleepily.

'All right,' Bex gives in. He can't be bothered to argue at three-thirty in the morning.

'Come on then, Hero,' she gives him a wan smile and gets up unsteadily from her chair, leaving the half-drunk mug on the table. Then she leads him up the stairs to her room.

# CHAPTER TWENTY-NINE

'I think we have done everything we could these last few days,' Bex remarks with satisfaction over his lamb chop, boiled new potatoes and runner beans. He is not a bad cook, Ant thinks without saying so.

'Yes, we have worked hard,' Ant agrees busy spearing a small potato with her fork. 'That's why it's doubly frustrating.'

She hasn't mentioned last night at all, as if it had never happened.

'What is?' Bex looks up from his plate. Ant still battles with a mouthful of potato. She grimaces at him with puffed out hamster cheeks.

'It's very tempting…,' he laughs, nodding towards her face.

She swallows several times: 'Don't you dare!' she protests playfully and then launches into her reasoning: 'The DNA result came through this afternoon on the computer.'

'Now you tell me…and what is so disappointing?' Bex narrows his eyes, suddenly focusing entirely on Ant.

'The murderer is definitely a male and likely to be a Brit, but they haven't found a match on the Police Data Base.' Ant sighs noisily.

'So, no previous conviction,' Bex deducts, shaking his head in disbelief. 'Damn!'

'It doesn't mean he hasn't done something like that before; he just got away with it.' Ant is not one to give up easily. Bex knows she will keep following the traces of the culprit tenaciously, doggedly, until she has found him.

'That means,' Bex reminds her, 'that we have to find the owner of that particular genome; dig up old case files, forensic and witness reports of similar unsolved crimes; plough through old witnesses statements... it's never ending,' Bex folds his hands behind his head and looks disillusioned. 'And I thought I had retired.'

Ant bites her lower lip, incredulous at what she is hearing: 'Couldn't we just leave it to the local police?'

'I can't, as you well know. I tend to finish what I started. I thought you felt the same.'

The answer surprises her: 'I don't need that sort of stress in my life anymore.'

Ant's eyes sparkle with defiance and disappointment: 'Why did you come down in the first place?' She can't believe that he is seriously considering abandoning a case halfway. He would never have done that in the past. Retirement really has changed him.

'You don't need me here, Ant.' She hears him mutter as he begins to clear the table, stacking up crockery in the Belfast sink, 'you are quite capable of carrying on by yourself.'

Ant is speechless. If this is an attempt at rousing her to contradict or plead with him, she won't oblige.

He waits, and when nothing more is said, he concludes: 'I think I'd better go back home and let you get on with your life, Ant. I am beginning to feel that I'm cramping your style.' The remark is half statement, half question. Ant can't believe what she is hearing. Surely, the lack of progress can't be the only reason for this change of mind; it has never stopped him before. She is beginning to suspect that there is another reason. Did he come to the farm with an ulterior motive?

'You can stay as long as you like,' Ant offers feebly, but she is beginning to doubt that she wants him around in this frame of mind.

The next morning, Bex is up early, packs his few belongings and orders a taxi to the station.

'I'll go via the school and say good-bye to Kathleen,' he mutters, looking around, as if he were still undecided. When he catches Ant's eye, she looks away, fiddling with the end of her ponytail. He waits another moment. 'Good-bye, then, Ant.' He makes a step towards her, but she has already turned her head away. 'Keep me in the loop if there are any developments.' What for? She thinks and stomps back to the house. He sighs and gets in the taxi, slamming the car door in frustration.

As it takes him away along the narrow, muddy lane, Ant feels a familiar coldness growing and tightening around her heart.

A few days later, she rings Kathleen for some solidarity, but it is the first day of the Easter holidays. Ant had forgotten. There is no reply. She doesn't even leave a message. Ant's anger and disappointment that Bex has abandoned her and the case, will have dissipated by the time Kathleen gets back.


Ant keeps herself busy with the animals. It's a lovely spring day, full of gentle, warm breezes without the fierce heat of the summer. The trees are in full leaf and their glorious green is satisfying, opening Ant's heart wide. The animals have missed her while she was consumed by the case. She has rung Sergeant Penhaligon several times, but there's no news, and it sounds, as if the investigation has been shelved for the time being. She relates her frustration to the best listeners she knows: her Girls.

They like her constant presence, reliable routine and personal care; her lovingly prepared treats and her sitting on the fence prattling on – not that they are interested in what she is saying. The latest topic, she has come up with, is the horrendous subject of the dispatch of their numerous off-spring. They would probably have trampled her to death if they had understood...though come to think of it, she has seen the sows rejecting their young when they had grown into rumbustious teenagers; there clearly comes a time when the sows had enough of having them around, needing some time to themselves before the next lot arrives. Just now they look at her, vying for more treats.

It really is a dilemma for Ant: to send piglets, she has lovingly raised and is immensely proud of, to an abattoir, however local and humane. Is there anything humane about killing? On the other hand, why, on earth, has she started to breed pigs in the first place? The initial idea had been to earn money, sending first class organic pork to posh restaurants, thus securing a decent improvement on her pension. Ant is confused on the subject. ...best not to think about it for a little while longer.


'Ant, I am back. Can I come and see you before I am being swallowed up by the school on Monday?'

What a nice surprise, Ant thinks, clamping the receiver between her shoulder and her ear as she was just unwrapping muffins. 'Hi, Kathleen! Great to have you back! Where have you been?'

'...Ireland, to visit my family. It was about time that I reconnected with them. It was touching how delighted they were to see me after such a long time.'

'That's nice.' Ant is pleased for her friend, and a little relieved that she hasn't made a detour via London. For some reason,

206

alarm bells had rung, after Bex had hurriedly left and Kathleen had gone away without telling her; it's embarrassing to admit – even if only to herself – that she has been paranoid. You are getting neurotic; a sure way of losing friends, Ant scolds herself. She has every intention to mend her ways, she

'Would you like to come up this afternoon,' Ant asks. Kathleen does: 'I'll bore you to tears with my new photographs and stories of my tribe,' Kathleen warns, sounding exceedingly cheerful.

'You can come right now, if you like. It's one of those mornings when she is brooding and could do with cheering up.

She can hear the engine of Kathleen's car roar towards the farm and something like an emergency stop. Ant grins; Kathleen is not the most subtle of drivers.

They embrace like two long lost sisters, pull chairs up to the Raeburn and sip from two steaming cups of tea, comfortable in each other's company.

'I missed you,' Ant says truthfully, although she doesn't mention the tiny suspicion of doubt she had experienced, too. She is ashamed of it now.

'Well, I didn't want to say anything beforehand, in case it went wrong, and I had to come back crying.'

'So they welcomed you with open arms?'

'They did, and I learnt one thing: we mustn't let relationships slip. It's so easily done, but it is much harder to re-build. As my Da put it, however busy you are, treat your relationships like tender plants, otherwise they shrivel up and die, and we are all the poorer for it.'

Ant gulps. She has never been successful with keeping relationships alive.

'…biscuits?'

Kathleen shakes her head: 'I must go on a diet. All these Colcannons, Irish Stews and Soda breads…'

They look at holiday photographs, and Kathleen explains affectionately who is who and what each of them is doing.

'Is Bex out?' Kathleen asks suddenly, looking around her as if searching for him.

'He has left. Sylvie's case was shelved again.'

'… but he'll be backs, surely?'

Ant shakes her head.

'What happened? Did you have a row?' Kathleen is bewildered. 'I thought you were a couple.'

Ant shakes her head. 'No, he has gone back to London.' Ant raises her hand to wipe something invisible from her eyes, to hide that tears are welling up in her eyes. 'We were not getting on.'

'Not getting on? What are you – children?' Kathleen scoffs. 'In my book not getting on looks different.'

'Never mind,' Ant smiles bravely: 'Let's change the subject…. Tell me more about your holiday.' There is silence between them, until Kathleen asks boldly: 'Do you two actually have history, you and Bex?'

It's not a question, Ant has expected, but she answers, however unwillingly: 'Yes, we had an affair once – and now… mind your own business.' It comes out more brutal than she had intended.

Kathleen is unperturbed: 'So, what happened?'

Ant is exasperated and almost shouts: 'He went back to his wife; when she became ill.'

Kathleen thinks for a moment, how to console her friend and opts for sympathy: '…very honourable, if I may say so, but it must have been hell for you.'

Suddenly, Ant's emotional armour crumples; her voice is hardly audible, her breath louder than words: 'I was pregnant, too,' old grief has resurfaced. It is the first time in years, she has confided in anybody. The last confessional was with Lucinda, whom she lost, too.

'Oh, you poor thing,' Kathleen stands up and throws her arms around her friend: 'So, where is your son or daughter?'

Ant presses her lips together in the hope that it stops the tears. She gulps and they flow -    . After a long pause, she confesses: 'I had an abortion.'

'And Bex agreed to it?' Kathleen is outrage.

'He never knew. There was no point in telling him: He was back with his wife, and I had a job to do.'

Only for a second, Kathleen looks horrified, before composure takes over: 'I can't imagine how you must have suffered – and still do; it never goes away, so I am told. …and you suffered all by yourself…When did you tell him? Is that why he came down here?'

'He doesn't know.'

'All these years…?' Kathleen is speechless. 'When are you going to tell him?' Ant shakes her head, but remains silent and stares at the floor.

'You won't?' she raises her eyebrows in expectation of a change of mind, but Ant shakes her head again.

Kathleen gets up. 'I better go,' she mutters and heads for the door. Ant closes the door softly behind her.

# CHAPTER THIRTY

'Ant,' Bex calls out of the blue from London: 'Have you got a minute? I think I found something going through old files. Ring me back as soon as you can.'

He seems to be picking up their relationship and the case where they had left it, without any trace of rancour.

Ant has run down the hill from the pigs' enclosure, hearing the telephone ring, but the message service has just kicked in. She rings him back immediately. 'What have you found?' Ant asks breathlessly, without greeting or polite conversation.

'It could be nothing,' he says cautiously.

'Bex!' she shouts in exasperation. 'You wouldn't ring if it wasn't promising! What have you found…anything new?'

'Yeah!' he draws out the word, savouring every moment he can keep her in suspense. This is the old Ant he knows and loves.

'There was a call from Cumbria,' he is serious now, 'a little town called Dufton in the North of England. A woman saw our appeal. She remembers the case of a prostitute, who she thinks, was murdered in a similar way.'

'…recently?'

'No, a few years ago.'

'Do you think it's worth pursuing? Sylvie wasn't a prostitute; and this is a totally different location.'

Bex doesn't reply and asks instead: 'Would you come with me to Dufton?'

'…when?'

'Ant, you know how important time is!'

'You mean tomorrow, don't you, Bex.' It is an informed guess.

'Tomorrow would be great,' Bex sounds relieved.

'Hold on. Before I can say yes, I have to find out, whether Felix is free to look after the farm, the pigs...'

'…and Boy, the cat,' he says with irony, and not a little exasperation. Bex would leave tonight if he could, Ant suspects.

'Yes - and Boy. They are my priorities,' she reinforces the principle.

'I know my place, Ant,' Bex laughs uneasily.

'I'll do my best, and let you know. In the meantime, ring the woman and tell her that we're coming.'

'I thought you first had to square it with the divine Felix?' Bex growls,

'If he can't stand in for me, I know somebody who wouldn't be my first choice, but would have to do.' She is thinking of Kathleen. At least she would be kind to the animals.

Ant dials Felix's farm, and he's happy to take over for a couple of days. She pictures his red curly hair falling over his forehead, and the stunning green eyes; in summer he looks cheekier than ever, because his face is covered in freckles. She knows he is most conscientious running his parents' farm and loves working side by side with his father, but he is tired of his parents telling him to settle down and start a family, when all he wants to do is tell them that it will never happen. The only person he has told that he is gay, is Ant.

Felix is delighted to escape his parent's clutches and stay for a few days at Ant's house. He loves her pigs, characterful, intelligent creatures who always cheer him up; his father's sheep are not half as personable.


The following morning, Ant has an early start to catch the seven o'clock train to Bristol Temple Meads from where Bex said he would pick her up.

'No point in dragging yourself all the way up to London,' he had said, showing his thoughtful side, 'and then we take hours to get out of it to the motorway. It will be much easier meeting you close to the M5. And once we are on it, it will be plain sailing.'

I wouldn't bet on it, Ant had thought the previous evening, but had kept it to herself. Various junctions on that stretch were notorious for clogging up the M5. Moreover, it would take five hours anyway without any traffic jams.

When her train gets in at Bristol, she is met by a most positive Bex outside Temple Meads Station, in spite of the early hour he must have left London. Bex is wearing a light-weight fawn suit and a contrasting floral tie, while Ant has made an effort to spruce up a bit, too, wearing light-blue chinos and a tunic in a stronger blue, whose long sleeves can be rolled up and held further up the arms by loops and buttons – not her idea, but the shopkeepers in Fore Street whom she paid a hasty visit just before closing time yesterday afternoon had thought it stylish and practical all at once. The woman also tried to talk her into buying the very expensive, labelled sandals – the foot bed was tempting - but Ant's feet were never presentable enough to be shown in public. She bought a pair of light-blue plimsolls instead and is wearing them now with white socks. She notices Bex's brief, but appreciative glance as he greets her. She half expects a peck on the cheek, but he turns away before she can see his embarrassment.

'Pleased you could make it,' he grins. 'Dragging you away from the company of your beloved zoo – not sure whether my company will be an improvement on them,' he chuckles. She feigns disapproval at his ill-judged jibe and doesn't reply.

'Is Felix safely installed?' he enquires.

She nods: 'He came just before I left.'

'Good man!' Bex looks amused; and is that a little whistle she hears?

'Tell me again,' she asks, matter-of-factly, unwilling to enter into banter, 'what are the new developments?'

He considers her question, quite serious now: 'A woman called Susan Thomas has rung Taunton Police Station to say that she has some information which might help in the case of the murdered French girl.'

'...a woman from Dufton? That's a fair way away from our crime scene,' Ant ponders. 'Was she on holiday on Exmoor?'

'No idea. We just have to ask her. I offered to pay for a trip to London or Taunton, but she is working and doesn't want to take time off; and, of course, she couldn't very well say anything of importance over the telephone.'

'...that's understandable,' Ant agrees. 'Let's hope it's worth the trip.'

Bex sighs: 'Most people think that what they have to say is important. The worst thing we can do is to ignore them, so that they bottle it up and never tell a soul.'

'Quite, 'Ant feels the same, 'I much rather have people talking who leave it to us to decide whether, what they have witnessed, is important or not.'

Bex nods.

'Where the hell is Dufton? Never heard of it,' Ant tries to find it in the AA Atlas on the Cumbria page.

'I switched the SatNav off,' Bex grins; 'I can't bear you arguing with it.'

'Satnav is only for people who can't read a map! Aha,' a cry of triumph, 'here we are; I found it: an Area of Outstanding Natural Beauty, it says here.' Bex drives stoically along the M5 leading to the M6. Ant seems bothered by something: 'Why would someone come on holiday all the way to Exmoor, if she lives next the Pennine Way?'

'Maybe to escape tourists,' Bex guesses.

'Very drôle...Or work or visiting friends or family?' Ant counts the possibilities on her fingers.

They stop to have a coffee at a service station.

'Why can't they make decent coffee like everywhere else?' Ant grumbles as they return to the car, 'why does it always have to taste like mud?' Bex isn't fussy as long as it quenches his thirst and gives him a boost. He looks over to his passenger. He has just started up the engine, when he catches her propping her feet up against the dashboard. 'Sorry, bit of back ache from doing the pigs in a hurry,' she mumbles and sits up hastily.

'You are not exactly a bundle of fun,' he remarks.

She is embarrassed: 'Sorry,' she says again, 'I just hate long drives.'

'You don't like flying either,' he points out. You have become a real country bumpkin...pigs, cat, meadows, muddy hills,' he is enjoying teasing her. He hopes it will make her snap out of her sombre mood.

'I travel, if I have to,' she defends herself and then immerses herself into the silent study of the case file copies she has brought along, just to refresh her memory.

When they finally turn off the motorway and begin a much slower journey along B-roads, Ant soon seems invigorated: 'This is pretty!' she exclaims and looks out of the window at the lush Cumbrian landscape. After a while, Ant turns to her driver: 'You wouldn't think, anything horrible could happen here, would you?'

'I don't think psychopaths choose their home turf for the beauty of the landscape,' Bex comments drily.

Ant looks at him to check whether he is serious or teasing again: it is a little bit of both. She nudges his arm playfully with her elbow.

'What have I said,' he grimaces as if in pain.

'Kathleen is back,' she starts off a fresh topic.

'How is she?' Bex doesn't seem particularly interested.

'She went to Ireland to reconnect wither family,' Ant reports and watches his face.

He doesn't reply.

Ant can't help herself and says: 'You know, at one time I thought Kathleen and you might hit it off.'

Bex looks at her in a strange way. When she doesn't say anything further, he simply states: 'Kathleen is a very nice woman, but she is your friend…and even if I considered a dalliance, I would have it hundreds of miles from you.' He stops talking to concentrate on the road.

'Nothing to do with me anyway,' shemutters..

'If you say so,' Bex replies calmly. He can play hard to get, too.

When they finally drive into the tiny village of Dufton, they are ready to concentrate entirely on Susan Thomas's statement.

# CHAPTER THIRTY-ONE

They stop outside a small terraced house built of grey stone. As soon as they open the car door, a fierce wind tugs at Ant's ponytail and ruffles Bex's cautiously combed hair to hide his hearing aids. They quickly make their way across the pavement. Susan Thomas has obviously expected them and opens shortly after they knock.

'Susan Thomas?' Bex enquires. 'We have spoken yesterday. I am DI Benjamin Cox and this is my colleague Antonia Bell from the forensic science team. May we come in?'

'Of course,' says Susan Thomas with a welcoming smile. 'Sergeant Penhaligon from Taunton rang, too, to say that you were coming. She is mid- to end thirties, not more than five foot two, if that. With her bleached, short blond hair tucked behind dainty ears and chic clothes she doesn't look like a woman who has lived all her life in a remote, rural village. The shape of her face is long and delicate, her skin is almost translucent and her brown eyes sparkle with vibrancy; she has chubby hands and curves comparable to those of Dolly Parton. Ant notices immediately a tracheostomy scar revealed by the V neck of Miss Thomas's black pullover which reaches almost down to her thighs. The scar is pink, well healed, but prominent as if displayed as a trophy. Their host's black and white patterned leggings and black, flat shoes show off her voluptuous figure. She is definitely a city girl, Ant thinks making mental notes; As Miss Thomas turns to open the door wide, so they can all enter, Ant notices that their host has a pronounced limp, as if one leg is shorter than the other. They follow her along the narrow corridor – they can see stairs to the first floor – and into a door on the left which leads to a cosy, cottagey sitting room, dominated by a wide chimneybreast and an open fire grate beneath. Pictures of babies and family groupings are displayed on the mantelpiece in pretty frames.

'Are these yours?' Ant asks nodding towards the baby photographs.

'Not my own, but they are family.'

'Are you married?'

'No.'

Ant nods with sympathy:   'Any particular reason?'

'When I have told you my story, you will know why,' she says simply. There is sadness in her eyes. 'I am forgetting my duties; forgive me,' she changes the subject, 'would you like some refreshments? You had a long journey. Would you like tea, coffee, something stronger, a soft drink, something to eat?'

'No,' Ant declines courteously. 'That's very kind, but we are not intending to keep you for long. You rang Taunton Police Station, didn't you?'

'Please, at least take a seat,' Miss Thomas insists. They flop into the comfortable cushions of a two-seater sofa by the fireplace. Susan Thomas sits opposite them on a mirror image settee. She nods: 'Yes, I rang the day after the television appeal on the BBC. That poor mother…'

'I know; It's horrendous,' Ant acknowledges. 'Why did you ring?'

'What do you mean?' Susan looks baffled from one to the other. 'Didn't Sergeant Penhaligon tell you?'

'What was it you wanted to tell us,' Bex takes over quickly, ignoring her question.

'I did say over the telephone that I have no idea whether this is relevant to your case or not, but when the mother and the policeman had told the background to the French girl's story, and how she was found, it triggered flashbacks; it reminded me of somebody I once knew.'

Now it's Ant's and Bex's turn to look baffled: 'What precisely was it that reminded you of the person you knew?'

'The brutality...'she stutters and stops, overcome by the memory, 'the viciousness... the cruelty towards a woman who can't escape,' and suddenly, Susan Thomas bursts into tears. Ant and Bex exchange a look; so far it sounds like thousands of other cases of domestic abuse. Susan Thomas takes a tissue from the box on the coffee table between them and wipes her tears.

'Did you experience the same at the hand of that person?' Ant asks as gently as she can and waits till the violent sobs abate.

'Yes,' Susan Thomas whispers, 'it happened to me.'

'I am so sorry, Miss Thomas! When was that?'

'Please, call me Susan,' she whispers through her tears as if reaching out to friends.

They reciprocate giving their names.

'That person, you were talking about, was that a man. You were close to, Susan?' Bex carries on probing.

'Yes, it was a man; a man I met, fell in love with and hoped to marry some day until I realised that he was a pervert.'

'What makes you say that?' Bex and Ant hold their breath, aghast at what they are hearing. It is a bombshell they hadn't expected – hoped for, maybe, but not expected.

'Let's start at the beginning. Susan, please tell us, how you met him; how your relationship developed'; what it was like; and how it ended.'

Ant and Bex know that it is a tall order to ask somebody to remember one of the worst times in her life.

'I hardly dare to tell you. You will think I am an idiot,' Susan snuggles into the cushions of her settee, almost curling up in defence.

'We wouldn't dream of it, Susan. We can well imagine what you have gone through, and it is very brave of you to be prepared to tell us about it!' Ant desperately tries to reassure her. 'I think we could all do with a cup of tea now, Susan. I'll make it, if you don't mind.'

Susan shakes her head and points to a wooden stable door which Ant assumes, leads to the kitchen. She gets up and disappears.

Bex thinks it best, to just give Susan some time to calm down and reflect before making her statement. He leafs without purpose through Ant's case file.

'…milk and sugar?' Ant's head pops round the kitchen door.

'Milk,' says Susan without focusing on the questioner.

A couple of minutes later, Ant reappears with three mugs of steaming tea, two with milk and hers black without sugar; she couldn't find any.

They take their first sips, and lean back. After a second sip Ant continues with the interview: 'Susan, I suspect that what happened to you is what we call *gaslighting*: a man comes into your life and is initially very loving and supportive, very caring and very protective, but ever so  slowly, he turns down your oxygen - like one would turn the knob to low on an old-fashioned gas lamp - so that eventually, you can't breathe; you feel stifled; and then one day you wake up and think, how did it come to this? How did I lose my freedom, my independence, my own decision making, my self-confidence, even my self-esteem? Every thought you have is controlled by that somebody; but you are the one who feels guilty, unable to protest because you have been told that he loves you as nobody else will; that it's all for your own good, that you need to comply because he knows best…' Ant looks straight into Susan's face: 'Rings a bell?' Susan is choking with tears and can only nod. The pain of her past flows out of her.

Ant is passionate about this. It is one of her hobby-horse topics; something she has met so often during her career – one person bullying another until they totally surrender.

'Very few women,' she continues, 'manage to extricate themselves from abusive relationships, and some women never get out, living in a straight-jacket all their lives, or they end up taking their own lives.' Ant, Bex and Susan Thomas sit in silence, as if honouring those poor souls. Ant has one more thing to say on the topic and hopes it helps to restore her host's self-worth: 'You have done enormously well under the circumstances, Susan. You can be so proud of yourself! Maybe this statement will give you the closure you crave.'

Bex looks at Ant in admiration. It would have sounded not half as convincing had this come from a man. Ant knows her stuff, and she knows what people need to hear. He has always envied her empathy and passion.

'Your story is very important to us,' Ant adds, 'and we are grateful that you called us, Susan. What I mean is that we know from experience what you went through, and we feel with you. You can trust us; we'll understand whatever you say.' She smiles at Susan in the hope that she does. The young woman sits bolt-upright on the settee, ready to tell her story:

# CHAPTER THIRTY-TWO

'I met Mike when he delivered a parcel – about three years ago'

'Was he a postman?' Ant asks, looking up from making notes.

'He worked usually in the Royal Mail sorting office, but sometimes he was asked to help out delivering parcels. He was funny and cheerful.'

'Did he live in Dufton as well?'

'Oh no, all that happened when I still lived in Leeds. I worked in a bank, and I also attended evening classes in accountancy. I was so busy that I hardly ever went shopping. I shopped on-line a lot. Mike made sure that I received my internet orders when I was at home, sort of late afternoons or early evenings or on Saturdays; it's such a fuss otherwise. He used to say; undelivered parcels often end up with neighbours or are left somewhere outside and get stolen or soaked; and if nobody takes it in, the item has to be returned to the depot and the recipient has to come and collect it.'

'So you were very grateful,' Bex reinforces the point, 'for your preferential treatment, to have your personal delivery man, were you, Susan' It's more of a conclusion than a question. She nods vigorously.

'You obviously kept in touch with him after your first meeting,' Bex states.

'Yes. He worked shifts, but he kept coming round when he wasn't working.'

'Did you mind?' Ant asks.

'No. It was nice to have somebody around. All my family live down south; he was company.'

'Did he move in with you?'

'Yes, although he said he had a house on the other side of Leeds. He had to return to it sometimes to do repairs and check everything was okay.'

'Did he have regular work at the post office depot?' Bex asks, poised to write down Susan's answers.

'I think so, but there were weeks when he said, work had dried up.'

Ant and Bex look at each other. At the Royal Mail's Parcel Force?' It sounds unlikely.

'And you worked during your bank's opening hours?'

'Pretty much so, until Mike insisted that I work part-time. Some weeks later he suggested that I should give up my job altogether. He thought that they underpaid me and didn't treat me well; so I handed in my notice.'

Ant looks up sharply: 'That is what I meant earlier, Susan. Ever so slowly, you became his prisoner.'

Susan stares at her knees in recognition and remains silent. It probably dawns on her that this had been far from being a healthy, loving relationship, Ant suspects.

'When did you have an inkling this was not normal?' Ant probes.

'I was so happy at first that I was blind to everything else. If he wanted to be the breadwinner, the head of the household or the man in the house or whatever it was he wanted, it was fine by me. To me it was just how relationships worked. He was so caring, did a lot of things for me like repairing taps, bleeding the central heating, fitting new locks; that sort of thing.'

'Did you tell your family about him?'

'They knew I was in a relationship. At first, I would have liked to show him off to my parents, but Mike always had an excuse: an extra shift, too far away for a weekend visit, or he preferred a cosy weekend in. Deep down I knew they wouldn't like him anyway. Later on, I didn't want to worry them; luckily they never saw the bruises, otherwise they would have stepped in.' Susan pauses, looking distressed and pleadingly at Ant to try and understand – why she didn't just end the relationship, leave him, chuck him out or run away. Why had she been so stupid? Susan answers the questions herself, her face red with shame and embarrassment: 'I didn't want to lose my boyfriend.'

'Absolutely, that his trick: he made you believe that you can't live without him, Ant reassures.

'Sorry having to ask this, but what was your sex-life like?' Ant asks as gently as she can.

Susan Thomas blushes and clears her voice elaborately before she can answers, and it is not clear whether what they hear are gulps for air between the words or sobs: 'We became intimate too quickly for my liking, but he loved sex and put pressure on me. I gave in; it's what people do who love each other, isn't it?'

Ant and Bex remain silent. From now on, their questions will get even harder to bear and to answer: 'Did you like his love-making?' Ant asks cautiously in the tone of a nursery nurse consoling a sobbing child: 'At first it was thrilling. I had never known anybody like him, with such a huge sexual appetite;' she hesitates between the words.

'For how long did it stay thrilling, Susan?' Bex continues with this line of questioning as sympathetically as he can.

'After three months he moved in; that's when it became unpleasant.'

'Did you tell him?'

'Yes,' she says under her breath.

'How did he react?'

'He was angry. He said that I obviously didn't love him as much as he loved me, and that nothing was taboo between people who loved each other.' The word 'love' is mentioned uncomfortably frequently.

'That old chestnut,' Ant mutters under her breath. 'And what was so unpleasant about his love-making?'

Susan's voice begins to falter and she croaks in a stutters: 'He… w-wanted me to d-do things, I had never d-d-done before.' She puts her palms over her face in shame.

'Susan,' Ant tries to console her, 'I know this is hard for you, but you need to tell us everything, so that we get the full picture. We need as much information, as many details as we can get to nail him. I am sorry, I have to ask again: what were the things, he did to you?'

'He totally dominated me; he humiliated and mocked me because I was inexperienced.' Her voice is barely audible.

'Were you a virgin before you met him?'

Susan nods almost imperceptibly: 'He said I was rubbish, and I would never make a good lover; I wouldn't even make a good prostitute. That stuck in my mind.' She pauses again until she picks up the courage to ask the burning question which must have plagued her ever since: 'Why did he suddenly turn on me like that?'

'He tried to undermine your self-confidence, to make you totally compliant and dependent on him,' Ant explains.

'What sort of things did he do or ask you to do, you didn't like?'

'At first it was only binding my hands behind my back, when we made love.' She shudders at the memory, 'it was terribly uncomfortable.'

'I would think it hurt!' Ant suggests.

'And you let him?' Bex enquires.

Susan can hardly belief her own words: 'Yes. He told me, not to be such a prude; I should trust him.' Her pale face has turned the colour of beetroot: '…and I wanted to please him.' Her hands fly up to her face again. 'I thought it was normal, making love in bed, on the floor, against a wall, on the coffee table… with my hands bound. And it hurt,' her sobs emanate from deep within and her face crumples.

'We all do strange things for love sometimes…' Ant mutters, not looking up.

'And did his brutality increase during your relationship?' Bex continues. Susan finds a tissue somewhere in the folds of her jumper's sleeve and blows her nose. They let her choose the time to continue.

'It got worse,' she speaks with a clearer voice and more composure: 'After a while, he wanted to shackle my feet as well… and then,' she croaks, 'he started beating me if I gave the slightest impression that I didn't like his advances; or if I didn't cook his steak to perfection; if I hadn't washed and ironed a shirt he wanted to wear. In the end, it felt more like rape than making love…' she can't continue and is instead groaning with inner pain. Ant goes over to Susan, sits next to her. She puts an arm around her shoulders until Susan's breathing calms and tears

226

stop. After a while, Susan asks to go to the bathroom to get more tissues.

When she comes back, she has splashed cold water on her face and looks a little more composed.

'Can you continue, Susan?' Ant asks warmly.

'Yes, I want to.'

'Good,' Bex re-starts the interview, 'what did you do when you were assaulted, Susan?'

'Nothing; I just covered up my bruises, and if anybody asked I lied about having bumped into the door or a cupboard; but I didn't meet many people anyway. I had given up my job and rarely went out.'

'Nobody from your bank every contacted or visited you?' Bex wants to know.

Susan shakes her head: 'No, they were cross with me, when I left all of a sudden.'

It is astonishing, how this Mike had managed to isolate his girlfriend so completely.

Here comes another difficult question, Bex thinks, and ploughs on: 'Would you know, Susan, whether Mike ever visited prostitutes? You mentioned he compared you at least on one occasion with them.'

She thinks about it, hesitates and finally says: 'I can't say for sure. He hated it if I asked where he had been. I only know that when the news was full of those prostitutes being assaulted in Leeds he was scathing, saying they were scum, and that they deserved it.'

'Did you agree?' Bex probed.

'Of course not,' Susan protests with all the passion she can muster. 'What a dreadful life they must have, and then one of their clients kills them. It doesn't bear thinking about!' Susan pauses and suddenly adds after a little while: '…but I kept it to myself.'

Ant takes over the questioning: 'When did your relationship end, Susan? What happened?'

'It all came to a head one day. I had befriended a neighbour, a lovely young woman. We met by chance when we both collected mail. She asked me questions; she wondered why she had never met me since she had moved in. She thought Mike lived there by himself. She gave me funny looks - mind you, the night before, he had slapped my face hard and that had left a red streak across my cheek. It made me think for the first time in months, that maybe this is not how other people live; how it should be; what a relationship should be like… I decided to confront him.'

'That was very brave!' Ant exclaims, dreading to hear what had followed.

Susan seems to be falling into a trance before finishing her story: 'I tried to be diplomatic, but I didn't get far. He was instantly beside himself with rage. He threw me on the bed, bound and gagged me and strapped me to the bedstead, my legs apart, and then he threw himself on top of me, pumping himself up and down, with all his weight. It hurt. By then I had managed to dislodge and spit out the handkerchief he had used as a gag. When I screamed at him to stop, he laughed and carried on, hurting me even more. I was sure he would kill me.' Susan pauses and takes a deep breath: 'I was so frightened! I panicked and in my desperation, I shouted 'help' and 'police', but he just laughed like a maniac and punched me in the face several times; I lost quite a lot of teeth. I know I shouldn't have provoked him, but I wanted to try to change things.' Susan looks pleadingly from Ant to Bex.

'You have done nothing wrong, Susan. You were enormously brave! None of this was your fault!' Ant puts her arm a little tighter around Susan's shoulder; she seems to lean in closer, too.

'His face changed,' Susan continues, 'I didn't recognise him anymore; he was like a wild animal in a feeding frenzy. He pushed the handkerchief back into my mouth and put his big hands around my throat and throttled me until I fell unconscious. And just that moment, my neighbour must have knocked on the door and wouldn't go away, threatening that she would call the Police. She had heard my screams.'

'What did he do?'

'I was told afterwards, that he bumped into her as he stormed out of the door, half-dressed, still trying to do up his fly. She thought I was dead when she found me.'

'Bound, gagged, raped and strangled,' Ant repeats, 'exactly like Sylvie.'

'Oh my God,' Susan groans into her palms.

'Did you see him ever again?'

'No never. Thank God! However, I was reminded of him, when a year later, two prostitutes were found strangled, exactly the way he did it to me; then two other women disappeared and another one was raped but survived.' She described her assailant exactly how I would have described Mike: a mountain of a man, almost six foot; huge hands; slightly balding; thin brown hair, stubbles; strange coloured eyes, pale brown with yellow flecks; and a weird weedy voice.'

'Did you tell to the police about your suspicion?'

229

'Oh yes, I did. I told them everything because men like him must be stopped!' Ant looks at her with a smile, amazed at the sudden transformation of this tiny woman: brimming with self-confidence, righteousness and compassion for others.

'Did they find him?'

'No. He simply vanished. They couldn't find the house he supposedly owned. He never told me where it was. I never heard from the police either. I rang a few times afterwards, but I was politely fobbed off. I think they were embarrassed that they still didn't have a clue where he was.'

'Didn't the post office depot, where he used to worked, know where he had gone?'

Susan shakes her head: 'It turned out that he was a casual worker there. They didn't know him very well.

'Very unsatisfactory,' Bex comments angrily and then promises, 'we'll do our very best to catch him this time… and, I am pleased to tell you,' he sees Ant's eyebrows going up in question and maybe a little disapproval, 'that we have a DNA profile.' He had to give that poor woman something to hold on to.

'Have you?' Susan looks up, hope glimmering in her red-rimmed eyes, and for the first time Ant observes how Susan sighs with relief and relaxes into the sofa cushions..

Ant sweeps her scruples aside, too, and nods, to reassure her.

'I have two more questions for you, Susan,' Bex breaks into the euphoria: 'Question one: what was Mike's surname?'

'Forester,' the word comes out of her mouth like a bolt. She stops and adds with bitterness: 'but now I don't even know whether that is true.'

'And my last question: can you remember with what he used to bind your hands and feet?'

230

'It was a kind of blue rope, cheap nylon type stuff – he said they were using it at the depot for parcels that had come apart.'

Ant and Bex exchange a glance. It seems quite possible that he's their man.

'One last thing, Susan,' Bex asks while he gets up from the far too comfortable sofa, closing the buttons on his jacket, 'would you happen to know the name and address of the woman who survived the attack?'

'Yes, I do,' she replies without hesitation, 'I visited her in hospital a couple of times, and when she was discharged and all the publicity frenzy had died down, we stayed in contact.'

'Did she know Mike?' Ant asks, hopeful.

'Yes, he was a punter. She recognised him from a police photo.' Then she remembers:

'I'd better go and look up her address and telephone number. You can ring her from here, if you want.'

'That's very kind Susan,' Ant and Bex say almost simultaneously.

She comes back a few minutes later, holding a piece of paper, torn off a writing pad.

'Here you are. Her name is Rose Powell. Give her my love, when you see her.'

'Shall do,' Ant reassures her, 'and thank you for your hospitality and frankness. We appreciate your cooperation immensely. You have been exemplary, such a great help!'

'Will you let me know…?' Susan can't finish the sentence, nor bear the thought of what the investigation might lead to.

'Of course, we shall keep you informed of developments,' Ant promises.

'If we catch the murderer and it turns out to be Mike, would you be prepared to give a witness statement and evidence in Court?'

Susan thinks for a moment, the horror of digging up the past etched into her face: 'I shall have to be even braver, won't I?' She looks pleadingly from Ant to Bex. They both nod and hope she comes to the right decision.

'It would help to keep him off the streets and to save many more women from experiences like yours.' Ant looks pleadingly at her.

'I have no choice, have I?' She doesn't seem to expect an answer from them.

'I promise!' Susan raises herself to her full height and proclaims with determination and a suddenly steely voice: 'I shall be a witness. We can't leave him on the loose to kill more women.'

Ant nods and smiles: 'Good decision. Thank you,' she says simply. '…and don't forget that from now on, you will be under our protection. You just give us a call… any time.' Ant knows how much it will cost the poor woman in emotional turmoil once they have caught Mike Forester and proceedings against him begin.

As they leave Susan Thomas's little cottage, the Cumbrian *Helm Wind* almost blows them back into the open door. They run to the car, falling into the seats, windswept, but happy that they have taken the trouble to come all this way.

# CHAPTER THIRTY-THREE

Finally things begin to move. They can replace suspicions with facts.

'Do you want me to drive to Leeds?' Ant offers.

'…if you want to?'

Ant has no idea why she asked. She doesn't really fancy driving to a town she has never been to, never mind had finding her way through it during rush hour. The longer she thinks about it, the more anxious she becomes. Is that another symptom of the bloody PTSD?

Yes, waking up to your house being on fire, may cause some distress, but months of nightmares, sleepwalking, compulsive security checks and now anxiety when faced with driving a car - what is happening to her? Does she really want to drive?

Bex has developed a way of grinning without moving his mouth; you would never know unless you noticed the skin at the outer corners of his eyes crinkle and a sparkle of amusement in his eyes. 'Don't worry, I'm happy to do it,' he says, turns the ignition key and roars off.


Ant makes a telephone call on Bex's mobile to Rose Powell from the car and is glad to find her at home. She is very eager to help with catching 'that bastard', as she puts it. At first the drive is scenic, passing the fringe of the Yorkshire Dales and Moors, but once they reach Leeds, the traffic is horrendous. They make the bulk of the journey in under an hour and a half, but lose the time saved negotiating the centre of town to get to the other side where their next witness lives. Ant puts a quick call through to her when they are close.

Rose Powell almost fills the front door frame. She is black, statuesque in a sort of gone-to- seed way. Her Afro hair surrounds her head like a frizzy halo and her strong, white teeth light up her face when she smiles in welcome.

'Rose Powell? I am Antonia Bell; and this is my colleague DI Cox.'

They shake hands, enter the Victorian terraced house and climb stairs to an attic flat. 'They call this a studio flat,' she says sardonically, shaking her head, 'so I pretend it is, but it is no better than a bedsit. Make yourselves comfortable wherever you like.'

There are two settees along a wall each, meeting in the corner, colourful bedspreads thrown over them to hide their age. There are also three collapsible chairs folded up, leaning against the wall next to one of the settees. The floorboards are bare except for a faux sheepskin rug in front of the settees. There is a little table at the end of each of the settees, big enough to put down a mug or a glass with a drink.

'I'll put the kettle on,' Rose Powell says in a mixture of accents, partly Jamaican and partly West Yorkshire. They nod gratefully.

Ant discovers the photograph of a tall, rather glamourous looking young woman on a portable television tucked into the corner next to the only window. 'Can I have a look at this,' Ant calls across the room, pointing in the direction of the picture.

'Help yourself,' Rose answers, stirring milk into the teas. Ant gets up, walks over and picks up the frame: 'A sister of yours?' she asks.

'No,' Rose replies with a curt chuckle of bitterness, 'that was me before the attack. I keep it to remind me what I am fighting for: to get back to being like this!'

'We are not keeping you from dinner, are we?' Ant asks politely, putting the frame back to where it was.

'No, no.,' and she laughs again, raucously, 'as you can see, I eat all day.' Indeed, she is built in 'the traditional way', as Mma Ramotswe, the Botswanan Detective, would describe her, and when she walks, she waddles a little like a matronly duck. She is dressed from head to toe in a long Kaftan-style gown which hides most of her, but, when Rose returns from the kitchenette at the other end of the room, carrying two mugs with tea, Ant cannot help noticing in the process that her host also limps and that her wrists are deformed and painfully rigid. Rose registers Ant's glance.

'This is a legacy of that monster. He broke my wrists, five ribs, my skull and my spirit, apart from raping me,' she says with passionate hostility.

Ant suddenly realises that Rose's left eye is unnaturally still; it doesn't move because it is made of glass.

'The doctors said that my recovery was a miracle, but here I am, grateful to be alive.' She sounds triumphant and down-hearted at the same time.

'Susan Thomas gave us your name and address,' Ant begins the official interview.

'Yes, so you said on the phone. She is a lovely person. She has helped me a lot not to lose hope.' Rose stares into the distance, lost in her own thoughts of past horrors.

'Before you were assaulted, where did you live and what did you do?'

Rose looks at them with incredulity: 'Hasn't Susan told you?'

'A little, but we need to hear it from you.'

'I lived all my life in Leeds, and I worked as a prostitute. It's a long story, but the short answer is, that as a teenager, I got into the wrong company, I got into drugs, didn't finish school and my mother chucked me out - so, not much choice for a career.' It is a brisk statement tinged with regret.

'So, when did you meet your assailant?' Bex continues probing.

'It was one evening, about eighteen months ago. He seemed charming, so I went with him in his car, and no sooner had he found a deserted, as he called it, beauty spot outside town, he turned on me and... do I have to go on with the details,' she asks, suddenly tearful.' I scratched and bit him to defend myself.'

'No. Don't worry. We can look those up in your case file at Leeds Police Station.'

'Oh good!' she sighs with relief and adds: They found his DNA under my fingernails, because I scratched him when he first attacked me.'

'That's excellent news,' Ant smiles at her witness.

Ant and Bex look at each other; Bex nods in agreement: 'we can let you into a secret: we have a DNA to compare it to.' Ant puts her forefinger over both her lips and Rose responds with a nod and a delighted grin.

'How would you describe your attacker?' Ant takes over.

'...tall, strange, weedy voice, thinning brown hair, a bald spot on the crown of his head. Huge hands! I remember his hands; I still have nightmares about them.'

'Any other distinguishing features you remember?'

'Yes, there was one, but my friend Susan Thomas can't remember it. I noticed it when he pushed his trousers down to rape me,' she stops.

'What was it?' Ant and Bex ask in unison.

'He had the Superman logo tattooed just above his penis; very distinctive in red, yellow and black.' '

Ant feels a wave of hysterical laughter coming on– bloody great bloke with a tattoo of his hero on his Willy - but she just about manages to remain stiffly professional. 'He might have got that done after he had left Susan.'

'Oh yes,' Rose hadn't thought of that.

'What are you doing now, Rose; how do you manage?'

'I am recuperating and catching up on my education, and I hope to work with wayward teenagers; to show them, how not to waste their youth as I did.'

'Will you be prepared to come to Court, if we find him?'

'You bet I will be there!' She looks from one to the other, hesitating to come out with a question which has burnt on her lips since the interview started: 'Why are you looking for our attacker now? We both thought, the local police had given up on our cases.'

Rose has obviously not read about the murder of the French girl.

'It begins to look as if we are hunting a serial killer. We are investigating the disappearance and murder of a 15 year old French exchange student; and her case led us to you and Miss Thomas.'

'Here in Leeds? I didn't hear anything.'

'No, down in the West Country; on Exmoor.'

'…that poor girl! What a tragedy for the family!'

'Yes, we intend to do everything to stop him this time, whoever he is.'

'Did the DNA reveal who he is,' Rose enquiries.

'No,' Bex replies, 'they couldn't find the owner of the DNA profile on the Police data base.'

'Do you think it could be Susan's bloke?' Rose has put two and two together.

'We really won't know until we find him.'

'Good luck then, and let me know when things are happening.'

Of course, they will keep in touch - they promise and thank her for her help.

'Good luck for your studies!' Ant shouts back to Rose and gives a little wave, as they walk to the car. Rose's beautiful, white teeth sparkle through the dusk.

# CHAPTER THIRTY-FOUR

They pop in at Leeds Police Station, but when they explain that they would like to speak to any of the Investigating Officers in the Thomas/Forester case, and, if possible, also in the cases of Rose Powell and the two murdered prostitutes, they draw a blank. To their relief, they come away at least with the names of Investigating Officers in each case and contact numbers; in turn, they leave their request for copies of all case files.

'E-mail attachments will do,' says Ant briskly, writing her e-mail address and telephone number on a page in her notebook and tears it out; 'As soon as possible!' she urges the duty officer at reception: 'The same perpetrator might have struck in our area.' They hope, the solemn nod means that he will give the request priority.

'Are you working from home?' he wants to know.

'Why?'

'Files are only sent to police departments.'

'You have seen our ID,' Ant protests.

'Still…We would prefer…'

Ant has already started to write down Sergeant Penhaligon's contact details at Taunton on a new page in her notebook and rips it out, too.

'Here you are,' she obliges with a strong dose of sarcasm.

Bex leaves his own contact details for good measure.

'Do send the files to all three of us,' he requests with well-rehearsed authority and grins when the young police officer's eyes widen, realising that he has just tripled his superior's workload.

'I shall see to it.' He confirms hastily and makes a move to come from behind his reception desk. Ant and Bex take the opportunity to thank him and leave.

It is late and Ant and Bex are getting hungry. All these cups of tea are not nourishing. They stop at a pretty pub on the outskirts of Leeds. It offers Bed & Breakfast as, too.

'Shall we stay?' Bex asks looking hesitantly at Ant. The hopeful raising of his eyebrows puts Ant off. Better not.

'No, traffic will be so much better at night than in the morning,' Ant points out.

Bex agree lamely. 'Right, in that case, I am going to have a big steak, lots of chips and a pint of beer.'

Ant laughs: 'You glutton! I fancy a Lasagne and salad.'

'How virtuous,' he pulls her leg which is answered with an ugly grimace.

When they have satisfied the worst of their hunger pangs, Bex has another sip of his beer and suggests: 'We might as well have a recap before we hit the road.'

'All right,' Ant puts fork and knife neatly side by side onto her empty plate. 'That was quite good,' she states and sits back in her chair. 'So what have we learnt?'

Bex launches into their list of things to follow up: 'We have to stay in contact with Leeds police about that string of attacks on prostitutes over the past three years; we must read the case files when they arrive; and we have to compare whether the DNA results from underneath Rose's finger nails are the same as the ones from Sylvie's grave when he urinated on it.'

'It might not be the same man's at all,' she warns, although she fervently hopes she is wrong. 'We also have to find out, whether anybody else has mentioned the Superman Logo on his nether regions,' Ant grins from one ear to the other.

'What a plonker,' Bex concludes and puts the last chip from his plate into his mouth.

'I don't think I'll have a dessert,' Ant mutters, folds her napkin and puts it on the table.

'Whatever the outcome,' Bex agrees, 'this Mike Forester seems to be a nasty piece of work, and should be stopped anyway whether he is our man or not.'

'Definitely,' Ant agrees with conviction, shutting her notebook with a thud.

'Next, we must organise a meeting with Sergeant Penhaligon and his team.' It's more of a statement than a mere suggestion.

'I'll ring him now, and make an appointment for tomorrow afternoon?' Ant picks up swiftly on the idea.

'He has probably gone home; it's late,' Bex reminds her. 'Let's hit the road.'

'I have got his mobile number.' Ant is already dialling.

Sergeant Penhaligon doesn't take the call. Ant texts a message from Bex's mobile: 'Big progress. We'll pop in at Taunton tomorrow afternoon.'

'I still like catching criminals,' Ant says on their way to the car, surprised by her own admission.

'So I have noticed,' Bex chuckles; he admires her stamina and enthusiasm for the job.

As they click themselves into the seatbelts, Bex has one last point to make: 'Only this time, we have to find the proverbial needle in the hay stack.'

'By the way,' he adds as he drives out into the night, 'have you rung the psychiatrist?' he asks with all the delicacy he can muster. He is too tired to have a row.

Ant frowns: 'Now don't spoil the evening!'

Bex shrugs his shoulders. Anyway, she seems happier than she has been in a long time.


They arrive back at Ant's Exmoor farm in the early hours of the morning and go straight to bed. By late morning, Bex notices two things: Ant has not woken him up while they were both, in separate rooms, catching up on sleep: no sleep-walking or screaming the house down; and secondly, she is cheerful, whistling while rinsing the breakfast dishes.

'Has Felix left already?'

'Yes, he has to make it up to his father. Coming to me is a holiday for him.'

They find that Leeds Police Station has already sent the case files, and the police officers in charge have made contact and left messages. It was thoughtful of them to copy everyone in at the same time.

'They sound keen and rather relieved that somebody else is looking at those seemingly hopeless cases,' she remarks, and Bex recalls: 'We both know how frustrating it is to be so close and not being able to close a case.'

'Let's have a quick look at the files, give Leeds a ring to say *thank you,* and then we better make tracks to Taunton.'

Sergeant Penhaligon has obviously put aside his reservations about working with two outsiders, and comes, hand outstretched to greet them: 'I am really grateful that you have taken the trouble to find new links. The three of them retreat to his office after telling reception staff that they will be unavailable for some time.

Ant and Bex fill him in on their recent journey and their progress. He had received copies of the Leeds files, but he hasn't had time yet to glance at them. 'It's one thing we need to establish urgently: are the Leeds and our DNA samples from the same person?'

'I have sent the Leeds results to the forensic team for comparison as soon as I got in,' Sergeant Penhaligon assures them. 'They promised I would have a call tomorrow morning.'

Ant and Bex look at each other, then at Sergeant Penhaligon in astonishment: 'Amazing, how quick they can be when it matters,' Ant comments drily. Still, the hours of waiting will test their patience.

# CHAPTER THIRTY-FIVE

Ant has just come in from feeding the animals, when the telephone rings. As she is still holding the huge tin plate and a couple of bowls, Bex picks up the receiver.

'Bingo!' Sergeant Penhaligon's voice booms over the phone as if his favourite football team had won the World Cup. 'Same bloke's DNA! So now we know for sure that we are looking for Mike Forester.'

'Yes,' Bex replies with irony, 'all we need to do is find him!'

'Easier said than done,' Penhaligon admits. 'Have you got any idea where to start?'

'Yes. We know he has or had a house in Leeds. I think we start with that. Maybe we find some clues where he might have gone, maybe to relatives or friends.'

'Friends – is he likely to have any?' Ant is unconvinced. 'Who wants to be friends with someone like him, weird and violent?'

'He does seem to find girlfriends...' Bex interjects.

'Yeah,' Ant barges in contemptuously spitting out the words, 'the vulnerable and gullible type.'.'

'Shall I send a few people up to Leeds?' Sergeant Penhaligon wonders aloud. 'Not enough, I know, but a small contribution.'

'That would be helpful, Bill. You don't mind me calling you by your first name, do you?'

'Of course not; call me Bill,' the Sergeant feels flattered to be on first name turns with a famed retired Metropolitan DI, apart

244

from the fact that both of them are a great asset to his thus far stagnating investigation.

Bex reciprocates: 'We don't answer to our proper names either; everybody calls us Ant and Bex; feel free to do so, too,' and then he begins to explain their plan:' 'Bill, we must liaise with the police in Leeds, get a warrant and search Foresters house from top to bottom. With some luck, Forester is there, and if not, we might get an indication of where he has gone.'

'That means I don't have to delegate more than a couple of officers?' Bill sounds relieved. 'We are a bit short-staffed,' he adds apologetically, 'holiday season and thousands of tourists coming down soon.'

'Bill, we understand. Now that we've got our teeth into it, we better carry on ourselves. Of course, we'll keep you informed at all times.' Bex is pleased that they will have full reins of the investigation – anything else would simply complicate matters.

'You had an early start,' Bex remarks turning to Ant who is waiting with baited breath.

He gives Ant a quick update on the details of his arrangements with the Sergeant and leaves the best to last: 'as Bill Penhaligon called it: Bingo – the DNA matches.'

'Congratulations! No rest for the wicked then,' she suspects. 'Leeds again, is it?'

'Well, hold on,' Bex stops her from the wrong conclusion: 'he offered to send a small team.'

'Do we need them?' Ant says without thinking. Bex grins: uncanny how we think alike; they rather rely just on themselves

'Not really. And the Leeds team will just have to do it our way.'

'Absolutely,' Ant confirms.

Ant puts the enormous pig dish into the sink, wipes her hands on her jeans, grabs both of Bex's hands and whirls him around the kitchen.

'Stop it!' he shouts with a twinkle in his eye. 'I am getting too old for your antics!'

Ant throws herself onto a chair, laughing. 'We better go up there as soon as possible to find this house.'

They are both relieved that things are moving forward. And, of course, they are excited to get closer to doing what they believe in: to do justice to the victims and their families.

'We first have to find his address,' Bex points out.

'That's easy,' Ant says lightly. 'I would have thought we should be able to find an address via the last census or the Land Registry or on the personnel list of employees of the local Post Office depot where he has worked at least for some time.'

'You should also ring Susan Thomas and Rose Powell. They or their solicitors might have kept some of the relevant cases files which were submitted to the Court, mentioning Mr Forester's address.'

'Did Susan ever take him to court?'

'No idea. If not, she might have collected newspaper articles of the subsequent murders, which could mention her ex-boyfriend's whereabouts. One of the reporters might remember something.'

'Good thinking. So, plenty for you to get on with before we make our way to Leeds,' Ant can hear one of Bex's heartfelt sighs: 'It will keep you out of mischief. I am afraid I'll have to be a farmer all day in preparation for another absence. I need to organise feed and straw and various other things like food for ourselves.

'Housewifely things,' he mumbles with a grimace. 'Exactly; somebody has to…' she says pointedly, grabs the car keys and disappears again.

By the evening, Bex has pulled out all the stops and has found out the address of Mike Forester. 'Blimey,' he groans, 'I went all round the county, but eventually, Rose looked through her stuff and found her solicitor's papers, and there it was – the defendant's residential address, and, even better, Leeds Post Office depot confirmed it.'

'Good work!' Ant is generous with her praise. 'I'm surprised they gave you the information over the phone.'

'I had to get Penhaligon to ring round, too, but everybody was cagey with him. Zac…'

'You spoke to Zac?' Ant interrupts.

'Yeah,' Bex chuckles, 'he was a great help: he threatened the Post Office branch manager with a visit and thorough inspection of his premises by the CID; that worked.' Nothing seems to deter Bex tonight from feeling smug.

'You can prepare dinner then, Hero, while I feed the Girls,' she points at an overflowing shopping bag. 'Is pizza okay?' He doesn't answer, still in thoughts about today's achievement.

'And a bit of salad and tomatoes,' she insists.

'What?' he says absent-mindedly.

'Pizza and salad for dinner,' she repeats firmly, 'you are in charge!' She grabs the pigs' paraphernalia from the sink.

He finally concentrates on what she says and nods: 'Fine by me.'

'You do it!' she repeats, just in case he had missed that bit. Before he can protest, she is out of the house, shutting the door with a loud bang.

'So what is his address then?' Ant asks munching on a slightly over-baked, crunchy pizza Margherita.

'It's a terraced house in Leeds.'

'I mean, what's the address?'

He grins with satisfaction: '23, Roman Gardens.'

'Off we go then! Tomorrow morning?'

He nods eagerly.

'You organise the warrant to search the premises and the garden if there is one, and I'll ring Rose Powell to let her know that we are coming. Maybe she knows where to find decent accommodation near Forester's house.' Bex looks doubtful. Does Ant really want to sleep near a murderer's house?

'Penhaligon rang,' Bex changes the topic. 'He won't be there himself, but he confirmed that his team will be.' Bex mutters uncomfortably.

'I thought, he was short-staffed,' Ant scoffs.

'So did I,' Bex replies and shrugs his shoulders. The Sergeant obviously doesn't want to be accused of slacking.

'Okay,' Ant gives the minor change short shrift: 'They'll just have to follow our orders.'

Bex hesitates: ' There was something else, Bill mentioned: Kathleen reported to him that she had a word with the Dulverton Post Office Master, and he confirmed that a couple of weeks before Sylvie disappeared, someone called Mike Forester had asked the Dulverton Post Office Master  whether they had a vacancy. He said he had past experience at the Le The Manager advised him to apply formally to the main PO Recruiting Office in Exeter. He seemed all right with that.'

'Most murderers have an obliging side if they want something,' Ant points out sarcastically and prepares to have an early night.


They set off early on the following day, knowing that it would take them once more the best part of four and a half hours to reach their destination. They head for the M5 leading to the M6 junction, only stopping once for a cup of tea from the flask Ant has brought along; they carry on to Manchester and only when they are near the city, do they stop for lunch in the knowledge that it will only be another hour's drive to Leeds.

'Do we know where Roman Gardens are?' Bex enquires.

'Once we are on the A 6720, you need to slow down because we turn off at the Roundhay golf course.'

An hour later she shouts: 'Left!' and he swerves into Park Lane. From there it is a right hand turn and a little further on left, right and left again. It is an area of long roads lined by nineteen-thirties, two-storey houses, interspersed with Victorian terraces.

'Not a bad area,' Bex sums it up.

'Interesting, isn't it,' Ant notes, 'the front gardens of the 1930's houses are well-kept, whilst most of the ones on the other side are untidy and overgrown. I am curious what Mr Forester's house looks like.'

Number twenty-three belongs to the cared-for side of the road with a grassed-over front garden and a drive leading to a fairly new extension which includes a garage and a first floor extension above it.

'…a good place to be anonymous,' Bex remarks and points at the green space it borders onto. There is even a little wood along the far distant edge. A great place to hide.'

Ant rings Rose to say that they have arrived and are beginning work. They arrange that they would take her out for dinner, leaving her to choose. Rose would come to Roman Gardens at the end of the day to pick them up and let them know the address where they would sleep.

The next call is to the police headquarters who promised to assist in getting entrance. There are also two SOCOs (she still can't get her head around the new title, CSI) who will assist and answer to Ant. The three officers from Taunton phone through that they are stuck on the motorway, but hope to be there as soon as they can.

It's time for the assembled team to get down to work. Instead of waiting around and kicking their heels. Bex and Ant decide to go ahead and approach the house -maybe someone does live there, although the drawn curtains indicate that it might be deserted. They knock on the simple, white door of number 23 Roman Gardens and wait. Nothing happens. They knock again and then a third time.

'I could open it,' Bex suggests.

'Better wait,' Ant says quietly. 'Let's do things properly. We want to nail him this time.'

Bex nods and begins to whistle just as a police car draws up and spills out a man and a woman in police uniform and two young ladies clasping their still wrapped white forensic suits and a bulging utensils' bag. They introduce themselves to each other – Karen Walliams, Pat O'Connor, Sergeant Jim Brown and Constable Valerie Cusack; then they march together to the door. They ring the bell another three times and then the local police ram the door open.

# CHAPTER THIRTY-SIX

Flakes of white paint and wood splinters fall to the ground as the door shatters and Sergeant Brown reaches inside to open what is left of it.

'Police – we are coming in!' he shouts like an army commander, loud and intimidating. There is no answer. He tries again: 'Hello?' Nothing stirs. Everybody present listens attentively, standing still, staring into the dark corridor. 'We are coming in now,' Sergeant Brown threatens again. He doesn't wait and makes the first steps along the corridor, not expecting a reply. His female colleague, Valerie Cusack, follows him, while the CSIs including Ant pull on their protective white uniforms, covering them from head to toe in pristine white; when they have slipped the covers over their shoes, they enter, too. 'Walk behind each other! We only want one line of our footprints, preferably all on the same side!' Everyone nods and does as they are told. The beige linoleum floor in a faded pattern is sticky underfoot. They will have to find out later whether it is just grime and dust or something else. All the doors leading off to the left are closed. Ant opens the first with a gloved hand. It swings open wide with a loud, complaining creak as if it hasn't been used for a while. The long row of windows out to the street have streaks of dirt which block out some of the daylight. Ant turns on a dirty light switch, and a lonely bulb dangling from the ceiling springs into action. As they look up to the ceiling, they discover stains, most likely caused by a water-leak on the first floor. The room is sparsely furnished with an old television set on a low, cupboard of dark wood in the far corner by the windows; a table of non-descript plywood which looks so rickety that it might have come from a junk-shop; two plastic garden chairs in black; the floor is un-carpeted showing worn floorboards with gaps between them; the walls are blank, hung with spider webs rather than pictures; there is a brick chimney breast which sports inside the hollow an electric one-bar heater.

Ant registers her first impression and then orders the two women CSIs to take swaps from every inch of the room. They are looking for any sign of human presence – shoe sole prints, finger prints, spilled fluids or dried up remnants of them. The slightest trace could be useful. Ant urges them to be thorough.

'Pity there are only the two of you,' Ant remarks; 'could you do one room each? Just call me if you need help or discover something. I'll check the rest of the house first, and then come and help you.'

The figures in white nod and a pair of blue and another of brown eyes sparkle with excitement and eagerness.

That's how I used to feel going to a new job, she recalls. That's the kind of people she likes to have on her team. They leave Karen behind, who is already extracting tools of the trade from her bag.

'You do this one, Pat!' Ant points to the still closed door of the next room. There is something sticky on the handle when they open it. A thick cloud of dust, flies and stink engulf them. Luckily they wear face masks. Bex takes refuge behind a handkerchief from his trouser pocket.

'Holy cow,' Ant exclaims. 'I bet we find something unusual here. Good luck! I'll go through the upstairs rooms. Give me a shout if you need me.' She shuts the poor girl in so that they can investigate the ghastly scene without fear of contamination.

Bex and the police team are just coming back downstairs. They have inspected the upper floor in case somebody is hiding there.

'…anything?' Ant asks in passing. They shake their heads. 'We'll have a look at the garage now.' The three head outside.

Ant in her white unflattering outfit stomps up the stairs. The colleagues have left doors to the three bedrooms open, including the one over the garage. Obviously, they didn't encounter a cloud of flies and unsavoury smells. She doesn't expect a great result from up here, but one never knows. She begins her inch by inch search of the first room: floor, bed, wardrobe, looking carefully at walls, window sills, curtains. There is not much more to examine; it doesn't take long. When she has reassured herself that she hasn't overlooked anything in the empty looking wardrobe, under the bed and matrass and in the creases of the curtains, she moves to the next room, the biggest one of the bedrooms. It is strangely bare, nothing in it, no bed, no wardrobe, no bedside tables; it could have been a double bedroom once, but now it is just an empty, airless space with drearily rough, scaffolding type floorboards.

Ant moves on to where the landing turns off to the right. This must be the extension above the new garage. This room looks as if it has been refurbished recently. The double bed is fully equipped with a duvet in a nice cover which looks as if it has been chosen by a woman: white with big swirls of summer flowers. The pillow cases belong to the same set and the bedsheet is crispy white. The pine wardrobe is empty apart from eleven wire hangers and one wooden one; nothing is hanging from them; there is only a blue overall thrown carelessly into the left hand corner at the back. Great, Ant thinks but is disappointed because it seems freshly laundered and the pockets are empty. She will take it with her, in case the Lab microscopes can detect traces of something, which are at this moment invisible to the naked eye. Hold on! She stops. There is something at the bottom of one of those pockets; something coarse. Ant pulls it out carefully and whoops.

'What is it?' she hears Bex shout up from the landing. 'I know that whoop!'

'Just a bit of rope.'' she shouts back cheerfully.

'What colour?' he asks; she can hear the suspense in his voice.

'Yep, it's blue, the same cheap and nasty stuff from the Parcel Depot.'

'Bag it!' he shouts up excitedly.

'As if I wouldn't,' she shouts back grinning all over her face.

'How are the girls getting on?'

'Shall we have a break and a little conflab in the garden?' he suggests

'Good idea,' she agrees bags and labels her finds and carries them downstairs to add to a pile of evidence bags.

'Any luck in the dining room?' Ant asks Karen as she appears in the door. Karen shakes her head: 'A couple of finger prints on the remote control for the tele, but that's about it. Total waste of time!' she sounds disgruntled.

'With some luck, these fingerprints place our suspect in this room.' Ant consoles her.

Karen answers with a weak smile.

'Tell you what:' Ant suggests, 'could you possibly help Pat in the other room now? She has a nasty task.'

Karen still smiles, nods and heads for the second door. 'Put on your mask,' Ant warns her, before the young woman opens the door. 'Oh my God,' Ant can hear her exclaim as soon as she has slipped in. 'Shut it,' her colleague yells above the buzzing, muffled by her face mask and whatever else she has wrapped around her head,. A cloud of flies has escaped into the landing where Ant and Bex swat them with their bare hands, and Ant tries to catch some in a couple of vials. They might yield something interesting under the microscopes.

'What's going on in here?' Bex enquires. He, Sergeant Brown and Constable Cusack have inspected the garage and found nothing out of the ordinary: no car, a few shelves on the walls with little cans of oil and carwash products plus a few unsuspicious tools in a box. It still smells fresh as if it hasn't been used much since it was built.

'The girls will definitely find things in here,' Ant grins and opens the door to what she named 'the dining room.' 'Holy shit,' Bex gags as if he has already swallowed some of the insects; Jim and Valerie shake their heads in disgust.

'You two can locate the kitchen and check that out for anything unusual,' Ant directs them, no need for everybody to be traumatised.'

Ant fully clad in protective gear hands Bex a white face mask to strap over his mouth and nose: 'Come on, no time for a beauty contest!,' she pushes him in the ribs, 'we can't just let the girls deal with this filthy job.' Bex looks with incredulity at her as he makes a step into the room of horrors.

# CHAPTER THIRTY-SEVEN

As they open the door not more than an inch, the horrible stench of putrefaction hits everybody's nose even though they all wear face masks. As they open it a little wider, just to be able to slip into the room, they are confronted with a cloud of frenzied buzzing. All they can see through the moving haze is a blood-spattered table. Droplets are sticking to the surface, gelled, dried and hard, like a rash. Someone has tried to scrub off the worst of a blood bath, probably with bleach, but has only managed to dilute the bright red stains to dirty smears of a pink layer all over the table top. Strangely, there seem to be animal hairs of various colours and consistencies embedded in it, too. Ant and Bex notice with glee, that a hoop of blue nylon-type rope is leaning against the skirting board on the opposite wall to the door. The floor boards are bare and of the same low grade quality as in the other room, with the difference that here they are covered in stains of various colourings; Ant suspects a mixture of blood, faeces and bodily fluids, diluted and spread in an inept attempt to clean up. Pat points to an open table drawer and its contents: a heavy meat cleaver, two butcher's knives and a metal sharpening rod. Again, a lonely bulb hangs from the ceiling, spreading a tight circle of light on the revolting scene. 'Can you see in this light?' Ant asks and, without waiting for an answer, orders Bex to get extra lighting from the car.

'You have taken pictures, I presume,' Ant asks Pat, the Leeds CSI, in something like sign language. The poor girl can only nod. Nobody wants the smell of rotten flesh, congealed fat and blood, of excrements, bodily fluids and death in their nostrils or mouth; the masks, they wear, are no shield against the revolting odours at all. It could put you off eating for life, Ant ponders, and nods back to Pat, who is unenviably working on a particularly nasty bulge of mess

'The curtains were closed when I came in,' Pat says, 'probably to hide the state of the room, should anybody bother to look through the window from the back garden.'

'Did you....' Ant begins, but Pat has read her thoughts and confirms that she has taken swabs from the light switch before switching it on and from the curtains before opening them to let a little daylight in.

Back from the car, Bex plugs in the daylight lamp, and when the room is flooded with light he goes to the window and looks out. It's a strange sight: unkempt; sparse growth of grass; unpruned, wildly overgrown hedges along the wire fences. The neighbours would have to make an effort to peep over to witness anything - if they were interested at all.

'Kitchen's clear,' Sergeant Brown reports standing in the door frame, brushing away flies from his face, eyes and nose, 'empty cupboards, pristinely clean sink and cooker; the fridge smells funny, but it's empty; the whole kitchen smells of bleach and detergent'

'I think we can find enough in here,' Bex makes a sweeping circle with his arm around the room, from which the flies are now trying to escape through the open door..'

'All right,' Sergeant Brown has a suggestion: 'Shall I start knocking on doors in the neighbourhood? The Taunton lot have arrived. They could spread out and cover the whole road. They might need to stretch their legs after the long drive'

'That would be a great help, Jim. Take Valerie with you; a friendly woman's face might help to get people talking'

Isn't that sexist?' Jim grins. 'Come on then, Val. Let's interview the neighbours.' They can hear heavy footsteps approaching. Bex goes out into the corridor, welcomes the two officers from Taunton and explains the situation. 'I am parched,' one of them mutters. They have come a long way.

'You don't want me to brew you anything in this place,' Bex points towards the room where most of the activity takes place. 'I have some tea in the car; let's go and get the flask.' The two nod gratefully and introduce themselves: 'Constable Adam Pike,' says one and almost stands to attention; 'Constable Paul Baker,' says the thirsty one. Bex introduces the team members to each other, before taking them to the car for refreshments.

Bex strolls back to the house after the brief respite, checks on the kitchen, just to be sure, and finds it indeed spotless apart from a rickety backdoor which has seen better days. It is locked and for a moment Bex is tempted to ram it - it would probably splinter into pieces like the front door. He decides against it: this seems an easy lock to pick; he has the back door open within a minute. Bex steps out into the unloved garden and let's his eyes glide over it the hedges are not only tall but spread almost to the middle; a few patches of grass, light-starved, limp and yellow, keep the soil from turning into mud. Bex looks upwards; he can hardly see the neighbouring house on the left. On the other side, as he remembers from the map, there is a large green space, merging with a narrow strip of forest, which in turn borders onto another residential road. Bex walks along the obscured path. Suddenly he notices something odd: a straight thin line in the soil disappears under the lower branches of the hedge; he lifts them, and as his eyes follow the line; it meets another line; this one is shorter at a right angle, which in turn merges into another, leading his eyes back to his feet.

'Ant,' he shouts with sudden urgency. She opens the window from the inside and leans out with a broad grin: 'Lovely view. Are you enjoying the fresh air?'

'Hardly!' he growls. 'Have you got a minute?' she knows that tone; it means: come out immediately and have a look at this. She is by his side within seconds.

He lifts the hedge again: 'Does that remind you of something?' he scrutinises her reaction.

'A grave.' she states, 'lines made by a spade.'

'Pat, Karen,' she shouts into the open window: 'when you have finished in there, we need you out here, digging!'

Karen is out first explaining that Pat was just packing up, securing the swabs and samples and stashing them away safely without risking contamination. She won't be a minute, Boss.' Ant's heart leaps: it has been a long time since somebody has called her boss. Those two women are much younger than her, but she feels a great affinity with them. They work hard in a job that would not be everybody's cup of tea; and they display the same excitement, sense of duty and understanding of the importance of their work that she had felt at the start of her career.

By the time the four of them have gathered in the garden, Ant and Bex have lifted more branches of the hedge and have discovered more lines.

'It looks like a cemetery,' Pat mutters and Karen nods in agreement.

'We'll start digging this side,' they offer, 'let's get spades,' says Ant, 'I have two in the boot.'

'So do we,' says Pat, and follows Bex into the house.

'Wait,' shouts Ant, 'could one of you secure the entire site including the house to restrict access?'

'I'll do it,' Karen springs up from her crouching position and runs after the other two.

'The chaps have already done it,' they report when they return with four spades. 'Police tape all over the fences, gate and front door. Everything cordoned off,' they report with pride.

'Catch!' Ant shouts, and two little parcels fly through the air: two still wrapped forensic uniforms. Karen has caught both of them. Ant hears: 'Thanks, Ma'am,' and smiles about another promotion. 'Bag up the ones you wear,' she reminds them.

They return to the house, quickly change into their fresh uniforms inside the cordoned off front door, stuff the used garb into forensic bags, amd Karen takes it all to their car.

Back with Bex at the back of the house, they find him erecting tents across the width of the garden. They need to protect the site from the elements and possible neighbours hanging out of their windows. After all, some have been alerted by the door to door enquiries. There are six graves on the one side. When Bex lifts the hedges on the opposite side, he discovers two more. They look at each other, steeling their hearts and souls against all eventualities of what they might find. They are ready and Ant gives the commando: 'Let's dig!'

# CHAPTER THIRTY-EIGHT

'We could do with Sergeant Brown's muscle power,' Bex complains.

'What do you mean?' Ant is merciless, 'no concessions for anybody, not even the elderly!'

'Ouch,' Bex laughs it off.

He is showing his age, she thinks with more charity than she is willing to admit to. Pat and Karen drive their spades with so much more ease into the dusty rectangles they labelled number two and three, next to where Bex has made an effort. He has not got far with digging up rectangle number four right by the fence at the end of the garden and breathes a sighs of relief, when the police team returns from their door to door enquiries. He stands up and offers his spade to young Constable Pike. Constable Baker offers to give Ant a break, too.

'If Mike Forester dug these holes he might have left a spade behind,' Ant uses lateral thinking and sure enough she find another in the under-stairs cupboard.

'Keep showing your digging power!' Bex encourages them from time to time, but he only earns himself rolling eyes and ribbing: remarks about old chaps who are better at giving orders than digging.'

'Don't worry, he is over the hill,' Ant quips. Bex ignores them, but it doesn't make him feel any better. It's not easy to admit that you are past your best.

'Someone has to oversee you lot!' he counters, and suddenly, stung into action, he shouts: 'I'll show you,' takes off his jacket, grabs the spade out of Pat's hand and rams it into the ground. They can't look at each other, desperately trying not to laugh. Ant has no such qualms, holding her sides, laughing so much that soon everybody is leaning on a spade shaking helplessly with merriment. Bizarre, aren't we, Ant thinks, laughing while digging up graves; she sends an admiring glance to Bex, whose back is turned towards her: Admittedly, he has still got it, she thinks, this ability to get everybody back to work simply by setting an example. His face is set in stone, his jaws are clenched, but when he looks up for a split second, she gives him both thumbs up. He doesn't react and only wipes a bead of perspiration from his forehead with the back of one hand.

'What did the neighbours have to say?' Bex asks the team, when they are all taking a breather.

'Not much. Most of them were out, and we left our leaflet to contact us. A couple of older residents said that they had never seen Forester. Only a young stay-at-home mum had spoken to him once, when she was struggling with the buggy.'

'…and?'

'He seemed all right; quite friendly and helpful. She used the word *charming.*'

'Yes,' Bex nods, 'so did his girlfriend and see what happened to her.'

'So, you are sure it's him who abducted the French girl?' Pat asks.

'Ah, you know about our case?'

'Of course, it's all round the Police Stations in the country.'

'Let's say, I would be most surprised if it wasn't him,' says Bex with a clipped voice and tight lips, sounding as if he regretted having said that much.

'I'll keep it to myself for now,' she promises, seeing his uneasiness. 'Oh, and I forgot: an old man, who has lived across the road from no.23 all his life, knew Mr Forester's parents. Nice people; hardworking. Mike was an adopted child and disappeared before finishing school. They were quite heart-broken, he remembers.'

'Good work,' Bex praises her. 'Leaving school without qualifications, that fits his profile.' They all look at Bex in expectation, but he doesn't elaborate.

Ant sidles up to him: 'You better have a look at that,' Ant points towards the hole she has dug.

'Found anything?' Bex steels himself seeing Ant nod.

'A body?' he guesses.

'…of a dog,' she says simply.

'What?' Bex is hugely disappointed. 'We are digging up the graves of his eight pets?'

'Looks like it,' says Ant and claps him on the shoulder as a gesture of commiseration. He is irritated and shrugs her off.

'If all these are graves for his pets, he must have been really unlucky losing so many of them,' Ant can't help being sarcastic.

Bex has seen this face before: 'Do you have one of your hunches?' He looks at her with intense scrutiny.

'Might have,' she jokes feebly, 'let's see, what the others found.'

It's as expected: they find three more dog cadavers in various stages of decay. Ant has a closer look at all of them, but when she gets to number four and pulls a piece of string from under its neck, she alerts Bex: 'That's not a dog lead. Let's empty them all.' Ant takes charge of lifting everything out of the graves;

carefully storing each gave content into a separate body bag, so that no cross-contamination can occur. Bex picks up more bits of string pressed into the damp soil of each grave.

'Why would he need string to bury his dogs?' Ant asks, baffled.

'It's the same string we found on his human victims: cheap nylon-type and blue.'

Ant is covering her face with both palms to give herself space to think, muttering: 'Why would he do that?'

'Just think,' Bex takes up her thought, 'the suspect used it to shackle and kill his human victims; put that together with the table inside, covered in smears of blood and gore and a vast number of dead dogs with the same blue string around their necks. What does that tell you?'

Ant understands immediately and whispers with a look of horror: 'He practised on the dogs…'

'Exactly…I don't think they were pedigree dogs; so where did he get so many….?'

'…dog rescue centres. They are desperate to place dogs with families. He couldn't possibly afford to buy that many puppies from breeders on part-time postman's wages.'

'He approached probably different dog homes, not to raise suspicion; but aren't they supposed to check out the applicants before they place an animal?'

'They might not always get round to checking everybody; and even if they did, this is not a bad place for a dog: garden, green space right next to the house…and you know what his girlfriend said: he could be charming if he wanted to.' Bex's laugh is short and bitter.

'I am surprised the neighbours didn't complain about barking,' Ant says and after a short pause continues with her line of thinking: 'He probably kept them in the house; or beat them into silence.'

'Somebody would have heard them surely,' Bex argues; 'there is always somebody who can't sleep and hears noises.'

Ant thinks about this, wrinkles her forehead and concludes: 'The only other possibility is either that he killed them soon after he got them or he kept them sedated.'

'…with what?'

'…Phenobarbitone. It's used for epileptic or any other form of fits in animals. He would have needed a hell of a lot though; it needs to be prescribed by a vet and it's not cheap either.'

Ant has goose bumps. 'Poor creatures!' she says sadly, 'we'll have to see what the autopsies throws up.'

Bex can see that Ant is biting her lip, making a big effort not to burst out with her hatred for this cruel man, a torturer of animals and most likely humans, too. It is surprising really that neither Ant nor he have ever lost their temper with any of the misfits they confronted with their horrendous deeds during their long careers - even if they were ever close to losing their temper, their professionalism had kicked in every time they were tempted – and that was often enough.

They call the others over and tell the team what they suspect: that Mr Forester has probably practised murder on his dogs before setting out to kill young women.

They are understandably shocked, but remain composed, getting on with the task in hand; there are still another four graves to be dug: two on the side where they have dug already and two on the opposite side of the path.

'I'll do the last two,' Ant insists. She has noticed something that intrigues her.

'Are you sure?' Bex says warningly. He is obviously thinking what she is thinking. When she nods with a grim expression, he takes off his jacket again, rolls up his shirt sleeves, grabs one of the spades leaning against the shrubbery, and mutters: I'll do the last one.'

Jim and Karen finish their grave digging before Ant and Bex have excavated theirs.

'…anything different?' Ant shouts across.

'Not really; just a smaller dog or a cat in mine,' Karen shouts back.

'…same here,' reports Sergeant Brown, '…and you?'

'Nothing yet… not long to go, though.'

Ten minutes later, Ant stares down into the hole she has dug with one last, big effort. The police tent is blocking out most of the remaining daylight and only throws a dull, eerie shadow over the scene. There are barely visible outlines at the bottom - a totally different array of bones: not so much a heap as a stretched out skeleton of…: 'That's a human,' Ant exclaims. Everybody rushes over to her and bends over to stare into the hole. Pat puts an arm around the shaking Ant.

# CHAPTER THIRTY-NINE

'Same here,' Bex has finished digging, too; 'more human remains…' He is exhausted, mentally and physically, so Ant finishes his conclusion: 'I think we have found the two missing women,'

'The hunt is on,' Bex takes a deep breath and declares, clearing his throat from the bitterness that has accumulated in his mouth, 'only a matter of time until we catch him,'

Ant looks at him with some doubt. She has rarely seen him so emotional. Maybe he is thinking of his daughter who must be the age of the murdered women by now? It's every parent's worst nightmare. She puts her hand on his shoulder and, to drag him back to reality, points out the obvious: 'He could be anywhere in this country; he might even have gone abroad to Europe or further afield. He might have changed his name, his appearance…the possibilities are endless, Bex.'

'Don't let's be defeatist,' he snaps, 'we have made a good start and I won't rest until we have got him.' Of course, deep down, he knows she is right. At least, she has pulled him away from the brink of tears. She can bear it if he is grumpy, but not if he cries. She has never seen him cry. Neither of them likes to admit to weakness. For example, she hates the thought that he has seen her living with nightmares.

Bex knows that she has witnessed his moment of weakness and strides away from Ant's consoling arm on his shoulder; he needs to pull himself together: 'Let's retrieve what we can, pack up and leave the rest to the pathologist,' he says gruffly to the assembled team.

They nod or mumble their agreement and get busy. No one wants to spend longer at the gravesides of six dead dogs and two murdered women.

Rose Powell arrives just as everybody gets ready to close up the house of horrors. She can see in their demeanour that they had a trying day. She doesn't even need to ask whether they have found anything; she can guess looking at their haunted eyes, dragging feet and grim faces.

'Rose,' begins Ant, her voice trembling as if overtaken by a spasm of pain. 'I don't think, I could…', but she doesn't need to explain:

'Tell you what,' Rose volunteers, 'you don't look as if you fancy dinner. I understand. I have actually cooked a pot of sweet potato stew, but I can freeze it. I'll move to my friend for the night and you can sleep in my pad.'

'That's not necessary,' Ant responds immediately, a little too abruptly with the weariness of the day. Bex feels obliged to smooth it over:

'It's really kind of you, Rose. I think we would both prefer to drive home and sleep in our own beds.'

'But that's hours of driving!' Rose exclaims aghast, genuine concern mirrored in her eyes. Their haunted expressions stop her from trying again.

'I am so sorry, Rose, but we had such a harrowing day,' Ant, pleads for understanding.

'I can imagine,' she says softly, her voice full of compassion.

'Why don't you plan a little holiday sometime and come to my farm on Exmoor; when this horrible case is closed. It shouldn't take much longer now.'

'That would be nice,' Rose replies with a watery smile. They all know that it isn't likely that they will see each other again.

'Sorry,' Bex feels that they have disappointed their witness, turned host.

'Don't apologise. I am so relieved that you are pursuing the trail of that monster!' Her sigh is heartfelt. They stand for a minute, looking at each other like a group of good friends who are reluctant to part.

The Leeds and Taunton police officers and their crime scene investigators approach the little group, too tired for words. Bex quickly introduces Rose as a key witness in the case, shakes them all by the hands and thanks them for their massive contribution to solving several murders. Shadows of smiles indicate that they appreciate the praise. Then the teams split up, walk back to their cars and roar off.

'I'll keep in touch,' Ant turns to Rose, labouring to find something else to say;' I'll keep you informed. You have my telephone number, Rose. Ring me any time you want me – any time!' Ant hopes she sounds sincere in spite of her exhaustion. 'And if you ever need that holiday…'

Rose nods and a little smile flutters around her lips: 'Thank you.'

'I promise…,' Ant adds unnecessarily.

'I know,' Rose assures her and pulls the straps of her handbag firmly onto her shoulder, ready to leave and go back home without them: 'I let you go then,' she whispers and steps back, so Bex can get into the car. Ant walks over to the passenger door. Just as she has opened it, she hears Rose's timid question: 'Have you found them?'

Ant simply nods and slams the door shut.

As Bex starts the engine, they can hear through the half-open window: 'That could have been me!' They have driven off before they realise that they should really not have left her there on her own with her traumatic memories.

'Home, James,' Ant jokes weakly. 'And don't spare the horses,' he finishes the sentence for her. A couple of minutes later, he can hear a little whistle: Ant has already fallen asleep.


They reach Ant's farm just after midnight. Ant stumbles out, drowsy and feeling a little sick from all that time in the car and Bex's adventurous speed, but they are both glad that they have pressed on as the motorways had been remarkably clear of traffic.

Ant dials Rose's phone as soon as she gets in and leaves her telephone number again, just in case: 'Rose, don't hesitate to ring me when you need someone to talk to or a shoulder to cry on, she feels compelled to reinforce her sentiments, ' I'll always be here for you. I mean it! And I was serious about you coming down for a holiday; it's lovely down here!'

This is the Ant Bex knows and loves. Even when she is on her knees herself, she will still consider the feelings of others.

'Has Felix left?' Bex asks looking around for any sign of him. He always feels like an interloper when that young farmer is around.

'Yes, I rang him before we left Leeds,' Ant reassures him. 'He was quite glad to leave early because his father needs him on their farm today.'

Bex yawns and declares that he is going to bed. Ant stays downstairs a little longer to leaf through the mail on the kitchen table.

'Ouch! Bloody cat,' she hears Bex exclaim as he tries to get into the guest bedroom.

'Don't you insult Boy; he will never forgive you,'' Ant shouts up the stairs, chuckling.

'Why does he have to sit in the dark by the door?' Bex yelps taking off his shoe and examining his sore toe.

'He considers himself to be the defender of that room: his territory and - come to think of it - mine, too.'

'Very droll…' she hears Bex mutter, followed by a determined: 'Sorry, M'lad,' a scuffle, an outraged meow and Bex slamming the guest bedroom door.

# CHAPTER FORTY

The gloom in their hearts has lifted by the morning. Boy sits at the bottom of the stairs and eyes up Bex with suspicion. Just as Boy makes a precautionary move to flee, Bex has reached him, bends down and gives him a gentle stroke between the ears. Boy lifts up his chin to indicate that the guest could ingratiate himself even more with a chin scratch; Bex obliges. When he rights himself up, Ant stands close to them and smirks: 'So you have made up, you two?' She has just come in from the pigs and is taking off her boots and socks. She has funny shaped toes, he notices for the first time; I wonder whether they are arthritic; it wouldn't surprise him considering that she is out working daily in all weathers.

'Sorry about last night...' Bex mumbles as he gets up from the step he is sitting on, walks into the kitchen, grabs the cornflake box and fills a cereal bowl to the rim. Ant, who stands by the fridge, opens it and hands him the milk bottle. One of Bex's little nods means 'thank you'. Well, if Boy can forgive you, so shall I, she thinks.

'Are you awake enough for a con-flab?' Bex asks staring into the remnants of his cornflakes, or do you need a break?' She shakes her head: 'Let's carry on with the investigation,' she says to his relief. When he doesn't say anything further, she continues: 'The pigs are done and had their little morning chat; in fact, they rather ignored me. I think they are beginning to like Felix better than me.' Bex groans and Ant looks at him in astonishment: 'What have I said?' she enquires innocently. He just shakes his head.

Bex begins to clear his Cornflake bowl and puts the bottle of milk back into the fridge.

'Is that all you are having?' Ant enquires. After all the exertions of the last day, she had expected him to indulge himself with bacon, eggs and baked beans.

'Have you had anything at all for breakfast?'

'Yeah, I had an apple with the pigs.' It's probably the truth. They both laugh about the absurdity of it.

'Let's get on with what we need to do, and when we have finished, I'll take you to a pub lunch.' Bex announces. He is in a really good mood. He has reasons: Ant is amenable; he is warming to the cat and vice versa; the sun is shining outside; Exmoor is at its best, lush and vibrant in a mysterious way, as only a Moor can be - he has to admit, that it is beginning to tug at his heart strings, too; and most importantly, they are at last making progress in solving the French girl's murder. There is one more area to improve , but that will have to wait.

'Let's get started,' Ant puts paper and pens on the kitchen table.

'List of things to do as soon as possible,' Bex mutters while writing and underlining his headline.

'Liaise with Taunton Police,' Ant provides item number one. 'I left an early morning message on Sergeant Penhaligon's answer machine to prepare him for my report. His people have probably given him the gist of what happened in Leeds.' Send report to Bill after lunch, she notes on her list.

'We also need to contact Leeds Police,' Bex reminds her, 'they are lumbered with all the forensics, and we need the results as soon as possible.'

'We also need them to contact the Human Resources Department of the Leeds Postal Services. It's easier for them to coax Forester's personal details out of them,' Ant lists number three. 'They have more chance of getting past the new data protection rules, than we do.'

'…absolutely. Someone must interview the supervisor of the PO Parcel depot where Forester used to work. We need questions answered: When was he employed - to do what? What was his work schedule and did he stick to it? Did he get on with his colleagues? Was he reliable and trustworthy? I want a copy of all his work schedules with times and dates while he was employed there. When and why did he leave his job? Was he sacked? Did he tell anybody where he was going or was he transferred to another Post Office? Where to? Or did he intend to do something totally different?' Bex pauses while Ant's pen is flying over the paper. 'Phew,' she sighs and looks at her long list. 'And, of course,' Bex is in full flow, 'we want to know, why nobody from the Post Office, and particularly that depot, has ever come forward after the appeals to report his weird behaviour, if they weren't happy with him. He certainly doesn't strike me as a model employee.'

'Having dished out task to Taunton and Leeds, what are **we** going to do?' Ant wonders.

'We need to find out whether Forester has been employed by a post office in the West Countr.'

'Maybe he still is?' Ant is getting excite; 'Bill could arrange to find that out quite easily. He has got the authority.''

'And are we agreed to check dog homes in the Leeds area, whether they remember a nutter who took on one dog after another?'

'That's again for the boys in Leeds.' Bex suggests and writes down: **dog homes** on his list, adding gleefully: 'They will be busy!'

'It's in their interest, too,' Ant reminds him.

'Quite! It's as much their case as it is ours. Same suspect, same method,' Bex agrees. 'With some luck, they might solve at least four cold cases with one swoop.'

'And if all that doesn't unearth Forester?'

'Don't be defeatist! In the unlikely event…, we'll just have to think again; maybe another Media appeal or something,' Bex has the bit between his teeth and won't let go now. 'For God's sake, we have nailed him down as the likely murderer; we know where he lives or at least used to live; we know where he used to work, and can assume that he is likely to seek work again; we have witnesses who are willing to testify against him; we have DNA which links him to these victims around Leeds, and most importantly…'

'…to Sylvie's murder,' Ant finishes the sentence for him. 'Remind me, why are we feeling gloomy?'

'Because we have no idea, where he is now, this monster called Mike Forester?

Ant nibbles at the end of her pen which already shows teeth marks, when they hear a knock on the door. Ant takes a moment to direct her focus to the door.

'Shall I go?' Bex asks, but Ant has already jumped up.

# CHAPTER FORTY-ONE

'I was just wondering whether you had returned from Leeds and how it went,' Kathleen's is brimming with hope.

'Better than expected,' Ant is happy to report. We didn't stay overnight. There comes a point when you don't want to be anywhere, not for another minute, to the murder scene,' Ant explains.

'I can imagine, poor you.' Kathleen commiserates.

'Come in. Bex and I are making a list of what we need to do next. We have identified him, we know about his private past and career path, but now we need to find the bastard.'

'Oh…I don't want to disturb,' Kathleen, who has already made a step into the kitchen, is about to withdraw.

'Don't be silly,' Ant gives her a little shove further in.

Ant returns to her developing-a-plan mode: 'You can help with the brain storming. How can we find Mike Forester?'

'Is that his name?' Kathleen asks, breathless with excitement.

'As far as we know,' Bex replies. 'Of course, there is nothing to stop him to call himself something else.'

'I see. And this is, of course, still confidential, is it?' Ant and Bex nod vigorously.

'I won't breathe a word,' Kathleen promises, and mutters: '…my goodness, haven't you done well!'

'Thank you, Miss,' says Ant, stands up and curtseys. Kathleen is a tonic; she always has a way to make even adults feel better about their achievements.

'The student exchange,' Kathleen elaborates, 'wasn't at the height of the holiday season but close to the summer school holidays. The locals would have noticed a stranger, hanging around out of the holiday season. He must have been at least two days in the area: one to abduct Sylvie and another to bury her.' Kathleen ends with a heartfelt sigh; then she stops to remind them: 'Well, at least we can count on one sighting,' Kathleen adds. They look at her, baffled.

'When was that?' Bex has definitely forgotten. Ant is wrecking her brains, too.

'Forester applied for a job at the Post Office, and they turned him down,' Kathleen recalls.'So they have definitely seen him.'

'Of course,' Ant slaps her forehead with her palm:. 'Clever clogs.' Come on, sit down. You have already earned your seat.'

Ant pushes the comfy chair from near the Raeburn close to their chairs. Kathleen is still tall enough to see across the table top.

'Who, it's lovely and warm,' she says and wriggles herself into the most comfortable position.'

'So he has definitely been seen in Dulverton on those dates. Maybe other people noticed him as well,' Ant summarises.

'Didn't young Peter - and, I think Kirsty, too – think they saw someone in the post van they didn't recognise?' Bex remembers.

'Yes, of course, they did…' Ant exclaims, pleased that he had remembered theinterview.

'Would you like me to do the round of shopkeepers again?' Kathleen offers. Ant accepts immediately: 'Absolutely! People know and trust you. They will open up to you more than to the police,' she says; there is rarely a good reason to refuse a volunteer.

'I'll start with the parents I know; then I make the rounds of the shopkeepers, pub landlords restaurant owners. Someone else must have seen him.'

'…and hopefully someone will be able to give a description.'

'Brilliant! The more the merrier.' Ant clasps her hands behind her head leaning back in her chair.

'…soon?' Ant begs.

'…as soon as you want me to. I only live a stone's throw away from Fore Street. I can start with the shop owners this afternoon, when customers have gone home to cook dinner. I'll ask the shoppers on Saturday when I have a good chance to catch most of them.'

'Good strategy,' Ant gives her the thumbs-up, '…and if you find something, take down their name, address and telephone number and ask them to see us.'

'What does the suspect look like?' Kathleen looks from Ant to Bex and back.

Ant opens and shuts her mouth with embarrassment: 'It needs a total novice. We need to get a photo of his revolting face,' Ant slurs her words in haste. 'We…'

'I have a picture,' Bex interrupts. Ant's mouth falls open.

'It's on my computer,' Bex explains sheepishly.

'Now you tell us…Where did you get it from?'

'Leeds Police sent it to me, and they got it from the Job Centre, which had sent Mike Forester for a job interview to the Leeds Parcel Depot.'

'…genius!' Ant is so relieved: 'It will be much easier to jog people's memories, if we can show them his mugshot.'

They realise, they have made another big step towards getting justice for Sylvie and her family.


When Kathleen has left with firm promises of asking the school secretary to run off posters and copies of the photograph, Bex gets ready to go out. He feels Ant's questioning look burning into his neck.

'My assignment for this afternoon is a visit to the local DIY centres and hardware shops in the area to find out whether anybody recognises Forester from the photograph and remembers him buying or at least enquiring about spades in June last year. It's a long shot, but it's worth a try. The stores have all CCTV cameras installed nowadays, and the tills register each and every transaction.'


'That's enough for one day.' Ant turns to Bex, fixes her green eyes on him and reminds him with a devilish grin: 'And what about that lunch you promised?' She has caught him out – he has forgotten. Ant watches his reaction and is relieved when he chuckles. 'We'll stay local, shall we? We'll just make it before the pub close for the afternoon.'

'Next time, we have to include Kathleen; she is a valued member of the team.'

'If you say so.' he replies lamely and walks out into the corridor to grab his jacket.

'Are you coming?' he yells back through the kitchen door. 'I am starving.'

'I'll better take my car, so that after lunch, you can drive straight to Tiverton.'

When Bex has returned from scouring the hardware establishments on the Tiverton Industrial Estate,, he and Ant have a calm look at Mike Forester's picture. They want to store it in their memories, so that they will be able at any time to pick him out from a big crowd. They stare back at the man who has caused so much pain, grief and heartache; they see a long, pale face with a prominent high forehead; thinning, mousy brown hair, swept back without a parting; the long, beaklike nose; his fleshy, bulbous lips and... dead eyes, drained of colour like the stains he had tried to scrub away with bleach.

# CHAPTER FORTY-TWO

'Do you mind if I stay a little longer at the farm?' Bex asks Ant at dinner. She has cooked one of her favourite simple, quick meals, a bowl full of nourishing and warming Colcannon - mashed potatoes with knobs of butter, shredded, steamed cabbage, decorated with a ring of fried bacon, onions and topped with two poached eggs each. For once they have laid the table properly and are not in a rush. Ant tidies away yesterday's newspaper from the table to the recycling bag, which hangs on a hook inside the broom cupboard. They haven't heard from Kathleen yet.

'The forensic results should be coming through soon,' Bex expresses hope and impatience at the same time, while attacking his mountain of Colcannon, adding some grated cheese, Ant has put on the table. She is a glutton when it comes to stodgy food.

Ant nods unable to speak with a full mouth. She chews a little while longer, swallows and finally responds: 'Leeds Police should have had a chance by now to interview the Post office manager – although, sods law, he might have just gone on holiday or been replaced.'

'He or she,' Bex grins reversing their usual roles on insisting on gender equality.

'Ha, ha; very funny,' she retorts. 'I have contacted everybody on my list.'

'I got through my list, while I had to wait for the DIY boss to scour through the old recordings from the security cameras. They were he had locked away and he took some time to find them.'

'…and…?

'He found a tape from around that time, but our suspect managed to avoid recognition. The girl on the till thought, she recognised Forester, when I showed her the photograph.'

'Did they find any relevant till receipts?'

'Not yet, but they'll give us a ring if they do. They set a young, conscientious apprentice on it – well they called him 'our nerdy Jim', but if he finds something, I am going to tell the boss that he is lucky to have him.'

'I hope the Taunton team are scouring the West Country Post Offices,' he sounds a little dubious. He finds it hard not to be in charge.

'Penhaligon is a good chap. Don't let's drive ourselves round the bend, just because for once we sit down and enjoy dinner. We'll hear from everybody when they are ready.' Ant is, to his astonishment, in a mellow mood, smiling between mouthfuls. It is nice, he has to admit, just sitting here, eating, and chatting … like friends or … other couples. There are not many women who would be equally interested to talk about the ins and outs of a murder case.

'I bet, the results will all come at the same time,' Bex grumbles.

Ant's plate is nearly empty when she reminds him: 'At least you have one result already: Forester bought the spade at the DIY Centre in Tiverton. That's something; and it ties in beautifully with our timeline – three days before the murder…'

'… just a memory of the girl on the till; we are awaiting the receipt to prove it,' Bex corrects her.

'… and Forensics confirmed that, according to Sylvie's stomach contents - traces of school lunch - she was killed on the day she was abducted,' Bex finishes the thought.

'Poor Bernadette,' Ant whispers sadly. Inexplicably, she is suddenly reminded of the enormous decision she has to make concerning the pigs. Should she...? She hesitates, waits till he has put his knife and fork on his plate; then she looks straight into his eyes:

'Bex,' she begins and takes a deep breath: 'I need to make a decision about the pigs,' she says flatly. 'Can I have your opinion ... about the pigs'

Bex is taken by surprise. She doesn't usually ask him for advice on farm matters. He looks at her, sees her frown and says kindly: 'I don't know how I can help you with that.'

'I would appreciate your opinion,' Ant mumbles uncertain whether this was a good idea. She has never been one for asking, never mind taking advice. It really must bug her, Bex concludes.

'I am no expert, Ant; it's your life as you keep reminding me, and I fully accept that.'

'Just have a go, Bex,' she pleads; 'I won't jump down your throat whatever you say.'

Bex clears his voice. He needs to be cautious, but truthful. Ant waits patiently, her eyes fixed on him, while he thinks how to answer. Eventually he replies with a question: 'Why do you find it so difficult to have them slaughtered? I thought that was part of your business plan.'

Good, old Bex: realistic and logical as always. 'Feelings, Bex; heard of those?' she winces.

'That's a bit unfair, don't you think?' he says quietly.

'I raised them,' she carries on, 'cared for them; I saw the sows through their pregnancies and helped them with the birth of their babies...' She doesn't mention how often their simple presence has kept her going.

'…but you are used to working without feelings, Ant. You were brilliant at it: focused, unemotional, pursuing only one goal: to find whoever had committed the crime.' He makes a consoling gesture, reaching across, covering her hand lying on the table with his.

Ant wipes an embarrassing tear hastily from her cheek with her other hand, sniffs, gets up and carries the plates to the sink.

Bex wonders whether there is another reason for her feelings – maybe in her past. As far as he knows, she has buried maternal instincts, and would pigs really be a substitute for a human baby? He has never thought about it until now.

'Ant, it's not a decision I can make for you; I know nothing about animals,' he says gently, 'you alone can decide whether they are your pets, a business proposition or a liability.'

They are silent together. 'How soon do you have to make a decision?' he asks eventually.

'I am running out of space,' she sighs. The current litter is their fourth, and each time they produce each up to twelve piglets,' she mumbles miserably.

'And money might be getting tight, too, I imagine,' Bex guesses.

'What are the options to get rid of at least some of them?'

'Slaughter, selling on at market or keeping them as pets,' Ant grabs a roll of paper towels to blow her nose.

'Money spinner, financial ruin or a lot of pets,' Bex states drily; 'great choice!'

'They breed like…'

'Don't tell me – rabbits?'

They burst out laughing, tears now rolling down Ant's cheeks. It's liberating.

When they have regained composure, Bex asks: 'Just out of curiosity, why did you start the pig farm in the first place?'

'To earn money to pay for the house and to concentrate on animals rather than horrible human beings,' she sighs. Ah, Bex thinks, then that didn't work out either.

'…a sort of therapy for past traumas?' Bex says calmly. Ant shrugs her shoulders.

'Tim Grace could sort that out in no time while he is at it.' He mentions the psychiatrist again cautiously.

'I love them,' Ant blubs, still laughing through her tears. She knows how ridiculous she sounds. Bex can only shake his head.

'Well,' he says, you have to get it sorted out one way or another.'

'What do you mean?' Ant is still thinking about her pigs.

'…your obsessions.'

'What obsessions?' She sounds a little outraged.

'Not to put too fine a point to it, I can hardly bear watching you, when in the evenings, you check for the umpteenth time that everything is locked, secured and switched off.'

Ant bites her lip, taken aback, as if he had caught her doing something she rather had kept secret.

'You are right. The pigs are my decision,' she has rallied and reverts to her true, independent self. '…time to think. Best go up to the Girls.'

'Just before you go, Ant,' Bex blurts out. She turns back to face him. 'I have a conundrum of my own,' he continues. Maybe you could think about that, too?' He raises his eyebrows in expectation.

'Try me,' she says flippantly.

'Do you mind, if I stay here some more time? I mean, I could always move to a hotel until we have solved the case and found Mike Forester. I don't want to outstay my welcome.' It had been a surprise to him anyway that he had ended up sharing Ant's house. A few days, maybe, but this was stretching her hospitality.

Ant still looks a little baffled, but then the penny drops and she grins: 'Yes, I remember, you asked before.' He is waiting for an answer. 'Another problem to submit to the Girls,' she says enigmatically and disappears through the door.

# CHAPTER FORTY-THREE

Two days later, the results tumble in one after another. Ant and Bex tick every question answered on their lists and add the answer:

Mike Forester's neighbours confirm that the dogs had been a great nuisance to them, barking, howling and whining at the oddest times of day and night until, so they thought, the dogs' owner had seen sense, and the house had fallen silent. They had felt a bit guilty and hoped fervently that he had returned them from wherever they had come – dog rescue centres, he had mentioned on a rare occasion of neighbourly chat. As for Mr Forester himself, they had hardly seen him since then; they had assumed that he had moved away, changed jobs – that sort of thing; however, they were sure that the house had not been sold – one neighbour's son worked in the local estate agents and kept a keen eye on bargains in the area; he would know, the police were assured, if it had been advertised. Other neighbours didn't even know whom the police officers were talking about. No community spirit by the sounds of it…

There was more concrete news from Leeds Police about where the dogs had come from: a member of staff at one of the dog rescue centres remembered the ever so kind Mr Forester, who had come to adopt one dog and had ended up – out of the goodness of his heart - taking three dogs home. She had been less forthcoming about any home checks on Mr Forester's address, and nobody else seemed available to answer that particular question. There was no trace of where the other three dogs had come from – maybe from further afield or puppy farms or through answering re-homing requests; the search was on-going.

Another report came through from Leeds Post Office Headquarters and their Human Resources Department: they had made every effort to contact most of their UK branches in a quest to find out whether someone called Mike Forester, or someone with a different name but looking much like the man on the attached photograph, had applied for a job within the past year and a half.

Taunton had drawn a blank with the local Post Office and Job Centre, so they now concentrated on bombarding job centres all over the country, particularly in the West Country, with the same request: to scour their brains and files for any man, similar in looks to Mike Forester who might have been asking for a low-skilled job, full time or part-time, with a background in sorting or delivering parcels. William Penhaligon sounds worryingly dispirited on the phone reporting his meagre pickings. No trace of Mike Forester. Still, the Sergeant promises, they would keep at it, although, he warned, the suspect could have long changed his name, his appearance and even his country. Yes, that had been mentioned before.

When Bernadette rings, Bex is only a moment on the phone, before Ant grabs the receiver from his hand: 'Bernadette, we are doing everything we can...' rattling off the latest news, results and plan of action.

'You want me to come over?' Sylvie's mother asks. Her voice is steadier, more resigned than before. There seems to come a time after bereavement, when anger and railing against the injustice of it all, subside to be replaced by resignation and calm acceptance; the stage, when the long festering cocoon of pain buried deep in the heart breaks to the surface only occasionally.

'Not yet, Bernadette, but thank you for offering. We might well need to do another media appeal to find this bastard. I shall keep in touch regularly.'

'Are you sure?' Bernadette sounds unsure whether they were just kind or fobbing her off.

'I promise,' Ant reassures her. 'I'll ring you next week when we should have more results.'

'Please, do not give up!' Ant can hear the agony in Bernadette's voice.

'Never,' Ant hopes that Bernadette can hear the determination in her voice.

At the end of the day, they have treated themselves to a comforting meal of lamb chops, new potatoes and French beans, and just as they have tidied the kitchen –together, Ant notices with glee – and are ready to go upstairs, each to their own bed, the phone rings again.

Whoever that is, has been working late, Ant thinks and picks up the receiver. She recognises Bill Penhaligon's voice immediately. She had expected him to sound weary and tired, but he is ebullient:

'You are working late, Sergeant,' Ant teases, and he replies sounding pleased with himself: 'So are you by the sounds of it… and please, call me Bill!' Touché!

Ant switches on the intercom button, so that Bex can hear as well, what Bill has to say: 'Someone else up in Leeds is working late, too,' the Sergeant continues. 'I just got these various messages: The lab has found conclusive proof, that the bodies from Forester's back garden are those of the two missing women: Eileen Kemp and Alexandra Peterson.'

'That's a relief!' Bex raises his voice, so that the intercom can catch it.

'It is indeed; and to the Leeds team, too, I can tell you.'

Great; another tick on the list, Ant thinks. There follows a tense pause.

'What else have you got, Bill?' Bex hurries him on, sensing that there is more to come.

'Leeds officers have spoken to the manager of the depot where Forester worked. They sacked him because he had stolen consignments which had turned out to be Phenobarbitone, tranquilisers vets had ordered from their suppliers. Those are always special deliveries because they are prescription drugs. The consignments are easily recognisable. When the manager of the depot investigated why some of those parcels had gone missing, he found that they went missing every time on Foresters patch and during his shifts. When he confronted him with the evidence, Forester told him a cock-and-bull story about one of his dogs being ill and that he couldn't afford the Phenobarbitone. It also turned out that Forester had visited the local vet demanding the drug for free, but the guy refused without examining the dog he had brought along. The vet remembers that Forester became quite abusive and threatening before he left the surgery; that's why the vet could easily pick him out from amongst his hundreds of customers.' Bill Penhaligon takes a deep breath after this slightly convoluted explanation. It gives Ant and Bex a chance to digest the news.

'Brilliant! We have solid proof of a triangle connection between the suspect, the P.O. depot and his vet's surgery

'There is more,' Bill goes on: ' A young colleague of Mike Forester at that parcel depot, admitted that several times, he was bullied by Forester into swapping shifts – due to unforeseen circumstances, as he put it; one of his dogs was supposedly sick;

290

or it was his girlfriend's birthday, although nobody had ever seen her. The lad was particularly upset the last time it happened, because it was on the day when he usually visited his grandmother; but Forester was adamant that the lad should swap the shift with him. The boss wasn't to know about it because he was known as a stickler for the rota he had worked out.'

'Poor lad,' Ant said, 'to have such an intimidating colleague.'

'Has anybody verified the dates and stories?' Ant asks through the intercom.

'Yes!' Bill sounds triumphant, 'the boy and his superior worked them out together; then our colleagues in Leeds compared them with the dates they had for the murders and assaults on prostitutes … and guess what?' Bill pauses dramatically.

'Come on, Bill; don't leave us in suspense!' Bill quite enjoys his present role as the bearer of good news: 'The dates are the same. Forester took time off work on the days of the murders, and nobody guessed.'

'And how about Sylvie's date?'

'They had sacked him by them, and he had disappeared. Nobody knows where he might be. He certainly didn't ask for a reference.'

'Good work, Bill!' Ant and Bex exclaim simultaneously.

'And there is one more thing,' Sergeant Penhaligon is still in full flow: 'I am not quite sure where that would fit in, but just so you know: three days before Sylvie's murder, a post office van was stolen from Plymouth's main Royal Mail depot, and was found two days after her disappearance in an Exeter car park.'

'That could have been any old thief,' Ant cautions.

'Yeah, it could, but Post Office Human Resources in Plymouth were interviewing applicants for jobs that morning before the van vanished.'

'Was Forester among them?'

'Not somebody by that name but somebody who very much looks like him. They are trying to hunt down his application form first thing in the morning.'

'That visit would have given Forester the opportunity to steal a van - he knows his way around Post Office depots,' Bex deduces.

'Exactly,' Bill agrees.

Ant has a light bulb moment: 'Bex, do you remember Kirsty Smith, the pupil who followed Sylvie and Peter after school, when those two were rowing in the street?'

'Yes,' Bex isn't quite sure why he is supposed to remember that.

'Didn't Kirsty say that she saw the post office van coming down the hill from where the host family live?'

Bex doesn't remember, but he recalls something else: 'Didn't young Peter Shelley nearly collide with the post office van, after his row with Sylvie?'

'Exactly; Kirsty seemed to think that there was something distinctly odd about the Post Office van and its driver.'

'What?' Bex and Bill say at the same time.

'There are only three posties in Dulverton and everybody knows them. That day, Kirsty didn't recognise the driver, but waved to him as usual; he looked grim and didn't wave back as they usually do/'

292

'That could mean that Forester is likely to be still in the West Country.' Ant speculates.

'He certainly hasn't turned up in Leeds again. They keep an eye on his property until he has been caught.'

'Oh, and I almost forgot: the Lab had a look at the dog hairs on or around the victim's body. Theoretically, they could have been hairs of other people's dogs; after all, Haddon Hill is a dog walker's paradise. But guess what: they matched up with the dog hairs found in the graves in Forester's back garden.'

Ant is ecstatic about the progress, about so many pieces falling into place: 'That makes sense. Hairs have a tendency to cling to all sorts of things: clothes, blankets, soil…' Ant is sure she could think of a thousand things more, but she is too tired; to think another thought. So is Bill; they can hear him yawn at the other end.

Ant grabs the receiver out of Bex's hand: 'Brilliant work, Sergeant… Bill. Thank you so much for letting us know. We'll sleep better for it. Speak again soon.' She puts the receiver into its cradle, as if it were on fire.

'What was that about – you suddenly ending the call?' Bex is perplexed.

'I am knackered,' she admits, 'my brain has come to a stand-still in the last few minutes.'

'Up you go to bed,' Bex orders; 'you do look washed out.' It doesn't happen often that Ant admits defeat.

She stumbles up the stairs, hangs her clothes over the little rickety chair, crawls under the duvet and is asleep within second. Very quietly and gently, Boy, the cat, snuggles up to her.

# CHAPTER FORT- FOUR

'Fire, Fire,' Bex hears a yell, followed by rumbling as if somebody was moving heavy furniture, truncated by another scream: 'Fire; help!'… Not again, he thinks. He can't smell any smoke, but he is out of his bed with one leap. He runs to the door, throws it wide open, but shutting it immediately again, just in case there really is fire spreading. The screaming and screeching is now at the top of the wooden stairs where he sees a small figure swaying. Downstairs, he can hear the cat flap beeping and shutting with a thump, as if Boy had run through it in panic. At least the cat is safe, Bex almost laughs. Ant's consideration for animals might be – in his mind - exaggerated, but it seems to rub off on him.  He grabs the swaying little figure of Ant and carries her into his room. She clings to him, still shouting 'Fire', kicking her legs, struggling to get out of his grasp, but he holds her tight and only releases her onto his bed, when she has stopped struggling, limp with exhaustion. He sniffs the air again: still no whiff of smoke or an acrid cloud of smouldering, melting white goods like the fridge freezer and the washing machine.  No flames are licking at the stairs. He rushes downstairs as quickly as he can without tumbling down. There he checks that everything is as it should be, and rushes back upstairs to his room and Ant.

'Ant, there is no fire; it's just one of your nightmares again,' he says soothingly.' There is no answer. Has she fallen asleep again? Her eyes are staring blankly at the ceiling, wide open; her breathing is rapid, but her body seems stiff with paralysis. He puts his arms around the slight frame in his bed, lifts her up and presses her gently against his chest, feeling the cold sweat that has drenched her pyjama top. As he brushes, almost lovingly, damp strands of hair from her forehead, he can hear sobs; at first intermittent, short gulps turning into racking, heart-wrenching, anguished wails, accompanied by a flood of tears. He is still holding her, when he decides that he has to talk to her soon; she can't go on like this; he'll just have to take a chance, even if she bites his head off and never speaks to him again: she must seek treatment. He is not an expert in the human psyche, but he assumes that the attempt on her life a year ago is not the only reason why her mind keeps going into these fits of panic. Her previous job as a crime scene investigator for over twenty years plays probably a part in it as well. Who would not be affected by always being the first person at a murder scene? Seeing another human being killed, cruelly murdered, mutilated? Seeing the horror in their frozen faces, imagining the pain and anguish they have goes through before the blessing of oblivion had set in.

One thing is clear to Bex: this is not going to go away without professional advice. It's just a matter of convincing Ant, too. He squeezes his body onto the edge of the bed, holding Ant tenderly until she is fast asleep. He will use the sleepless hours to think over several things.


The next morning, they sit at the rough-hewn kitchen cum dining table with a half wilted bunch of wild flowers in a vase, half-full with brown water between them and dried up rose petals gathering around its base. Outside, the sky is pastel blue; the sun has recovered its ability to warm the air and brighten up the day; and the fierce, cold winds of winter and spring have calmed and retreated. Most trees are in full leave, newly awakened, their fresh  green the harbinger of a new beginning; even the birds can't hide their delight, tweeting songs of happiness in between their efforts to build nests.

Bex looks at Ant. He doesn't seem to notice any of it. She looks sleepy, even drowsy and far away in thoughts.

'We must talk, Ant,' Bex begins to talk quietly. He wants it over and done with, and then she can do with it what she wants.

She looks exhausted after the disturbed night which she spent in Bex's bed, snuggling into the crook of his arm – just to make her feel safe. He won't misunderstand, she knows. He is an honourable man. She shouldn't put him through this; she is cross with herself.

'I know the flowers need to go in the compost.' She says to his astonishment, gets up from her chair. He ever so gently takes the vase out of her hand, puts it in the sink and presses her back down into the chair: 'That's irrelevant, Ant.' 'You know, that I don't mean the flowers.' Bex says seeking her eyes, but they are fixed on the flowering horse chestnut tree outside the window.

'Thank you for last night,' she replies eventually without looking at him. She knows he means well, but she can't bear somebody, particularly not Bex, witnessing her weakness. She wants to be anywhere but opposite him. She doesn't know how to respond to his concern; she doesn't want it; she despises herself for rousing his pity.

'You can't go on like this, Ant,' he ploughs on, 'having interrupted sleep; sleepwalking, having nightmares and running the risk that you might throw yourself down the stairs or out of the window.' How can she function at all, never mind run a pig farm and solve a murder case?

'So you said before,' she snaps and stares at the table top. '

Ant,' Bex, moves his chair closer to her, takes her hand from her lap like a kindly father and whispers: 'Ant, you need help¬ nobody gets through post-traumatic stress alone. You were in a dreadful situation and could have lost your life. You need to tell someone, talk to someone who knows what to say to you.'

'You mustn't let it get out of hand, Ant,' she hears him say.

Bex is right, but when would she spare the time to go to a psychiatrist? Tears are rolling down her cheeks again. Ant hates self-pity, rips a sheet of paper towel off the kitchen roll and blows her nose loudly, a signal that she is trying to pull herself together.

'There is no shame in seeking help, Ant.' Bex's compassion makes her cringe and more tears roll down her cheeks. 'You will drive yourself into a total breakdown! Please, let me ring Tim. He is a good bloke. Just see him once and see what he has to say.' Ant has scrunched up her paper towel and kneads it with her fingers.

'Thanks, you are very kind, Bex, but I don't need a psychiatrist,' Ant says without looking at him. She has no idea what possesses her to reject his offer out of hand. She knows it upset him, but she says it anyway. He gets up, pushes his chair roughly out of the way and storms up the stairs. She can just hear him mutter with fury and disappointment: 'Please yourself.'


Ant and Bex avoid each other for the rest of the day. Just after school, Kathleen rings and reports that she had shown Mike Forester's picture to the pupils in assembly and that afterwards, one of the girls had come forward to say that sometime during the last days of the French exchange, a postman in a post office van, whom she didn't recognise as a local, had stopped her on her way home from school and had asked her for directions. She had found it strange that a postman didn't know his patch, but she had assumed that he was new to the area. Thinking, this was odd she followed her mother's advice and suggested that he should better ask one of the adults, who were approaching, but he drove off.

'Did she identify him from the picture?' Ant asks with baited breath.

'She said that she could only see his head and shoulders, but she thinks it could be him. She also noticed his enormous hands on the steering wheel.'

'She doesn't remember the exact day and time?' Ant asks.

'She is not sure, but she thinks it might have been the day before Sylvie disappeared.'

'If that was Forester, the girl had a lucky escape,' Ant mutters.

'Had anybody else in Dulverton seen him?' Bex mouths to Ant, and she repeats the question to Kathleen.

'Somebody's friend has a B&B where he stayed. Evidently, Forester was charm personified and leaving his room impeccably neat and tidy. He said that he was sent from Exeter tohelp out at the Dulverton Post Office.'

'Lovely,' Ant can't help herself being sarcastic, back in working mode, quite a different person to the one last night. She won't mention her tiff with Bex nor her latest panic attack to Kathleen, but she has a sixth sense, like Lucinda had: 'Are you all right?' she asks out of the blue.

'Yes, just busy. Why do you ask?' She tries to provoke an answer she can rebuff. Why? Has she become that nasty? Just as she tries to smooth things over, Kathleen says warmly: 'You know where to find me, if you want to talk.''…must go. Keep me informed, especially if I can help,' Kathleen hangs up before Ant can say another word...

A couple of hours later, the phone rings, and for a moment, Bex feels tempted not to receive it. Ant is out feeding the pigs

298

and, he presumes, having a jolly good rant to them about Bex wanting to send her to the psychiatrist. It would be interesting what they thought, but they probably don't care one bit.

'Not you again,' Bex quips, when he hears Sergeant Penhaligon's voice.

'It's Bill from Taunton,' he hears the Sergeant's excited voice.

'I know. Good to hear from you, Bill,' Bex smiles.

'They found forensic traces all over the van in Exeter and it's smothered in Forester's fingerprints. He must have been in a hurry to get rid of it without wiping everything with bleach.'

'Fantastic!! That proves at least the theft of the van. Any trace of Sylvie or a blanket with dog hairs or bits of a Polypropylene rope?'

'Yepp,' Bill confirms proudly, 'the rope was kept in the boot, no blanket, though, and, as I said, lots of his fingerprints; and one final nail in the coffin: he seemed to have pulled Sylvie by the hair, because they found quite a lot under the passenger seat.'

'Have they checked the DNA?' Bex can't wait to hear the answer, rubbing his chin nervously.

'Of course, 'says Bill smugly.

'…and?' Bex's voice almost somersaults. He can hear the front door open and being slammed shut, probably with a sock-clad foot.

'Hi, I'm back.' Ant calls out, in a surprisingly good mood. Amazing, the effect the pigs have on her. Maybe it would be a mistake to get rid of them…

Bex has just put the phone down and meets Ant in the narrow corridor of her cottage.

'They have examined the van,' he beams, 'Mike Forester left clear traces behind: blue Post Office rope in the boot and dark human hair under the passenger seat.'

'Good.' Ant raises her eyebrows, not half as excited as he is.

'Is that all?'

Bex waits a moment for effect, like an actor with a killer line: 'The hair has Sylvie's DNA!'

'That deserves a hug,' Ant grins and puts her arms around his neck. 'Sorry about this morning. I know you mean well, but…' with Ant there is always a 'but': '…but where the hell is Mike Forester now?'

# CHAPTER FORTY-FIVE

'Bernadette?' Bex rings Sylvie's nother in Morlaix, where the English children had had such a wonderful experience on their school exchange visit; it seems years ago. With Sylvie's disappearance and death, the exchange had sadly died; it was a great disappointment to the pupils who had been too young to participate the first time round and had set their hearts on a trip to France the following year.

'Ah, it is you, Bex?' Bernadette greets him; 'You want me to come to England?'

'Yes. We have all the proof we need to have the subject convicted, we just must find him. Can you take time off, Bernadette?'

'You tell me date, and I shall come,' nothing else seems to be more important in her life.

'Next week?' he asks cautiously? We'll arrange the TV appeal in Plymouth, and then you can come back with us to the farm and see what happens.'

'And I want to take Sylvie 'ome,' she says quietly but with a firm voice.

'I shall tell the staff at Taunton, so that everything is ready for you.'

'I come with ferry Monday afternoon, I think, one o'clock,' Bernadette confirms.

'Ant and I will be there to pick you up from Plymouth Harbour. Our appeal will be on Tuesday, so we'll have to stay there overnight. Don't worry about accommodation; we'll arrange that. The appeal will be on Tuesday lunchtime on local and national TV, Radio and Social Media.'

'Excellent!' Bernadette says in French with a grateful sigh of relief.

'See you on Monday, Bernadette; safe journey!'

'Thank you,' she says, more cheerfully than when she first came to the telephone.


Ant proceeds to the front door. Bex follows her: 'We better prepare for next week. I must ring Felix; Monday is not his favourite day to cover my absence, but I hope, he can make an exception.' They both jump when the phone rings next to where they stand. It's Sergeant Penhaligon again: 'Just one more bit of news,' he says bright and breezily, happy that things are progressing: 'The Post Office staff in Plymouth have finally located the application form. Forester applied for a job there under the name of Sam Peregrine.''

Just in time for the TV appeal, Bex tells him, and invites him to join them on the following Monday.

'I'll see what I can do,' Bill remains vague.


They leave on Monday mid-morning to avoid the worst of the rush-hour. There was a last minute change of plan, and, instead of driving down to Plymouth in two cars, Sergeant Penhaligon picks up Ant and Bex from the farm before winding his way back to the M5 southbound, on the narrow Tiverton road along the river Exe.

'I thought it might be a good idea to go over arrangements for the next couple of days,' had been his argument, and they agreed.

Maybe his long legs were also more comfortable in his own car. Each is glad of the others' support.

'I also brought an arrest warrant – just in case,' Bill mentions with a huge, satisfied grin. They are impressed by his foresight. They were going to arrange one on location.

Ant gives him the thumbs-up when he looks in the rear view mirror and is rewarded by an appreciative smile. The atmosphere in the car is fizzing with excitement and anticipation.

They have timed it right: after just over an hour and a half, they arrive at the ferry port to pick up Bernadette. From there, they will make their way to the hotel near the studios, check in, maybe have a bite to eat and prepare for the big day.

While they are standing in the reception hall of the ferry port, waiting for the ship to dock and for Bernadette to disembark, Ant notices for the first time, that Sergeant Penhaligon is cutting quite an impressive figure: tall, sturdy in his impeccable uniform; his thick, wiry brown hair tamed by a fresh cut in a sort of hedgehog fashion, which makes him look younger than he is; his brown eyes are sparkling underneath bushy, black eyebrows; she also notices for the first time that he has uncommonly delicate hands for his stature, which he keeps folded on the back of his jacket like an old-fashioned school master walking up and down the exam hall. While they are still waiting for Bernadette to disembark, Bex gets coffees from a machine which they sip, standing around, looking out for the arrivals. They are too restless to sit down. When Bernadette finally walks through the exit doors, Ant catches sight of a wry smile on Sergeant Penhaligon's lips. Well, well, she thinks with amusement and puts it straight out of her mind - they have more important things to think about right now. Bernadette looks still as tiny and fragile, as Ant remembers her, but walks with determined steps and a wistful smile towards her little reception committee, dragging a small suitcase on wheels. They kiss each other on both cheeks like old friends, a band of confidants here to right a wrong. Bill Penhaligon's hazel eyes shine with a warm welcome.

By the time they get back to the car, it is mid-afternoon. Everyone is ready to go straight to the hotel, freshen up and have a little rest.

The Sergeant is down by the reception desk first, a few minutes before the appointed time. He might as well pick the brains of the receptionist for a nice place to eat dinner. She has come up with some interesting possibilities, close to the city centre; maybe they could afterwards go for a stroll along the Hoe – the weather is clement enough. However, when the three others come out of the lift, and he makes his suggestions for the evening, Bernadette says that she is exhausted from the six and a half hour ferry crossing, and would rather stay put. Luckily, the hotel has a rather grand dining room and offers a reasonable selection of food on the dinner menu.

'I want to sleep early, to be ready for TV tomorrow,' she says and they all see her point; only Bill looks a little disappointed, but he hides it quickly. 'Quite right,' he agrees bravely, 'we are here to work. We can celebrate afterwards.'

Yes, Ant thinks, when we have found the murderer of her daughter; until then, everything else comes second. Suddenly, the excitement of the drive down to Plymouth, the confidence and positivity drain away and there is only one objective weighing heavily on their minds.

They order without much interest in the food and eat listlessly which is not the fault of the cook. All their senses are focused on tomorrow. After the meal, they go briefly over the arrangements of the following day; they read through and approve of Bernadette's short, prepared speech, the words with which she wants to stir the hearts of the viewers. She is worried; she wants to get it right, and they help her to tweak a word here and there, until Ant, Bex and Bill reassure her, that her speech is perfect, ready to be read out in front of a camera and millions of viewers. Bernadette's tiny frame and misery written allover her face will do the rest to invoke pity, compassion and hopefully, cooperation.

Ant accompanies Bernadette to her room, while the chaps go to the bar for a nightcap.

'Do you want me to go over the plans for tomorrow again?' she asks, not because she thinks it will be necessary, but to convey reassurance and peace of mind. Bernadette shakes her head. Ant hopes she can manage a good night's sleep. Ant has many more questions about her son, how she has adjusted to life without her daughter; was she still working as a cleaner with a Saturday stint in a local shop; she wants to tell her about her journey to Algiers and meeting her ex-husband; but now is not the time; it will have to keep until after tomorrow.

'My speech is good?' Bernadette asks one last time.

'It couldn't be better,' Ant replies and gives her a hug. 'Sleep well!'


In the morning, the men tuck into an English breakfast, while the women can't face anything more than a cup of coffee. The appeal is set for midday to be repeated during the evening news.

They arrive an hour earlier than requested and are welcomed in the so-called Green Room by a breezy, most charming young woman with a blindingly white smile, offering drinks. Bernadette and Ant first shake their heads, but when the chaps opt for a cup of coffee, Ant and Bernadette agree to a glass of mineral water. Ant is glad that she has spotted a 'ladies' just opposite the Green Room. After a few minutes, a glamorous man in a spectacularly well-tailored suit and freshly coiffed blond hair comes in and introduces himself as Crispin something or other, the presenter of the programme. He talks them through the sequence of the broadcast: First make-up room, then changing room – they won't need the latter as they haven't brought a change of clothes; they didn't think clothes were important. Crispin looks a little stunned, but then mentions helpfully: 'They will tidy you up if at all necessary. Then you will be led into the studio – we call it the Floor. You will all be seated at a long table in front of the central camera. Will you need a tele-prompter? We can put on there what you want to say, in case you dry up?'

All four shake their heads in unison. They can't cope with technical complications on top of the stage-fright which is already overwhelming them. They don't even want a make-up artist to make the best of their features, as Crispin put it, but they are told that it is necessary to at least take the shine off their anxious faces. When they leave the Green Room behind, they leave behind half-drunk cups of coffee and most of the mineral water.

And then, all of a sudden, it's time to go into the studio feeling like lambs being taken to slaughter. The studio seems to be full of cameras and people behind them, and they can see more people walking back and forth behind a huge glass wall. Crispin directs the four guests to a long table with four microphones at precise distances from each other, and points to the padded chairs on which he wants them to sit down. Crispin introduces them to the staff who nod in welcome; only a few are preoccupied, still busy preparing their recording equipment for the broadcast - and suddenly, all goes quiet, people become stationary at their particular spot and a lone voice counts down. Crispin alone springs into action and introduces his guests to the viewers. Very diplomatically he encourages each of the guests to tell the heart-breaking story of Sylvie's exchange visit to

Exmoor, her disappearance, the search for her and the gruesome discovery of her body on Haddon Hill. Then he addresses each to describe their personal level of involvement in the case: Sergeant Penhaligon outlines the enormous efforts the Taunton Police and forensic teams have made and praises the efforts of Ant and Bex, who, though retired, have lent their expertise to the investigation, quite voluntarily, for the past twelve months, no less. Then it is time to introduce, very gently, the grieving mother: Bernadette offers a powerful picture of her beloved daughter Sylvie, and the heartbreak her disappearance has caused; yes, Sylvie had been at times a moody teenager, but she was a great girl, generous, loving and a great support to her mother and brother, 'a lovely girl, just like your son or daughter,' she says directly into the camera. 'Just imagine, if your child were to disappear from a school trip and found murdered,' Bernadette drives the picture hom. Then suddenly, she stops, wide-eyed as if the truth had just hit her. Bex nods encouragingly at her, and when she doesn't say any more, as if no more words could ever escape her lips again, he takes over: 'Yes, it could happen to any family, and that's why we need to find this man, we have identified as the main suspect: a man with the name of Mike Forester, calling himself lately Sam Peregrine.' A photograph flashes up on the monitors and the cameras focus solely on it for as long as Bex speaks. 'Mr Forester alias Sam Peregrine, is originally from Leeds,' Bex explains further. He has worked in the past in Post Office Parcel Depots, but he could work anywhere, if indeed he does work. However, we have reason to believe that he is still somewhere in the West Country. He is dangerous, so if you know where he is, don't approach him; rather contact the police or get directly in contact with us on the telephone number or e-mail address now flashing up on your screen. We shall be in Plymouth for several days and would be most grateful for any information you can give us about Mike Forester's whereabouts.'

All of a sudden, the presenter springs into action again, and the cameras focus on Crispin, who repeats the name 'Mike Forester' and the contact telephone helpline number, the e-mail address and the studio's website address, urging the viewers once more to help if they can.

Afterwards, the whole event seems a blur, particularly to Bernadette. The earlier high of tension due to the occasion can't go any higher leaving them in an emotional void. They feel flat and tired, until they are asked to help man the telephones. As they realise that there is an even more important task ahead of them, their energy levels replenish and the feeling of purpose overrides their emotional slump.

'Off we go,' Bex takes charge, 'and let's hope somebody somewhere knows where Mike Forester is.'

They don't have long to wait. One of the first calls is from a young woman, who needs to talk to them urgently.

# CHAPTER FORTY-SIX

'Are you the police from the TV appeal?' a muffled, hesitant voice breathes the words hastily into the receiver. Bill can hardly hear her.

'Yes, Sergeant Penhaligon, speaking,' Bill replies. 'Would you mind giving me your name?'

The person at the other end of the line ignores his request and comes straight out with what she has to say: 'Can I speak to the woman detective, please?' she says in a whisper.

'Could you please speak up a bit?' Bill requests. He can just hear a clearing of the throat. 'Do you mean Antonia Bell?' he tries to keep the conversation going.

'I think someone called her Ant.'

'Yes, that would be Miss Bell,' Bill confirms and wonders when his colleague's nickname had been made public.

'Just a moment, I'll get her for you,' he says making a note that Ant should be made aware of the fact that her nickname has slipped out. In their profession anonymity is invaluable.

'Thank you,' whispers the woman hastily.

'Antonia Bell speaking...' Ant has swapped telephones with Bill. 'How can I help you?'

'I haven't got much time, but I think I can help you,' the nervous voice races through the words.

'It's very kind of you to ring, Miss - Mrs...'

'I can't give you my name. I'll get into trouble...'

A bell rings in Ant's head. This call fits perfectly, she thinks, remembering all the women she has met in connection with this case: intimidated, frightened and robbed of any self-confidence.

'Would you like us to come and see you, so we can speak in private?'

'Oh no,' Ant hears panic vibrating through the line, 'you can't come here.'

'We would come in civilian clothes, not in uniform. We could simply make it look like a visit from a girlfriend.'

'I don't have a girlfriend,' the little voice slumps and stops.

'Could we meet in town for a coffee?' Ant tries another line.

'I rarely go out. I haven't got a key.'

'Who keeps the key?' Ant asks carefully.

'My boyfriend,' is all she volunteers.

'Could I speak to him?'

'Oh no, please don't! He might get angry.'

'Is there a way you could sneak out the back?'

'It's locked, too.'

'Are you a prisoner in your own home?' Ant can hear a bitter laugh escaping from the poor woman's throat; then comes the horrifying answer: 'Yes,' followed by a sob which wells up from deep down, like a tsunami; as if something frozen solid, a glacier perhaps, is melting, breaking into pieces and falling into her ocean of tears..

'Listen: I understand if you don't want to give me your real name, so I shall call you Cindy. Is that okay?'

'Yes,' the answer flutters through, thin as a breath.

'Cindy, do you want to give me a telephone number?' Ant knows that the chance that a victim of domestic abuse and imprisonment owns a mobile phone is remote, but it's worth a try; she might have owned one before she met her jailor, still hiding it in a dark corner he doesn't know about.

Ant can imagine her shaking her head, followed by a dispirited: 'No!'

'Well, if I ask for Cindy on your landline, you will know that it is me and if someone else receives my call, I just say I dialled the wrong number.'

'No, please, don't...' the caller whispers, panic-stricken, pleading fervently.

'Right, Cindy. I shall now do something, I do very rarely: I shall give you my mobile number. Keep it somewhere safe, and if you change your mind and want to meet me or want to speak to me, just ring.' Ant dictates the phone number of her decoy mobile. That at least should facilitate further contact, even though Ant has no way of knowing whether it would ever be used. Often, subjugated women can't keep secrets; they blurt them out to ingratiate themselves to their torturers; to show they can be trusted; to prove loyalty; and in many cases, to avert harsh treatment, at least for a while.

'Now tell me, what do you know about Mike Forester or Sam Peregrine?' Ant comes to the most urgent point. Where is he? Where does he work?'

She can hear a horrified gasp at the other end of the line, a bout of half-finished words, and then, hardly audible:

'I don't know a Mike Forester, but my boyfriend looks very much like him.'

'What does he call himself now?' Ant just wants to check that they have the correct alias.

311

'Sam Peregrine.'

'Since when do you know him, Cindy?'

'…since last year.' The voice seems to shrivel, about to disappear.

'When did you meet him, Cindy – at the beginning, the end or in the summer of last year?'

'…summer.' Somehow, Ant gets the impression that Cindy wants to get away from the phone, wants to end the conversation. Maybe the woman suddenly thinks it was a bad idea to ring at all.

'Could it have been in June?' Ant perseveres.

'No, it was beginning of July; actually, I met him on my birthday in my local supermarket: I was out shopping for a nice meal for myself. I dropped my basket, and Sam came and helped me pick it all up. He was joking; really funny and nice.' How extraordinary it sounds to listen to this waterfall of complimentary words about the man, who has enslaved her ever since; as if she can't believe how much he has changed.

'So what's your boyfriend's surname again?'

Ant knows very well, that Cindy has given it to her already. She waits patiently.

'Peregrine,' Cindy giggles incongruously and strangely affectionate: '…that's how it started: he introduced himself, and I said: you don't really look like a falcon…and it went from there, we both laughed, and I ended up sharing my birthday meal with him.'

'Did he stay the night?'

Cindy gulps, a little outraged: 'Of course not!' There is an uncomfortable pause.

'So, how come, you live with him now?'

'It just happened gradually.' Obviously, Mike Forester wormed his way into her life as usual… Cindy seems to have floated away down memory lane, remembering the good times, when Peregrine had still wooed her.

'Does he live with you now?' Ant calls her back to reality.

'He comes and goes; but he doesn't like me to go outside.' I bet he doesn't Ant thinks with fury.

'So,' Ant stretches the word, as if not sure whether to ask this next question: 'Where does Sam Peregrine work?' However, the answer is disappointing: 'I don't know. I did dare to ask him once, but he is very private; he said I shouldn't worry my little head about such things.' So that nobody can trace him, of course, Ant suspects.

'You have really no idea?'

'No,' Cindy says sadly, and then to Ant's surprise and disappointment, Cindy whispers hurriedly: 'I must go!' and the phone goes dead in a gentle way, as if the receiver has been place back very carefully.

'Shit,' Ant scolds herself and repeats in quick succession: 'shit, shit, shit!' They all look at her.

'…anything?' Bex and Bill have hurried over and now look at her in hope.

'Zilch!' she cries out, so cross with herself. For a moment, she buries her face in her palms.

'Forester has just interrupted us, and I have no way of contacting his girlfriend again' and as a thought occurs to her she shouts: '……quickly, ask the others whether anybody can trace the call.' Five minutes later, Bill comes back to her desk shaking his head before she can ask the question. 'She must have dialled

141,' Ant speculates, just in case he comes in, so we can't ring back. She is obviously terrified of raising his suspicion.'

Bex looks worried; he has seen this scenario many times in his career: 'I just hope he doesn't use her as a hostage as we get closer.'

Ant wails. It wouldn't be the first time that one lover uses the other as a human shield.

'So we can't interview her at all?'

'Nope,' Ant is furious with herself. She should have made sure that she could keep in contact with Cindy – in some way.

'Couldn't she meet one of us away from the house?' Bex asks.

'She is locked in all day.' Ant is distraught.

'Did she give any hint about his workplace?' Bex asks cautiously not to upset her even more. She just shakes her head.

'Let's wait and see, what happens tomorrow. She might ring again.' Bex knows that recriminations won't help. They have to face the situation as it is.

'I have given her my decoy number,' Ant suddenly remembers; 'but now it depends entirely on her to stay in contact. I have no way of finding out where she lives, where he lives with her, and who has given him a job!' Ant is gutted and hits the desktop in frustration. 'I can't believe I have been so stupid!'

'Well, giving her your decoy number is something,' Bex tries to console her, but it doesn't.

They all know such moments well: you feel like a total novice, totally incompetent and in the wrong job; you want to disappear with your shame and never be seen again; and no commiserations however sincerely meant, will make a difference.

314

Bernadette comes over from her desk with a big smile putting her arms around Ant: 'Why are you upset?' she asks.

'I messed up,' Ant says brusquely, 'don't ask. I am so embarrassed!'

For some reason, Bernadette still smiles, and declares cheerfully: 'I think I know where Mr Forester work.'

# CHAPTER FORTY-SEVEN

'A lady, 'is boss, ring me; she do not like him.' Bernadette scrambles the sentences in her excitement.

'That must be him,' Ant jokes in desperation and hope. 'What name does he go under at the moment?'

'Sorry?' Bernadette has not understood the question.

'No, I am sorry, Bernadette. Let me rephrase that: What name has he given to his new boss?'

'I write down; the lady spell it for me. I have paper on desk.' She rushes back to her telephone position and comes back waving a sheet of paper. 'Craig Best,' she shouts before she has even reached them.

'Is that what he calls himself now? And where does he work, this Craig Best?'

'In Plymouth, main depot for…for… rubbish,' Bernadette says proudly, pleased that she has proved to be a useful member of the team, not just the grieving mother. She looks radiant and happy to be able to do something for her girl.

Bex is already checking on his mobile where Plymouth's main litter depot is located; he even finds the name off the person in charge: Jenny Tuff.

'Did you get her name, Bernadette?' Bex wants to check to make sure they are both talking about the same person.

'She say something like *Shenny*.' Bernadette furrows her brow, unsure.

'That's her, Jenny Tuff! Well, done, Bernadette! I'll ring this Jenny Tuff and prepare her for our visit.'

'Forester won't be at work now,' Ant interrupts; 'he just returned home half an hour ago when his girlfriend put down the phone on me. We can't afford to lose time, it might be a good idea to go and see his boss right now.'

Bex makes a quick call. 'Let's go,' he says when he has switched off his mobile. 'She's expecting us.'


'Are you sure, he won't turn up in the middle of our visit?' Ant is nervous. She doesn't want anything to go wrong again.

'No, his next shift is tomorrow morning at six.'

'Let's just hope that he is oblivious to the fact that we are on to him and that he doesn't harm his girlfriend tonight,' Bill reminds everybody of the danger poor Cindy is in constantly, in the same way the other women had been, some of whom hadn't survived their acquaintance with Mike Forester.

'I 'ope, Cindy stay strong, not say she call police.' Bernadette obviously feels deeply worried about the young woman.

'And I just hope, Forester hasn't seen our appeal,' Bill brings up that possibility to everybody's horror.

'Oh God,' Ant groans, 'I hope he doesn't watch the evening news. If he sees himself, he will take it out on Cindy.'

When they reach what looks from the outside like a well-run, neat and orderly litter depot, huge, fortified gates open as if by magic, slowly folding themselves back. Someone must have spotted them and pressed a button. Bill drives through. As soon as he parks in front of a neat, large hut with an OFFICE-sign over the door, a tall, middle-aged woman with a high forehead, short, bottle-blond hair tucked behind her ears, pretty blue eyes and a heart-shaped mouth, appears. She wears the obviously standard company uniform - blue overalls, clean, pressed and unflattering. When she reaches them, she takes off her hard-hat and a pair of heavy-duty gloves. The ripples in her sleeves indicate strong arm muscles, as if she was visiting the gym every day. It is probably the job which gives her a daily workout.

'Are you the detectives?' she asks straight to the point.

This is not strictly true, but they nod and Bex shakes her hand first before introducing her to Ant, Bill and Bernadette.

'We believe you might have our suspect working for you,' Bex explains the visit.

'I saw the appeal during my lunchbreak, and it confirmed all my worst fears.' The visitors look at Jenny Tuff, hanging at her every word. 'There is just something about the bloke, I can't stand; he gives me the shivers,' she says with a gratingly shrill voice. He can be quite charming, but when he doesn't get what he wants, like time off, he tries to put the fear of God into you. He didn't win so far, and that annoys him.'

'How does he get on with other colleagues?' the Sergeant asks, looking rather dashing in his uniform in this land of overalls and refuse bags.

'Oh, they are all blokes; he gets on well enough with them!' she laughs sarcastically, 'although one of them said to me the other day, that Craig or Mike or whatever he calls himself, is a weirdo.'

'Did you get anything more out of him?' Jenny shakes her head. 'They are not talkers.'

'Can we have a look at his application and the personal papers he has handed in?'

'Be my guest,' Jenny says and leads them into her office. A wall of neat files promises a quick search. However, the pickings turn out to be meagre: 'There is only an application, dated January this year, with a photograph attached. Did you not ask for other papers, like references from previous work places?'

'He promised he had applied for new ones because he had lost the old ones in a house fire at his last address.' Liar, Ant thinks; the last time we saw his house in Leeds, it was still standing, with lots of dead bodies – animals' and humans'- in the garden.

'Why is his Plymouth address crossed out on the application form?' Ant looks at the sheet, Bex has handed to her

'He said he was moving in with his girlfriend. He would let me have it later, when he knew the postcode.'

'Am did he?'

Jenny shakes her head, slightly embarrassed: 'You know, most of the people we employ, don't lead orderly lives. I try to keep on top of things, but this one slipped past me. Sorry!'

'Don't worry,' Bex smiles amiably. 'Has he ever rung your office from a mobile or a public telephone box or maybe from his girlfriend's house?'

'No,' Jenny says regretfully, 'not that I can remember.'

'Did you instigate a security check when he joined your depot?' Bex is becoming rapidly suspicious of the seemingly perfect organisation, which is developing enormous hole of inefficiency, not to say incompetence. Jenny Tuff is obviously not coping well with her lonely role at the top.

'I did, but it goes to Headquarters, and that hasn't come back yet.' She begins to sound flustered. Not surprising; her superiors don't seem to give her much support.

'Did your employee say where he had worked before he came to you?'

'At a Post Office depot in Leeds; but after the house fire, he said, he was ill, something to do with his lungs, and was advised to take a sabbatical. He came down here for a holiday and decided to stay.' Interesting, Bex thinks; I wonder whether Jenny was his original target, when he told her his sob story. A female boss, showing compassion... rich pickings

Jenny must have read Bex's thoughts: 'I stopped our chats during the morning coffee breaks after a couple of days. He got on my nerves! He freaked me out! So I began to avoid him apart from the daily distribution of duties. When he still tried to be familiar, I reminded him that I was his boss, and that he was here to work; nothing else.'

'How did he react?' Ant grins with Schadenfreude.

'Sulking; he definitely doesn't like to take orders from a woman. We have settled on ignoring each other, as long as he does the work he is paid for.' There is a pause. 'I am actually working on getting rid of him...' Jenny adds to everyone's surprise. It sounds like a confession.

'Why? Isn't that a bit drastic?' Ant asks.

Jenny Tuff sighs like a mother who has been called to school to discuss the behaviour of her child for the umpteenth time: 'He is a bully. The others don't like him either; they just tolerate him. He won't improve.'

'You saw the TV appeal, didn't you, Jenny? Your intuition was spot-on!' Ant looks her straight into the eyes, and Jenny nods: 'Murder' she whispers, incredulous and horrified.

'So, when is his next shift?' Bex returns to the purpose of the interview.

320

'…tomorrow morning at six.' She seems to know her staff's schedule by heart. 'I can call him into the office.'

'We don't want to alert him, parking police cars outside the office,' Ant warns.

'Okay, we'll come after he reports for work; is seven all right,' Bex looks at Jenny for confirmation.

'Perfect,' she replies looking apprehensive, almost frightened of the next day. She is totally in the hands of these people who are on the hunt for her ghastly employee. She truly hopes it is him; after tomorrow, she never wants to lay eyes on him again.

Ant shakes Jenny's hand warmly. It is surprisingly delicate and beautifully manicured underneath those heavy-duty gloves. Obviously, Jenny tries to rescue a little bit of her femininity amongst the brawn and testosterone. 'Look on the bright side, Jenny: you might get rid of him sooner than you think.' Ant is so pleased when she sees Jenny's dark mood lift and her face brighten like a sunrise lights up the sky.

'Thank you so much,' Bernadette whispers to this woman who had the courage to stand up to the man who very likely murdered her daughter.


Back at the hotel, they make plans over dinner for the next day and determine timing and who will play which role. They have to expect the unexpected. Bernadette absolutely refuses to be left behind in the safety of the hotel. She wants to stare into the eyes of the man, who has killed her daughter. She has no idea what she will do, how she will react, but at least, she must be there. They understand; it will make things more difficult, as they will have to provide additional protection, but how can they deny her this fervent wish?

They will meet at six-thirty a.m. in the lobby, skip breakfast and drive straight to the litter depot, where Jenny will receive them. She will call Mike Forester to her office via the site loudspeakers; they will ask a few questions of identification; they will read to him the oh-so-familiar words while arresting him and deliver him to Plymouth Police HQ for an initial interview; when all the formalities of a hand-over are complete, Sergeant Penhaligon and Bex will drive the suspect to Taunton for further questioning, where they hope to charge him with the murder of Sylvie Karim. They are prepared that Forester will deny everything and claim false identity, plead innocence or repeat ad nauseum: 'No comment'. Nowadays, criminals are rarely overcome by feelings of guilt, remorse or fear; they know their rights better than most ordinary citizens. The team can't wait to put this criminal behind bars as soon as possible.

Just before seven o'clock the following morning - they have almost reached the depot - Bex's mobile rings shrilly.

'Cox,' he answers brusquely, followed by a few snappy yes – yes – I understand. Thank you.'

'Damn!' he bursts out while the others hold their breath.

Bex remains silent, sitting in the front passenger seat, staring angrily out of the windscreen; it takes him a while until he can trust his voice: 'Mike Forester hasn't reported for duty, nor has he rung in with an excuse.'

'Oh my God,' Ant exclaims. 'I hope his girlfriend hasn't spilled the beans.' She pauses when another horrendous thought occurs to her: 'She is a witness…he will kill her!''

# CHAPTER FORTY-EIGHT

'He might opt for abducting her or using her as a human shield,' Bill suggests. It would mean that she would still be alive when they came face to face with him.

'Where would they go?' Ant speculates; 'Back to Leeds?'

'I doubt it; he doesn't have any friends left there either. Your guess is as good as mine.' Bex replies, his brain flooding with possible scenarios.

They arrive at the depot where a most apologetic Jenny is waiting. They reassure her that she has been a great help.

'Morning, Denis' she says miserably to a passing lanky youngster in work-overalls. 'Morning,' he shouts back, 'all right?' he asks his boss politely.

'Not really,' she replies miserably, 'Craig hasn't turned up.'

'I am not doing his shift again; I can't today,' he is adamant about something only Jenny seems to know about.

'No, that's fine,' Jenny responds hastily to placate him.

'Forgive me for asking,' Ant experiences a sudden moment of déjà vu; and then it strikes her: Mike Forester used to lumber a young colleague at Leeds Parcel Depot with some of his shifts. Ant steps towards the young lad: 'Have you ever swapped shifts with Craig?'

He nods, disgruntled: 'All the time. Sometimes he rings me late at night at home, just because he has something better to do than coming to work early. My girlfriend is really pissed off with him... and me.' Jenny looks aghast at these secret swaps she knew nothing about, happening probably when her deputy was on duty. Jenny's face drains of colour as she realises the multiple shortcomings of her organisation. The guests stay silent; It's not their place to criticise; someone else will have to sort out this rather faulty personnel policy. Jenny realises what Ant wants, and begins to riffle through the diary on the desk for her deputy's contact details. She writes them down on a pad, tears off the paper and hands it over.

'Thank you,' Ant whispers. Bex has this intense look on his face, she knows well – a bit like a dog that has identified a smell and wants to run with it... They are both probably thinking the same thing. Ant takes the bull by the horn and asks the all-important question: 'Denis, have you by any chance stored Craig's telephone number he rang you from?'

'I think so.' The lad digs in one of the overall pockets and pulls out a cheap supermarket mobile, before switching it on and furiously scrolling down the list of his contacts.

'You are not supposed...' Jenny splutters and stops mid-sentence - another nail in the coffin of her inadequate system. Ant had seen the lockers, where presumably mobile phones should be stored during shifts. Young Denis is deeply immersed into finding his colleague's number. It takes him a few minutes, before they all breathe a sigh of relief: 'Here it is!' he exclaims triumphantly and grins all over his thin, sweaty face.

'Denis, you are a star!' Sergeant Penhaligon claps him manly on his bony shoulder. 'You might have just saved somebody's life.' Denis beams with the cockiness of youth and even Jenny looks at him like a proud mum.

Denis hands over his phone, so that the policeman can write down the telephone number of this pest of a colleague.

'We'll keep you informed,' Bex promises, suddenly in a great hurry to end the visit. Bernadette, Bill and Ant take this as a sign that they should return to the car as quickly as they can. They mumble a few apologies and thank yous, but they don't see Jenny's little wave anymore, as the doors close with a hasty bang and the police car roars off. Life is rarely that exciting, Jenny thinks wistfully; certainly not at her litter depot.

Bill is driving, putting the siren on the car roof and steps on the accelerator. Bex is immediately ringing for identification of the phone's owner and corresponding address and possibly a landline number. After a very short time, he is given all three by Bill's team back in Taunton HQ. Then he re-directs the Plymouth squad from rushing to the litter depot to the new venue, asking for reinforcement, and possibly an ambulance in case Cindy is hurt. 'See you there in a few minutes,' he ends the call, and Bill increases his speed, sirens blaring.

# CHAPTER FORTY-NINE

They race across town to the other end of Plymouth, a respectable but slightly run-down part. There are occasionally glimpses of the docks, the harbour and the sea, but Ant's, Bex's, Bernadette's and Bill's attention is not focused on sightseeing; they know that a life is at stake; Bill thrashes the accelerator pedal accordingly. As they arrive at the address they were given, he stops the police car with screeching brakes, runs towards several waiting policemen and women from the Plymouth squad, some of which are already ringing one of the doorbells where Cindy is supposed to live, while two other policemen sprint to the back of the building. There is no answer to the bells. They try only once more, peeping into the ground floor bay window. No response. Colleagues bring the battering ram and don't hesitate to smash the front door. They were told by headquarters scouring the most recent census lists, that three parties live at this address: upper ground floor a retired chap, Mr. Pettigrew; first floor a family of three; and on the top floor the attic apartment is occupied by a young woman; the basement flat was unoccupied at the time of the census.

'Top floor,' Bex shouts, but asks Ant and Bernadette to knock on the doors of the other residents to inform them of what is going on. There is no one present on the first floor; they assume the parents are at work and the child is at school. The old chap doesn't seem to be at home either. Good, Ant thinks; it's always easier to explain goings-on after the worst is over and no by-standers and fellow residents have come to harm. They can hear that an ambulance has arrived outside, sirens blaring and suddenly being switched off. Heavy boots of the ambulance crew follow those of the police team up the stairs to the attic flat. They find a baby-stair -guard across the top of the stairwell. It is locked with a chain and padlock. Now they know for sure that this is the right spot: Cindy's prison. They listen: not a sound from behind the door; no one opening the door trying to escape or peeping out, curious who the visitors might be. They all stop and listen: total silence. One of the burly Plymouth policemen smashes the silence and the guard with one swipe of his battering ram without even bothering to cut through the padlock chain. Everyone surges forward and within seconds, the front door to the attic flat is smashed open, too: 'Police. We are coming in. Police! …anyone in here?' They yell, then they listen for a reply or noises of someone to hide or escape, but all they can hear in the silence, is a shuddering groan followed by whimpering. The police team fan out to check each room, the ambulance team close behind them. It clearly sounds as if they are needed.

They find Cindy, or as they now know from the census, Tessa Brinkman, each foot and hand shackled to one of the four bed posts; she is naked, her face bloody, her eye lids swollen, her nose askew and she has scratches all over her breasts and belly as if a rake had scraped over them; Tessa is frothing at the mouth, a mixture of nasal and throat excretions combining with rivulets of blood. The mattress she is lying on is drenched with fluids her body has expelled in panic and distress; there is also a variety of yet unidentified stains and smears. That will be Ant's unenviable task.

'Tessa,' Bex addresses the victim with a warm voice. 'Tessa, Ant is here with me. The police are here, too, and an ambulance crew. We are here to help you and get you into hospital. You are safe now. Your ordeal is over.' Bex waves Ant to the bedside.

Ant steps closer: 'Cindy, I am Ant, the woman you spoke to on the phone. We are so glad we found you. It's all over. You have been so brave. We'll keep you safe.' Until this moment, Ant has no idea whether Cindy/Tessa has heard her. Suddenly, the heavy, swollen eyelids flutter, but Tessa can't manage to open them.

'Tessa, you have seen Sergeant Bill Penhaligon from Taunton Police in the TV appeal. He is now going to release your arms and legs from the chains.

Bill had had the foresight to bring chain cutters from the boot of his car. 'Tessa, I am Sergeant Penhaligon from the Taunton Police,' he introduces himself, in case she hasn't heard or understood Ant's introduction: '...this is what will happen next: I shall release your arms and legs; don't worry; it will be quick, and it won't hurt. After that, Ant will cover your body with blankets for warmth.' He throws a blanket to Ant, which he had also in his car. Then he begins to sever the chains around Tessa's wrists and ankles. She remains immobile like an ice sculpture. Ant arranges Tessa's arms and legs in a more natural, comfortable position and drapes the blanket ever so gently over and around the victim's body. A deep, low groan escapes Tessa's mouth like the roll of thunder above the clouds after lightening has struck.

'Shsh,' Ant smooths a dark, wet lock of Tessa's hair from her clammy forehead. 'You can say all you want to tell us later, when the doctors had a look at your injuries.' Another groan is all the confirmation Ant needs to give her hope that Mike Forester's latest victim will survive. Ant suddenly spies a roll of familiar blue rope under the bed, wound around a piece of cardboard which tells the world that it comes from the *Royal Mail City Parcel Delivery Office, Leeds*. She puts on surgical gloves and holds it up triumphantly:

'Another piece of evidence,' she announces cheerfully to no one in particular. 'This time we'll nail him, Tessa. Pity you had to go through all this first.'

The paramedics appear to prepare Tessa's transfer to the ambulance.

'Tessa, it's Ant again. The ambulance people are ready to take you to hospital, but I can't come with you. I shall visit you later in the day when I have finished here. I need to give the forensic team a hand.' She takes a deep breath before continuing: 'But Bernadette is here', Ant pushes Bernadette close to the bedside, so that Tessa might be able to see her from underneath her swollen eyelids.

''allo, Tessa,' Bernadette says softly, bending a little over the patient, 'I am Bernadette.'

Ant continues: 'You know Bernadette from the appeal. She is the French girl's mother. She will stay by your side in the ambulance and in the hospital, until I can join you.' Turning to Bernadette she whispers: 'Do you mind?'

'...of course not,' Bernadette waves any doubts away; she is glad to be given a task which will be a distraction from her own grief. Everybody round the bed is springing into action: the paramedics secure Tessa on a stretcher and take her down the three flights of stairs to the ambulance, followed by her new vigilant guardian Bernadette.

Ant turns back to the little attic studio which is now buzzling with CSIs. Bex has put Ant in charge with the words: Your turn, Ant. Do the stuff you do so well.' As she scrutinises the group of people in their protective, white suits, covering them from head to toe to avoid any possibility of contamination, she can't believe how young they all look. For a moment, she panics. Will they be experienced enough to do the job? The next moment she scolds herself: I was young once; we all have to start somewhere. However, she will make damn sure, that nothing is overlooked. Like a Drill Sergeant she bellows: 'Full forensic sweep! And don't leave an inch unturned! We need enough evidence to put this bastard away for life.'

As she opens her own tool kit, she wonders where Bex and Bill have gone; all she knows is that after a quick word with Tessa, they had stormed out just after she and Bernadette were taken away. She smiles to herself with satisfaction and the pleasant feeling that they are very near to closing the case, close to solving the crime, close to saving the women of the world from Mike Forester – not quite there yet, but almost.

# CHAPTER FIFTY

The feeling of elation evaporates, when Bex joins the three women at Tessa's hospital bedside in the late evening.

'Any news of his whereabouts,' Ant whispers full of anticipation. She hasn't seen the Bex and Bill for hours.

Bex shakes his head. He looks distressed and dog tired. His cheeks have sunken and the forehead and eye regions are criss-crossed with deep worry-lines saying: no rest until we have got him. They can't bring themselves to speak his name.

'Why? Did you follow his trail?' Ant enquires, a little too loudly, so that Bernadette puts a finger to her lips.

'Oh, Sorry,' Ant whispers hastily. She is exhausted, too, after hours of swabbing Tessa's flat.

'No sightings at train stations, airports and no trace of the car registered in his name.'

'Boat,' they suddenly hear a weak voice emanating from the swollen face on the pillow, rasping and crunching like footsteps on gravel, but they can understand what Tessa is saying: 'Boat'.

They turn to the patient: 'Tessa!' The patient has woken up from her delirium. Ant takes the young woman's hand and gently squeezes it. 'You are awake. We are so pleased, Tessa!'

The shadow of a tiny smile plays on her split and swollen lips, and she winces with the effort.

'Tessa, I am Bex, Ant's partner. Does your boyfriend own a boat?' He hadn't thought of that possibility; it would explain why he managed to disappeared from the landscape.

Tessa nods with great difficulty and almost imperceptively.

'Is the boat in Plymouth Harbour?'

A sideways nod dashes everybody's hopes, when Tessa suddenly utters another word: 'Torquay.'

'You are an absolute star,' Bex says for the second time today. If she wasn't so fragile he would hug her. What that girl has gone through in the last few months, and now with all the pain she must be in, she concentrates and comes up with the one important piece of information they need! 'Thank you!' he says with all his heart. The next moment, Bex has rushed out of the room, undoubtedly resuming the hunt for the man who has created so much heartache. The sooner he is behind bars the better, Bex sighs walking fast along the corridors and to the car in which Bill Penhaligon is waiting for him. He is busy to listen into the police radio announcements and messages, picking out anything useful.

'That was a short hospital visit,' Bill teases him. How is she?'

'She has woken up, and you won't believe it,' Bex is already opening the passenger door and throwing himself into the seat, 'and the first words she said were *boat* and *Torquay*.' Bex's face beams; all tiredness has evaporated.

'Well, well,' Bill grants himself one of those long, loud whistles which workmen on scaffoldings are not allowed anymore.

'Torquay,' Bex says brusquely. 'We might still catch him on his boat.'

'Who would have thought, the bloke owns a boat...' Bill shakes his head and brings the engine back to a roar.

When they arrive, the harbour master dashes all their hopes: No, the boat they describe, was docked here for a few weeks, but it must have left the harbour early this morning; she was gone by the time he started his shift; so he has no idea where she has gone. She is called *Tessa*, that's all he knows.

'Charming,' is all Bex can think of. Calling your boat after the woman you have just mutilated. But then, murderers are a different species to the rest of us, beyond the understanding of all human logic and compassion.

'Back to Plymouth then,' Bill asks and Bex nods.

'Don't worry, we shall get him!' Bex says with ill humour and without much conviction. How satisfying it would have been to wrap up the entire case tonight. It was not to be. Bex feels like hitting something with clenched fists but of course he doesn't.

The women are disappointed, too, when then men arrive back at the hospital.

'I stay with Tessa,' Bernadette insists; the same hope is mirrored in Tessa's bruised eyes imploring everyone to agree.

'Do you mind?' Ant asks Bernadette once more.

'No, I stay, until Tessa is well.'

'Are you sure? You must be exhausted, too.'

'Non, I stay!' Bernadette is adamant.

'Just ring, any time, if you need a break. Either we pick you up or we send a police car to take you back to the hotel.'

Bernadette shakes her head with a rueful smile: 'I stay. I not leave Tessa alone.' Tessa wouldn't be alone, but they realise that the women have formed a bond which mustn't be broken; both are victims of the same monster; no wonder, they feel solidarity; they need each other.

'That's so good of you, Bernadette,' Ant smiles. 'We are so grateful. We'll phone you in the morning and keep you informed all day,' Ant promises, 'and of course, we'll come back, as soon as we have caught him.'

It is well past midnight when they leave the hospital. The carpark is still full of staff vehicles of all shapes and sizes, but eerily empty of people. As soon as they are outside, out of earshot of the receptionist, Ant explodes: 'I can't believe it has come to this. We were so close; how come we still have no idea where he is?' Ant feels like kicking out – a stone across the hospital car park would have to do. Bex knows the feeling.

The Sergeant has again waited patiently for them in the car. He has used the waiting time to make further enquiries about possible sightings of a boat called *Tessa*.

'Back to the hotel?' he asks. 'We might as well. He could be in any of the harbours along the Devon and Cornwall coast.'

'Coming from Leeds, would he know his way around the coast,' Ant questions.

'We don't know,' Bex sighs.

'If he doesn't, or tries to avoid registering in a harbour, he might head for the open sea…' Ant suggests. Both men shake their heads. 'He is more likely to seek shelter in a big port – safety in numbers and all that.'

Bill ends the guessing game: 'Let's be patient, have a good night's sleep and wait for the answers to the questions, I have sent out.'

All three doubt that they will have that good night's sleep.

# CHAPTER FIFTY-ONE

When two days later, they are still waiting for answers to Bill's enquiries, Ant and Bex decide to drive back to Exmoor. They can wait there should any new information emerge.

Bernadette prefers to stay with Tessa, and Sergeant Penhaligon will keep an eye on both women, whilst continuing with his enquiries at several more West Country harbours. The wheels turn slowly down here, inconvenient, if one is in hurry, but charming to thousands of holiday makers, who seek peace and beauty. Unless the *Tessa* was taken abroad, she had to be somewhere close. Taunton and Plymouth HQ have united and gone into overdrive in their hunt for Mike Forester and his boat. They alert harbour masters and local police stations that there might be a serial killer on the loose, preying on young, female tourists. Nobody wants that to hang over the small villages and towns during the holiday season. It is useful that Sergeant Penhaligon is still in the Plymouth area, so that he can be dispatched to places at a moment's notice, where it is difficult to get hold of anybody in charge.

In the meantime, Ant and Bex arrive back at the farm and find Felix at the kitchen table writing furiously on a pad, frowning with the strain of it.

'Any luck?' he asks, but looking at their glum faces, he concludes it's a no.

They tell him a little about their mission and the lack of success; about the young woman who is now languishing in hospital, watched over by Bernadette; about their hopes that she will fully recover from her ordeal, so that one day, she will be well enough to testify against her tormentor ;

'Well, you saved somebody's life – that's something!' Felix looks astonished at their self-deprecation, 'you'll catch the criminal soon enough.'

'We are just worried that he could harm some other people before we catch him. I would imagine he will put up a fight when he is cornered,' Bex concludes and Ant adds: '…he knows that he will be put away for a long time. All the evidence against him is in place.'

'So there you are,' Felix tries to cheer them up, 'excellent work all round.' He couldn't do what they do. He brushes his red curls from his forehead, smiling in admiration.

'We let you go then. Thanks for looking after the Girls and their multiple off-spring,' Ant claps him on the shoulder. 'I wouldn't have the freedom do this job without you, I hope you realise, Felix that you are as much part of our team as we are on the front.'

Felix seems moderately flattered and remains inexplicably seated. Usually he rushes off to catch up on the endless tasks on his father's farm.

'Can I talk to you about something that bothers me?'

'Oh dear', Ant groans inwardly. 'Of course you can.' She pulls a chair next to Felix. Bex busies himself with making tea for everybody, only half listening; while he is waiting for the water to boil, he goes over the events of the past few days in his head.

'You know, I love working on the farm…' He pauses, and Ant's heart sinks: he is going to quit; he is going to say that he can't help anymore; maybe he is too busy on his father's farm. Ant is in a state of silent panic. She doesn't want to lose him. He is reliable and flexible; the Girls like him; he lives close by which makes it easier when she needs him at short notice. .. Ant looks at him, worried, her lips pressed together. Maybe he is leaving the farm and Exmoor altogether? We haven't had a good chat for weeks; almost since this case began and Bex moved in. Has he found someone he likes? He has told her last year that he is gay, but unattached...and his parents have no idea. They have never really discussed it, and he never brought it up again. Maybe that someone doesn't want to live with him on a farm? Ant's brain is running riot...'but I need something more,' he breaks into her thoughts. She looks at him with trepidation. Felix recognises that look and laughs: 'Don't worry! I am not going anywhere.' Ant's sigh of relief is audible, so that Bex turns round towards them. 'I need something more inspiring in my life than just following my father's orders. I know he tries to include me in his planning, but it's still his farm, the plans are the same every year, and I am just the farmhand. I have no project of my own; something I can develop; something I can get passionate about; something to look forward to do every morning; something that is my responsibility, my creation. I know Dad doesn't see it like that, but when I watch you two doing something really worthwhile, , helping people, having an aim and getting results, I feel ...well, it's hard to put it into words,' he ends in a stutter, gazing into the void between Ant and Bex.... 'useless, might be the word,' he whispers.

'Have you thought of going back to what you were doing before,' Ant suggests, 'or something totally different? Maybe study something else? A total change of careers?' Ant has forgotten her own worries. Yes, it would be inconvenient to lose him, but he is her friend and is entitled to the life he chooses, he craves for. She twirls her ponytail as she does when she is confronted by a puzzle. The pigs know it well.

'One thing is clear,' he says into the silence, 'I can't leave my father now and to be honest, the work I did before wasn't that fascinating – a lot of driving up and down the motorways.'

'Would your father agree, if you tried out something new on the farm?' Ant beams all over her face, because she has just had an ingenious idea:' Bex, standing by the kettle, brings the tea cups to the table, looking apprehensive, fearing that Ant just had another one of her inspired ideas, which meant a lot of work for all concerned. And then, as feared, he hears her voice loud and clear: 'Would you like raising my piglets?'

You cunning creature, Bex laughs out loud. He can see her plan. Ant and Felix ignore him. Felix is baffled: 'Why? They are your pigs. I thought you want to develop a charcuterie business…' It is an astonishing suggestion, he hadn't ever expected.

'To be honest, Felix, I am running out of space. I can't keep them having one litter after another. I will always have the Girls and maybe a few of their little ones, but…'

'…but weren't you going to sell your pork to grace London's finest eateries?'

Bex grins, curious about the answer as much as Felix. Ant blushes, swallows hard, twirling the end of her ponytail furiously and opts for honesty: 'One of my dilemmas!' she admits. Felix looks from one to the other, until Ant explains: 'I can't rear them and then send them to slaughter. Bex knows that I have been bellyaching about this for weeks.'

'We know she is squeamish,' Bex comments drily. 'She can deal with dead people, but not dead pigs.'

Felix looks decidedly stunned about such a quick change in his fortunes.

Bex sits down: 'I am getting an earful most days, he confirms, 'Ant just can't make up her mind. I'll be over the moon, when she has finally reached a decision.' Felix can't believe his luck. His prayers were answered quicker than he could ever have hoped.

Ant leans toward him and asks in a soft, conspiratorially low voice: 'If you take on the piglets my Girls are producing, would you be interested in being the business brains?'

'You mean that I would work for you?'

'No, Felix. I would work with you, be your supplier until you have piglets of your own. You will run your meat business, and I'll do my bit for rare breed conservation, maybe in collaboration with research and the Exmoor National Park Authority. I would enjoy that a hell of a lot more than a charcuterie!'

'Stop,' Bex shouts in exasperation. 'Your ideas are running away with you.'

Ant shrugs her shoulders, grinning smugly.

'What do you say, Felix? Shall we shake on it?'

'Give the poor man a chance!' Bex warns.

Worryingly, Felix looks as if he is having second thoughts holding on to his tea cup with both hands: 'Can I sleep on it?' he says eventually.

'Of course, you can. And you will have to talk to your dad as well.' Ant says, confident that the old farmer would see the benefits of the new project. 'It might give him a new lease of life and a new purpose to the farm… and it will keep you here.' Another thought worries him: 'He might get the wrong end of the stick and think that we are finally getting married,' Felix says sheepishly looking at Bex apologetically.

'I tell you what, Felix. I shall come over to you tomorrow morning, and we can have a look at your land, see which part is suitable, how it could work. And then we could possibly submit our ideas to your father, who - knowing him - has his own contributions to make.'

'Great,' Felix gets up from his chair, looking relieved. There is a new fire in his eyes, a new vigour in his demeanour. 'I'll tell Mum to cook us a nice lunch.   '...and Bex, you must come, too. My parents are very curious about the man who lives with Ant.' Felix chuckles, slightly embarrassed. Yes, Ant thinks to herself, at one stage they thought that I might become their daughter-in-law. 'You are crafty, Felix,' she teases him. 'It will break their hearts!'

'I'll just join you for lunch. I have things to sort out here.' Bex accepts the invitation.

'Come when you can. Lunch is about midday.' Felix is fizzing with spirit and renewed confidence in the future.

When the door shuts behind him, Bex observes a certain smug expression on Ant's face: 'That's one of your problems solved,' he teases, and continues pointedly: 'Only two more to go.'

'What do you mean?' Ant's eyes narrow trying to figure out what he refers to, and then it dawns on her: 'I'll ring Tim, when the case is closed.'

Bex doubts it.

# CHAPTER FIFTY-TWO

They are sitting amiably around the big oak dining table at Felix's family farm on the following day, having just finished a delicious meal of lamb stew, home-grown vegetables of beans, swede, carrots and roast potatoes, crunchy on the outside and soft enough on the inside to melt on the tongue, when Bex's mobile rings. He hasn't turned it off because he didn't expect there to be a signal. It's a shrill, demanding sounds and everybody stares at him. Just as he wants to turn it off, he sees that the call is from Sergeant Penhaligon. 'Sorry!' he mouths to the people around the table, gets up stiffly and heads for the door out into the corridor, where he takes the call: 'Yes, Bill?' he says still not quite focused on the conversation.

'We have located him,' Sergeant Penhaligon shouts into the phone, 'we know where Mike Forester is hiding out. It's on a yacht in Falmouth harbour. Can you come?'

'Of course,' Bex says and notes down where they will meet. He returns to the dining table without sitting down, looks at everyone apologetically and says: 'Sorry, duty calls.' Ant gets up, too, and follow him: 'That's a taste of our job,' Ant smiles apologetically and thanks them for a delicious lunch. 'Next time, you will definitely have to come to us! So sorry to leave so abruptly, but we definitely need to put this man behind bars!' Felix's parents, his self-effacing mum and taciturn father, nod with understanding and some confusion. Farming life is rarely that dramatic. 'And you, Felix, Ant says, 'go ahead and draw up plans with your father for the new business.' Delight shines from Felix's face and even his dour dad hazards a lopsided smile; his wife, sitting next to him, keeps her hands folded in her lap, grateful that her son has such good friends.

Ant and Bex rush out of the door, apologising several times more, and then roar off in Ant's Land Rover to join Bill Penhaligon in Falmouth. It will take them about three hours.

'Be quick,' was Penhaligon's request, and as soon as they reach the motorway, Bex encourages Ant to step on the accelerator of her bone-shaker. She is an excellent driver.

'I wish we had a siren,' Ant mutters.

'…on a Land Rover?' Bex chuckles and then he dials Bill, racing down from Plymouth in the same direction, most certainly using his siren. He dials the Sergeant for an update. 'Do we know where exactly he is?' Bex asks.

'Forester got himself a job on a luxury yacht; the harbourmaster recognised him from the appeal.'

'Excellent!' Bex replies, 'Nice to know that these things work and that at least some people pay attention.'

'Have the owners of the yacht been informed?' Ant wants to know without looking anywhere except straight ahead. Bex repeats the question to Bill.

'I informed the local police, but if uniform turn up on the yacht, Forester will smell a rat and abscond again,' Bill worries, but just as Bex wants to make a suggestion, Bill continues full of optimism: 'I told them to lure the family away from the boat under a pretext and meet with police officers somewhere safe where they can explain to them what's happening.'.'

'Good thinking,' Bex agrees; 'how many members of staff are on the boat?'

'I'll find out,' Bill promises and adds: 'We must avoid a hostage situation, don't we?'

'Definitely,' Bex agrees whole-heartedly.

Bill seems to ask a question to which Bex answers: 'We are half-way down to Cornwall. Stay in touch!' Bex ends his call,

'What was that about?' Ant gets finally a chance to ask.

'Falmouth Police are staking out the yacht where Forester is now working, but first they have to lure the family away without raising anyone's suspicions.' Bex puts his mobile in the glove compartment.

'They might inadvertently tip off Forester. They need a good excuse why they are leaving the boat so suddenly and all together. Are there children involved?'

'I don't know. The harbour master talked about a family,' Bex states unhappily.

'If Forester suspects something, he will take them hostage,' Ant continues painting the worst possible scenario. 'He has nothing to lose now, has he?'

Bex doesn't hesitate and dials Bill's hands-free again to find out. The family consist of father, mother, a teenage son and a daughter in her early twenties,' Bex reports back to Ant, 'and there are three crew members on board, too.'

'...one of whom must be Forester. When will the family leave the boat?'

'Right now, they told the crew that friends had just arrived and were docking at the other side of the harbour and that they were going over to their yacht to welcome them.'

'Sounds plausible,' Bex feels some relief that the family are taken to safety. The mobile rings again to confirm that everything has gone according to plan and the family are safely installed at the Police Station, having coffee and biscuits.

'Are the crew members still on board?' Ant whispers. Bex forwards the question.

'There are three who are preparing for the family's departure tomorrow morning,' Bill replies.

'Where are they going?'

'France, I think.'

'Who is coordinating when we board the boat? We mustn't raise suspicion,' Ant wants to know and Bex repeats the question into the phone.

'The Falmouth Police leave that to us,' Bill reports. He doesn't seem perturbed.' It will be you, me and Ant, if she is up for it,' the Sergeant suggests.

'I'm not going to put that to Ant,' Bex laughs, 'my life won't be worth living.'

'I take that as a yes then,' Bill allows himself a tense chuckle. All he wants now, is to bring this case to a swift end.

Bex hangs up and is straight away bombarded by Ant's fury: 'I hate it when you joke about me, and I have no idea what it is about!'

'Calm down,' he laughs even louder as Ant takes one hand off the steering wheel and tries to hit him on his arm, missing it a few times.

'Autsch,' he cries when she finally hits her target. 'I defended your honour: I said you are boarding the boat with us,' he

344

explains, still chuckling: a rare glimpse of the old Ant is worth a bit of pain: spirited and eager to be in the scrum, that's her.

They meet up with Bill Penhaligon in The Chain Locker Pub in Falmouth on its terrace overlooking the busy harbour. It is crowded with hundreds of vessels from tiny punts, private fishing boats to luxury yachts owned or rented by wealthy holiday makers. Most of the boats on the water sport cheery bunting in bright colours, fluttering in the gentle breeze; masts stretching proudly into an incredibly blue sky, reflecting the colour of the ocean. Ant has never been so far south in the West Country and is intrigued by the brightness of the light, and its intense reflection on the water's surface. No wonder, artists like to settle down here.

Bill, Ant and Bex are soon joined by the local Sergeant Steve Winston, who briefs them about his plans. They listen with concentration, aware of the seriousness and danger of what they will have to fac. They nod acknowledgement of the plan. Ant, Bex and Bill add some of their own suggestions and - to everybody's relief – they can finally exhale all the pent-up tension and set off with determined strides to execute what they have agreed on. Sylvie's murder would not remain one of those tragic cold cases. The French girl will have her justice.

# CHAPTER FIFTY-THEREE

Bill - who has changed in the pub's toilet from his uniform into his yellow Bermuda shorts, trendy, a labelled white T-shirt, expensive leather sandals and sporting an expensive wrist watch – is almost apologetic about his appearance: 'Just trying to blend in,' he grins when he sees their surprised faces, '…getting into my role.'

'You go ahead, Romeo' Ant jokes, 'and we Exmoor farming folk totter behind like an old, arthritic couple.'

'We could be your parents,' Bex chips in. The Sergeant shrugs his shoulders, unsure what to make of those two – one moment they are super-efficient and tenacious, the next, they behave like kids. He just catches Ant as she boxes Bex on the upper arm: 'Don't be so childish,' she chides him, and he just shakes his head, grinning like a Cheshire cat. It's just their coping mechanism with tension, Bill suspects; he wouldn't mind a relationship like that…

They set off, Sergeant Penhaligon at a pace, whilst Ant and Bex amble a few paces behind him along the harbour promenade, looking to all intense and purpose like a group of tourist strolling in the summer sunshine. They are looking for a yacht called *The Mermaid* and have been directed towards the end of the quay. Soon they spot it, Ant and Bex hang back, their faces inscrutable behind sunglasses. They let Bill go ahead. They will act as the back-up.

'He really looks like a beach bum,' Ant sniggers. 'Who would have imagined that he cuts such a fine figure of a man?'

346

'I can't possibly comment,' Bex extricates himself being drawn into jibes about the Head of the investigation; 'I am sure, he enjoys himself. It beats spending the afternoon at the station in Taunton in full uniform.'

Bill has reached the boat and stops, pretending to look at his clipboard, seemingly comparing registration numbers. It was agreed that Bill would pretend to be sent by the harbour master to check docking licences for the night on all yachts present; he would also have to ascertain when each boat would leave – in the case of *The Mermaid*, sometime during the following morning. Ant and Bex watch from afar, pretending to consult a tourist guide.

A young boy, who seems to aim to look like a pirate, dressed in torn jeans and a washed-out string vest, his blond, lanky hair reaching to his shoulders, held out of his face by a red and white spotted Bandana, emerges from a cabin below deck as soon as Bill sets foot on deck.

'Excuse me,' the young pirate says imperiously, 'you are trespassing.'

'I am the harbour master's deputy, and I have come to check your mooring docket.' The boy hesitates, in two minds whether to believe the stranger. 'Wait a minute,' he says eventually, turns round and disappears through the swinging cabin door, obviously leading downstairs. For a second, Bill can unfortunately only see blackness through the gap as it opens, and on the second occasion when the young pirate reappears waving a receipt.

Bill takes the docket from his hand, scrutinises it before transferring the details onto paper on his clipboard and ticking things off. 'All in good order,' Bill says with a reassuring smile, and hands the docket back to the teenager who is now leaning languidly against a mast.

'Can I speak to the owner of the boat?' Bill smiles amiably.

'They have gone out to see friends on another yacht,' the boy volunteers.

'You are stuck here?' Bill commiserates. The pirate looks at him with a bored expression and nods.

'Any other crew members on board,' Bill probes casually, as if the question is only a formality. He waits for the answer, strolling just a little away around the deck, averting his eyes from the boy, who promptly says: 'Two.'

'That makes you three?' another bored nod.

From afar, Ant and Bex watch Bill and the young man negotiating, occasionally gesticulating, nodding or shaking heads. They are waiting for a sign to join him.

'He is leaving it a long time…' Ant remarks impatiently, turning her back to the boat. Bex shrugs his shoulders. Bill knows what he is doing.

Suddenly, they see the agreed wave of Bill's hand to come and join him. Ant and Bex quicken their pace and jump without invitation on board.

'My boss said not to let….' The young pirate look-alike stutters helplessly, because at that moment they are already surrounding him and whispering in his ear: 'We are the police. We are looking for a man called Mike Forester; we think he is working on this yacht.' Bill holds the photograph from the appeal in front of the young pirate's eyes. He blushes furiously, his eyes wide with shock. He can only nod.

'What's your name?'

'Ben,' the boy is about to lose his voice. Good. He won't alert anybody.

'That's easy to remember: it's my name, too,' Bex takes over quietly. 'Ben, where is he?' Ben's arm shoots out as if to

348

distance himself from this uncomfortable situation and his index finger points to the cabin door leading below deck.

'Is the other fellow down there as well?'

'Yes,' Ben whispers.

'What's his name?'

'Sam,' they can hardly catch what Ben is saying; time is running out: 'They are playing poker,' Ben whispers and sidles up to Ant as if trying to hide behind her back.

'How old are the two men?' Ant whispers close to his ear.

'Sam is about twenty and Bert is as old as my dad.'

In his forties, she guesses; that fits.

'I am getting fed up with all these different names…' Ant mutters, but nobody listens.

'Right,' Bill prepares for action, 'you leave the boat now, and we do the rest, oaky?'

'What happens, if the family come back?' The young pirate is surprisingly astute and touchingly protective of his employers.

'They are safe at the police station.' Bex whispers to him.

Suddenly the door to below deck swings open violently and they all hold their breath.

'Okay, Son?' the emerging twenty-something, tanned and bleached hair asks the youngest crew member. Young Ben looks like a rabbit caught in headlights, turns round and jumps off the boat.

'What the heck …' the three of them hold their finger over their lips in synchronisation to indicate to Sam that he must not say another word. Bill proffers silently his police credentials.

'You better follow Ben' Bill whispers urgently. We are here to make an arrest - it could get nasty...' They have rarely seen someone jump off a boat that fast, as if a rabid dog were after him.

Without further hesitation, Bill, Bex and Ant run through the flapping door and storm down to the cabins. At the bottom, Bill collides with the third crewmember, a man in his early forties, strong arm muscles, large hands and the spitting image of Mike Forester.

'Mike Forester, I am arresting you ...' but before he can finish the sentence, Sergeant Penhaligon feels a sharp elbow dig into his midriff and a blow to his groin where a knee just made contact. 'You bastard,' Bill screams before sinking to the ground, but as he falls he grabs one of Forester's legs who promptly looses balance, too. Bex pushes his body past the two on the floor and approaches the suspect with a menacingly stare. 'Help me,' he shouts to Ant and both heave Forester up with a jolt, grabbing his arms, twisting them to his back and putting hand-cuffs around his wrists. Forester is still kicking out, wild and desperate to leave the boat.

'If you don't stop that,' Bex hisses, 'I'll give you a taste of your own medicine. 'Of course, Forester doesn't stop: his foot has just connected with Bex's shin. 'Right, you bastard' he screams, 'you had it!' Bex pulls out a sturdy piece of blue rope from his trouser pocket and lashes it around Forester's ankles. Ant recognises it as coming from under Tessa's bed. Bex must have cut off a piece before it was sent to the lab. 'Recognise that? Useful, isn't it?' he spits the sarcasm into Forester's face.

Bill gets up, dusts himself down and repeats: 'Mike Forester, I am arresting you on suspicion of murdering Sylvie Karim in June 2019 in the vicinity of Dulverton on Exmoor. There are other Police Forces who are eager to charge you with other crimes -

murders, attempted murders, rape, assault, bodily harm, not to mention cruelty to animals.' Forester's face tightens at this last accusation, but Bill continues regardless: '…you do not….' he rattles off the well-known litany. Once Plymouth and Taunton will had dealt with him, the other police forces, which have their own grievances against him, will have to re-arrest him and bring him to justice in their own jurisdictions. What happened today was just for Sylvie, Bernadette and Tessa.

'You must have got the wrong guy,' Forester suddenly changes his tactic, playing the innocent victim, pleading it's a case of mistaken identity. Bill continues unperturbed until he comes to the end of the - oh so monotonous but satisfying - script.

Forester's face mirrors bewilderment and fury. How could this happen to him?

'Let's go,' Bill can't help giving Forester an impatient, sharp push in the ribs to get him moving. It's divine justice that, with the blue rope around his wrists and ankles, Forester can only shuffle like an old man.

'You are not the police. You are not in uniform,' Forester shouts at the few by-standers who have slipped through the cordon. 'I demand the protection of the Falmouth Police!'

'You called, Mr Forester?' a young officer, waiting on the quay, replies courteously. 'Here we are.' There are about ten officers, who help everyone down from the boat and then bundle the stunned suspect into a police van which had blocked the promenade more or less successfully.

'We'll deal with him now,' says the Falmouth Sergeant, who had introduced himself as Sven Mullet, 'and then you can take this beauty to Taunton for your own amusement. The Police van and three accompanying cars drive off at speed with their unsavoury cargo.

Ant, Bex and Bill look at each other: Bill has come off worst with badly grazed knees, a shin turning blue with bruises and the left hand side of his face, eye and cheek, turning purple from the impact of Forester landing on him, not to mention the pain in the more vulnerable regions of his body. As they walk along the quay, they notice that Bill limps, probably a result of Forester's knee; for once, the fine figure of the man looks dishevelled and dazed. Bex's attire has also suffered in the scuffle of the arrest: the tie hangs loosely round his neck like a rope, his light-tan jacket is ripped around the top of the right arm, so that the sleeve is hanging off; he also has scratches on his hands and a bloody lip – he is not sure how that has happened. He looks at Ant: she is absolutely fine; only her face is grim as she returns his look of concern. 'Come on, Ant,' Bex urges her as she seems rooted to the spot. 'It's all over!' He walks a few steps back and puts his arm around her. 'The world is a little safer,' he says, and she nods wordlessly.

'Can I have your mobile,' she asks suddenly, as if woken from a deep trance. Bex hands it to her, and she dials the hospital in Plymouth. While she waits for the call to be connected, she mouths to Bex: 'I want Bernadette and Tessa to be the first to know that we have got him!'

# CHAPTER FIFTY-FOUR

A week later...

'I never knew that Bill Penhaligon isn't married,' Ant muses aloud. They've heard that he has taken a further week's leave to support Bernadette in looking after Tessa. They'll all come to Ant's farm when the patient is discharged. Tessa is making good progress - although the mental scars of her ordeal will take a lot longer to fade - and expects to leave the hospital in a matter of days.

'Hm, gossiping, are we?' is all the reaction she gets from Bex, who looks at her over the thin rim of his reading glasses. For once they are sitting in arm chairs in her tiny and rarely used sitting room, opposite the kitchen. It was Bex's idea to make use of this bright, airy part of the house with double aspect windows and a look over the front garden where the last of the daffodils and tulips rule in a totally unplanned way. Apart from the two soft-furnished arm chairs, there is a small fire place with a grate, stacked with logs, ready to be lit, and a two seater settee in front of it. Bex has sunk into the second arm chair opposite her and is reading a book, a rare occurrence, indeed! Ant - and probably Bex himself - wouldn't have classified him as an avid reader of literary tomes.

'What are you reading,' Ant looks curiously in the direction of the book cover which is half hidden by his hands.

'Oh, nothing,' he says sheepishly. She laughs and walks over to him.

'Come on; let's see,' she insists, and Bex holds it up a little shyly, for her to see. She reads aloud: 'How to Combat Post Traumatic Stress'.

'When did you buy that?' she asks.

'I borrowed it from the library.'

'Have you got PTS?' she teases but with a frosty, warning undertone. 'Seriously, Bex, I can take a hint. I appreciate your concern, but this is my PTS, if that's what it is, and I deal with it in my own way, in my own good time!' She looks defiant. Bex is getting annoyed, too; he doesn't need a lecture. He just wishes she wasn't quite so stubborn and combative.

'In your own good time means: not at all,' he retorts angrily, shutting the volume with a thud. Pity! Just when it gets interesting... 'I'll return the book to the library tomorrow,' he says sulkily.

It really was interesting: For example, he hadn't known that there were so many different ways PTS Syndrome could manifest itself: Ant's nightmares, panic and anxiety attacks combined with inexplicable sweats and her paranoia about locking and checking everything obsession ally, are only the most common signs. Sudden symptoms of angry outburst, uncharacteristic tendencies to violence, or the opposites - being withdrawn, depressed or frequently, worryingly forgetful; or an impenetrable mist shrouding past events, are all serious warning signs which point to some if not a total change of personality  caused by Post Traumatic Stress. The condition is particularly hard on the families, who want to help, but are only met with hostility and denial by the patient. The only way to put an end to the suffering is professional therapy. Bex is quite certain now that this is the right way to go; if only Ant would agree. According to the book's index, there are specialists in London, Bristol, and – of all places - nearby Minehead - very convenient, should Ant not want to make use of Tim Grace's generous offer. Bex has written down Tim's telephone number and has left it on the hall table next to the telephone.

'Pigs are calling!' Ant declares and gets up from her cosy armchair. 'Hold on,' Bex stops her: 'As we are just clearing the air of awkward topics, I want you to know that I will be leaving shortly. You have been very patient and generous to let me stay here, but it's time to go.'

'What about our expert statements to the Court when Forester will be tried?'

'That's still weeks away; you don't want me to hang around that long,' Bex looks at her provocatively. 'We can meet at Court when they call us.'

'Well, if you must…' Ant doesn't finish her sentence. They don't look at each other, no one says a word. Ant turns, collects the pigs' paraphernalia from the kitchen and trudges up the hill, like she does every day at least twice. As Ant opens the front door, a quite unseasonably cold draft reaches Bex in his cosy armchair; he gets up and shuts the door quietly behind her.

When she comes back, she seems to have forgotten all about their conversation and chatters happily about the titbits, Sergeant Penhaligon has let slip on the phone that morning about the first couple of interviews with Mike Forester. 'No comment,' featured a lot and the solicitor doesn't seem to help much either, advising his client to stick to it.

'I would love to know what is really going on,' Bex admits wistfully. It often used to be the pinnacle of an investigation, to grill the suspect and finally get to the truth. Bex envies the Sergeant, but he knows he can't interfere, however much he would love to have a go at dragging a confession out of this nasty piece of work.

'He said he would ring you tonight,' Ant mentions cryptically; and sure enough Bill calls mid-evening.

'The things is,' Bill begins, 'I am not getting far with Forester. He knows his rights, and his solicitor is shielding him. I know it shouldn't happen, but Forester is running rings around us. There is something I am missing.' It's very good of Bill to admit such a thing. 'It should be so easy with all this evidence,' he sighs audibly, 'but this one is a more slippery customer than most.'

'We all have our off-days,' Bex consoles him. 'Don't forget, you were quite seriously battered yourself only a few days ago.'

'Yeah, but I had several bad days,' Bill confesses. There is a pause. 'Could you have a go, Bex?' It's a silent cry for help between colleagues.

'Of course, I can,' Bex jumps at the chance to get from under Ant's feet for a day or two, before he leaves the area altogether. In the middle of that thought, Bex hears what else Bill has to say:

'Could Ant come as well? I think a female perspective could be helpful; and of course, she is a scientist who can make it crystal clear to him and his solicitor that they really haven't got a chance in hell to get him off those charges.'

Bex calls Ant to the phone. She is trying to catch up on animal husbandry paperwork at the kitchen table.

'Hi, Bill. …things going well?' In a few words, Bill repeats his request.

'Thanks for your confidence,' Ant laughs. 'When do you want us?' She can hear his sigh of relief.

'…as soon as you can… tomorrow?' Bill replies, jumping at the offer.

'You are on!'

'I'll inform the solicitor and his precious client,' he ends the call much more hopeful than he had started it.


The next morning, bright and early, Mike Forester looks angry when he appears in the interview room door. He had planned to have some more fun with Sergeant Penhaligon and the wispy-voiced young Constable. Seeing Ant and Bex instead has rather spoilt his plans and wiped the smug grin from his lips. He can feel that they are in a different league.

'Good morning, Mr Forester.' Bex greets him breezily, as if he was pleased to see him, but didn't have much time to deal with him. Forester grunts something and flops down on the chair next to his solicitor. He doesn't know that his counsel arrived some time earlier and was appalled at what Ant and Bex had to tell him. Forester is now sitting at the table, opposite the new team, leaning nonchalantly into his chair and wrapping his long legs round the front legs of his chair. He might not know it, but there is very little hope that his solicitor can be of use to him.

The recorder starts to whirr.

'So, tell me, Mr Forester...' Bex begins but is interrupted:

'Mike, call me Mike,' he says in a thin, high-pitched voice which is in stark contrast to the coarse, burly hulk of his body. No one knows what Forester means to achieve with this, offer of familiarity, but Bex obliges: '...tell me, Mike: how do you explain that we found six dogs' carcasses and two female human bodies in your back garden?' Bex asks with a straight face as if he is talking about items stolen from a gift shop. Bex doesn't like the face opposite and would like to smash it in, but of course, he won't. His own face will remain inscrutable throughout the interview.

Foresters changes tactics and scrutinises Ant's face opposite him. There must be a chink in its blandness. He usually can wrap women round his little finger, apart from his butch boss at the litter depot and this police woman in front of him. He smirks: 'Do you know anything about female corpses in my back garden?' he addresses Ant directly.

'Indeed I do, Mr Forester. I dug them up and identified them.' Ant stares at him, triumph blazing from her eyes. One-nil to her, Bex grins and repeats his question: 'So, Mike, what can you tell us about the seven dogs?'

'Six,' Forester corrects him.

'Six dogs and two women you murdered?'

'I didn't,' Forester replies sulkily and earns himself a stern look from his attorney. '. ...no comment,' he says, quick as a flash.

'Let me answer your question from our point of view: we paid a visit to your property Mike. Can you confirm that you are the only person who has access to it? Does anybody else have keys?'

'Someone could have broken in...' he stops because his solicitor has just sent him another sharp look which tells him to shut up. 'No comment', Forester corrects himself.

'These murders of dogs and women must have occurred over a great number of years, Mike. So, if there were burglaries and strange people digging in your garden, you would surely have noticed and reported them to the police, wouldn't you?'

'No comment,' Forester is beginning to wriggle uncomfortably in his chair, unfurling his legs and stretching them out under the table, almost touching Ant's feet. She immediately pulls them back closer to her chair. The solicitor looks uncomfortable, too.

Bex ploughs on: 'We have several witnesses who can testify that you have physically and mentally abused them during their relationships with you. You seem to follow a working pattern; a unique and quite distinctive one, which – very conveniently for us - connects all these cases under re-investigation. Have you got anything to add to that?'

Forester looks baffled and then tries once more to fight his corner: 'I live up in Leeds anyway. I haven't even been in the back garden in Plymouth.' Forester says triumphantly, but nobody can see the connection why he thinks this is helpful to his cause.

'Yes, we know, Mike. We were talking about your house in Leeds all along. The one in Plymouth isn't yours. So, to finish what I was saying: we did a thorough house search and dug up your garden; and while we were up there, we visited those witnesses, your victims, who are still trying to get justice. I am sure you know who they are.''

Forester looks flustered: 'I thought you were talking about Plymouth'. He is sulking now.

'Yes, we'll come to Plymouth in a minute, Mike. That flat you share belongs to your latest girlfriend, Tessa, and she is another victim, isn't she? I am pleased to tell you that she has survived your horrific attack on her life; so that in her case, you will only be charged, lucky you, with attempted murder and incarceration. Had she died, it would have increased the number of murders on your conscience, if you have got one. You can thank us that we found her just in time to take her to hospital.' Forester shrugs his shoulders, which could mean anything from I don't know about this to I don't care.

Sergeant Penhaligon joins the interview room and positions himself by the door like a barricade. Mike turns round and sneers at him, until his solicitor taps him on the shoulder and whispers something in his ear.

Mike Forester's eyes narrow with fury: 'She is lying. It wasn't me. I found her.'

'...and left her lying there, gagged, shackled, bruised and battered? That's hard to believe, Mike. Why didn't you call an ambulance, if you were so concerned? You are talking about Tessa, aren't you?'

Mike ignores the last question and tries to make his reaction look reasonable: '...because you would have blamed me anyway.'

'That's a flimsy excuse if ever I heard one,' Bill contributes from near the door.

'...and why was she bound and gaggled with the same Post Office string you used to strangle all the other women you killed and the dogs you practised on? I mean: in Leeds, in case you get confused again.'

' They can see the rising desperation in the solicitor's pinched face and hunched shoulders. Forester looks at his brief for reassurance, but the man stares at his file on the table instead.

'No comment,' Forester takes refuge in the familiar phrase.

'You mentioned mistaken identity, when you were arrested,' Bex continues the interrogation and looks once more disapprovingly at Forester.

'Yes, that's right,' Forester sounds hard-done-by - and hopeful: 'Yes, I think you mistake me for somebody else. You are pinning this on me because you can't find anybody else.' He looks triumphant as if he had just saved his own skin. His solicitor puts his hands over his face in despair, realising that his client is about to walk into a trap.

Bex addresses Bill: 'Sergeant Penhaligon, have we established the identity of Mr Forester one hundred percent?'

Bill grins and replies formally: 'Yes we have, Sir.

'Apart from the clear DNA matches from various murder scenes and the houses in Leeds and Plymouth, was there anything else which pointed clearly to this man, Mike Forester?'

'Yes, there was one thing, Sir.'

'What was that?' Even Ant looks curious.

'Not many people can say that they have several witnesses to their body art.' Bill finds it hard to suppress a smirk.

'...body art?' Bex plays along, and even the duty solicitor looks up.

Sergeant Penhaligon has the great pleasure to reveal the result of his findings: 'As several witnesses described, Mr. Forester has a large Superman logo, bright red, yellow and a little bit of black tattooed just above his penis. It is so striking, that they noticed it while he raped them... and he is very proud of it.' Bill can hardly hide his Schadenfreude..

At first Forester doesn't seem to understand the implication, and, tellingly, looks down towards his nether regions. Then the penny drops and he is shouting with outrage: 'You bastard. I thought, body-checks were normal procedure. And you said you liked my tattoo.'

All present, to the consternation of the interviewee, burst into derisive laughter. Even the solicitor is amused, trying to hide his mirth by pretending to look for something in his briefcase.

'I would hardly stoop that low,' Bill rejects the suggestion out of hand; 'I like art, but a Superman tattoo is not one of them.'

Ant takes over to dampen the hilarity and to get them all back the serious matter of nailing the suspect: 'And then there is, of course, a mountain of forensic evidence. You very kindly left traces where ever you operated. Remember the blue parcel post string you nicked from your place of work? We found it everywhere; in the car, under your bed, around the previous victims' necks including the dogs'; we found blue fibre even on the hedges on your way to bury the French school girl's body. Do you remember taking a leak on her grave on Haddon Hill? The dog homes you bought the poor creatures for a pittance? They all remember you. Your dead dogs' hair were transferred from your dog blanket to the dead body of Sylvie Karim? …Shall I go on, Mike?' Ant pronounces his name with disdain. 'Your solicitor will be given the full list of forensic examinations and their results.'

'What would you know about it, Bitch?' Mike shouts angrily, disappointed that he can't't win her over to his side..

'Mike, it might have escaped your attention that most women are very smart,' Ant enjoys rubbing it in. 'I am the forensic scientist on the case, and I can tell you, that it doesn't look good for you. All your denials have been proved wrong. My team and I have all the evidence a judge and a jury needs to put you away for life. We found mountains of evidence, all unique to you, which you left carelessly. We can prove one hundred percent that you committed all those crimes!' Ant takes a deep breath. She has said her piece and hopes it trickles into Forester's thick skull.

Mike Forester looks sullen, but far from crestfallen. Bex reminds himself, that this is a hardened, dangerous man who won't give in ever. It's for the judge to deal with him now.

The solicitor looks horrified at the change in his client's demeanour after the realisation that the first stance of denial and 'no comment' just isn't working any longer. The self-assured cockiness has been replaced by something much more threatening: a primeval urge to save his skin and desire to annihilate his opponents. The lawyer also realises that he is the nearest person to this menace: If Mike Forester loses his rag and lashes out; his representative will be the first to feel it.

'I think we better adjourn the interview,' the lawyer requests, 'it will give me time to advise my client further.' Forester could not look more disgusted with his brief, folding his arms like steel rods over his chest and staring menacingly at the man with narrowed eyes.

'It will be interesting whether the defence lawyer will return in the morning, Ant thinks.

'If you wish,' Sergeant Penhaligon says graciously and nods towards Ant and Bex. 'Are we all agreed to an adjournment?' Everybody nods glad to be given a break from the presence of this vile individual.

'I'll let you know tomorrow, what the two of them come up with,' Bill promises. 'A confession might be in order.' He chuckles with relief.

'Don't count your chickens, Bill,' Bex warns and claps him on the shoulder before they leave the interview room.

Bill has definitely lost his dour expression; Ant speculates what the reason might be – wrapping up the case plays surely a big part, but she can't help feeling that there is more to his good humour?

# CHAPTER FIFTY-FIVE

Ant is quiet in the car while Bex is driving. 'I really don't mind you staying on a bit longer,' she surprises him.

'No, I better get back to London. You have your life, and I have mine, although yours is definitely more interesting.'

She laughs out loud: 'Pigs, mud and muck? Stop playing hard to get. I am not repeating my offer.'

'Yes, pigs and mud and Felix and Kathleen and the village and the little town of Dulverton... There is a purpose in your life – they all need you in one way or another; you all care for each other. I haven't found that sense of community and purpose yet...,' he sounds almost sad. '...not in retirement, I haven't...and everybody promised that the world would be my oyster...'

'Oh, stop grumbling. You'll be all right. It's early days yet!!' she slaps him on the shoulder, as if that would help to make him snap out of his mood. 'You have just cracked a murder case,' she reminds him.

'**We** have,' he grumbles and then says as an after-thought: 'We are still good when we are working together.'

'Yes, not bad,' she admits, a little hesitantly, a little doubtful and then she pauses. 'It can get awfully quiet down here,' she says out of the blue.' Bex grins at the incongruity of what she has just said and the events of the last couple of months.

'Routine gets boring everywhere,' she tries to explain and gives up. Everybody has to work out life for themselves.

'Tell you what,' Ant says: 'I am willing to make a fresh start if you promise to give me the freedom to be myself, not to make demands. Let's just see how we get on.' The next moment, she is regretting her impulsiveness; she is frightened of her own courage, but on the other hand, she is not entirely sure that she wouldn't miss Bex's company more than she could ever admit.

He smiles, not quite willing to feel elated; he knows how quickly she can change her mind.


Several weeks later: The Court proceedings are an open and shut case. There has never been much doubt that Mike Forrester would be found guilty of all charges. The witness statements, forensic and factual evidence cannot be disproved. The case is solid and the murderer is sentenced to life imprisonment with a minimum of thirty-five years before parole can be considered.

# CHAPTER FIRTY-SIX

Tessa, who had absolutely loved to be with them all on the farm to celebrate the verdict, has already left. During several evening conversations, she has run past them what she plans to do: she will move to Exeter and catch up on the education at the University, she had denied herself in the past; sociology and social care for battered women were mentioned. 'Good for you!' they all agreed and declared that she was well on her way to mend.

Soon it is time to say good-bye to Bernadette, too, who will finally take the ashes of her daughter with her to France. Before Bernadette departs to catch the evening ferry to Roscoff, Kathleen has organised a remembrance celebration at the school, a very special assembly with all the pupils present, many of whom remember the French girl. When all the songs are sung, self-written poems have been recited, memories have been told and fervent prayers have been sent heavenwards for their friend's eternal peace, and a few tears have been shed, everyone goes in orderly groups out into the school's new vegetable garden where a plaque is revealed in honour of Sylvie, a simple granite square with Sylvie's name and dates. The French girl, who came to visit and never made it home, will not ever be forgotten.

'Thank you,' says Bernadette and shakes everybody's hand. When she comes to the last person in the row, it is Kathleen. The two women embrace: 'We'll stay in touch,' they promise each other; 'and you must revive the exchange with Morlaix,' Bernadette says. 'I will speak to the Principle in the school.' Nobody had thought of that out of fear that it might be

366

insensitive and rejected out of hand. Bernadette is full of surprises. '

'Life must go on,' Kathleen hears her say and nods, unable to overcome the knot in her throat. She gives her a hug and Bernadette responds by kissing her on both cheeks: 'I want to come back, too,' she adds cheekily.

They drive the short distance back to Ant's farm to collect Bernadette's luggage. Among the many good-byes, good wishes and promises to stay in touch, Ant invites her back for the following summer.

Bernadette blushes: 'I cannot promise,' she says in her endearing accent with a shy smile. 'Bill has invited me and my son Bertrand to go on holiday with him.' Her English has certainly improved, they notice with pleasure.

She looks at Ant's face and realises that her friend has suspected developments in the romantic department for quite some time: The French lady and the strapping English protector – a perfect match.

'You not surprised?' Bernadette giggles like a school girl, 'but you and Bex…?'

'It's a trial,' Ant whispers into her ear, while Bex puts Bernadette's luggage into Bill's car. Bernadette beams at her complicated but oh so dependable and loyal friend Ant: 'Be 'appy!' she urges her; 'you are good together, like Bill and me.' They embrace one last time and walk to the garden gate.

Bex joins them, and gives a last hug to Bernadette, before she rushes with a joyous spring in her step to Bill, who is already revving the engine. As they drive off, Bex puts an arm round Ant's shoulders. It's bold, something he hasn't done for a long time. He waits. She doesn't look at him, but she doesn't shrug him off either. As they wave and the car disappears, they stand there a little while longer. Suddenly, he feels Ant's arm wrapping itself around the back of his waist, and when he looks at her from the side, she smiles.

The End